To I.

CH00456564

Ackn

I would like to thank my wife, Irene, for her encouragement and invaluable help in identifying errors and inconsistencies in the text; also Tony van Breugel for the excellent design of the book cover, and to Gladys van Breugel for her interest and support. And to Alison, Justin, Euan, Alasdair and James for their inspiration.

Also By Robert Buntin

Oceans Apart
Travelling in Hope
Oceans Apart (Screenplay)
All in the Family (Stage Script)

Robert (Bob) Buntin lives in Skelmorlie, North Ayrshire with his wife, Irene. He is the author of two novels, a non-fiction travel book, a full length feature film screenplay, and a stage play. He can be contacted at rhb66@msn.com

Chapter One

I'm an atheist -I think - or is it an agnostic? Anyway I'm not sure but it's one or the other and I'm too apathetic to find out. There we are; I'm an apathetic atheist or an indifferent agnostic.

Don't get me wrong I've got beliefs. I believe that, I really do. Okay, I gave up on Santa Claus but I held on to that longer than most. Thirteen's not bad although it would have been longer if my eight year old sister hadn't spilled the beans and anyway I believe that there's a Santa Claus in all of us, so there.

I believe in love although God knows my patience has been sorely tried on that point. I thought my mother loved me but it turned out not quite as much as she loved the ledger accounts manager in the bank where she worked, but I think at least she quite liked me. She used to put Smarties in my school lunchbox; and a map, but I think she wanted to make sure I couldn't get lost on my way home from the swimming pool, which was seventeen miles away.

My dad loved me, I know that; he told me so every Saturday night through drink soaked tears over the phone when he felt lonely and needed a comforting shoulder to cry on but when I got older I didn't really need that type of love. Neither did he; a bottle doesn't answer back.

I do believe in love, the love between a man and a woman; the overwhelming, passionate, all consuming union between two bodies, or three if your luck is really in.

But I don't believe in much else. I think that you've pretty well got to make it on your own in this world without the aid of divine intervention to fall back on. Divine help didn't do much for the coastal dwellers of south-east Asia when the ocean rolled in or the brokers in New York when some jihadist nuts managed to board a couple of airplanes and wiped them and half of downtown New York out. It didn't do much for me when I lusted after Linda Craig whose head was turned and knickers removed by Barry Marshall who was only marginally better looking than me and, okay, he had a car - oh, and a job. Oh, and a credit card.

See what I mean about divine intervention? It's never there when you really need it. Maybe it's just bad timing and I don't suppose God can be everywhere at once. Maybe there were more pressing matters on Alpha Centauri that prevented the All Powerful from hinting to the inhabitants of Pompeii that now would be a good time to pack their cases because that hill in the background was belching smoke for a reason.

Except, and I don't really know if I should admit this, but well, I do believe that I am the proud benefactor of a guardian angel. It sits there, invisible for the most part, on my left shoulder guiding me into the right choices and generally smoothing the way. I say for the most part because there have been one or two occasions when I have been very tired or very emotional, or indeed, very tired *and* emotional, that I may have glimpsed the slightest sensation of her.

She was right (my guardian angel is a she) about not assisting in my liaison with Linda Craig who turned into a sour harridan with a face that could turn milk, to the extent that Barry upped and left with Lesley Bell upon whom, incidentally, I also had unrequited designs. Barry got me a date with Lesley's distant cousin (distant only in the respect that she lived in Taunton and was here on holiday) who lived down to my every physical expectation. And she was better looking than Linda Craig. Barry is now my closest friend and a gentleman; he's even going to let me have Lesley when he's finished with her.

Anyway my guardian angel has consistently guided me, much like an automatic pilot on an unmanned airplane, to being in the right place at the right time despite my every effort to the contrary and fucking it up royally when I get there.

The first example of that was when I first applied for a job in a travel agency. I had no experience, of course, other than a C level in geography, but the attraction of free travel to exotic Club 18-30 locations was too hard to resist. I got the job; I was the only applicant who turned up for the interview. I assume that they didn't know where Ingram Street was, not a good sign for working in travel.

Fuck up number one was when I got my Boulogne's and Bologna's mixed up resulting in two old dears who had planned their first (and probably last) trip away from these green and pleasant shores to visit their grandson's wedding in northern Italy. Well, it's an easy mistake to make. The problem wasn't helped by the fact that the old man persisted in asking directions based on instructions from the Collins Gem Italian Dictionary which led the French to believe that he was quite mad. Apparently it went downhill from there.

Number two wasn't my fault; not really. Well, maybe really. A honeymoon couple that I had booked on holiday to Mexico took out insurance to cover themselves against medical costs and personal loss. When they got there hubby took a severe dose of Montezuma's revenge and spent the first week sprinting between the bed and the toilet bowl, sometimes confusing the two. A doctor was called and prescribed the usual expensive medicines with the exception of any that could actually cure the problem. Meanwhile his wife, sunbathing on the beach in front of the hotel, got third degree burns on ninety-eight percent of her body which, coincidentally, was the exact amount not covered by her Donna Karen bikini. Just to put the tin lid on it, while they were both recovering in their darkened suite, the marriage still unconsummated (no major problem since they'd shagged themselves senseless long before the nuptials) someone sneaked in and stole their money, their passports, their tickets home and for good measure, his diahorrea pills and her sunburn lotion. They had to be flown home in a private jet specifically covered under the generous terms of their travel insurance. Which I had forgotten to take out on their behalf.

Over the few months that I was employed there were two or three other minor glitches but nothing to write home about, mainly because the clients didn't get away from home in the first place.

I'm now doing a course on computer programming and IT at Cardonald College with a view to setting up my own business. I feel as if I have an affinity with computers; I usually go to sleep after twenty minutes of inactivity too. I'm actually quite bright but, to be honest, just can't be arsed. I have a memory like lint and if you're looking for a partner at trivial pursuit, I'm your man. If you're looking for someone you can sit down and get a job done for you, well my mind tends to wander and...sorry, what was I saying?

If you are wondering what I look like, and there's no earthly reason why you should, I am just on six feet tall, floppy brown hair that I keep having to sweep from my eyes in a rather dashing and carefree manner even though I do say so myself. No-one else will. My eyes are also brown; I'm quite tanned, or possibly just weather beaten, because I have that sort of skin, and I make no concessions to incipient melanomas by the wimpish use of poncey fifty factor suntan lotions. I've grown into my looks, which is to say that as a teenager I left a lot to be desired. The ears hadn't quite decided how much lift they should generate but thankfully they settled a little closer to my head. My front teeth could bite an apple through a tennis racket, but either they got smaller or my mouth got bigger and I'm told, somewhat unkindly, that it's the latter. Consequently I was never in the running when it came to the really great looking girls who reserved their favours for those guys who, metaphorically speaking, graced the upper half of the premiership whereas I tended to float around the nether regions of the lower division.

Janis Ian captured it all perfectly in her seminal song 'At Seventeen', a wonderful description of teenage angst that, while written for girls, is equally applicable to acned, tortured youths in their late teens like me. When she wrote about waiting hopefully for the Valentines that never materialised she must have had my address because Valentine's Day and the non-existent rattle of a silent letter box and the smug smirk of my sister as she opened a mail-bag full was almost too much to bear. (However, years later I received a Valentine that had on the front the title of the 'West Side Story' song, 'There's A Place for Us'. Inside was a picture of a double bed. I never did find out who the sender was although I was tempted to hire a private detective.) For me, the years between sixteen and twenty-one were like driving a car with faulty steering and brakes at speed along a motorway filled with other cars with the same defects. I was not alone in this and yet, like most of us, I emerged unscathed into the hilly uplands of adulthood only to find things, well, not that much different really.

My name is Gordon Lorne. I have a generous mouth and most of my teeth that could be saved after years of slavish addiction to Mars bars and Barr's Irn Bru, that delicious golden concoction brewed solely for the purpose of relieving the effects of alcohol excess. I am around twelve stone give or take (and let's be generous here) which is amazing given the amount of fatty junk I eat, but I do like to run which helps burn it off. I even dabble in the guitar if you count the three chords which can be used to bash out any song and with judicious use of a capo I can even make it sound interesting with a voice to match. Hum me a 'b' and I'll flatten it myself. I know it's a bit passé but I like the Gordon Lightfoot, Tom Paxton sort of stuff with a bit of early Dylan thrown in. My party piece is 'Early Mornin' Rain' but Barry Marshall says I murder it. He is being a touch unfair but I will admit to grievous bodily harm.

I am still single and pushing thirty-five but I do have a girlfriend of the long suffering sort who follows me not from any sense of loyalty but mainly out of simple curiosity. She's around five feet five, reddish auburn hair

7

and blue eyed. When she's sexy she smoulders, when she's mad she smoulders, when she's sleeping she smoulders. I've got the fire brigade on speed dial just in case. Her name is Christine Hill and I call her Chris because that way people such as my grandparents don't turn up a Roger Moore eyebrow when I say I am going away for a few days with Chris. At least that's what I innocently thought until my Grandma on my father's side asked what I was doing for the weekend.

'Doing anything nice, Gordon dear?'

'I'm going to T in the Park with Chris.'

'What's that, dear?'

'Oh, just some rock groups and a bit of a lark.'

'Drugs?'

'Of course not.'

This was true in the strictest letter of grammatical purity since it was a drug in the singular, namely a little dope that I had planned on using to ease the pain and lighten the darkness and generally improve upon drug free life in general.

'Oh.'

I sensed disappointment in her tone.

'Who's Chris?' She wasn't giving up.

'My friend.'

She looked at me oddly.

'What?'

'Gordon dear, you're not a pillow muncher, are you?'

'What?'

'Shirt lifter, horses hoof, - you know very well what I mean, Gordon. - oh for God's sake - a homosexual.' She said this in much the same way that Dame Edith Evans said, 'A handbag?'

I assured her that I did not take it up Bourneville Boulevard and that Chris was short for Christine with whom I was having a normal sexual relationship, even abnormal at times when I was in luck.

'Thank fuck for that.'

And with that the matter was closed. My Grandma never ceases to amaze me. Dear old Grandpa, Gordon senior, was in awe of her until he died and ruined her bingo night.

Anyway, Chris will do until something better comes along or Barry Marshall gets tired of Lesley Bell and just in case you're shocked by my cavalier, chauvinistic attitude to women, I should point out that the aforementioned Christine doesn't view me as the rock upon which she'll build her life either. I know for a fact that she lusts after Barry, because he told me, and he added just a little too much in depth detail for my liking so it's pretty clear he's literally had hands on experience.

Chris and I rub along okay, we both know where we're going, probably not together, and can live with each other's faults for the time being or whoever gets fed up first. She's also very inventive in bed, crafted by much experience, and I, without sounding too smug about it, I'm pretty hot stuff in that department as well. Okay, she sometimes thinks I'm grumpy when I wake up sleepy and dopey and I'm not always happy and I have to remind her that this isn't the seven dwarfs here and she's definitely not Snow White herself in any shape or form. Besides, statistically six out of seven dwarfs are not happy.

Grandma's inquisition was before last weekend and a lot had happened in the intervening days. Like T in the Park and like I was now out of a job. It wasn't that I had

9

screwed up again, although I had (a small matter of miscalculating the exchange rate on five hundred pounds worth of euros resulting in a woman getting ten times more holiday cash than she expected. Honestly! - the quality of calculators nowadays). No, it was the fact the agency had gone into liquidation and we were all out of a job. I don't understand it; they seemed to be doing so well.

One pleasure the agency instilled in me was the love of travel and for the time I was employed there I indulged it well courtesy of cheap air travel and complimentary accommodation. Airlines and tourist boards co-joined to promote destinations and invited agency personnel on fam trips as they were know in the trade and jollies as they were known outside it. By that means I was able to sample the delights of such diverse places as New York, Bangkok, Hong Kong, Disneyland and virtually all of Europe. I went to Nova Scotia once but it was shut. I even got to turn left at the end of the jetway to where those big comfy chairs that uncoil like a snake into a bed are. After you've had the steak Diane, the Sancerre, the Chateau Palmer '97, the vintage port and the petits four, of course. And all on the company dollar.

I also got freebies through my dad's British Airways concessions. If I ever design a family crest the motto will be 'Upgrade or Die'. I got to visit The Hermitage in St Petersburg and the Musée D'Orsay in Paris, which is way better than the Louvre, by the way. Look, I may be a total arse but I'm not a Philistine, okay? The owner of the agency was delighted to recommend me for these trips; it kept me out of harm's way.

One thing about being exposed to the wider world thanks to having a British Airways captain as a father, even at a young age it gives you an appreciation of the culture of various times, people and places. Being dragged through a variety of museums and art galleries, temples and cathedrals, bored and protesting, somewhere along the way some of it rubbed off. I recognise and even enjoy good art and music on a different level to my usual more base tastes, much to the astonishment of Chris or Barry who tend to view anything that hints at classical culture with a deep suspicion. I'm not actually a culture vulture as such but even at the tender age of thirty-four I get what some of the older wrinklies see in some of that stuff. I just keep quiet about it.

New York, that was the place to go. New York is a city, all the rest are just villages. Except Paris, of course. New York blows the mind, but Paris, Paris steals the heart. Then there's Venice which is just like eating a box of Black Magic in one sitting, except for the coffee ones, of course. Now I fart about with computer codes and the nearest I get to Paris is Paisley. How the mighty are fallen. Ozymandias was not alone.

Before they lost their way, their jobs and each other, Mum and Dad were a useful source of income although my father had long since got wise to me and anyway since he was grounded, the money wasn't there. My dad used to give me tips on enjoying my teens and early twenties with the members of the opposite sex.

'Don't put all your eggs in one basket, son,' he'd say. 'Don't put all your eggs in one basket. You're only young once – play the field.'

As I wasn't putting eggs into anyone's basket no matter how hard I tried the advice seemed a little redundant but I thanked him anyway and went back to reading last month's Playboy.

We all once lived in genteel domesticity in Clarkston, a bijou corner on the southern edge of the city much sought after by those seeking to ensure decent schooling for their offspring. Dad had been a British Airways pilot and mum had been a stewardess when they met and got cosy on a Lisbon stopover. Net result – me. I have a sister, Lara, my mother's idea having once seen Doctor Zhivago and fancied Omar Sharif, and Lara has proved much less of a disappointment than her elder brother, obtaining a coveted two-one at St Andrews, a position as a marriage guidance counsellor, a house in Newton Mearns, and a husband, Keith, who obeys her every whim of which she has a constant flow. It's the secret of a happy marriage she says, and I dare say she's right. Says it all, really. She is far and away my father's favourite but my mum still has a soft spot for me.

'You spoil that boy, you know that?' my father would frequently scold my mother in between jaunts to Sydney. 'Why couldn't he be more like Lara, that's what I want to know? Are you sure he's mine?'

I once heard my mother reply under her breath, 'Believe it, kid, Lara however...'

She left the sentence unfinished.

I flew the coop much to the relief of everyone and took up residence in a rented bedsit near Partick Cross, ambitiously advertised as "charming" but would be more accurately described as "condemned". But it was mine so long as I paid the rent and there was nobody, nobody permanent at least, to nag at me for such transgressions

12

as not making my bed and peeing in the sink. (Okay, it only happened once).

There seemed to be nothing else for it. I couldn't hang around my squalid bedsit all day. Not that the dishes were piling up in the sink or anything since all my food came in those little disposable foil cartons although I have to say that *they* were piling up in the sink. Time to get off my arse and do something serious; like go to the pub.

It was called the Horseshoe and was the last remaining original pub in Glasgow, known colloquially as a 'howff'. Don't ask, I haven't a clue, but that and the Saracen's Head Tavern on the Gallowgate, a pub that no self respecting down and out like me would be seen dead in, are probably the only two real drinking dens left in the city . It's a man's pub and I say that without a hint of sexism as most women will agree with me, even those who frequent it. They serve serious beer here, not your luvvie real ale stuff, but pints of McEwan's, Belhaven and Tennents. Any short, other than whisky, invites an opinion on your sexual orientation. A request for a drink that requires fruit in it usually elicits a long hard look from the bar staff - and don't even think of asking for ice.

It also has a contraceptive machine in the gents with the inevitable graffiti scrawled across it. You know the type of thing; where it says "approved by the British Standards Institution" and some comedian has felt tip penned in, 'so was the Titanic.' However, it had one very funny line. Someone had written on the whitewashed wall next to the machine, 'I am black with a twelve inch dick'. Someone else wrote underneath it, "I am green with envy".

This tavern is my usual watering hole where I can be found whiling away my increasingly frequent leisure time. I like the ambience and the easy camaraderie. I'm not an alcoholic, no, really. Actually, no – really! I like a pint and a dram or two but I rarely go over the score and often enough, particularly when I'm a bit boracic, I go for days without having a drink at all. Mind you, I'm not exactly the life and soul of the party then, but the point is, I like a pint, I don't need it. This, then, is where I agreed to meet Barry Marshall.

Barry's direction in life had led him down a different path to mine. Whereas I had chosen a more bohemian, carefree, devil may care road, eschewing the bourgeois principles and capitalist greed and was, as a result, an enthusiastic proponent of wealth redistribution and consistently doing everything possible to have it redistributed in my direction, Barry was a highly successful financial advisor leaching off the wealth of the downtrodden, one of which was me. I saw it is my social duty to try and re-educate him by the simple expedient of letting him buy the drinks whenever possible. He has a rather nifty BMW 500, a comfortable town house in the west end, and an Amex Platinum credit card. He is around my height, perhaps slightly smaller, and doesn't have my rakish good looks or devil-may-care charm, although he does have a certain, shall we say, style, if that's your bag. Frankly I don't know what Lesley sees in him.

However, adhering to custom borne out of years of experience we each bought our own drinks. Mine was a half pint of light, the quantity of which conveyed evidence of my current fiscal problems to Barry's trained eye. A previous similar situation had prompted a search between the cushions of the third hand settee in my bed-sit that had yielded a trove of mixed coin to the tune of two pounds thirty-six pence, a lint covered Rowntree's orange fruit gum, the top of a Bic pen and, interestingly, a condom, sadly unused. However, that particular source of funds was now exhausted. Barry had a pint of heavy, already a third consumed, and a large whisky in front of him on the soiled table. He lifted the whisky to his lips and appeared to exaggerate the sensation of satisfaction derived from it.

'Aaaah...not just Glenmorangie, but Glenmorangie matured for fifteen years in Madeira wine casks nurtured by the mid Atlantic sun and imparting that subtle flavour of je ne sais quoi.'

He pronounced it wrongly, putting the emphasis on the penultimate syllable, Glenmor*an*gie.

'It's Glen*mo*rangie.' I downed half of my half pint.

'What?'

Good, I'd got him on the back foot already.

'It's okay – better to make an arse of yourself in front of me than doing it before an audience.'

'Wee bit of financial trouble?' he retaliated, nodding at my already depleted glass.

'No, no...just cutting back.'

'Yeah, right. That's quite far back.'

He drew another large gulp of McEwan's and eyed me, no doubt sizing up some new line of attack. He played a trick with a beer mat, positioning it half over the edge of the table, flicking it up and catching it mid air between thumb and forefinger. He did this three times but on the fourth it skittered out of his hand and onto the floor.

15

'And how's the lovely Christine?' He raised an enquiring eyebrow.

'Oh, fine...you know.'

'No I don't know. That's why I asked. Why don't you tell me?'

'Same old, same old.'

Barry looked at me. 'Same old, same old?' What's that? You been watching American soaps again?'

'Maybe I need a change of life.'

'What, you want the menopause?'

I looked at him with what I fancied was disdain then took a sip from my beer, depleting the glass by half.

'I'm in a rut. I need some adventure in my life. Chris's fine but it's just mindless sex when we're together.'

Barry looked at me open mouthed. 'And your point is?'

I really hadn't thought that this was a problem up until now. In fact it wasn't a problem at all – it was a major plus so I have no idea why I said it. I guess I was in a weird mood. Lack of cash maybe had something to do with it. Barry changed tack. He leaned forward.

'How old were you when you had your first sexual experience?'

'What, you're Marjorie Proops now?'

'Come on.'

I sighed, took a swig from my depleted drink.

'Fifteen,' I said with unconvincing and exaggerated insouciance, knocking a couple of years off it.

He snorted. 'Who with?'

I paused, just a beat too long. Barry spotted it.

'Don't tell me you were on your own!' he howled. 'And you're complaining about all the mindless sex!'

16

I downed the rest of my half pint which was a mistake in that it was now obvious that I would either have to sit with an empty glass in front of me or leave. I'd only just got here and, besides, I needed the bank of Barry's help. Barry, in a fit of unusual benevolence, or perhaps just pity, looked at the glass and then at me.

'Fancy another?'

Pride and convention demanded that I refuse. Hopefully he would ask me again at which point I could 'reluctantly' accept, honour intact.

'Nah- you're fine.'

He sat back in his chair and peered at me through narrowed eyes. Surely he wouldn't leave it at that? Please?

'Sure?'

'Oh, go on then.'

He gave me a knowing look and a half smile and went over to the bar to catch the eye of one of the bartenders.

I looked around. Nothing had changed in the many years that I had been coming here except for the absence of coils of cigarette smoke meandering upwards to form a floating blue haze between the heads of the punters and the ceiling. Recent legislation had prohibited smoking in pubs and now you had to push your way through a half dozen chain smoking, asthmatics at the door. Pretty soon they'd ban drinking in pubs.   I hadn't really noticed the decor before. The pub had recently undergone a badly needed redecoration. Gone was the nicotine stained paint above the high dado rail and bright magnolia had replaced it. Below the dado rail was mahogany panelling framed with ornate wooden carvings. The large mirror at the back of the bar still proclaimed 'The Horseshoe' and a magnificent wooden statue of a horse, freshly varnished, adorned the top of the Edwardian island bar. It's the longest continuous bar in the UK, apparently, a useless fact I must have picked up during one of my sessions. There's even a terrazzo spittoon trough all around the base of the bar although all it collects now is city dirt from the soles of shoes. Glasgow has come up in the world; spitting is frowned upon and is now the sole preserve of Latino footballers. The ceiling was painted a fresh burgundy and all around the walls were hung paintings and photographs of old Glasgow street scenes. The floor was tiled which made it easier to wash away the blood and other detritus from the day's events. All they needed to do now was refurbish the clientele and the place would be a treat.

Barry came back with a couple of pints, disappeared again and was back seconds later with two doubles. I swear I nearly sobbed in gratitude but limited myself to an effusive Glasgow thank you.

'Cheers, mate.'

He nodded, took a large draught of ale, leaned back and looked at me.

'You're a fuck up, you know that?'

'Your friends speak highly of you too,' I responded wittily, downing half of the Scotch, Glenmorangie for me too, I noted gratefully.

'If insulting me is the price I have to pay for you buying me drink, fill your boots.'

'I'm worried about you, Christ, even Lesley's worried about you.'

I pricked up my ears at this. Clearly there was still hope on the Lesley front yet.

'Why would anyone worry about me? Lesley? Really?'

'How do I love thee; let me count the ways. It's the beginning of two thousand and seventeen, you're thirty-five, you're broke, jobless, you live in a room that looks like giant petri dish, you're in debt, your arteries are hardening cement and a vegetable is an alien life form. Want me to go on?'

'I like sushi.'

'Deep fried haddock is not sushi.'

'Anyway is that all? I thought I was in trouble for a minute.'

'Mate.'

'What?'

'I'm serious.'

I looked at him for a long minute. Christ, he was serious. What's more he was right.

'Look, I'm just going through a bad patch at the moment, happens to us all. How much do I owe you anyway?'

'It's not about the money. It's about you.' He took a sip of beer. 'Two hundred and thirty.'

'Two hundred and thirty what?'

'Pounds. That's what you owe me.'

'What?!'

'It's okay. I'm not chasing you for it.'

'Two hundred and fifty quid?!'

'Thirty; two hundred and thirty.'

'Well, I was going to tap you for another twenty.'

Barry rolled his eyes. 'You're un-fucking-believable. How much are you into Chris for?'

'That's none of your business. Besides she sees me as an investment. She knows I've got potential.'

'You're a potential bankrupt. How much?'

'A couple of hundred give or take.'

19

'Give or take what?'

'A couple of hundred.'

'Jesus, so four hundred plus what you owe me.'

'Her parents are rich. Just look on it as redistribution of wealth.'

Barry groaned. 'Who else? Credit cards?'

'Let's not go into that.'

He sighed and leaned back on the stool then looked at me with a mixture of despair, sympathy and concern and what could almost have been anger. I'd never seen that look before in Barry. He looked at me for a few moments.

'There's something you should know.'

I tried a lame attempt at humour. 'Don't tell me you're broke too?'

'Lesley and I are thinking of getting married.'

'Fuck.' It was the only thing I could think of.

'Most people just say "congratulations".'

'"Thinking" of?'

'Well who gets engaged now? OK, I'm buying a ring.'

'Fuck. Yeah, yeah. Congrats and all that. No, seriously, that's...that's great...yeah. A ring – Jesus.' I looked at him, dumbfounded. Well, that was Lesley clearly off the menu. A thought struck me. 'She's not pregnant or anything?'

'Piss off, Gordon. No, not anything.' He paused. 'You okay with that? I mean, I know you kinda liked her.'

'No, no. Fine. Totally. I mean, yeah. Totally.' I leant forward and gave him a chuck on the shoulder. 'Let me buy you a drink.'

He dipped into his back pocket for his wallet. 'Here, you'll need this.' He handed me a twenty.

'Thanks, mate. You'll get it all back, promise. When's the big day?'

'Probably April, she's looking at venues for the reception as we speak.'

I finished my drinks and nodded at his glass. He shook his head at the pint but nodded at the dram. I got up and went over to the bar, head reeling and not with the drink either. He was the only one left. It never occurred to me that Barry would get married but then again, why wouldn't he? He was my age, good job, flush, and Lesley was perfect for him in a way that I could never be for her, so why wouldn't he? And, truth be told, he was a better friend to me that I had been to him. Two hundred and fifty quid, Christ!

'Two Glenmorangies, when you've got a minute, make them large ones,' I called to the barman, any barman.

Well, I had to do something. I had to pay him back for a start. He was right, I was a loser and a big time loser at that. If I was to be best man I'd need to pull myself together. Wait, he never said anything about best man. Well, I'm his best mate. Has to be me. Just has to be.

I took the goldies back to the table. 'Well, here's to you mate. And tell Lesley here's to her too, sorry she had to settle for second best. And here's to me, last man standing.' We clinked glasses and drank.

'So, big wedding then? Lots of bridesmaids? Anything shaggable for the best man?'

Barry looked into his glass and swirled the whisky around without saying anything, not looking at me.

'I am the best man, Barry, amn't I? Barry?'

21

He looked at me. 'You're my first choice, mate, but there are problems.'

'What problems?'

'Well, remember when I said she was looking at venues? Well, she's looking at them all right. There's two in Barbados she likes and another in St Lucia. And the Maldives isn't out of the running either. So the thing is, yeah, I want you to be best man, Gordon, but we're looking at a couple of grand for flights and accommodation for you and you're on your own there. See what I mean?'

'Christ.'

'I mean, I wanted something special too but I was thinking more like Lochgreen or Cameron House or even Andy Murray's place, but you know Lesley.'

'So who are you thinking? Not that wanker, Kelso? Don't tell me you're going to ask Brian Kelso. What sort of speech do you think you'll get from him? He's no' a real mate, Barry.'

Brian Kelso was a peripheral friend in our diminishing ragtag, dissolute band. For someone who hung out with us, a group that didn't treat anyone more foolish than us gladly (and there weren't many), Brian was the exception. Well, every village needs an idiot. He was an authority on everything with information gleaned through listening to Cliffy on 'Cheers'. One week he would assure us he had started writing a new and ground-breaking opera (seriously) yet didn't even know the words to 'Doh, a deer'. The next week he would have started his magnum opus revealing the real truth behind Kennedy's assassination, apparently by a hit man hired by Joe DiMaggio who bore a grudge against the Kennedys and believed they had conspired to have Marilyn murdered.

It wasn't a bad concept but never got past the working title 'A Nation Turns Its Lonely Eyes to You'. He was also cross-eyed.

Barry shrugged.

'Come on, Barry. Brian! He can stand in Monday and see both Wednesdays. Have you ever seen a squint like that? His last girlfriend dumped him because he was seeing someone on the side, literally. Anyway, you've never seen eye to eye with him.' I was outraged.

'OK, cool it. Enough of the cross-eyed jokes already. I haven't asked anybody yet. I only proposed to her at the weekend and anyway Brian can get himself out there. He might have a squint but he also has a bit of cash. Lesley suggested her brother, Tom. Remember Tom?'

'Tom - oil slick Tom? You're kidding. He's so up himself I'm surprised he doesn't disappear through his own arse.'

'Look, I'll make a deal with you. Once she's got the details sorted, if you can come up with the green for your ticket and the hotel, you're the man. I'll sort it with Lesley.'

'OK, you're on.' I paused mid drink, 'What do you mean, "sort it with Lesley"? Does she not want me there?'

'Of course she does. No, it's just that, well, she doesn't know if you're up to it these days. I mean, well, as I was saying, you've let yourself go a bit.'

He was right, of course, and I knew it. I just didn't want to see it but if Lesley had been talking about it, well that just hurt my pride, whatever of it there was left.

'Anyway,' he continued, downing his drink, 'Got to go. Meeting her at John Lewis. Don't ask.'

'Well don't look any further. I'm your best mate and your best man. Whatever it takes, I'll be there, you can count on me. And you can tell Lesley that. You don't need her smarmy brother or that skelly-eyed tube, Kelso, either.'

Barry smiled unconvincingly and stood up to go. 'OK, I'll keep you posted. Consider that twenty a starter, I don't want it back. You've got a tenner left, now as the good book says, go forth and multiply, and you can take that anyway you like.'

I watched him push through the swing doors out into the weak January light of Drury Street. Fuck, what was I going to do now?

Chapter Two

Sitting there alone finishing my drink. I knew I had reached some sort of watershed in my life. Barry was the only real friend I had in the world and now he was going to transfer his priorities to another. Not that I am saying I was ever his number one priority but once you decide to get married there is a dramatic shift in perspective. As a girlfriend, Lesley was disposable, just as he was to her; as a fiancé he was committed; as a husband he was bound body and soul; as a father he was history. Sure, he would always be my friend, and a great friend at that, but he had to cut me loose. He couldn't afford me *and* a family.

I drained the dregs of the malt and stumbled into the dank, dark Glasgow air and made my way to Renfield Street and walked down Union Street to Argyle Street. A flash was followed a few seconds later by a rumble of thunder and a few fat raindrops started to slap into the pavement so I hooded up and headed for the sanctuary of Central Station. I wasn't looking for a train to anywhere but it was under cover, bright and anonymously welcoming like a minister at a watch-night service.

I liked trains, always did. I don't know whether it was the trains themselves or the tracks. I loved tracks. They took away responsibility. You went where they chose to take you and that choice was made by invisible gods pressing buttons and pulling levers from a box far away.

When I was a boy of around twelve my pride and joy was my model railway and don't, don't ever, make the mistake of calling it a train set. It had a four platform station; it had a complex layout with bridges, a viaduct and a tunnel. It had points and sidings and signal boxes and signals in semaphore and aspect lights. It had four engines, a Stanier Pacific "Duchess" class 4-6-2 and if you don't know what that means then fuck off and don't annoy me. It had a class 4MT 2-6-4T tank engine for local working. It had a class 30 diesel locomotive. There were six classic carmine and cream coaches, three maroon suburban coaches, an assortment of goods wagons, guard's vans, houses and Dinky toys. I even made up an operating timetable. Christ, I even went out on sympathy strike with ASLEF.

God knows what happened to it. There's that hazy period in my late teens when I sort of lost my way (still haven't found it, wherever it is) and I put away childish things. Problem was that I never found adult things, just other, more grown up toys, like booze, sex and rock and roll, and, let me tell you, model trains find it hard to compete when you discover them. Once you've had your first shag the two-fifteen to Little Innocence can go piss up a rope.

But Central Station always stirred the soul in me. I looked up at the big electronic board straddling the main concourse. The destinations hadn't changed since first I haunted the platforms but there were some new ones that piqued my interest: Whifflet, North Berwick - when did they start? The concourse was covered in a marble tile terrazzo substance and there was any amount of new shops and cafes; in fact the place looked more like a shopping mall than a station. There was a shiny Virgin silver and red Pendolino sitting at platform one going to London stopping at Carlisle, Oxenholme, Lancaster, Preston, Wigan and Warrington according to the listed calling points. Oh, to be on that. I could hear a sprinter ticking over on a distant platform. An electric multiple unit moaned going out to wend its way around the Cathcart Circle. It would be back here in under the hour and there would be at least one inebriate who slept the whole way instead of getting off at Mount Florida. I'd done it myself. In the distance a bank of red signal lights were punctuated by a couple of greens and an amber.

I mooched around the concourse for a while mulling over my life and what a waste it was. I knew I needed to change it but I couldn't figure out how. I needed money; to get that I needed a job; to get that I needed a kick up the arse and maybe, just maybe, Barry and his pending nuptials with the heavenly Lesley, my Lesley (well, I did have dibs on her) was the kick up the Khyber I needed. I really, really wanted to go to the Caribbean for the wedding. A single ticket would do; who wants to come back to this place?

I looked up at the board again and the digital clock clicked over to nineteen fifty-one. Christ, I had been meandering about the streets and the station for nearly three hours since Barry left me in the Horseshoe. I looked around again and made a resolution. No matter what, no matter how, come hell or high water I was going to be Barry's best man and I was going to Barbados, St Lucia, Guantanamera, Guantanamo, wherever the hell, I was going, and with that thought I looked at the large Victorian clock dangling from the roof of the station and walked under it heading for the

27

Hope Street exit just as the big hand swung onto three minutes to eight.

And in an instant, all was dark! Remember the Burns' line from Tam O'Shanter, just after he shouts out to the witches, 'Weel done Cutty Sark!'? And in an instant all was dark. Then an instant later all was light again. Christ, what just happened? Did I pass out? I looked around me.

I was on the ground trying and failing to get up, a bit like a drunk wondering which way up was the sky, and I should know. Somebody grabbed me by the elbow.

'Are you all right, son?'

'I don't know, I think so. I don't know what happened there.' I felt my legs, my arms and head and everything seemed to be functioning. Other people hurried over. Some looked up at the clock.

'Did ye see that?' someone said.

'Looked like lightning,' said someone else.

'Get an ambulance. This man needs an ambulance.'

'Is he deid?' asked a woman with a sense of the macabre.

'Don't think so.'

'Must be deid if he got hit by lightning.'

Everybody seemed to be talking at once but I managed to stagger to my feet. I shook my head and looked around trying to focus. I looked at the gathering crowd then I looked at them more closely. Strange. All the men had ties on except some who were wearing overalls. Some wore flat caps, others wore hats; all wore jackets of some sort. There were a number of women looking worried and concerned. They all wore a coat over a dress or a skirt. A few had a scarf or a hat on. The air smelled different, grimier, sootier somehow. I looked around. I was still in the station but it wasn't the same

28

station. Well, it was but it wasn't. It was Glasgow Central all right but not my Glasgow Central. Gone was the destination indicator board, gone was the flower stall in the middle of the concourse; gone was the terrazzo flooring. I whirled round. The long curved building which housed a wine shop, Krispy Kreme Donuts, Costa Coffee, and a bar restaurant on the upper floor now had the same thirteen windows on top except they were all numbered Platform One, Platform Two and so on to Platform Thirteen. Some had large printed destination boards in them and above them a departure time or so I presumed. There were a couple of men inside taking boards down and putting new boards up. My kindly Samaritan clearly saw my mad eyed bewilderment.

'It's okay son. Take it easy. Someone will get ye an ambulance.'

'I DON'T NEED AN AMBULANCE!' I sounded frantic.

'It's okay, it's okay - calm down, ye don't have to shout, we can hear you. Can you hear me?'

There was a ringing in my ears but it was easing. 'No, no. I mean yes, I can hear you. No ambulance. I'm fine, thanks. I'm fine. What happened?'

'Hard to say but it looks like it was lightnin'. A big flash seemed to come down out of that clock up there and the next thing you were on the ground. I think it hit you.'

I followed his gaze and sure enough, the clock looked a bit blackened. The hands were still at three minutes to eight.

'Is that the time?'

'No, it's just after eight. I don't think it's workin' now.'

I just needed time and space to clear my head. I felt physically okay but something was definitely messing with my brain. I've had my brain messed with before, five pints and a couple of voddies will do that anytime and a couple of puffs of the wacky baccie will get you there without passing go, but this was different, in the past my brain was screwed up but everything else was fine. This time I was pretty sure my brain wasn't the problem, everything else was.

'I'm good, honest. Thanks. I just need some air.'

I pushed my way through the gathering crowd towards the Union Street exit and out onto the street to cross it. I needed a drink. That's when it hit me, or in the case of the approaching car, nearly hit me. I must be in some sort of mind disconnect. The car screeched to a halt with me leaning over the bonnet.

'Hey,' I screamed, 'Where are you going?! This is a one way street. Prick!'

But it wasn't a one way street. As I looked beyond the car, which was a Wolseley, for Christ's sake, with a little motif on the bonnet, I saw a line of three tramcars moaning their way up the street. Tramcars! One was a Coronation type and the two behind were the old "shooglie caurs" that I had seen in picture books. I eased my way back to the kerb, my mouth hanging open. I let the car past, the driver looking at me as if I was some sort of idiot. This time I looked right and, sure enough, a couple more cars and then a van approached from the direction of Argyle Street. The tramcars stopped, one behind the other, some people got off, others boarded and the trams rumbled off across Gordon Street and up the slope of Renfield Street. Traffic was light now in both directions so I made my way as if by osmosis back to where the Horseshoe was in Drury Street. Thank God, sanity prevailed, there it was, just the same as I had left it. As I turned to go in a couple of locals slipped out and held the door for me.

'Thanks, Mac.' I entered and nearly choked on the smoke.

A light blue haze wafted above the punters at the bar, all of whom seemed to have a cigarette between their fingers. The bar was a lot grungier than I had left it previously and I didn't recognise any of the bar staff. I caught the eye of a barman, not difficult since they all seemed to be staring at me.

'Pint of heavy, mate,' I said wearily.

He looked at me oddly before moving to the pump. I turned round and looked at myself in the mirror on the wall. I had on a navy hoodie covering a tee shirt that loudly proclaimed 'I fuck on the first date'. Well, I thought it was funny. The thing was, most of the others in the bar, and they were all male, just had jackets, donkey jackets, white shirts, dungarees or sweaters. There wasn't a pair of jeans on sight or anything with a message on it. They all looked, I don't know, I couldn't put my finger on it. Then I got it; they all looked old.

'That's some shirt, pal,' said the barman putting the pint down in front of me, 'Mind covering it up with your jacket?'

I tugged at my zipper.

'Right, one and fourpence.'

'What?'

'One and fourpence,' he repeated.

I had no idea what he was talking about so I fumbled in my pocket and brought the fiver I had from my change of the twenty earlier.

31

'What's this?'

'Em, Sorry, I've nothing smaller.'

He picked up the note and looked at it. 'What's this?' he said again.

'It's one of the new ones, I think it's plastic.'

'Are you tryin' to be funny?'

'No, no. Wait, lemme see if I've change.' I dug into my pocket and dragged out three one pound coins and some silver. 'How much did you say?'

'Haw Alec!' the barman shouted over to someone who appeared to be the boss.

'Joker here's tryin' to palm off some funny money.'

Alec, whoever he was, sauntered over. 'Oh, aye. Let me see.'

Okay, I'd had a weird day. Things hadn't gone well with Barry, I had got soaked in the rain and nearly fried with some sort of lightning strike, nearly killed by a vintage car going the wrong way, but even I could see that there was a problem here. I was here and I was the problem. Alec held the note up to the light and examined it. He picked up the coins and turned them over and over.

'Where did ye get these?'

'Eh, when I was in here earlier, in my change.'

Alec turned to the barman and in a voice everyone could hear, even people in Kirkcaldy, shouted, 'Anybody remember this guy in here earlier?'

There were a lot of mumbled 'naw's and head shaking.

He turned back to me. 'I don't know what your game is but you'd better get your arse out of here and take your Monopoly money with you or you'll be needin' a get out of jail free card.'

Bewilderment descended heavily on me like a tramp on a hot pie. 'But that's a fiver.'

'It's no' a fiver on this planet, now move your arse.'

'Do you take credit cards?' This was a long shot as my only card was pretty well maxed out, but you never know.

'What the fuck are you talking about, credit card?'

'Look I'm just trying to buy a pint. What's the problem?'

'Do you want me to call the police?'

'Okay, okay I'm going.' I dragged the coins and the note back and put them in my pocket.

As I turned away I saw an Evening Tines on the bar counter and picked it up. It blared a headline, 'EDEN RESIGNS! *Prime Minister Anthony Eden Tenders His Resignation to Queen'*. I looked at the date; Wednesday 9th January 1957. Oh, dear sweet Jesus. Well, that explains everything: and nothing.

By this time it was after half past eight and I had said I'd see Chris at nine. If I tried to use this as the latest excuse for being late there would be serious repercussions, like the withdrawal of sexual favours for an indefinite period. She'd be fine, she'd just make other arrangements. Pulling my mobile from my back pocket which had about eighty pence left on pay as you go, I dialled her from my contact list. When there was no sound at all from the phone I realised that I didn't have 2017 on my contact list. I could dial person to person but not year to year and I was going to have to talk to these good people at Samsung about that.

Dragging myself back towards the station I had time to look around me. Union Street was made up of large granite setts and the rain glistened on them reflecting the

33

colours of the changing traffic lights. Even though it was getting late a horse and cart trundled by me, the horses hooves ringing off the stones, the carter sitting huddled on the cart giving the horse a desultory tap with a cane. A tram trundled south with 'Crossstobs' on its destination panel, the three s's oddly running together. The road was eerily quiet, just a couple of tramcars and half a dozen cars, all black, slipped by. I crossed Union Street with the lights and went back into the station.

Glasgow Central Station on a dreary January evening in nineteen fifty-seven was the last place I thought I'd ever be and the curiosity of the railway buff in me took it all in. A large dark green Standard Class Brittania, 70021, 'Morning Star', hauling eleven carmine and cream coaches from Birmingham eased to a halt a few yards from the buffers of platform ten and belched out a sigh of smoky relief. Doors opened noisily and a sea of people descended, most lumbering large brown or black suitcases, the kind my grandma had under her bed for storing old bedclothes and smelling of camphor and gin. A couple of ticket inspectors stood guard at the wrought iron barrier making sure no one passed through without handing over a one inch square piece of cardboard that passed as a ticket. Above them hung a massive hoarding advertising 'Askit for Headaches' just in case you thought it was for grouting. They knew how to make up catchy slogans in those days. A shrill whistle screamed as a guard waved a green flag to a grimy driver whose engine chuffed in acknowledgment and inched forward like a groaning mastodon lumbering across the plains. Thick smoke poured out as the wheels slipped and struggled to get a grip on the damp rails. Semaphore signals clanged back and bounced to horizontal.

A line of old, black taxis stood at a stance on an inside roadway behind the odd torpedo shaped building that housed the departure and arrival information boards. In the middle of the station concourse there sat a large burnished first world war fifteen inch shell on a plinth about six feet tall surrounded by a six smaller six inch shells topped each topped with a two inch bullet. On the main shell was a slot for charity coins for the Royal Sick Children's Hospital at Yorkhill. Almost directly above it was the clock that I had walked under when the lightning or whatever it was, struck me, the hands still stuck at three minutes to eight. Just below it the tarmac was a bit charred.

Where was I going when it hit? Think man! I remembered I was walking towards the Hope Street exit where now a couple of taxis sat waiting for traffic lights to let them out. Trying to figure out the angles I walked slowly towards the point directly underneath the clock, closed my eyes, and continued on.

Fuck me, hello 2017!

Chapter Three

Chris slumbered not so gently beside me after a rather substantial bout of sexual calisthenics which left her satisfied and me exhausted. I looked up the definition of nymphomaniac in the dictionary but it didn't seem to quite cover her requirements, not that I'm complaining. I think the idea of coming to the Caribbean with me fuelled her libido although she didn't give me time to tell her that financial limitations would preclude her unless she could come up with the cash herself. In fact she might even have to sub me.

I looked at her lying there, mouth open, dribbling slightly onto the pillow. She looked so cute. She snored softly, gently rattling a window pane or two. She was a simple soul with simple needs, food, a roof, and sex; lots of sex. Oh, and a fair amount of Bacardi, a steady supply of new clothes, unlimited access to Daddy's credit card and other bits and bobs. There were times when she reminded me of Eartha Kitt singing 'Santa Baby'. God knows what she saw in me since my ability to keep her supplied with any of these things, with the exception of the odd Bacardi, was severely limited, and I had detected prior to today a certain waning enthusiasm for my debonair charm, if not my body. Maybe the mention of Barbados had postponed what eventually must be inevitable. That would be a pity; she was a major source of income.

I hadn't told her about what had happened earlier because it was beyond doubt that she would think I'd been on the magic mushrooms. I was beginning to wonder if I hadn't been hallucinating myself.

'Where have you been today?'

'Oh, just to 1957 and back.'

No, it wasn't going to wash. Besides I wanted to see if it was real, if I could do it again. This time I would be prepared; I could take a proper look round and see what the place looked like sixty years ago. Maybe I could look up my great-grandparents. OK, maybe not. I was brought up in Clarkston. What was it like in the old days? What did people do? Were there disco's? Did people really like Max Bygraves? What were the Rangers like? Maybe I could take in a game. How much did things cost? The barman at the Horseshoe said something about 'one and fourpence.' I thought he meant one pound fourpence and I thought that was cheap. It didn't matter, I didn't have any of the fifties money. (I didn't have any 2017 money either, come to that) although I still had about ten pounds left over from Barry's largesse but that was worthless back in 1957 in its present format.

I tried to understand what had happened. Clearly what had taken place was some sort of hiccup in the space time continuum. But what was the space time continuum other than a whole load of sci-fi babble conducted by some guy in a wheelchair and a synthesised voice?

I tiptoed into Chris's kitchen not wanting to disturb her although the massed pipes and drums of the Royal Scots Dragoon Guards backed by the Grimethorpe Colliery brass band playing reveille would be hard pushed to get a response. Chris's computer was on sleep so I was able to get onto Google without any problem.

Typing in 'space time continuum' brought
bunch of sites, mostly all papers from scientis
full of diagrams and the sort of algebraic eq
turn a normal brain to porridge. Even Wikipedia, which I
regarded as the font of all wisdom and the officially
recognised way of settling bets and arguments at the pub
started out by stating 'In non-relativistic classical
mechanics the use of Euclidean space instead of
spacetime is appropriate...' I mean, why can't they just
talk fucking English?

Then I saw a site that explained it quite simply.
Imagine a cine camera taking a reel of thirty-five
millimetre film of you at the standard twenty-four frames
per second. Each frame would be time stamped at the
exact moment in time it was taken, down to the last
twenty-fourth of a second. Now imagine taking a film of
an entire day of your life. Then cut the film into its
2,073,600 individual frames and stack them into a pile
one on top of the other from the first at the top to the
last at the bottom. (Just imagine, okay?) This, in effect, is
a depiction of space time since that pile of frames shows
you where you were three-dimensionally, i.e. exact
longitude, latitude and height above sea level, (length,
breadth and width), but also *when* at any given point in
the pile. The pile is, in effect, a depiction of a space-time
continuum of a twenty four hour period. Life is exactly
like that except you can't go forward other than at the
existing pace of our lives and you can't go back, period.

Except, at three minutes to eight last night, a bolt of
lightning had struck the station roof, travelled through
the clock and zapped me so that now my body was hard
wired to 1957 instead of 19.57 so that every-time I
walked through the exact spot where it all happened, if I

.d it at the same time, namely three minutes before eight, I'd wind up back in 1957. And it must work in the other direction because even although it was more like half past eight when I came back to the present, the hands of the clock still stood at three minutes to eight because it had stopped due to the strike. The lightning had created a disconnect in the time part of the space-time continuum so that last night when I had come to I was in the exact same place but I had slipped back in time like the needle in a record player (remember them?) jumping backwards when you give it a jolt. And, even more amazing, I understood all this.

So where did that take me? I recalled the heated discussion with the bar staff in the Horseshoe. They wouldn't take my money and I could now see why. But what, I wondered, was a tenner in today's money worth back then, and more importantly, what could I buy with it? The first site I checked on the computer was moneysorter.co.uk and sure enough all I needed to do was type in the year and the amount and – Jesus Christ! – one hundred and sixty seven pounds eighty pence. *Really?* So I asked Google the price of a pint in 1957. Bingo! One and fivepence. That seemed about right; the guy in the Horseshoe wanted one and fourpence and the Horseshoe always was a bargain basement pub. At that time in the morning and with my brain a bit befuddled by generous attention to Chris's well stocked supply of alcohol, it took me a good few minutes to work out that a pint of beer back then cost about seven pence in today's coin. Jesus, I could get about a hundred and forty pints for a tenner! First round's on me, guys!

Rummaging about Chris's cupboards I found a jar of instant coffee so I put the kettle on, let it boil, then made myself a brew. A quick raid in the biscuit tin yielded up a couple of KitKat's so that was breakfast sorted. The next problem was, of course, how to get hold of whatever passed for money back then, so back to the all knowing computer for the answer. eBay was the obvious place to start so I had a trawl through that. It didn't take long to find that Scotland had no less than six banks each printing their own notes back in the old days. There was the Royal Bank of Scotland, The Bank of Scotland, The National Bank of Scotland, The Commercial Bank of Scotland, The Clydesdale Bank, The British Linen Bank. (maybe that's where they laundered money). It was a counterfeiter's wet dream. Then there was the Bank of England. Anything printed under the auspices of Preppiat or Beale as the Chief Cashier of the Bank of England would work, in fact any note as long as it was printed before 1957 and not out of date would fit the bill. As for coins, there was ha'pennies, pennies, threepenny bits, sixpences, shillings, two shilling pieces known as a florin, and half crowns. Since a florin was ten pence in today's money I could buy a pie and a pint with one and still have change for the juke box, as they say. All well and good, but where do I get yesterday's money?

There was stirring from the bedroom. Chris had come out of her coma and I could hear the mental wheels ticking from here trying to work out if it was Paisley Road or Tuesday morning.

'Gordon?'

I ignored the call.

'Gordon!'

Birds across the street took off in fright.

'Good morning, my little barracuda.'

'What are you doing? Come back to bed.'

40

'In a minute.'

'Are you using my computer?'

'Just checking something.'

'Are you watching porn again? If you are, bring it in here where it could do us both some good.'

'No. Give me a minute.'

'What time is it?'

I checked my watch. 'Quarter to eleven.'

'Shit, I'm on at twelve.' Chris worked as an auxiliary nurse at the Royal Infirmary. 'Maybe I should throw a sickie.'

That was the last thing I wanted. I needed time on my own to try to develop things further, like testing out if I could pay another visit to the good old days. Like trying to put some money into the Bank of Yesterday.

'Maybe you shouldn't. You had one already this week.'

I could hear muffled curses and groans but she eventually shuffled into the kitchen in all her naked glory. Suddenly my research didn't seem quite so pressing.

She yawned, 'Christ, I've got a mouth like a camel's crotch.'

Ah well, perhaps on second thoughts.

An hour later and I was walking along Argyle Street towards Glasgow Cross where I knew there was a wee shop that sold anything as long it was useless. You could buy 2010 calendars and gas mantles and clay pipes. If they didn't have it they could get it in a day. I think it did a handy line in redundant 747's for emergent African dictatorships. If you wanted to buy dust this was your place. It had it by the bucket load. The door had a spring mounted bell that alerted someone from a Dickens' novel to my presence and he looked at me somewhat malevolently.

'What?'

Right enough, there was no 'Welcome Host' sign on the door.

'Do you sell any old coins or notes, fifties like?'

'Nae notes but ye can look in that jaur.' He nodded to a large sweetie jar packed with coins on a shelf. 'An' there's merr in that biscuit tin.' He pointed to a McVittie's tin beside it.

'Mind if I have a look?'

'Fill your boots.'

'This could take a while, that all right?'

'Ah'm no gaun anywhere.'

Three quarters of an hour later I had unearthed two pounds ten and six in old money that was issued on or before 1957.

'How much for these?' I asked, interrupting the proprietor from his 'Daily Star'.'

He looked at the coins of which there were about thirty. 'Ten pounds.'

'I've only got eight pounds on me.'

'Right, give me the eight and leave me in peace.'

Done.

Outside I did a swift calculation. What I had weighing the pocket of my only jacket down had the buying power of about thirty-five of today's pounds in 1957. At one and fourpence a pint I could buy...I could buy...well, a lot of pints. Jesus, how did they manage before decimalisation? I started back towards the station thinking that if this didn't work I was going to be left with just a couple of pounds and a pocketful of shrapnel.

The station was moderately busy. A train bound for Birmingham was about to leave and a few latecomers scurried towards platform two. The main difference between now and yesterday was that the weather was reasonably fine and bright, otherwise it was just another day in the life of trains. What started to nag at me was my confidence that all I needed to do was repeat yesterday's manoeuvre but today there was no thunder and lightning. I saw the clock, now repaired and working normally just ahead of me. Anyway, I took a deep breath, closed my eyes and ventured forward on the light, as the bard would say. Nada, zilch, nothing. The Birmingham Voyager started to pull out and a sprinter gurgled to a halt at platform three. Shit. This wasn't in the script. Trying a different tack I figured out the angle of approach that I used last night. Eyes closed, forward. Still nothing. All I was conscious of was the rattle of thirty coins as they distorted my pocket.

Think Gordon. I thought. Of, course. I needed to wait until three minutes to eight. I could only enter and exit at the exact time of last night's lightning strike. I checked the clock again; three thirty. Chris was working, Barry was doing what fiancés do, whatever that is, so I had four and a half hours to kill and less than two present day pounds with which to kill it.

Some time later, nursing the dregs of a half pint under the withering gaze of Peggy, one of the Horseshoe's delectable barmaids, a harridan with all the charismatic allure of a Paisley postcode, I saw that the clock was slowly creeping past half past seven. Time to make a move.

Just before twenty to eight saw me in the station concourse looking nervously around.

'Gordon! Gordon Lorne!'

Oh Jesus, no. It was Jerry Frame, a long lost quasi buddy from my travel days.

'Gordon, long time no see! Good to see you, what are you doing with yourself since, since, well never mind that, how are you?'

'Great to see you too Jerry,' I gritted with fake sincerity long borne of practice. 'How's, eh, eh, how's Jane?'

'Oh, ancient history. We just sort of drifted apart.'

Actually I had heard that he'd been caught shagging a teen who had just turned seventeen and was lucky to escape the sex offenders register, her parents, and an appearance before the court since the offence took place on a well known dogging site on the south side of Glasgow.

'Time for a pint?'

A glance at the clock told me that it was nudging past the quarter to mark and I had to get rid of him.

'Great idea, Jerry, but I need to find a cash machine. Why don't you get the first round in and I'll catch you up.' I nodded towards the station bar.

'Don't worry about it, my shout – come on.' He pulled me by the elbow.

'Eh, okay. Tell you what. Need a pee. Catch you up.'

'Good idea. I need one too.'

Christ, this guy was on to me like Velcro. I hurried down to the downstairs toilets, Jerry hard on my heels and after a quick handshake with the vicar we came back up and made our way to the bar. I glance at the clock showed that it was six minutes to the hour so I needed to think of something fast.

'So you're with Christine now. Lucky, lucky,' he leered suggestively.

Clearly he hadn't changed much in the intervening years but he had given me an idea. I took out my mobile.

'Sorry mate, glad you mentioned her. Meant to call.' I fumbled with the phone. 'Shit, no signal, give me a sec.'

Without waiting for a reply I nipped out of the bar. Four minutes to. The clock hung suspended above me and I slowly approached it as if I was walking towards the Hope Street exit. As the minute hand moved on to three minutes to eight I walked under it. A nano-second later there I was, back in the good old days. This time I walked past people unnoticed. I had dressed a little more conservatively, a T-shirt covered with a dark sweater and an anorak, although even the anorak seemed a little out of place. A pair of dark, shapeless trousers and old trainers topped off the outfit and while I wouldn't win any prizes in a well dressed man competition most of the men passing by wore coats and suits and shirts and ties so I wasn't too conspicuous.

I took a little more time to familiarise myself this time. Then I had a worrying thought. I was going to have to wait until just before eight tomorrow night before I could get back again. I looked up at the clock. It was still stuck at seven fifty-seven so it hadn't been repaired. That's okay. I could get back anytime as long as the clock was still at that time.

I took the Gordon Street exit this time. To my left were ticket windows where in the future there would be a Virgin Trains ticket lounge and information bureau. Taxis lined up on the ramp just outside the station, the old black cabs with a single cubicle for the driver and a small open platform to his left for stacking luggage.

Turning to the right for a few yards I came to the junction of Union Street and Gordon Street and stood at the lights. The pavement was covered in bird shit and I looked up to see dozens of birds, starlings, roosting on the overhead cables running from the lampposts. A couple of old standard trams rumbled up towards St Vincent Street and stopped, one behind the other, at a post with a red 'fare stage' sign attached to it. A couple of black motor cars pulled up to allow two or three passengers to cross to the tram. I was entranced. I looked down Union Street and took in what I had missed before. The shops were all quite classy; Dolcis Shoes, and A&J Ferguson on the right hand side looked like quite an expensive food store. A large tearoom, Peacock's, Smart's Furniture Store, John Collier tailors with well dressed dummies in the window, all kitted out in suits with shirt and tie or tweedy sports jackets and cavalry twill trousers stood out all brightly lit down towards Argyle Street. Burton's was on the other side of the road but the display was more of the same.

It was dry but cold so I made my way back up the street. A wedding group entered the Ca d'Oro building and at its corner was a huge City Bakeries. I'd heard of them; my mother used to tell me about their cream buns. This was a Glasgow I had never imagined before and I rather liked the look of it. I always thought of it as dirty and grimy, and to be sure there was a lot of that, but, on this little stretch anyway, it had a touch of faded class. It looked a lot better than all the junk shops and pound stores and boarded up places that there is now; or the future now if you know what I mean.

Just before the Ca d'Oro there was a bar, Laing's, and it looked like my sort of place so I went in. It was all men, of course, dressed much the same as the Horseshoe crowd the night before. In fact the place had a sort of Horseshoe feel to it, people standing smoking, reading the 'Evening Times' or 'Citizen' and generally shooting the breeze. The drinks in front of them were almost all exclusively beer or whisky, and some lager. There was a snug and I looked in the partly open door. Two men and a woman were deep in conversation. So that's where they're kept, I thought.

Standing at the bar there was a group of four youths exchanging details of unlikely exploits with the opposite sex. They were dressed in longish draped jackets and drainpipe trousers and their shirts were knotted at the collar with string ties. Their shoes, almost identical, were elevated by means of an inch of crepe rubber. Each sported a greasy hair style that featured a forward combed quiff. One of the group constantly adjusted his with a comb. Clearly this was the style of the day.

There was an empty stool between a couple of worthies at the bar so I plonked myself down. One of the two barmen came over. He was stocky, ginger haired and in need of a dentist, evidenced by the fact that he had a false front tooth that didn't keep time with his mouth when he spoke.

I waited till his tooth caught up and in my most nonchalant voice I said, 'Pint of heavy.'

I turned and looked at the guy on my right, a working man of about fifty who was staring intently at his half full glass and the empty whisky glass beside it.

'Aye,' I nodded.

He nodded back at me, his face as cheerless as a prescription note for haemorrhoid cream. At that my pint was placed in front of me. 'One and fourpence.'

I fumbled in my pocket and brought out a small selection of coins and examined them before picking out a shilling and a sixpence. It was taken without comment and he came back a moment later with a couple of coppers in change.

'Any food?' I asked. Realisation dawned, occasioned by rumblings from my stomach, that I hadn't eaten anything since this morning sixty years hence.

'Aye, there's pie beans and chips, or peas. Ah think there's mince.' He shouted at a door in the back wall, 'Any mince left, Maisie?'

There was a muffled 'aye' in return.

'Aye, mince,' he confirmed.

Pie, beans and chips sounded good so he shouted the order in. Five minutes later out came Maisie, her hair in a turbaned headscarf and wearing a wraparound apron, bearing a generous steaming plateful. 'Which wan o' youse is this?'

I caught her eye and she put it down in front of me together with some cutlery that suggested that Uri Geller might have paid a visit recently.

'That was quick.'

'Aye, ah keep them warm a' day. You've got the last o' it.'

I didn't quite know how to take this but, God, it was good.

'No' seen you in before,' the barman nodded at me as he dried a glass with a dirty cloth.

'Never knew this place existed,' I said, which was no less than the truth.

'Well, ye know noo. One and tuppence.'

'What?'

'Pie, beans and chips – wan and tuppence.'

48

'Oh sure. Don't know how you do it for the money.'

I gave him another shilling plus two pennies. I was getting used to this. 'Have one yourself,' and I gave him another one shilling and two thruppeny pieces.

'Thanks, I'll save it for later if that's okay.'

My God, dinner, a pint and one for the barman and so far all for twenty pence. Actually more like seventy five pence taking into account my exchange rate but I could get used to this. I downed my pint and ordered another - and another.

It seemed that the guy on my right hadn't moved in half an hour other than to lift his pint, the same one he had been drinking when I came in. By this time I felt quite convivial, what, with having dined well on Glasgow's culinary delights and knocking back three pints of McEwan's best.

'What can I get you?' I offered to the man.

'Half and a pint,' he said without the slightest hesitation.

'A pint for my friend here and another for yourself, my good man,' I said in that jocular fashion that only alcoholic bonhomie can induce. 'And another for me.'

The barman raised an eyebrow but poured the order without question.

'Gordon,' I said and offered a hand to my new friend.

'Naw, Davie.'

'Sorry, I'm Gordon,' and I offered my hand again which Davie reluctantly shook but clearly felt it was a reasonable reward for a drink.

'Thanks for the drink.' He downed the scotch in one, a quarter gill whatever that was but it looked like a large one.

'This your local, then?' I asked.

He didn't answer but pulled another gulp. I was about to ask again assuming he hadn't heard me but he beat me to it.

'Naw.'

Clearly conversation wasn't his strong point but I persisted. I had bought him a drink after all; courtesy demanded some pleasantries.

'So, just finished work, then?'

'Just startin'.'

'Right, what do you do?'

'Ask a lot of questions, don't ye?'

Oops, touchy.

'Just making conversation, like.'

'Is that a fact?' He took another pull at the beer and looked at the clock. 'Engine driver.'

I nearly choked on my pint. Here was a guy who had just shifted a couple of pints and two serious whiskies about to drive a train.

'Really?' I squeaked, 'Really?' Lower this time.

He pulled a navy cap from his pocket and sure enough there was a little enamel light blue totem on the front with its British Railways logo written in that distinctive sans serif font.

'Ten twenty to London.'

'You're driving a train to London?'

'Only as far as Carlisle.'

That's all right, then. I was momentarily stunned. Fast forward sixty years and a whiff of mouthwash would lose you your licence for a year and cost you your job.

'I don't want to appear, well, concerned or anything but, eh, is it okay to drive a train with a, well, you've had a couple?'

'Nae law against it and anyway it steadies mah nerves.' He downed the last of his pint.

No *law* against it! He saw my look of astonishment.

'Look, it's no' nuclear science. The train steers itself – ah just go when it's green and stop when it's red, okay?'

He picked up his cap and headed erratically for the door shunting a couple of chairs and a table en route. I looked at the barman who just shrugged. The clock ticked over to ten past nine and the barman took a look at it and called out to everyone, 'Last orders, gents.'

'What do you mean, last orders?' I was just beginning to enjoy myself.

'Drink up, it's closing time in twenty minutes.'

'Closing time? I only just got here.'

'Licensing hours, sure you know that fine well.'

'Let me get this straight, you've got to shut up shop at half past nine?'

He looked at me strangely. 'I think you've maybe had enough, don't you?'

'Is there anywhere else I can go?'

'Aye, home.'

'It's only just after nine.'

'Just that. It's the law. Where have you been?'

You wouldn't believe me if I told you, I thought. So that was it. Back in the good old days they shut the pubs at nine-thirty. It reminded me a line from that old Tom Paxton song about Toledo, Ohio where the sidewalks get rolled up at ten. Maybe this wasn't going to be as much fun after all. I still had the best part of two pounds burning a hole in my pocket and that could do a lot of damage these days.

'Have you no' got a home to go to?' the barman asked me rhetorically but now that he said it I realised I hadn't, not in this century anyway.

Glasgow was eerily quiet as I stepped out into the winter chill but at least it was still dry so I decided on some air before catching the clock to the next century. I walked down to Jamaica Street and turned right into Midland Street under the railway bridge. On my right there was a windowless shop with 'Turf Accountant' painted above. I wondered what they did there – count grass? I liked coming across all the same places I knew but weren't the same. Besides it gave me time to think. I was beginning to realise that there were opportunities to be found in this new situation. How many times have we all said if I only knew then what I know now? Well I knew a lot of things now that they didn't know then. I could predict their future. And if I could predict their future there was money to be made.

Eventually I found myself back at Central so I strolled around. There was a little machine at the entrance to platforms one and two that dispensed platform tickets for one penny so on a whim I splashed out and bought one. By now it was ten past ten. There were two trains occupying the platforms, both London overnight expresses scheduled to leave within five minutes of each other, the first at twenty past ten. Was that not the train Davie was driving? I sauntered up to the top of the platform where two magnificent Pacific 'Duchesses' oozed steam as they waited for the off. Sure enough, there, holding the regulator on one of them was Davie, well fortified with whisky and beer. He caught my eye just as the whistle blew then opened the regulator a little and the massive engine eased forward in a miasma of

52

hissing steam and smoke. I gave a little salute, two fingers touching my forehead in greeting, and he gave me a two fingered salute back.

Chapter Four

Having manoeuvred the transition back to the twentieth century without any difficulty I was now lying alone in my own bed in my cheerless bedsit, Christine clearly having other plans that didn't include me. My mind was taken up with possibilities of profit from my time travel facility. Clearly there were many opportunities. Armed as I was with a computer, albeit so old that it was powered by coal, and an iPhone, I could easily check on events in 1957; like who won horse races, who won football matches. I could predict any future event from the past with pinpoint accuracy. I could make myself rich in pretty short order. In fact, I could easily make the three thousand I needed to go to Barbados or wherever for Barry's forthcoming nuptials. I could even have enough to take Christine and try to make Lesley jealous. Okay, that last bit was pushing it.

Right, supposing I could get hold of a couple of hundred pounds in 1957 currency, that would probably cost around seven hundred or eight hundred now, maybe less if I shopped around, but it would be worth about sixteen times as much as today, around three thousand three hundred. I could then parlay that up with some judicious betting and make some serious money. I lay awake staring at a trail of cobwebs dangling from the ceiling, Irish lace my Grandma called it in her non politically correct innocence, trying to think this thing through.

Firstly I needed to get hold of a couple of hundred pounds. I could either borrow it from Christine but I was already into her heavily and I would need to let her in on the deal, and I didn't want to do that, not yet anyway, or I could wait until my subsistence Giro came in at the beginning of the week. Secondly, I would need to find where I could exchange it for old money cheaply. Thirdly, I would need to have a betting strategy as I couldn't bet too much in one place or they'd get suspicious if (when) I kept winning. But even if I won a thousand, a huge amount then, it wouldn't go very far today. Clearly this would need a lot of planning.

Barry called to see if I fancied a pint later. Does Pinnochio have a wooden cock?

I spent some time wondering if I should tell him what happened after I left him a couple of nights back but I knew I would; it was hardly something you can keep to yourself and secrets and me are like money and me; easily parted. I went for a run around Kelvingrove Park just to get the endorphins to kick in and clear the head. It was clear but cold and my breath traced patterns in the air as I ran. Running gives me time to think properly and the more I thought of the opportunities that the loophole in the laws of physics presented, the more excited I became. There's something about running that concentrates the mind. You get wrapped up in your own world and your own thoughts. Some people like to run with ear buds in pumping music into their brains and run to the beat, each step keeping time. Others, like me, use the rhythm of the steady pace to think, to imagine, to dream. Some of my most productive ideas come to me as I run, I'm just damned if I know what I do with them.

There was money to be made here; big money. There was also fame. Think of all the songs I knew that weren't written back then. They'd never heard of Bowie or Queen, never listened to the Eagles or Rod. Christ, imagine Christmas without Slade! I could write them myself and not be accused of plagiarism. How can you plagiarise something that hasn't even been written? Jesus, *The Beatles!* John, Paul, George and Richard Starkey were still kids at Quarry Street school. I could be a Beatle! (Things were beginning to run away from me a little). I could take a train to Liverpool, contrive to sit next to a sixteen year old Paul and start singing and humming under by breath. 'Hey Jane, da da de da. Take a sad song and make it da da dee. Remember to take her into your dum dum de de... Man, wouldn't that just fuck with his brain!

And what about Elvis? He was just about starting to make it in '57. I could send him lyrics and music for 'Girl of my Best Friend.' The possibilities were endless - a bit like the empty space between my ears.

The Art Galleries slipped by on my right as I ran on to Kelvin Way and turned up towards Gibson Street then right and put on an extra push up the hill past the statue of Bud Neill's Lobey Dosser and his two legged horse, El Fideldo. Dreaming dreams of the impossibly possible, I turned into the closemouth entrance to my humble hovel for a shower, a shampoo and a shit although not necessarily in that order.

We sat in the usual far corner of the bar with a pint generously sponsored by Barry. I should get a shirt with that message printed on it. Pleasantries had to be observed so I went through the motions of asking how the plans for the forthcoming big event were going which he thought I meant weekend poker school before he realised I was talking about something which was likely to put the hems on his poker school for all time or hell freezes over, whichever comes first.

'Oh you mean the wedding?'

'How soon we forget.'

'Oh, yeah well, fine I suppose. I'm leaving it all to her.'

He looked totally bewildered at the way that events seemed to be overtaking him. A casual post-coital, throwaway line about him being happy to spend the rest of his life like this was apparently interpreted as a pleading proposal, immediately accepted, and before he figured out what havoc he had just wrought, he was desperately trying to keep up as she blew a trail of devastation through John Lewis looking at wallpaper and brass toilet roll holders. He looked at me and I could see a hint of desperation, like someone trapped in the Hampton Court maze after midnight when the janitor has gone home with the map.

He tried to assert some authority. 'So, still saving for the trip? I heard her mention the Almond Beach in Barbados. Pretty pricy.'

I affected an air of studied nonchalance. 'Doesn't look as if it'll be a problem so you'd better tell the strabismally challenged Kelso and that greaseball brother of Lesley's not to keep their hopes up.'

'Strabismally?'

'I believe skelly-eyed is the technical term.'

'So he may be disappointed yet?'

'The tears will be rolling down his back,' I said.

'Pray tell.'

'I have cunning plan, to quote young Baldrick.'

Barry leaned forward He clearly needed to talk about something other than the colour of bridesmaids' dresses.

'I'm all ears.'

I took a long pull at my pint for fortification; this would be a hard story to sell let alone buy.

'Okay, you know after you left a couple of nights back?' He nodded. 'Well, I dodged into the station to avoid the rain and the weirdest, I mean the *weirdest* thing happened to me, man.'

I told him about the clock, the time, the lightning. I told him about my subsequent visit and I told him I thought that I could see a way to make big bucks. He looked at me for a long, long moment and took a swig of his beer. He looked at me again without saying anything.

I helped him along. 'I'll need some seed money, of course, but I'll cut you in.'

'Seed money?'

'Seed money.'

He sighed with the kind of sigh that only a long suffering Scotland football supporter at the prospect of a World Cup qualifier against England could sigh. A "here we go again" sigh.

'Let me get this straight. You need a sub so that you can travel back in time, put it on a horse or two in races of which you know the result, somehow bring the winnings back so that you can be my best man?'

'That's it exactly. Or I could wait on my Giro but that's kinda spoken for.'

He picked up his mobile and scrolled down the list of contents.

'What are you doing, mate?' I asked.

'Just thought I'd give Brian Kelso a ring to see if he's going to be free in April.'

'Aww, Barry. Do you not believe me?'

'How can I put this? Oh, I know. *Are you out of your fucking mind?*'

'Look, I know it sounds incredible,' Barry looked at me with one of *those* looks, the kind that says, 'You think?' but I steamrollered on, 'but it's true. Look, here's the money I changed if you don't believe me.' I pulled out the coins and notes that were still in my pocket. 'Now do you see?'

'What are you talking about? You told me yourself that you bought them down the Saltmarket. It doesn't prove anything other than you're a certifiable nutter.'

'What if I could prove it to you.'

'How? How are you going to prove it to me?' He was clearly pissed off. 'Look Gordon, mate, I seriously don't have time for this. I've got some heavy duty things on my mind right now. So how, exactly, are you going to prove it to me short of taking me with you. In fact, there's an idea, take me with you, it'll get me away from a trip to John Lewis.'

I looked at him as if he was the demented one. 'I can't do that.'

'Why not, exactly?'

'Because you weren't hit by lightning in the station.'

'So I just take your word for it?'

'Have I ever let you down?'

I knew this was a mistake the minute it had left my mouth. Barry looked at me with an expression of incredulous amazement.

'Okay, okay, maybe I have once or twice.' My haste was almost embarrassing, 'But I just can't.'

Barry drained his glass. 'Well, that's it for me Gordon, old son. Got to be going. Say hi to the other inmates at Carstairs for me.'

'Wait a minute, come on, wait. Tell you what, let's have another and by that time it will be nearly eight. We'll go to the station and I'll disappear while you watch and then I come right back. Okay?' I pleaded.

'I don't believe I'm having this conversation. I'm supposed to buy you another pint, accompany to you to Central, and watch while you walk into a black hole and wait till you come back?'

'What have you got to lose?'

'My sanity.'

There was a fire in his eye when he put his face a couple of inches from mine.

'Here's the deal. I'll buy the pint, it goes on your tab, we go to the station and go through this smoke and mirrors routine, then when I finally confirm that you've caught the last train to la-la land and gone right off the cuckoo scale, I phone Brian Kelso and we both get on with our lives. Deal?'

I clinked my empty glass against his. 'Deal.'

Chapter Five

We crossed Renfield Street dodging buses in silence and made our way into the station through the main Gordon Street entrance. The time on the clock above the concourse was seven fifty. A party of teenage girls dressed for January weather in sleeveless tops and pelmets chattered excitedly by, all set for a night, any night, on the pull.

'So what now?' asked Gordon.

'We wait.'

'Till seven fifty-seven, is that it? At the third stroke it will be nineteen fifty-seven A.D? That it?'

'You'll see.'

I hoped to God he would.

'Okay, let's get this straight. You're going to do some David Blaine disappearing trick for about a minute then just reappear? How do I now that you've actually gone back in time and not just pulled some stunt?'

It was actually a reasonable question. Assuming the clock on the other side had been fixed I would only have one minute exactly before it changed to two minutes to eight and I didn't want to be stuck for twenty four hours before getting back to the present. Besides, Barry would have given up in disgust and gone home.

I gave the matter some thought. 'Okay, I will have one minute. How about if I buy the evening paper and bring it back. That'll show the date. Proof positive – how about that?'

61

He mused on this for a while.

'In your own time, Baz.' I nodded meaningfully at the clock which was approaching the allotted time.

'Okay then, let's see you.'

At that the clock minute hand slipped onto three minutes to and with a quick look around, I stepped underneath – and into the past. John Menzies had a news kiosk between platforms one and two crowned with another huge clock and I sprinted over to it. The girl behind the counter was having an animated chat with someone who clearly wanted to recount the gory details of last night at the Plaza. I gave it a few seconds, grabbed an 'Evening Citizen' and threw down a coin, a shilling.

'Keep the change.'

Running back to the centre of the concourse I nearly came a cropper when an old codger, well he looked old, and breathing more than a hint of stale beer, stopped me just before I ran under the clock which by now had been repaired.

'Haud oan ther, son. Ye wouldnae huv a light, wid ye?'

He had half an unlit cigarette dangling from his mouth.

'Sorry, no,' and perhaps a little too roughly I pulled him out of the way and ran through the space under the clock. I would have given anything to have seen his face when he witnessed the most amazing disappearing trick since Glenn Miller stepped aboard his winged cardboard box tied up with string and sealing wax.

'Jesus H Christ!' It takes a lot to impress Barry but I could see I had done it big time. His face went through more contortions that a Picasso cubist portrait.

'Ta da!' I waived the paper in his face. 'They seek him here, they seek him there.'

'Let me see that.' He grabbed the paper and scanned the headlines. MacMILLAN SET FOR PREMIERSHIP screamed the banner.

'Read the date.'

'What?'

'The date, read it.'

Barry read it and reread it and reread it again. 'Friday 11th January 1957.'

He looked at it again, looked at me and shook his head. 'This is impossible. I don't know how you did it but it's not possible to go back or forward in time. I'm no physicist but I sort of got what Einstein said. The arrow of time only goes one way and all that.'

'But you can look back in time, we do it all the time.'

'How so?'

'The brightest star in the night sky is Sirius. It's about seven light years away so that means when we look at it we see it as it was seven years ago. It might not even be there now.'

'Yeah, but you can't actually go there, can you?'

The clock was now at eight. Directly under the centre of it on the glossy, tiled concourse there was still a scorch mark, faded now but still visible.

'See that?' His eyes followed my gaze. 'That's where I nearly bought the farm.'

There was serious doubt in his eyes now. 'It's really not possible.' But he was talking to himself now.

He scuffed the mark with his shoe not really expecting anything to change. Then he ran underneath the clock himself but, of course, bugger all happened except he looked like a right dick, confirmed by the strange look and a tut-tut from a woman scurrying to her train who almost collided with him. He looked at me again as if either I was mad or he was and he was reaching a rather worrying conclusion.

Egging him on I said, 'If Penn and Teller were here themselves they would be amazed too. They can pretty well explain away any trick but when there's no trick to explain...' I let him figure the rest out for himself. 'Back to the 'shoe?'

'Back to the 'shoe,' he agreed.

Savouring the warm glow of success all the more sweet for its scarcity, I led the way.

'And don't look so fucking smug about it either.'

Enjoying another pint this time bought without demur by Barry, I bided my time. I didn't need to wait long.

'So what happens now?'

Bingo! Barry was beginning to see the light.

I went over with him how I could find a way of changing two or three hundred into pre '57 money. I could probably get around fifty pounds worth in various denominations which would be the equivalent of around eight hundred pounds. The problem was that people didn't throw their money around very much back then. If I was going to use some of it for wagering a bet of any more than a pound it might raise a few eyebrows when a good bet was a couple of shillings each way. I would have to look to placing some sort of accumulator with about three horses with accrued odds of around thirty or forty to one. Three horses each at three to one would do it.

'How does that work?' asked Barry, a novice in these matters.

'You select three horses with those odds to win and all three need to win otherwise you lose the bet. Your pound goes on the first horse at three to one and wins so you get three pounds plus your original pound going on to the next horse and it wins at three to one. So now you have twelve pounds plus your stake of four pounds...'

'Four pounds?'

'Yes, your first horse returned a total of four pounds, remember?'

'Right, I think so.'

'Do keep up, Barry. So now you have twelve pounds plus four pounds, sixteen altogether going on to horse number three at three to one. Sixteen times three, Barry?'

'Er, forty-eight.'

'Right. Plus the sixteen pounds stake. That's a return of sixty-three quid for a one pound bet,' I explained.

'Christ, do you do this all the time?'

'Barry, this is two thousand and seventeen – I don't know who wins now and that's why I lost most of the time. That's why I actually don't bet at all now. It's a mugs' game unless you know what's going to win. And we do.'

He mulled this over, the gears in his marketing brain crunching with the cogs in his accountancy one like a learner driver grappling with clutch, brake and accelerator all at the same time. He spotted the fly in the ointment and added another one for good measure.

'So supposing you put all this into action and win, say, a couple of thousand which, as you point out, was a fortune then, it's a handy wee sum now but hardly earth shattering. And you've still got to sell it back to modern cash so you'll not be that much better off.'

Actually a thousand pounds now would be a bit of a life saver but we both left the thought unspoken.

He continued, 'What you need to do is to figure out a way to bring it back so that the value is equal to what it was then. So if you have a grand in yesterday's money which is worth about – what – Jesus – fifteen thousand then - now you're talking.'

I nodded in agreement; the point had occurred to me.

'I could open a bank account and leave the money in it to accumulate with interest,' I suggested.

'Nah, it would be declared dormant and how could you prove it was yours? And anyway, who knows what the interest rates would be on the account over the years.'

Barry tugged at his pint pensively then sat back in silence. So did I.

'Okay,' he went on, 'we'll park that bus for now and think of something later. But there's another problem.'

I looked at him, 'Oh, what's that?'

'Have you ever considered that you might get stuck back there?'

That was a thought that I hadn't really considered. I just assumed that this was a two-way street but he was right. Maybe I could just walk under the clock on my way back in nineteen fifty-seven and walk out the other side still in nineteen fifty-seven. Fuck! What would I do then? I could hardly phone home. 'Hi mum, I'm in nineteen fifty-seven –send help.' What if they took the clock away? What if...what if?

Thinking about that made me wonder if that would be so bad. If I had wads of cash I could be king of the heap, cock of the walk. As long as I had made sure that I had enough information to earn myself twenty or thirty grand I would be set for life. Hell, I remember that they used to have something called the pools then where you bet on a number of draws in the football leagues on a Saturday. Gran always used tell me of the things she'd do if she 'won the pools.' Now that I thought of it none of it included me and I'm pretty sure it didn't include granddad either. I tried to remember how much you could win. I'd heard of some woman who won well over a hundred thousand and spent it all in a couple of years. They made a television programme about her. That would be the equivalent of well over a million, maybe two.

Maybe the life of a multi-millionaire back then wouldn't be too bad come to think of it. I was conscious of a voice intruding on my musings.

'Earth to Gordon, Earth to Gordon. Do you read me? Over.' His voice interrupted my reverie.

'Sorry. Miles away.'

'I said, what if you get stuck back then and can't come back?'

'Don't worry about it. One way or another it'll work out.'

'I'm not worried about you, I'm worried about the money you owe me. You can hardly mail it to me.'

'Gee thanks. Listen. There are ways and means. I just need to figure it out.'

Barry gave the sort of throat clearing that precedes any major decision a bit like when Truman went, 'Hhmm, hmm, okay, listen up folks, we're going to nuke Japan.'

'Hhmm, hmm, okay, here's what we do. I come up with three hundred, you figure out how to change it, you research some winners at the time and use your system to win some money. Meanwhile, I'll come up with some

67

thoughts on how you can bring it back so that it's worth something. Oh, and we cut it fifty-fifty.'

'Fifty-fifty?' I protested. 'I'm taking all the risks here. Seventy-thirty.'

'And I'm providing the cash. Besides, the profits are limitless according to you. Fifty-fifty.'

'Sixty-forty?'

'Fifty-fifty.'

'Deal.'

'Deal.'

'I can't believe I'm falling for this. It has to be a scam.'

'Come on, Barry – you know it makes sense.'

'Well, you'd better be careful, that's all. You might end up shagging your own grannie.'

That thought took the gilt of the gingerbread a bit but we agreed to meet the next morning and he'd give me the cash. Meanwhile I would find out where I could get a bunch of yesterday's money. Then, all being well, I'd take the seven fifty-seven from Central to my own personal ATM.

'You couldn't sub me a twenty to tide me over, could you?'

'Jesus, Gordon, this had better work.'

Chapter Six

That gave me the weekend to do some serious research and I vowed to set upon it with a will. Christine and I hadn't seen each other for a couple of days and she was getting antsy. She got like that when she hadn't had the beef lance for a while; she said going without gave her a headache. Given my plans for the next few weeks she was going to have a serious migraine. Or there again, maybe not; I didn't think Christine was the monogamous type when the itch came upon her.

She suggested I come over to her place; she had an apartment in a relatively modern building on Tantallon Road just a couple of hundred yards from Shawlands Cross where we used The Granary as a local. This suited me as the mould on the dishes in my sink was beginning to look as if it might stake a claim to squatters' rights. This was a serious mould. It was a mould that would put the fear of death into Alexander Fleming. So I bussed it over to the south side and made my way to Chris's place where she opened a bottle of a fruity Tesco white that had been chilling in the fridge.

'So, any further forward on our little Caribbean trip?' Christine didn't waste time on small talk.

'As a matter of fact I was just talking to Baz and it looks like a go.'

'How much is that going to cost? I thought you were broke.'

'A temporary hitch. I have an opening that will take care of it all.'

She looked at me the way a lioness looks at a baby antelope, like, I know I could but is it really worth the bother?

'So it's still on?'

'Yup.'

'Where exactly?'

'Barry doesn't know yet. Her ladyship hasn't decided.'

She paused then took a sip of Chateau du Plonque and shrugged. 'So what's the opening?'

'The what?'

'You said you had an opening somewhere.'

'I'll tell you when things start to move, okay?'

'Gordon, right now I'm somewhere between telling you to fuck off and holding on until we see what happens.'

'If you tell me to fuck off you'll never know. Plus you'll be mega pissed off when I jet off to sunland without you. Oh, did I mention first class?' I thought that last bit was an inspired touch.

'Oh well, you've maybe just swung the balance, Gordy boy, but if you fuck up on this I'll hand you your balls in a jiffy bag.' She wasn't kidding either, not if the look in her eye was anything to go by.

'So why don't we seal the deal dans moi boudoir and bring the cheeky little white with you.'

It was obvious she had no intention of throwing me out; she wasn't wearing any underwear so that we didn't need to waste time. The little minx had been bluffing all along.

I pride myself in my inventive stamina in the bedroom a result, I think, of all the long distance running. It's like

70

I could go on forever and I think the promise of a Caribbean delight added a frisson to the next hour or so.

Sated and spent we eventually lay in a post-coital glow each lost in our own reverie. She was in Barbados and I was in nineteen fifty-seven.

'Penny for them.' She twirled some chest hair, mine, not hers, through her fingers.

'You know this opening I said had come up?'

She eased herself up onto one elbow. 'Yes.' It was drawn out, almost like a question.

'Well, I might have to go away for a while, a few days, maybe a week or so.'

'When?'

'Soon. Next week maybe.'

'Why?'

'I told you, I can't say too much right now.'

'Is it legal?'

'Of course it's legal,' I said.

'I mean, I wouldn't mind so long as nobody got hurt and you didn't get caught.'

Jesus, wasn't she just full of surprises!

'Gordon, do you have a bit on the side?'

She didn't sound as if she'd be terribly bothered if I said yes and I suspected it might salve her conscience on the assumption that she might ease the pain of a week or two's separation with a quickie or two. Or three.

'Just business,' I said.

We showered and then she rustled up a spaghetti carbonara that we washed down with the sister red now that the white was long finished. A couple of pints in the Granary guaranteed a fuzzy head that we cleared by another bout between the sheets before drifting off into oblivion.

71

All in all it had been a very successful day.

I got up earlyish and let Christine lie on while I made use of her computer to trawl through some sites. I found a number of offers on eBay of old coins and notes and took a note of them for future reference. There were also some dealers offering period notes. The best bargains were to be had in the higher denominations and I wrote down the dealer names. There was an antique fair on at the SECC and I thought I'd take a look at that tomorrow. All in all I thought I might be able to pick up about eighty quid for Barry's three hundred; easily plenty to be going on with. More research revealed that I could probably pick up a bed and breakfast for no more than ten shillings a night, fifty pence, and a decent hotel, of which there were few, wouldn't set me back more than two pounds ten shillings a night, about fifteen pounds at most after conversion costs. Meals would be about twenty pence or so. Anyway, with what I had planned it wouldn't matter.

It took me about half an hour to find sites that had information on race results way back when. A couple of the race courses had their own archived sites and there were also other historical horse racing sites that gave me some results at Lingfield, Kempton Park and Wolverhampton and there were a number of other courses that gave me the results for the upcoming weeks. I printed these out. There was also a site www.worldfootball.net that gave me every result in the UK for any week. Christ, Queen of the South beat Celtic 4-3 this same Saturday sixty years ago.

By this time it was getting on in the morning so I raided Christine's larder for coffee and generously made her one and took it to her but just got a bollocking for my trouble and she turned over and went back to sleep. By the time I drank the coffee, showered and dressed she had come to a bit and could communicate orally.

'You're a dinosaur, you know that?'

'I'm not the one that looks like an asteroid just hit.' She groaned and stretched. 'I'll have that coffee now.'

'No you won't, it's cold.'

'Make me another.' Not so much a command, more of a plea.

'Okay, but it's instant.'

'Fine, fine.'

I made her the coffee and told her I'd see her later. Things to do.

'Yeah, yeah. I don't want to see you until you've got those first class tickets in your hand.'

'I love you too.'

I met Barry for a quick coffee in a branch of Aulds where he handed over three hundred with a look at me that seemed to indicate that he was questioning his sanity. I thought he might have joined me at the SEC but a prior engagement with Lesley at the foreign events section of a wedding planner took precedence. Maybe that accounted for his look.

The SEC in Glasgow stands for the Scottish Exhibition Centre and is a large, bleak, grey structure that resembles an aircraft hangar. It used to be painted red and had a strap line that read, 'It's not just a big red shed.' Some genius in an ad agency probably earned about fifty thousand for that flash of inspiration. It's on the Clyde in a complex that houses a newly erected indoor arena custom built for concerts. Called the Hydro it seats around 12,000 people and if you are in the cheap

73

seats you are in serious danger of a nosebleed, plus the entertainer you paid a hundred and twenty to see is further away than you go on your holidays. He, she or them is usually backed by a couple of huge television screens which rather begs the question of why you don't just buy the DVD and save yourself a fortune.

Nearby is another auditorium called, probably by the same advertising star and for the same price, The Glasgow Auditorium. It looks rather like an armadillo and is therefore called by the great unwashed, the Armadillo, and could have been officially named that for no charge whatsoever but that's not how things are done in Glasgow. The SEC itself can be split into a number of exhibition halls of various sizes and in one of them over this weekend was an event called 'The Glasgow Antiques Fair'.

If, a week ago, anyone had said I would be browsing through brass candlesticks, ceramic wall ducks, toby jugs, and general assorted junk I would have called them mad. How things change. Had anyone said I would nip into the last century and back and was now planning a financial raid there I would have called a man in a white coat with a hypodermic needle and a jacket that ties at the back. But look who's president of the USA and nothing can be crazier than that.

There were about half a dozen tables laid out with collectors' items such as stamps, old coins and notes. The good thing about these events is that the stallholders are invariably eager to get rid of their stock in as short a time as possible and are agreeable to a bit of bargaining.

At the first table the coins were sorted by value; there were halfpennies, pennies, threepenny pieces, sixpences and so on up to half crowns and I spent ten minutes sifting through them for ones dated 1957 and before. I was able to find about ten pounds worth and with a bit of judicious bargaining got the bespectacled, moth eaten cardiganed seller down to forty quid the lot. Turning my attention to the notes I was able to get twenty one pound notes issued by various Scottish banks for seventy-five pounds and felt I had done all right. The next couple of tables yielded a reasonable trove of twenty pounds in coin and notes for seventy pounds and by the time I had finished I had about eighty old pounds for just over two hundred and ninety and all this without having to go on line. I couldn't believe my luck.

I thought I'd give it another day to plan out a campaign of action and head for the past on Monday. I'd plan on spending three or four nights which should be enough for my first foray. There were things to be done such as opening a bank account. I didn't want to carry around big money and I needed to work out some plan of action to convert it to present day funds at present day value. I thought I would maybe scout round for a private flat to rent, something decent for a change because I thought that sooner or later I might end up spending a few weeks just enjoying some big time luxury. There were places to go, sights to see, things to do in this new land. There were people to meet and ladies to impress although Barry's warning flitted briefly to mind. With these myriad ideas spinning through my head I headed back to the joys of present day Partick.

Not once did Barry's concern trouble my thoughts. The question of whether whatever portal would still be open and let me through to '57 never entered my mind.

No thought of could I get there.

No thought of could I get back.

Chapter Seven

Glasgow Central, half past seven, stone cold sober, Monday evening. I sat in Costa Coffee supping a last latte psyching myself up for the big adventure. I was wearing a pair of faded jeans, a blank, grey T shirt with a plain long-sleeved casual shirt on top open to the waist. I had a pair of unbranded trainers on and I felt that I wasn't going to be too conspicuous. I had a three day old stubble and my hair covered my ears and was a bit on the shaggy side but it was reasonably tidy. A very small back-pack held a couple of spare pairs of socks and underwear and a fresh T shirt. Stuffed into the foot of the bag were a number of closely typed pages with details of race winners for the foreseeable future, more than I felt sure I needed. Also at the bottom of the bag were most of the coins and notes I had changed.

In my back pocket I had an old battered wallet in which I had enough money for immediate use, enough and more, probably, ten pounds, and some coins in another pocket. I had no identification. In 1957 I wasn't even born yet.

Having gone through a mental check list and finished the last of my coffee, I got up and walked towards the clock, looking around to make sure there was no one around I recognised. I didn't want to go through that again. It was approaching the appointed minute as it were so I strode forward just as the hand reached three minutes to and, et voila, here I was, just as planned, sixty years back in the past.

The sensation was just as thrilling, more so now that I knew what to expect. I took a few minutes to let my senses, my real senses, sound, smell, sight, take it all in. I hadn't realised it before but it smelled different. It smelled –old, it smelled of soot and smoke. There was an almost sulphuric aura to it.

Walking out into Gordon Street, it looked different. It looked - black. The buildings were stained almost jet black. The same buildings I had left, those still standing anyway, were a dull golden colour, some were grey. Now I felt sure if brushed against one now my clothes would be stained sooty black. And the noise was – quieter. At first I couldn't place it but then I realised. There was no background hum. Twenty-first century Glasgow carried a million automated noises in the air. Buses, cars, people talking all at once, music from shops and pubs, the noise of a modern city. Now the clanking of steel tram wheels on steel rails seemed to echo and the noise from the street was muted; even the starlings were quiet. This was a city that put out the lights, tucked itself in and went to bed early.

It was past eight o'clock and I needed a place to stay. Money wasn't a problem, finding a hotel was. Behind me was the dark, gothic edifice of the Central Hotel. I thought about it but it looked like the sort of place that would look down its nose at someone like me. So I wandered along Gordon Street to Buchanan Street, nearly getting hit by a black taxi, horn honking angrily for me to jump out of the way. Shit, of course, nothing was pedestrianised. A couple of cars followed it, both Henry Ford black, and I was fascinated by their indicators. Instead of a winking orange light back and front, a little arm flipped out from the pillar between the doors. It was all so quaint. On one car the little arm moved up and down like a signal as if to show off some new technological advance. I turned left onto Buchanan Street and strolled up the hill. Halfway up on the left hand side I saw a place that seemed to fit the bill. It looked smart but unassuming and equally welcoming. A sign with the letters reading vertically downward proclaimed it to be The Ivanhoe Hotel so I made my way inside to the registration desk where a pleasant looking lady of indeterminate age smiled at me.

'I'm looking for a room.'

'Well you've come to the right place then, haven't you?' She spoke in a lovely lilt redolent of a croft in the shadow of the Cuillin in Skye.

I smiled with relief. The first hurdle seemed to be over.

'Just the one night?'

'Actually, four nights if you have it.'

She leafed through a large ledger and not a computer in sight.

'I've a single on the second floor at nineteen and six a night. If it's a bath you're looking for I've a room with bath on the first floor at a guinea. Breakfast included.'

'A what?'

'A guinea, if that's alright. Per night, of course.'

'Of course. A guinea you say?'

'That's right. A guinea.'

Just as it was going so well, too.

'I've only just got pounds, shillings and pence with me,' I said hesitantly.

'That's right. Twenty-one shillings.'

'Oh, a *guinea*! Sorry, didn't catch what you said there. No, that's fine. I'll take the room with the bath. I didn't know they came without.' I was babbling now.

She looked at me like a mother looks at a simple child and smiled accordingly.

'The first two nights in advance if that's alright, seeing as you don't have much luggage. Company policy, I'm afraid.'

Pulling my wallet from my pocket I took out a couple of pound notes and delved into my side pocket for some change. In the manner of a tourist in pre Euro Greece, I examined my change for a two shilling piece and handed it over. She took the money and started to hand write an ornate receipt.

'Who shall I say the name is?'

'Lorne, Gordon Lorne. Because that's my name.'

'I'm sure it is, Mr Lorne. And have you an address?'

I was about to blurt out my Partick pad details but that would have seemed odd. She caught my hesitation but I carried on.

'18 Staffa Place, Rothesay. Just over for a bit of a job. Might take a few days and I don't want to trust the ferry in case of the weather, you know. It can be a bit risky at this time of year.' I was babbling again, it seemed to come easy.

'That's fine Mr Lorne. Rothesay, is it?' She tore out the page and handed it to me, a smile playing the corners of her mouth.

'You mentioned breakfast. Is the restaurant still open?'

'You'll just make it, half past eight but I don't know what the kitchen will have left. Oh, and as you're a resident, you can order a drink from Davie up until eleven o'clock.'

She handed me a large key weighed down by a chunk of metal that would safely anchor an oil tanker at Coulport and pointed me the way to the stairs singing in the island tang. 'Better hurry, now.'

The dinner menu was printed on small piece of card and consisted of a meagre choice of three starters, one of which was juice, three mains two of which were finished and a couple of desserts all for the princely sum of three shillings and ninepence. The wee waitress wore a black dress covered with a white apron and had a sort of paper tiara on her head. Judging by the way she washed my feet and offered to let me sleep with her daughter I guess I over tipped. Davie was the doorman, drinks waiter and elevator operator. He had a maroon serving jacket and by the sound of his wheeze I think he may have been a first world-war gas victim and his accent seemed to indicate that he was on the losing side.

The bedroom decor was a sort of institutional green similar to that found in hospitals and government ministries but relieved by a couple of prints of a child with huge eyes set to cry. It was lit by two fifteen watt bulbs but the bed, when I located it, was comfortable and I slept. Breakfast was a much better affair than dinner after which I slipped out into the murky light of a grey Glasgow January morning.

Horse racing didn't start until the afternoon so I had a few hours to kill which I did by taking my first ride on a Glasgow tram to Auchenshuggle just because I didn't believe the place existed. Then I walked a mile or so back to where Celtic's magnificent stadium was only to find a rather run down arena uncovered at both ends and with little more than a corrugated shed covering the central terracing. How times would change. I felt like walking in the main entrance and telling them that big things awaited in 1967 against the Italian champions but as they had just been humped that weekend by Queen of the South, I decided against. By the time I took another tram back to the city centre and grabbed an excellent salmon sandwich and a pint at a pub called Sammy Dow's in Mitchell Lane it was time to place a bet.

It turned out that a Turf Accountant was just another name for a betting shop and I found one upstairs in a building in St Enoch Square. I loved it the moment I entered. The bookies like William Hill or Ladbrokes that I was vaguely familiar with boasted computer terminals, television screens with listed runners, and television coverage of the race itself. You could also bet on anything that took your fancy like who would be the next prime minister or whether Mr Blobby would be the Christmas top of the pops. This was different. A guy with obvious skills as a signwriter wrote up in coloured chalks the runners for a given race on a blackboard and continually erased and rewrote the changing odds. A radio blared out the commentary on a given race mostly to groans and curses and the sound of betting slips being torn. A blue smoke fug obscured the ceiling. Almost everyone had a cigarette between their fingers or dangling from their lips. I had the names of three horses that I knew were going to win, two at Lingfield, Jack the Lad at two to one in the two fifteen, and Safe Harbour at three to one in the two forty five. The other was Windmill at three to one at Kempton Park at one forty five.

To ease myself in I thought it best to put ten shillings on a horse that I knew would lose, just to allay suspicions, so I picked the favourite at Kempton at one fifteen, a horse called Fairhaven at two to one. I watched a couple of punters as they wrote out their lines on the slips provided then picked up a pencil and wrote out mine. I wrote the name down and put 10/- against it and took it to the grill covered counter. A clerk, for want of a better word, took it and looked at it. He was reedy looking with a face cratered with acne and teeth that were painful just to look at. A Fair Isle pullover strobed with the acne enough to induce a fit of epilepsy.

'To win?' he asked in a flat voice.

'Sorry?'

'Just checking. Is it five bob each way or is it to win?'

'Oh, sorry. Aye, to win.'

'OK. You need to put your nom de plume on it.'

'What?'

'Your nom de plume. Your pen name. Unless you want to use your real name.' He pushed the slip back at me as if I was a child.

'Sorry, I forgot to add it.' I wrote a name on the slip and pushed it back.

He looked at it. 'Bic Biro?'

'It's my pen name.' He didn't get it.

'Right.' He stamped the slip and gave me back a copy.

It was just a few minutes to race time and I sat and waited for the off. This race wasn't on the radio so after about five minutes a voice on the radio simply gave the one, two three and, of course, my horse came in third. I feigned annoyance as I tore up my slip.

'Nae luck son?' I got a sympathetic nod from a fellow punter. 'Ah'm fucked an' a'.'

I shook my head in agreement. Having by now laid out my credentials I wrote out another line with the three horses I knew were winners and marked it with £1 treble. The clerk made no comment at all as he took the line and stamped it just as before.

An hour and a half later, just as I had planned, all three horses romped home. On the last race I even shouted encouragement. I was a bit nervous as I took my slip back to the window and handed it over. By my calculations I should get forty eight pounds back including my one pound stake. The clerk took it.

'Give me a minute.' he said and took himself and my slip into a back office.

Oh shit. He came out two minutes later. 'Had to go to the safe.'

The acned one counted out eight large white five pound notes and eight singles.

'Your lucky day, eh.'

'Luck had nothing to do with it.' That was a bit bold but I was feeling euphoric.

'They all say that,' he said with a shake of his head.

Day one: mission accomplished.

Leaving the bookie's I made my way towards Union Street. I had my eye on a natty sports jacket and slacks that looked good on a tailor's dummy in John Collier's window. It was the sort of thing that I wouldn't have been seen dead in the Glasgow of 2017 in case my friends saw me and assumed I had got a job as a bank clerk. But the gear I was wearing now, anonymous by any modern standard, definitely stood out; and I also needed a haircut. Collar length hair was strictly limited to the opposite sex.

So it was that an hour later I sauntered up Renfield Street carrying my latter day togs in a brown paper bag and feeling rather pleased with myself. Over the clanking of steel wheels on steel rails I heard various conversation snippets. A female voice called over to a friend 'Gordon, is that you?'

Walking on, the calling became more insistent. 'Gordon?'

The next call as she caught up with me brought me to a heart-stopping standstill.

'Gordon. Gordon Lorne. Is that really you?'

Chapter Eight

I should have run. I should have but I didn't. I turned around instead. A lady dressed in a dark green overcoat with a shoulder bag draped over her left shoulder, loose, sandy brown, wavy hair down to her collar caught up with me. Did I say she was gorgeous? She looked quite slim even under the bulky coat and she would be around five feet six tall. Did I say she was gorgeous? She reminded me at first glance of Rachel Stirling, with just enough of a hint of Juliette Binoche to change a beautiful face into a phenomenon, just as a distant glimpse of a red sail on a beautiful blue sea creates a perfect picture. Did I say she was drop dead gorgeous?

Then I saw the shock, disappointment and embarrassment on her face, three emotions I recognised; I had seen them often enough. She put her hand to her mouth. I was worried that she might be sick.

'I'm so sorry. I thought...you look like...I'm sorry, really. I thought you were someone I once knew. You look so much like him.'

Once knew? I'd like to know her a few times.

'That's all right, happens all the time.' I don't know why I said that but she smiled.

Then it hit me. How did she know my name?

'How did you know my name?'

'Oh my God, is it your name?'

I had to think of something fast. 'Eh, no.' Nice one.

'Oh.'

We both looked at each other.

'This is a bit surreal,' she said, clearly confused.

She certainly got that right.

'Sorry, actually my name is ...' I had to come up with something quick. I could have kicked myself for giving my real name to Highland Mary at the Ivanhoe. A bit of forward planning wouldn't have gone amiss. '... George, George Clooney.'

Well, fuck it; why not?

'Katie McWilliam.' She held out her hand and I shook it. It was probably too soon for a kiss. 'I'm sorry, it's just that you are the image of... of a friend.'

I caught the hesitation and figured out that whoever he was, and I was beginning to have a terrible suspicion about that, he was, or had been, more than a friend.

'Don't worry about it.'

'Well, sorry again. I should be going.' She turned away to cross the road.

'Wait.' I caught her by the arm. 'I don't suppose it would do any harm for you to have a coffee or a tea with the image of a friend. You could just make believe for a little while. '

She looked at me, then laughed. 'I really shouldn't.'

'You really should.'

'Okay then, just a quick one. Reid's is round the corner.'

In a few moments we were in the cosy warmth of a tearoom that I remembered as now being a Carphone Warehouse. The waitress came over dressed in exactly the same outfit as the one in the Ivanhoe last night. There must have been a job lot at an auction house.

'Yes?' she asked, a pencil and notepad at the ready.

Katie ordered a cup of tea.

86

'I'll have a Cappuccino.'

'A what?'

'Cappuccino.'

'What's that when it's at hame?'

Oops. Katie was looking at me strangely.

'Just make it a coffee with milk.'

When the waitress left I looked at Katie who was looking at me, eyebrows raised. Clearly she expected me to make the running.

'So tell me about Gordon Lorne then. I take it he's exceptionally good looking.'

She laughed a little and coloured. 'And why do you want to know'

'You thought I was him whoever he is so I suppose I have stake in the answer.'

She considered her response. 'We went out together for a few months, that's all.'

'I see. You seemed very disappointed when I wasn't him.'

She looked away. 'Sorry, I just felt a bit of an idiot. I should have known it wasn't him. He was offered a job in Canada a year ago September and he wanted to take it. I was sorry to see him go. I rather liked him.'

So that was it. By the most amazing stroke of chance Katie had gone out with my granddad. I remembered him telling me that he had tried his luck in Saskatchewan for a couple of years, didn't like it, came back and almost immediately met my grandma and got married. He had been tall and athletic like me in his younger days and I had his same aquiline nose and high cheekbones. Jesus, Barry's warning wasn't too wide of the mark. I'll say this for the old goat, he had great taste in women.

87

The waitress returned with the coffee and tea, which came in a pot with a dinky little strainer. Katie poured her tea through it, added a half spoonful of sugar and a little milk then carefully stirred it. I watched, fascinated.

'So you didn't fancy going with him, then?'

'To Canada? No. What would I do in Saskatchewan? I hardly know where it is.'

'It's in Canada; prairie land. Flat as a billiard table.'

'I knew it was in Canada. What do you know about it?'

I couldn't admit that I'd hitch-hiked across it on my way to Vancouver where an acquaintance I knew rashly invited me to drop in if I was ever out his way. Boy, did he regret that. So did his new wife.

'I have an old auntie that lives there. She had a dog that ran away from home and she watched it go for three days. We're talking seriously flat.'

Katie laughed and it was a lovely sound. I needed to hear more.

'Yes, she says that if you look at the horizon long enough you can see the back of your own head. Did I mention it was flat?'

Now she really laughed. I was on a roll.

These were all throw away jokes that granddad use so many times that they had whiskers on them but behind the jokes he would sometimes let slip some more wistful thoughts and a faraway look would come into his eyes. I once asked him why anyone would want to go there if there was nothing to see. There's everything to see there, there's nothing in the way, he replied so softly I hardly heard him. He talked about how big the sky was, how the huge prairie sentinels, the large brooding grain elevators stood guardian over the golden prairie swaying like the sea in a breeze. In those moments I realised the old man had come back not because he didn't like it, but if he hadn't come back when he did, he would never have come back at all. Or maybe there was a woman involved. He was gone now to the great prairie in the sky and I'd never get the full story now; he'd been a good bit older than my grandma. Piecing together bits and pieces over the years I realised that the old roué had been a bit of a lad in his time and grandma had been hard pressed to keep him in check, although, truth be told, I think she might have had her moments. Who knows, maybe granddad had to make a sharp exit or a shotgun waving prairie farmer might have put paid to his exploits for ever. Good lord, this lovely woman opposite dated my granddad. She might even have...no, no, don't go there.

Katie was saying something and I realised that I hadn't been listening for a few moments.

'Sorry, say again?'

'I was asking what you did, for a living I mean.'

Again I realised that I hadn't prepared a full back story. I had thought I would be here for a few days, make a killing and then go forward to my own time and live the life; I hadn't expected to make friends. This could only complicate matters but complications and I went hand in hand; like death and taxes. In for a penny in for a pound, a 1957 pound at that.

'I'm self-employed, I work for myself.'

'Oh, doing what?'

'Research forecasting, statistical analysis, that sort of thing. Crystal ball stuff.' It was as near to the truth as I could get.

'How does that work? Do people pay for that?'

'Oh yes. Think about it. The telephone company needs to know how many phone lines to plan for, how

89

will demand expand - airlines need route analysis - what will the advances in health be? You need to know these things to plan for insurance and pensions. Who knows what the future may hold.' Well, me for a start.

'And you know all these things?'

Oh, yes, and how.

'I don't know for sure, but that's where the research comes in. Plus, and I say this with no sense of false modesty, I have a knack for logical analysis, you might say fortune telling, but when you break it all down, you can see the rationale behind it.' I was in full flow now. I almost believed all that shite myself; she certainly did.

'That's so interesting. Can you give me some examples.'

Careful now, Gordon. 'Well Katie, can I call you Katie?' she smiled and nodded, 'Think of what people want and need more than anything else. Other than food, sleep, clothes a house and sex.' She blushed slightly at that but I bulldozed on. 'Communication. Everybody needs to communicate. Ten years ago nobody had a television, hardly any phones, nobody travelled. Look at it now.' I was winging it here. 'I bet you've got a phone.'

'Yes, but it's a party line.'

I had no idea what she was talking about but I sailed on.

'There you are, but it's still a phone. How about TV?'

'I rented one last month. Sixteen inch.'

Sixteen inches! Barry had a forty two inch ultra HD hanging on his wall with speakers everywhere you looked and a thirty-four inch flat screen in the bedroom. Even I in my penurious circumstances had a ten-year old plasma that was handy for late late night Dutch television channels.

'How many channels?'

'Two of course, BBC and Channel 10.'

Haud me back.

'Okay. Phones. In ten years most people will have a phone and there won't be any shared lines.' I had figured out what party lines were. 'Also you won't need an operator to go long distance. Add another ten years and you won't have to dial. You'll just press number buttons. And you'll be able to call America, Europe. Australia even.'

'How do you know all this?'

'I don't, but I can figure it out. Twenty years ago nobody flew anywhere, not really. Now there are planes to New York in a few hours. You have to think forward, add a touch of science and, most of all, imagination then...' I snapped my fingers, '...you can do anything.'

'That's amazing. I never thought of it like that. What about in fifty years?'

I wasn't going to go there so I put the ball back in her court.

'What do you think?'

'I'm sure I don't know. Colour TV?'

I just laughed. 'How about 3D?'

'Now you're just taking the mickey.'

She had a lovely laugh and even lovelier smile. I basked in them both then she said, 'With your skill you could maybe make a win on the horses. You could win a fortune'

My false laughter was almost manic. I could hear echoes of Private Fraser of Dad's Army morbidly moaning, 'We're doomed, we're doomed I tell ye – doomed!'

91

The subject needed changing, 'Seems like I've been doing all the talking. What about you?'

A shadow darkened her eyes. 'Not much to tell, really. I lived with my mum in a tenement house in Calder Street, Govanhill, you know. She died last year so I'm on my own. I still live in the house, though, they can't just throw you out.' She paused then looked at her watch. 'Look at the time. I really should be going. It's been lovely talking to you, George.' She drained the last of the tea and got up to leave but then she paused. 'I'm sorry to say this again, but it's uncanny just how much you look like Gordon. You could almost be brothers.'

She was much nearer the mark than she could possibly have imagined.

'Don't rush. Let me settle the bill and I'll walk you out.'

'No, that's okay.'

I couldn't let her just leave.

'Can I call you?'

'Call me?'

'Yes, like on the phone.'

She thought about it. 'And do what?'

'I don't know. Whatever you like. A drink, a meal.' A visit to Paris for the weekend but, of course, I didn't say that.

'Okay, phone me and we can talk about it. You probably already know my number since you're so telepathic.'

'I'm not that good.'

'I'm at Govanhill four two one three.'

I had no idea how I would dial that.

'Could you write that down for me?' I asked.

She took a pen and a slip of paper from her bag and wrote GOV4213. I wasn't sure I was any further forward but I'd manage.

'I'll call you tomorrow evening.'

And with that she left. All I was left with was the bill and Private Fraser.

'Doomed I tell ye – doomed.'

Chapter Nine

The buzz of a dreich Buchanan Street woke me from a fitful sleep. My watch said it was nine o'clock and my stomach agreed so I threw on a shirt and trousers and made it to the breakfast room just in time to ruin the cook's day by ordering the full Scottish just as he was about to shut up shop.

I had filled in the dark hours when sleep was elusive by trying to firm up some plans. I was booked in for two more nights which gave me a couple of days to show the bookies what I was made of. That was all well and good as far as it went but while it gave me money to live in the here and now like the lord of the manor, it wouldn't go all that far in the twenty-first century. I had bought an evening paper on the way back to the hotel and I browsed the pages over my bacon, sausage, egg, black pudding, tomato, beans and mushroom, tea and toast, the waiter hovering in the background like a kestrel waiting to swoop. Two items caught my eye, an advert for Littlewoods Pools telling me that I could win a fortune, £100,000 plus, for forecasting eight draws at a penny a line on Saturday's football matches, and a list of houses for rent in the private house lets classified ads.

So, I wrote a to do list for the day.

        1 Rent a suitable property.

        2 Send away for a football pools coupon.

        3. Open a bank account.

        4. Place bets at bookies.

5. Phone Katie.

I was sure there was something else but couldn't remember. Now you see why I needed a hearty breakfast; I had a busy day ahead and I needed fortification.

The first property I had marked was a red sandstone tenement in Hyndland and was being let by a firm of lawyers in St Vincent Street so I went to see them where a woman no older than, say, one hundred and eleven, presented me with a single sheet of A4 paper with the specs of the flat written down but other than that she couldn't tell me anything, like the price for instance, until Mr Conway came in and she didn't know when that would be. Mr Conway was the senior, you see, and he needed to be there before she could give me any more details, you see. I didn't see.

Property number two was let through another legal firm, but one that specialised in house letting and conveyancing. I thought at first they maybe hired out taxis on the side. Anyway, a visit to their premises on West Regent Street, proved to be more successful and they had full details of a place I liked the sound of on Nithsdale Road around the corner from Darnley Street. I liked the area, the nice lady who smiled at me when she confirmed that she could offer a three month short term lease at eighteen guineas a month plus a ten pounds security deposit payable one month in advance, and the fact that the flat was fully furnished. She even had a couple of black and white photographs so I signed the deal there and then and plonked down seventy pounds. Plenty more where that came from. I knew I wouldn't need the three months lease but who cares; toffs are careless.

95

She pulled a set of keys from a drawer and smiled again as she handed them to me

'Thank you Mr Clooney. Keep in touch if there's any problems.'

There won't be, don't worry, I thought.

I still had over fifty pounds left so I went into the first bank I came to, the National Bank of Scotland in Gordon Street to open an account. Christ, I thought I had slipped back another hundred years. There was a long row of tellers sitting behind a wrought iron grill that ran the length of polished wooden desk some thirty feet along the length of the cavernous hall. Behind them there was about half a dozen more clerks sitting on high chairs at tall desks. I couldn't be sure but it seemed to me they were using quill pens but that was probably my imagination. Everyone spoke in hushed tones as if someone had recently passed away and the way the clerks were dressed seemed to confirm it. One of Dickens' characters leapt off the written page and nodded at me.

'Can I help you?'

'I'd like to open an account if that's possible.'

'Of course.' He took a printed sheet from a drawer. 'I just need your name and address.'

'George...,' I was about to give him my film star alias but then I realised that I would need to be Gordon Lorne if I was somehow able to get money back to the future.

I cleared my throat. 'Hmm, Gordon Lorne, sorry.'

He looked at me quizzically like a goblin teller from Gringott's then began writing. I gave him my new address.

'Do you need a deposit account or a current account? A current account may take a little longer. We need to get a cheque book printed although I can prepare some temporary ones for you,' he offered.

'No, deposit is fine.'

'Just give me a moment Mr Lorne.'

He eased off his stool and disappeared. This all seemed so easy. No appointments with financial consultants, no copies of passports, no evidence of residence. Clearly laundering drug money hadn't hit Scotland yet. He reappeared with a passbook in his hand with my name and account number written on it in copperplate .

'I'll need two specimen signatures,' he said pushing the forms towards me. I duly signed them.

'Very well, Mr Lorne, and what will you be depositing today?'

'Forty pounds?'

'As you wish.'

It was all as simple as that. Now I understood when I heard the phrase "the good old days".

Next on the list, the pools coupon, was easy. I simply filled in the request in the paper, bought a stamp and envelope and posted it. That left me with another visit to the bookie. Like casinos in Las Vegas, bookies figure out very quickly when they are being fleeced so I found one out near Ibrox and went through the same routine as before. It was a seedy little place in Copland Road in the shadow of Rangers' Ibrox Stadium and I doubt if there had been a bet placed for more than two shillings each way before I arrived. Three horses all romped in to give me a treble that yielded a net profit of fifty seven pounds seven shillings and sixpence to be exact. This was concurrent with a treble that I knew would lose so as to throw the bookie of the scent. It still wasn't enough.

'Got a wee tip, did ye?' said the cashier, looking at me.

'No, I just study form.'

'Is that right? Maybe you should study it somewhere else.' He counted out my winnings which I folded and put in my jacket pocket. I had just turned to make my way out of the door when it crashed open with some force and three of Glasgow's finest came in. There were two constables and an inspector with scrambled egg on his cap and a smirk on his face.

The inspector spoke first. 'All right lads, you know the routine.'

He was wrong there. This was one lad who had no idea what routine he was talking about. I was pretty sure it wasn't something from Strictly Come Dancing. There were eight other punters plus the clerk and me in the shop. That made nine who shrugged resignedly and one with a sudden urge to pee. The door to the back office opened and out came a very small man with a very big attitude. Inspectors with scrambled egg on their caps and smirks on their faces didn't faze him. He was wearing a black suit, the trousers of which had never heard of a Corby trouser press, a white shirt slightly frayed at the collar and a tie that could be thrown into a pot to make soup. The top button of his shirt didn't meet the hole at the top and the tie knot dangled below the neck. Cigarette smoke curled from an untipped wedged between his fingers.

'Fuck's sake, what is this? This is twice in wan month we've been done.'

'Pressure's on, Sandy. Targets to meet.'

The inspector started to usher every one out of the premises.

'Meet your targets somewhere else. Is there someone's palms I havnae greased or somethin'?'

'Don't know what you mean Sandy, just doing our job.'

'Is that right? Didnae see youse doin' it when mah Jag got nicked. Found him yet, have ye?' He shook his head in disgust. 'Didnae think so.'

'Right, lads, hurry up - come on. In the van.' One of the constables was anxious to get on with it.

'Me too?' I pointed to myself.

He pushed me in the back. 'Just get in the van.'

All of us, the one called Sandy included, were herded into a black van, the doors were closed behind us and we rumbled off.

Sandy spoke, 'Okay lads. Don't concern yourselves, you ken the score. Ye'll get five bob each for your trouble and all bets honoured.'

He had made a point of sitting next to me and he eyed me up and down. 'I'm told you got a wee windfall.'

'Lucky I guess.'

'Right, right.' He paused. 'We don't see much luck like that round here. Lucky at St. Enoch's as well if I'm no' mistaken.'

I sensed a veiled threat there.

'You'll no' be worried about your five bob, I don't suppose.' It was a statement rather than a question. 'Ye see, a' the lads in here, I know them all. They're in two or three times a week, maybe more. They get lucky now and then and walk away with a pound or two. I've never seen you in my life before and you waltz in and take us for sixty quid near enough, and no' just the once. See mah point?'

It was clear I wouldn't be welcomed back. I just nodded.

'Good, just so's we're clear.'

Nobody in the van seemed overly worried about their situation, in fact five shillings could feed a man for a couple of days, or a family, come to that so no harm no foul.

The van slowed and my body weight moved as it turned and bumped over some cobbles. After a few moments the doors were opened and we were ushered into a dismal looking building that turned out to be Govan Police Station. The nine of us that were the customers were put together in a cell while Sandy and his boy were taken elsewhere. The cell was tiled and smelled vaguely of urine and disinfectant although in fairness that may have been from one of the punters.

I broke the silence. 'What happens now?'

Nobody spoke for a moment or two then an old looking man, probably in his sixties said. 'Nothin'.'

'Nothing?'

'They'll let us stew for an oor or two and gie us a caution and let us go. Sandy'll gie us five bob each for wur trouble. You've never been lifted before?'

'No – first time.' I looked around. 'What happens to him?'

'Sandy? Och a wee fine and he's back at the shop.'

'So they don't close him down then?'

'Och it's just a game. Occupational hazard. Happens every month or so but if they shut the bookies doon it wid just cause trouble. They're talkin' aboot makin' it legal but they've been talkin' aboot it for years.' He clearly wasn't overly concerned.

I sat back and mulled over the events of the past hour. Not once in my history of minor transgressions since I was born in 1982 had I as much seen the inside of a police station and yet here I was in a prison cell within a day or two of my time transfer. I looked at my fellow inmates and made sure my back was to the wall. I wondered where the showers were. The talk became desultory and sure enough, after an hour had passed the desk sergeant returned.

'Right youse. Up to the desk and you'll be cautioned, you know the form. Don't let me see you in here again. Until the next time'

The wee man I had talked to said to me quietly, 'See? It disnae matter. They always say that.'

Relief flooded through me. 'So I haven't been arrested?'

'Not at all. They just keep your name in case you're in trouble elsewhere. Serious trouble like.'

'You could give a false name,' I pointed out.

He just shrugged. Soon enough it was my turn and I gave over my details, my George Clooney alias and my new address and was sent on my way with an admonishment from the sergeant, a big bluff red haired man with a highland accent. I was going to ask him if he knew the receptionist at the Ivanhoe but thought the better of it.

'Aye, and get a haircut.'

Damn it. That should have been number six on the list.

Chapter Ten

Taking the sergeant's advice I got a haircut in a barber's shop in West Nile Street by a man with a club foot and a scythe. It was brutal; men have died for less. I looked like an army recruit. By now it was time to call Katie and there was a bank of old red telephone boxes outside Central Station.

This was the first real test of my ingenuity. Inside there was a large black box with a dial on it and an old black handset. On the front of the box was a large press button above which was written a capital letter 'A' written inside a circle. On the side of the box was a similar arrangement except with the letter 'B'. The box had a slot for coins and a notice indicated that the cost of a call was four pennies. Apparently the idea was to lift the receiver, put four coins in the slot, dial the number and wait for an answer. If there was an answer then you pushed button 'A', the coins dropped and you got on with the call. If there was no answer you pushed button 'B' and the coins reappeared into a receptacle below. It was all very Heath Robinson.

Anyway I did as instructed and sure enough the whole thing worked and as soon as I heard Katie's voice I pushed the button and got the coins back. Fuck it. Wrong button. I did it again and this time when she answered I got it right. I tried to sound light and airy and not like some criminal who had just got out of jail.

'Hi, didn't know if you'd be home yet.'

'Who is this?'

'Go... George. Remember me?'

'Of course, I didn't think you'd call.'

'I had to pass up a heavy date with Marilyn Monroe.'

She laughed. 'Yeah, right.'

'So?'

'So what?'

'Are you ready for a night out?' I asked.

'What? Tonight? It's Wednesday.'

'Is there a law against Wednesdays?'

She laughed again. I liked that. 'No, it's just that...'

'Just that what?'

'Just that it's Wednesday. What would we do?'

'How about a drink and a meal?'

'Are you serious?'

'Why wouldn't I be serious?'

'I've never just gone out for dinner before. Well, maybe something on a special occasion like a dinner dance at the Plaza for a birthday or outing or something, but not just like that. It's usually the pictures or the dancing,' she said, unsure.

I wasn't really interested in sitting for a couple of hours in a cinema when I'd rather be talking and I wasn't sure about dancing.

'There's a first time for everything, you know. What about a nice restaurant?'

There was a silence on the end of the line and I panicked a little wondering if I'd run out of time but then she spoke.

'The only places I've heard of are the One-0-One or there's Guy's or the Malmaison but they're all very posh and would cost the earth. Most people usually don't eat out.'

103

'I know the One-0-One. Why don't we go there?' I'd never heard of the place but she couldn't know that. 'You know where it is, don't you?'

'Hope Street, just opposite Central Station.'

I looked around and sure enough, there it was just a hundred yards across the road from me. I could walk across and book it.

'That's the one. Right, it's half past five now. Meet me outside at eight o'clock, okay?'

She was silent again.

'Hello?'

'I'm thinking. If you're really sure. I mean, it's awfully expensive.'

'My treat, I'll see you outside. Eight o'clock, okay?'

She giggled, 'Okay.'

I still had a couple of nights booked at the Ivanhoe but I thought I'd take a run out to my newly rented pad to see exactly what I had signed for and as I still had plenty of time I decided to walk it. Everything was a revelation. This was Glasgow, but not like I'd known it, as Spock would say to Kirk. I loved the trams rattling along and the black cars with running boards for police chases. I seemed to remember reading that Henry Ford said of the model T, you can have it in any colour you like as long as it's black. They took him seriously over here. It was tenements all the way out to Eglinton Toll with the railway appearing on my right. Steam engines really did 'chuff-chuff' as they hauled old maroon coaches out into the suburbs. The tramcars rattled and moaned and it seemed every one was full. I resolved to ride one back to town.

When I reached Eglinton Toll I saw the ballroom Katie had mentioned, the Plaza, on my left. It was flanked by a couple of advertising hoardings each showing a couple dancing on air like Ginger and Fred. I couldn't have been more thrilled. It looked so authentically fifties, but then it would, wouldn't it? I turned right along past a tram depot and found Nithsdale Road and the flat that I'd signed for. It was on the first floor landing and looked quite genteel. The Yale key turned easily and I entered a hallway which led to a large lounge nicely furnished with a large and a small settee and a comfortable easy chair. I've often wondered why it's called an easy chair; is it possible to buy a difficult chair? A large corner bay window looked out over the street where to my left I could see over Darnley Street to the railway tracks. There was an occasional table (what was it on other occasions?) in the middle and an empty bookcase against a wall. The room was carpeted in a heavy pattern which didn't quite match the wallpaper. The owner was clearly no aficionado of interior design but it was fresh if a little hard on the eyes. On the other side of the hall there were two bedrooms, both well furnished if a bit dated, well they would be. There was also a decent kitchen with a gas cooker. I didn't waste much time there; dining out was the thing and anyway, I just needed the whole place for a bolthole for when I dipped in and out. Truth be told it was far too good for riff-raff like me.

After about fifteen minutes I figured that it was just as advertised and would do fine and with that I headed back to the city centre upstairs on an old tramcar where a nippy wee woman in a green uniform with a leather money bag hung around her shoulder and a steel contraption that dispensed a bit of paper when she turned a handle took twopence from me and rung up a

105

ticket. There was even a sign screwed to the woodwork; 'No Spitting.' Damn, it was my sole intention. I thought there might have been others proclaiming things like, 'No Farting' or 'No Nose-Picking', or 'No Ball Scratching', but the restriction for some reason only applied to spitting.

I mused about the events of the day. I had nearly seventy pounds in my pocket and plenty in the bank, well over a couple of thousand pounds worth in the value of the day. For the first time in my life I was rich and I had a date with a piece of perfection that I intended to impress the hell out of later. Perfect just.

Chapter Eleven

The One-0–One was named for and located, unimaginatively, at 101 Hope Street, just opposite the Central Hotel much as Katie indicated, so it was outside there, dressed in my new clothes and sporting a haircut normally ordered on American G.I.'s immediately upon induction by a gorilla posing as a drill sergeant and by means of a sickle, that I stood at precisely three minutes to eight. I made especially sure that I was nowhere near the station clock; I didn't want to accidentally land back in tomorrowland. The minutes passed and I felt chilled in the cold January air without a coat but warmed when I saw Katie walking towards me, right on time.

She hurried over. 'Sorry, I had to wait for a tram.'

Why she was apologising I don't know.

'Perfect timing. Shall we?' I ushered her inside.

The restaurant was hushed and warm and reasonably busy, perhaps eight or nine other tables in use. A maitre d' took Katie's coat and unctuously showed us to a table. She looked radiant in a salmon pink sort of twin set and I never thought I'd hear myself say that before. My grandmother used to wear them but this was different. Maybe I was just adapting to the period.

'Oh, George this is so fancy. I've never been in a place like this,' Katie whispered.

'Really?'

'People I've been out with don't have the sort of money for this. I mean, look at it.'

'Not even Gordon Lorne?' I teased.

'Gordon is just an ordinary guy. You may look like him but that's about as far as it goes. Other than that you're worlds apart.'

Didn't I know it? I watched her as she settled into her seat and generally made herself comfortable.

She looked at me and smiled. 'Got your hair cut, I see. Much better.'

'Really, you think? I was just about to order a hit on the guy.'

She laughed again.

'How about a glass of something to relax before we order? Champagne, cocktail?'

Boy, was I revelling in this new role. It sure beat asking for a pint of heavy and a pie and beans in The Horseshoe.

'Champagne? Really?' She looked amazed.

'Why not? It's a special occasion.'

'I've never had champagne before. What's the occasion?'

'It's Wednesday.'

'So?'

'You don't go out on Wednesdays. So – special occasion.'

A waiter came over and I put on my best suave and debonair impression, which, so far as I know, never fooled a waiter yet, and certainly not one in The Horseshoe let alone the One-0-One.

'We'd like two glasses of champagne, please, then we'll order.'

'Certainly sir.' A slight nod of the head and he left.

Wow, first time for everything. Two minutes later two flutes of champagne fizzed in front of us.

108

'Cheers, here's to Wednesday.' We clinked glasses.

'Mmm that's lovely. I feel so posh. Wait till I tell my friends. Who would have thought it, me drinking champagne?'

She closed her eyes as she sipped at it. Truth be told, I can't be arsed with champagne, it gives me heartburn and makes me fart, but noblesse oblige and all that.

We exchanged a bit of small talk for a few minutes about how nice and plush the place was, and plush was the word for it. Red velvet curtains folded back with ties covered a far wall, the sort of curtains where, when they close, you sing a couple of hymns and you know you'll never see your grannie again. The waiter brought over two leather bound menus. Katie took another sip of champagne then opened a menu and nearly gagged.

'Oh my God, George. Look at these prices.'

I looked. They seemed pretty good to me.

'That's fine. Just order what you want. Do you see anything you like?'

She scanned the menu.

'Do you like steak?' I asked.

'Yes, but I hardly ever get to have it.'

'What if I order us both smoked salmon for a starter and steak Diane as the main?'

'That sounds great – wait, oh God – it's seventeen and six for a steak Diane and – oh, would you look at the price of the smoked salmon.' She was shocked.

The whole meal was probably going to set me back about a fiver in old money, quite a lot right now, but buttons where I came from, and besides, I had an unlimited supply.

I caught the eye of the waiter, who by now, had twigged that this was a guy who knew his way around a restaurant menu, and he hurried over. I placed the order and asked for the wine list.

'George?'

'Yes?'

'What's Steak Diane?'

I smiled my know it all smile. 'It's a fillet steak battered thin and smeared with mustard. Then it's flambéed in a mushroom, onion and wine sauce and a little tomato puree with some brandy. They do it at the table. It's quite a show.'

'Oh my. Is there anything you don't know?'

The man about town smile came out again and I selected a bottle of Fleurie from the menu knowing it would be pleasantly light. Looking around the restaurant and considering the events of the past couple of days I revelled in all the changes in my life between that of the twenty-first century and now, here in the mid nineteen hundreds. For the first time in years I felt vibrant and active. I felt that I had some sort of purpose, and more than just making money although that part was fun. I was enjoying myself. I really wasn't looking forward to returning to 2017. I was having too much of a good time here. It occurred to me suddenly that it wasn't just that my circumstances had changed; I had changed. I was the person I always wanted to be, confident, solvent, independent, in charge of events. I was George Clooney, twentieth century bon viveur, not twenty-first century Gordon Lorne, waster. I liked the new me and what's more, so, I think, did Katie.

The waiter returned with the wine and poured a taste into my glass, which I swilled around for a second or two, held it to my nose and then sipped it knowingly, then nodded. I had no idea what I was supposed to be testing for but, hey, hello George. I seemed to remember not having much time for all that pretentious shite about wine having legs and allowing it to breath and savouring the body. I was once given a bottle of a reasonably expensive vino and advised to lay it down for a while. I laid it down, covered it in a blanket and gave it a pillow, almost shagged it, then drank it the next day. You'd have thought it was a film star. But I could get used to this. The waiter filled our glasses.

'You never told me what you did.' I said to Katie.

'Oh, nothing exciting. I work in a bank.'

I hoped it wasn't the bank I had been in.

'Really? Where?'

'The National Bank of Scotland in Gordon Street.'

Jesus, it was.

She went on, 'I'm on reconciliations.'

'Right,' I said, none the wiser. She could have been talking Portuguese. Maybe she got the manager and the chief clerk back talking again if they had an argument. We nattered for a bit and the waiter took our order.

Looking around I saw the other diners engaged in general conversation but something was different and I couldn't quite put my finger on it and then it came to me. There wasn't a mobile phone in sight. I was so used to seeing three or four people at a table all of whom had a mobile in their hands and prodding away at it with their thumbs or sliding a finger across the screen. I had been guilty of it myself and Christine was almost an addict. She had even once sent me a text when I was sitting opposite her. So I decided there and then to add mobile phone users to my cull list. This was a mental list I had prepared that was designed to reduce the world population problem simply by a process of elimination of all those people and groups who I deemed should not be allowed to exist. The list included men with waxed moustaches, women with tattoos, women with tattoos and waxed moustaches, rednecks with "I Voted Trump" bandanas so that was a few million right there,, Jeffrey Archer, and people who went on all inclusive holidays and wore coloured bands on their wrists to show what priority of catering they were entitled to. 'What colour band have you got, Fiona? Blue? Oh we're gold so we get the premium drinks package - a little bit more expensive but it's worth it.' Oh, fuck off.

The list also covers people who ask for upgrades at airports for no good reason and Boris Johnson obviously. It also includes Kenny MacKay. Kenny MacKay was in my class at school, a knuckle trailer who took a particular delight in giving me Chinese burns, charley horses, and punches to the solar plexus. He was, in short, a bully and like all bullies, a coward who surrounded himself with Neanderthals for safety. All the others on the list would be eliminated by means of a switch. Kenny MacKay would suffer unimaginable pain and the last voice he would ever hear on this earth would be mine saying, 'Hi Kenny, remember me?' Kenny was rescued and put on the back burner by the arrival of the waiter with our starters.

Now, I've had smoked salmon many a time but this was something of a different order. According to the menu it was wild salmon from the Tay, cured in a smokehouse in Dunkeld. Nowhere, but nowhere in the twenty-first century can you get smoked salmon that hasn't been farmed. I'm sure they use sheepdogs.

Katie was hesitant. 'What knife and fork do I use?'

'Just start at the outside and work your way in and if there are none left at the end then you know you've cracked it.'

Katie was admiring the surroundings as she ate. 'I feel like I could be somewhere glamorous like New York or Paris.'

This was a woman who was clearly on my wavelength.

'You like New York?'

'Only from scenes that I've seen in the pictures and magazines. It seems so, I don't know, so atmospheric.'

'What films?'

'Oh, you know. 'Guys and Dolls', 'The Seven Year Itch', 'Marty'. That one was black and white but it was still great. It won an Oscar.'

I knew what she meant. To me New York was a black and white city. Woody Allen, New York through and through, captured it perfectly in his film 'Manhattan' with Mariel Hemingway which he made in black and white because he saw the city that way, and he's right. Every time I see the iconic poster of the film with the two of them sitting on a bench silhouetted in the shadow of the Fifty-ninth Street Bridge and the title name echoing the Manhattan skyline I feel the city calling to me in my bones.

'Yeah, it's a great city.'

She looked at me in astonishment, a forkful of smoked salmon halfway to her mouth. 'You've been?'

I hadn't meant to go down this road but in for a penny in for a pound.

'New York? Yes.'

'Well don't just leave it there. What were you there for? What was it like?'

113

I had to make it up as I went along but I had been there so I knew what I was talking about except there must have been a lot of changes from between now and when I had last visited. Keep it simple.

'Remember I told you I did research and forecasting. Well the Americans are away ahead of us in so many ways. What they have now, we'll get in a couple of years. It was my job to see what the new trends were so I spent a couple of weeks meeting people and so on.' That didn't sound too bad.

'Did you sail on the Queen Mary?'

'No I flew.' Were there jets then? I couldn't remember, probably not. 'Flew out of Prestwick. Had to refuel on the way. It took forever. I'm sure we stopped at Gander to take on coal.'

'And?' She was agog.

'It was great, it really was. Times Square, the Chrysler Building, 5th Avenue. It's everything you ever imagine except it's bigger.'

I wasn't exaggerating. I told her about the dirty water dogs that taste like heaven that they sell on the street corners, I told her about Central Park, about Broadway. I didn't tell her about the spectacular dose of the galloping clap I caught from an enthusiastic amateur in a bar on 57th St. that had me pissing razor blades for two weeks and put me off sex for, well, three days at least.

'You're quite the sophisticate aren't you, George. The One-0-One, New York, whatever next?'

She forked the last of her salmon to her mouth. I poured some more wine, mostly for me, she hadn't taken too much.

'I'd love to travel- see the world. I love that song about the pyramids along the Nile. 'You Belong To Me' I

114

think it is.... market place in old Tangiers and all that. Da, de. da de, da....Jo Stafford,' she went on.

She looked wistful for a moment and it was lovely. She continued, 'You see pictures of the Taj Mahal and the Pyramids and the Colosseum and so on and you think - how wonderful. Who knows, maybe one day, one day when I'm rich and famous. Or just rich.' She laughed again. 'I don't know anybody who's been further than Jersey.'

The waiter reappeared and removed our plates and then set up for his pièce de resistance. He lit a small burner under a pan at the side of our table into which he spooned a knob of butter and let it sizzle. Then he sautéed some chopped mushrooms and onions, added some tomato puree and a little red wine. When they were ready he put them to the side and added the two mustard coated thin steaks and quickly seared them before stirring the mixture over them. He finished it off by adding cream then flaming it with brandy which was more for show than anything. The flames shot up a couple of feet from the table drawing admiring glances from the other diners and thrilling Katie. We ate for a few minutes in silence, just savouring the taste of the meal.

'This is so good, George. I've never tasted anything like it. It doesn't seem that long ago when this sort of thing was still rationed, and now look at us. Dining like kings and queens.'

I supposed she was right. Now, in 1957, it was still less than twelve years since the end of the second world-war and here we were...Christ, the war! The WAR! I forgot all about the fucking WAR! It was only a matter of time before she got around to that.

115

'So where were you during the war, George?'

See? I should have anticipated this. I was almost thirty-five now, that would make me seventeen when the war broke out, a bit young but I'd be twenty one in nineteen forty three, old enough to have been called up. I had to have been doing something. But what? Think Gordon. Okay, I could have been in the RAF. I could have been a dambuster, I'd seen the film years ago. No, that wouldn't work, I'd be famous or dead. I could have been on the reserved employment list. I'd heard people in certain industries like the railways or mining who didn't have to go and fight in the war. Or, I know, I could have been a prisoner of war, that's it, I'd seen The Great Escape every Christmas since I can remember. I knew all about Tom, Dick and Harry and sifting tunnel dirt through holes in my pockets. So that's settled. I had been in Stalag Luft III.

'I was a secret agent.'

Jesus Christ. Why is it my brain and my mouth never talk to each other? My mouth my brain and my dick are all part of the same body but it's like all three don't know the others exist. A secret agent? Where the fuck did that come from?

'A spy?' Katie was agog with excitement. 'Really?'

'I can't talk about it. I'm still bound by the Official Secrets Act.'

'But what did you do? Can you tell me anything?'

'Not much. It was to do with Operation Tosca. Very hush-hush, still is. It was to do with trying to use a hypnotist to get Hitler to order the Luftwaffe to bomb Rome by getting him to believe that Mussolini was a gay, black, Jew. I advised against it.' I could tell by her face that I'd over-egged it a bit.

116

'That's OK, George. If you can't talk about it just say,' she said coolly.

The waiter rescued me from what could have been a difficult moment.

'Can I interest you in dessert?'

'No arguments, Katie. You have to try the Crepes Suzette. Let's see how high they can get the flames this time.'

We talked more and more and the time passed. We talked about likes and dislikes. She said she loved 'Oklahoma' and I said I'd never been there and she said, no, the film, silly. She liked going to the cinema which she called "the pictures".

'You must have seen 'The Ten Commandments'?'

I shook my head.

"High Society?' No? 'The Man Who Knew Too Much' with Doris Day and James Stewart?'

I hadn't but I tried a Jimmy Stewart impression. I'd heard of him.

'My God, George, where have you been?' If only she knew. 'The Oscar winner –'Oklahoma?'

'Of course I know that.' I hummed a couple of bars of the signature tune.

She just looked at me oddly. The problem was that I hadn't prepared for this. I thought I would dip in, make a fortune and then dip out again. I hadn't bargained for social intercourse and I certainly didn't expect the other kind.

She said she'd heard of a new singer on the go called Elvis Presley and he had a film out called 'Love Me Tender' but she hadn't seen it. That was a pity because it was just about the only thing I could have talked about.

117

'His nickname is Elvis the Pelvis. I'm a bit old for that kind of music. I like Sinatra and Ella Fitzgerald.'

'Just you wait. He's going to be the king,' I said rashly, the wine and champers having taken effect.

'How can you know that?'

'It's my job, remember. Predicting trends. Young people are going to have more money, more freedom and they're going to like a different kind of music. We all rebel against our parents, even if it's only a little bit.'

She supposed so. 'I suppose that's what Bill Haley's doing with his rock and roll.'

'There you go,' I said and took another sip of the last of the wine of which I had had the lion's share.

'What's the difference between an alligator and a crocodile?' I asked.

'I don't know.'

'An alligator will see you later and a crocodile will see you in a while.' She thought this was funny. So did I the first time I heard it. Coffee came and went and we laughed and joked.

'Honestly George, I can't tell you when I have had such a good time,' she said as I paid the bill with a five pound note and a single which gave me enough left over for a ten shilling tip and some change. She looked aghast at the cost but I assured her it was a special occasion. Next time it would be The Horseshoe.

I helped her on with her coat and we headed for the door which the maitre d' held open for us. I felt as good as I've ever felt. Nothing could spoil the moment.

'Good night madam, good night Mr Lorne.'

Shit.

Chapter Twelve

I must have given the wrong name by mistake when I called in and made the reservation.

Katie looked at me. 'He just called you Mr Lorne.'

'I know. Isn't that odd?'

'It's more than odd, George. When I first saw you I thought you were Gordon Lorne, and you do look very like him, although I see the differences, but why would he call you Mr Lorne?'

By this time I had manoeuvred her away from the restaurant and over towards the station.

'I have no idea. Maybe he knew Gordon Lorne too.'

'That's very unlikely. Gordon hardly had two pennies to rub together and you've just spent the best part of a week's wages on one meal. Besides, Gordon has been gone well over a year.'

'Well, I agree that it's certainly weird.'

'There's something strange about all this, George.'

'What do you mean?' I knew fine well what she meant.

'First of all I bump into someone who is the spitting image of a previous boyfriend. Another thing, now that I think of it, when I called out his name, you turned around. Then you call and take me out for the most incredible meal I have ever had in my life and spend a fortune on me. Why?'

I opened my mouth to speak.

'No, I haven't finished.' She went on, 'And when I ask you about what you did in the war you spin the most incredible nonsense about Mussolini and being a secret agent when it's obvious you must have been making a killing on the black market.'

I have to say the girl was pretty perceptive.

'I'm not saying you're a spiv, George, you're far too nice for that, but I don't know what's going on. Oh, and another thing.'

There's another thing?

'You seem to have no idea what's going on today but you seem to be able to predict the future remarkably well. 'Oklahoma' didn't win the Oscar last year, it was 'Marty.' What on earth is that about? It's like having dinner with Rip Van Winkle.'

Who, in God's name, was Rip Van Winkle? I had no idea how to respond other than with a weak, 'I suppose it must seem a bit strange.'

She gave me what is colloquially known as an old fashioned look. We were at the head of a taxi rank and she didn't object when I said I would see her home although we didn't say much in the cab. When we pulled up outside the close she said she was all right from there, but I, ever the gentleman, got out as well and I paid off the driver.

'It's all right,' I said, 'The walk will do me good and it's not too far.'

'George, I've had a lovely night, really, the best I can remember. I hope you don't mind if I don't ask you up.'

I smiled my best Bogart smile, 'Here's looking at you, kid.'

She laughed, 'Finally, a film he remembers.' She leaned up and gave me a peck on the cheek. 'Thanks.'

She turned to go into the close and I turned to go but as I did she hesitated.

'George.'

I turned back.

'George, or Gordon, or whoever you really are let me just say this. I work in a bank nine till four Monday to Friday and up until lunch time on a Saturday. I live on my own and maybe once a week go to the pictures with Joyce and Margaret and sometimes to the Plaza or the Playhouse for the dancing. Up until now Gordon Lorne was the best thing that had ever happened to me but he ditched me for a better life elsewhere and I can't say I blame him.'

I listened without interrupting as I had no idea where this was going.

'On a Sunday I listen to 'Take it From Here', or 'Ray's a Laugh' or 'Educating Archie' which is listening to a ventriloquist on the radio if you can believe that.'

'At least you can't see his lips move.'

She shot me a warning look.

'Sorry.'

'I suppose, all in all it's not a bad life, a damn sight better than what my parents had, what with the war and all, do you understand what I'm saying?'

Actually I didn't but I nodded yes.

'But the thing is, George, it's boring and there are times I look around me and think, is this all there is? And then you come along and paint your pictures of New York and Paris and music in the clouds and double decker aeroplanes and so many things. You've been to New York and you've been to Paris and you know how to treat a woman and it's ...it's exciting.' She paused and looked away and said almost to herself, 'And God knows, I could do with a little excitement in my life right now.'

I still said nothing because I knew she hadn't finished. I was right.

'So here's the thing, George. I know you're not Gordon Lorne, not my Gordon Lorne anyway, and I can walk away now and say thank you for a lovely evening. Or I can tell you that you have my number and you can give me a call, and I think, to be honest, that I'd like that. I think I need a bit of adventure right now so I'll stick around for the ride to see where it goes, if that's okay.'

Then she took a step towards me, put her hand behind my neck and planted a big kiss on my lips. Then she turned away and disappeared into the close.

Walking back to the hotel my mind was in turmoil. There was nothing I wanted more than to take things further with Katie. I had money now, I could show her the things she talked about. I could take her on the Queen Mary and sail past the Statue of Liberty or take the "Golden Arrow" to Paris and stroll around Montmartre and I was sorely tempted. But that's not why I was here. I had promised Barry, and let's not forget Christine, that I would be back like the proverbial prodigal and my pockets full of green.

I had two more nights before planning to go back to my real world although the plan was to make another two or three trips and literally scoop the pools. I also still needed to figure out a way to get the fortune sixty years forward and I was no further ahead with that. I was trying to figure out how to get the best of both worlds. Katie said she wanted adventure and excitement; well I could provide that. I could take her to Paris for a few days. Why not? I wasn't planning to string her along, I would lay it on the line for her and let her decide. Hell, maybe we could even get to New York for a trip. Now I was just getting fanciful.

I decided to call Katie again tomorrow and tell her I was going away for a few days but would call when I got back. Tomorrow I'd go to the bank and deposit most of the winnings and then pay a visit to another unsuspecting bookie although maybe a trip a bit further afield wouldn't go amiss. So resolved, I saw a tram pulling up to a stop heading for the city and got on just behind a wee Glasgow man, bunnet cap on his head and drawing on a hand rolled cigarette which appeared to be mainly wrinkled tissue paper. He went upstairs immediately behind the conductress, his head immediately under her rear end and unavoidably looking up her skirt on the ladder steep step.

'Aw Isa, full moon the night ah see,' he joked.

'Aye, and there'll be a wee man in it later.'

123

Chapter Thirteen

The next day was crisp and clear although I knew that was just false promise as so many before. I had a few hours to kill before finding an unsuspecting bookie and I thought Clydebank was a reasonable distance out and there were plenty of buses, trams and even trains to choose from. I went to the bank and put in most of what was left from yesterday and kept twenty five pounds and change in my pocket which was far more than I was going to need.

It was on the stroke of eleven as I passed the Horseshoe so I nipped in for a quick half pint to ease an incipient thirst and think out the plans for the day. A few others meandered in with the same intent including someone sporting a camera, something that in 2017 might be found in a bric-a-brac antique shop but the owner was proudly showing it off.

'It's a single lens reflex,' he informed the barman and a couple of others who showed an interest. I wondered how he would react to my iPhone. 'You see the exact same image through the viewfinder as the lens sees. It's a Zeiss. Top of the range.'

'Where did you get it?' asked the barman.

'Won it in a poker school up at the Calton. I bluffed my way wi' a pair. Silly bastard had three whores.'

I assumed this was three queens. 'Stand there and I'll take your picture,' he instructed the barman. 'Kid on you're servin' a pint to him.' He pointed it at me.

I raised my half empty glass as the barman held a glass under a pump and the new David Bailey took a snap.

'Perfect. The light just caught your face.'

There was more detailed chat on the merits of slow exposures and shutter speeds as I finished my drink.

'That's you preserved for posterity, son. In another fifty years people will look at your photie and wonder who the hell you are.'

They all laughed at that and I smiled ruefully as I walked out the swing door.

Trains called; large steam engines, small tank engines, coaches, signals and all the associated paraphernalia of a railway. I had a small stock of railway books stacked on the floor of my flat, mostly photographs and most of them shot in England somewhere.

Lizar's in Buchanan Street was a camera shop that caught my eye and I spent a useful hour there looking to buy a decent single lens reflex like the one the Horseshoe poker player had and picked up a similar Zeiss for eighteen pounds, plus five rolls of thirty –five millimetre black and white film. I figured that should do the job but I couldn't help thinking that life was going to be so much easier for professional hopefuls when digital hit the streets but that was going to be a long time coming.

Photographs of steam locomotives have to be in black and white. It's the only medium that captures the brooding majesty of them, night or day. It highlights the white steam against the black of the engine and the sooty grey smoke. Colour tends to reduce the impact and the atmosphere. It sacrifices mood for realism. So with a fully loaded camera and a penny platform ticket I joined the ranks of the anoraks, a title not yet bestowed on them, at the end of platform one to record the action.

A gleaming 'City' Pacific, City of Birmingham stood at the head of the Mid Day Scot, the crack 1.30pm express to London getting there in a stately seven and a half hours. It even bore a headboard with the name on it. My last trip to London had been in a Virgin Pendolino and hurtled down at 125 miles an hour in under four and a half hours but with none of the magic associated with this scene before me. I snapped away happily, even persuading the driver and fireman to pose for me. Behind it snaked eleven carmine and cream coaches each with a side board affixed above the windows proclaiming the train's name and destination. The first class coaches sat in front of the restaurant and kitchen cars. The restaurant car offered white tablecloths, gleaming cutlery and white glove table service and a menu which, rather riskily, always offered soup as one of the starter choices, usually Brown Windsor, whatever the hell that was.

Precisely on time, the guard blew his whistle, waived a green flag, and with a wave of acknowledgment from the driver, the huge driving wheels eased into action, slipping occasionally until they gripped, and it slowly, very slowly, pulled out of the station and into the afternoon light. I watched it disappear over the bridge then turned my attention to a Black '5', another Pacific heading a stopper to Carlisle. Any number of tank engines scurried back and forward and I stood so long snapping away that a Cathcart Circle that had left about an hour earlier came chuffing back in. Half a dozen trainspotters oohed and aahed orgasmically as a previously unseen engine appeared and another tick went against the number in the Ian Allen trainspotters' bible. It was, simply, not quite but almost, very nearly, well maybe not *very* nearly, better than sex.

126

I can't believe I just said that.

After a quick pie and beans in a pub across the road I dumped the camera at the hotel and made my way over to Queen Street station where I got on a local train to Clydebank. Once there I couldn't but help think, uncharitably, that the Germans had improved the place. Halfway up Kilbowie Road I saw the welcome sign hand painted above a door, 'Turf Accountant', so rubbing my itchy palms, I entered.

It was simple enough. Once again I followed my set pattern and pushed the slip through the window slot where the clerk looked at it and stamped it. As I turned away I should have noticed him picking up the telephone and dialling, or if I did, it didn't register as important. I listened to the commentaries on the radio and watched as disappointed and disgusted punters tore up their slips in frustration and headed out of the door. Others more lucky claimed their few shillings gratefully and bet again on another sure thing only to listen in agitated disbelief to the inevitable outcome.

An hour and sixty two pounds later I was back out onto Kilbowie Road where the light was fading. Twenty yards away there was a set of traffic lights and I walked towards them to cross over. I never made it. Four very large hands attached to four very hairy arms bolted onto two six foot six, eighteen stone frames dragged me into a nearby lane and pinned me face first against a rough brick wall, one that had relatively recently been used as a urinal. That wasn't my biggest worry.

'Sandy says hello.' A steel voice rasping over gravel greeted me. So did a sickening punch in the kidneys.

They turned me around and the other one sank a huge fist into my solar plexus. It seemed to go so far in that I'm sure I felt it against my spine. I retched and crumpled onto the dirt ground of the lane. Bad idea. Steel toe caps battered my ribs and by now I realised that this could be more than just trouble. This could be life changing. Like life changing into death. They dragged me up to my feet while where one held me up and the other gave me a double whammy across the jaw. I was no clairvoyant but I could see dental work figured somewhere in my near future, if there was a near future.

'Some folks cannae take a tellin'.'

'Some folks need tae get the message.' Another fist disappeared into my gut.

The first one spoke again. 'So here's the message. Sandy say's if he ever sees you in any of his shops again, ye might find yerself takin' a wee holiday doon the watter. Get the drift?'

I nodded. I got the drift.

'See, we don't know what you're up tae, but yer up tae somethin'. We're no' daft. So Frankie here'll just take back what you scammed us for.' He turned to Frankie who, in the eerie light of a distant street lamp, looked like Lurch, and told him to go through my pockets.

'Right, and a wee bit extra for wur trouble, if it's all right. We'll just take the foldin' paper stuff if that's okay wi' you.'

A quick knee in the balls ensured that I wouldn't be chasing after them any time soon so I just sat there, my arse in a puddle, and tried to breathe. Eventually I managed to stand up, back against the wall for support and checked my pockets. All the notes were gone but they were as good as their word; they left me with a few coins that amounted to just over five shillings. That would get me back to the hotel where I could assess the damage.

Fortunately, by this time darkness had fallen and once the pain, and it was everywhere, eased enough to put one foot in front of the other, I attempted to move. My kidneys were arguing with my testicles as to which were the worse off. Fortunately I had two of each. Clearly sex was off the menu off at least, well, we'll see. My jaw ached and a couple of back teeth wobbled precariously. My nose was bleeding and one eye was swollen enough to cause me difficulty seeing. Other than that, it could have been a lot worse. How, I'm not sure.

I dragged myself round the corner into Kilbowie Road and saw a giant clock above a large factory and a sign that said 'Singer' and I remembered that Singer station was just next to it, so hugging the shadows, I stumbled around to it, bought a ticket and when a train arrived ten minutes later I found an empty compartment at the back far away from curious eyes and clambered in.

My first thought as the train trundled through the dreary suburbs of western Glasgow was to get to the hotel as quickly as I could as it was just around the corner from Queen Street, but I thought the better of it when I realised there would be questioning eyes at the reception desk and the possibility of a chambermaid wanting to turn down the sheets. So when the train pulled in I made my way up the stairs as quickly as my bruised body would allow and got into a taxi. There was just about enough to pay the fare by the time it dropped me off at Nithsdale Road where I found the bedroom by some sort of osmosis and collapsed unconscious or asleep or in a coma onto the bed.

It was daylight when I next looked at my watch. I calculated that I probably had fallen on top of my bed at around six o'clock so I must have been out for about fifteen hours or so. Congealed blood had cemented my face to the pillow and it took some delicate surgery to free it. It took another ten minutes for me to summon up the nerve to move my body but when I at last got to my feet I didn't feel quite as bad as I imagined I would. The mirror told a different story. My face looked like an old British Empire map of the world, liberally dotted with red and blue. I would have killed for an hour in a shower but there wasn't one, but I ran a bath after managing to figure out the intricacies of the geyser and gingerly lowered myself in and soaked the worst excesses from my body.

Mulling over the events of the previous day I figured out a few things. One: Sandy had a chain of bookies and I had managed to use three of them in three days. That, apparently, had not gone unnoticed. Two: bookies adhered to their own code of rough justice without involving the constabulary. Three: If I wasn't careful in what I was doing I could be in serious trouble. Like dead. Four: It was maybe time to take stock and head back to 2017 for a few days. If I did that I could update Barry, satisfy my burgeoning lust with Christine, and come back the next week and fill in the football pools coupon which should have by then arrived. The plans involving Christine very much depended on the functioning ability of that part of my body that had been in contact with a steel toe cap delivered at considerable velocity. Gingerly, I thought I'd just see how they felt. I wonder if the neighbours heard the scream.

130

Later that day I called Katie and told her that I would be out of town for a few days.

'Oh, international man of mystery?'

'Nah, just something I've got to do.'

'Going anywhere nice?' she asked.

I thought about what to say to her. Anything was going to involve a lie and I wanted it to be as little a lie as possible which is a bit like saying you're a little bit pregnant. A lie is a lie is a lie.

'Not really. Tell you about it when I see you.' That was just delaying the inevitable.

'Okay. Do you want to make a date now or will I wait till you call?'

'I'll text you.' It was out before I realised what I had said.

'You'll what?'

'Sorry, my head's full of broken bottles. I was just reading some text when I called you.'

'I'm glad I'm the full focus of your attention,' she said tartly.

'Of course you are. I'll call you Tuesday or Wednesday. Promise.'

I hung up, made my way around to Laing's and had a pint before heading back to the station and my trip to the other world. It was all so uneventful that I was beginning to take this toing and froing between past, present and future, or should I say present future, or hell, pick your own tenses, that I thought nothing of it when I found myself standing under the 2017 clock and almost on top of a much astonished a middle aged lady shopper who had thought herself quite alone when whispering some vague obscenity into her mobile.

The bedsit was cold and slightly damp when I finally made my way in and the dishes were still congealing in the sink. Oh 1957, missing you already.

Chapter Fourteen

Barry called first thing in the morning. 'Well?'

'Are you asking after my health or looking for an update?'

'How did it go?'

'Successful up to a point.'

'Please tell me the success was in the financial side, Lesley's spending money like I've got a home printing press. She doesn't know that you're the printing press.'

'Okay, give me a couple of hours and meet up for a pint?'

'I take it you're flush?' he asked hopefully.

'Yes and no.'

'What does that mean, Gordon?'

'I've got cash, the only problem is that it's in a bank account sixty years old. No problem though, I think my Giro's in so I'll manage a pint.'

'Jesus, Gordon. This had better be good.'

A hot shower helped ease the bruising pain and my face, never a Michelangelo at the best of times, resembled more of a cubist Picasso, but the swelling had gone down and my eye functioned despite the lurid colouring. At least I could play the pity card when I went round to Christine's later.

Glasgow looked a bit worse for wear through a watery light punctuated by the occasional glimpse of blue as clouds scudded across the sky. As usual in February or July the weather couldn't make up its mind. It was only when I looked more closely at the streets and shops as I meandered round the town that I could see the differences between the two centuries. Union Street was a mess. It was full of cheap pound shops, tack stores, video game shops and the like. Argyle Street wasn't much better and Sauchiehall Street was awful. There was litter everywhere, plastic bags dancing in the wind and discarded take away cartons cluttering doorways. There was just a sense of decay about the place. The city that I had left last night was so different. Granted, buildings were black and soot ingrained but the streets seemed so much more vibrant. I had noticed classy stores in Sauchiehall Street like Copeland and Lye, Treron's, (Tréron et Cie, would you believe?), C&A. There was a theatre, the Empire, that I recalled was the stuff of legend where English comedians trembled in fear. It was said that a comic called Des O'Connor faked a faint just to get off the stage, and a mime artist was somewhat nonplussed when five minutes into his act someone shouted, 'For fuck's sake, tell us a joke –ah'm blind!' It looked, well, prosperous, and this in the fifties. I had always imagined that era as a time of poverty and privation. Well, it looked just fine to me, I can tell you. Right enough, I hadn't gone into the tenement suburbs like Springburn and Possilpark, or Govan or the east end, places like Calton and Oatlands so I was probably being unfair, but looking at Glasgow right now it didn't seem to have a lot going for it. The city in 1957 appeared to have a warmth about it, not like now.

I walked out to Nithsdale Road to see if my rented apartment was still there, and by God, it was. I was tempted to walk up the stairs and see if the keys still worked but thought the better of it. I took a bus back

134

into town. Well, at least the Horseshoe was still standing. Talking of which...

'The wanderer has returned, alert the media.' This was Barry at his sardonic average. Then he noticed my injured state. 'Jesus Christ, what happened to you? Do they have forty-tonners in 1957 too?'

I told him the story of my Clydebank adventure embellishing it a little for effect in as much that I had inflicted no little damage myself and only lost on points.

'Okay, okay, start at the beginning.'

So I did; from finding a hotel, renting an apartment, opening a bank account, winning at the bookies, being recognised by Katie as my grandfather, dinner, ending up in jail, and lastly getting a thumping in Clydebank. To Barry's credit he didn't interrupt me once. In fact he didn't even touch his pint until I was finished.

'Jesus, Gord, mate, that's some story.'

I nodded modestly.

'So, this bird. Kate.'

'Katie.'

'Whatever- so?' He raised an inquisitive eyebrow.

'So - what?'

He looked over his glass as he sipped, 'Well?'

'What?'

'Did you shag her?'

'Oh, for God's sake, Barry. Is that all you think about?'

'Actually, I was under the impression that it's all you think about.'

'I didn't even try. Besides, I don't know what the protocol is then.'

'Protocol never stopped you before. If I remember right you once tried to put the bite on Lesley's mother.'

'Good looking woman.'

'Lesley was still in the room.'

'I may have been influenced by alcohol somewhat.' I recalled the event in question and I was so bombed I didn't know whether it was New York or New Year.

'You mean you were drunk.'

'I wasn't drunk but drink had been taken.'

Barry sat back to take stock and another swig.

'So, how much of the stake do you have left?'

'A hundred pounds in the bank. That's worth about one and a half grand back there. Don't forget the rent money I handed over.'

'Fuck all use to us here though, isn't it?'

'Don't forget those thugs took all my readies, maybe about forty quid. Anyway, that's not the point is it? I'm going back to fill in the pools coupon, it should be there by then.'

'And that's? Remind me.'

'Could be well over a hundred thousand,' I said.

'Jesus!' he exclaimed in astonishment.

'Yeah, and the rest. The buying power of that then is a million and a half today, maybe two.'

We both mulled this over and the same problem still concerned us. How do we invest it then so that its worth can be realised today?

'So, by and large it's all going to plan?'

'This time next year we'll be millionaires, Rodders,' I said with my best Del boy accent.

'This time next month, I hope.'

'You got it.'

We both relaxed and he was big enough to insist on buying me a large one. I looked around the bar noting the changes over the years. For all that, it was the same

136

Horseshoe I was glad to note. The difference was in the style. The fifties bottles behind the bar were virtually all whiskies, maybe a couple of gins and a vodka in the optics but that was about it. Now when I looked at the shelves there was Malibu, six different flavoured vodkas, green drinks, blue drinks, red drinks, drinks with little gold speckles in them.; it was like a Jackson Pollock painting. The only thing that there wasn't was blue cigarette smoke. I couldn't help thinking that a cigar would have been nice, just to celebrate, you know. I didn't want to inhale it, I wanted to feel the texture, smell the aroma, enjoy the general contentment that a once a year cigar brings but I couldn't and I thought, you know, this is so fucked up, they really will ban drinking in pubs next.

'So how are the wedding plans coming along?' I asked.

'They're coming along just fine. Actually I've left it all to Lesley. We're going to stay at my place for a while at least.'

Barry's place was a rather nice two bedroomed apartment on Queen Margaret Drive befitting his status in life, business and society in general. Financial advising clearly had its advantages and he was certainly advising himself pretty well. It had its own ground floor entrance with, would you believe, stained glass panelling on the interior door. It had a large lounge and a separate dining room and a kitchen area that would have Lesley in paroxysms of planning delight.

'Yes, I'm up to my knees in colour charts. I had to put my foot down and tell her to leave me out of the fine details. I'm a big picture man.'

'Big picture, huh?'

'Oh, yes.' He paused and took another mouthful, a gulp this time. 'Did you know there was such a colour as taupe?'

'Taupe?'

'Yeah.'

'Never heard of it.'

'Me either. Also I thought aubergine was a thing you ate.'

'It is,' I said. 'I ate one once.'

'It's also going to be the colour of the wood panels under the window. It's something like the colour of your eye, as a matter of fact.'

'You're in trouble, man.'

He was silent as he gazed into the distance with the thousand yard stare of people who know that for them life has changed forever. Like Vietnam vets.

'Frangipane.'

'What?'

'Frangipane, it's the colour of a curtain material she likes.'

'What colour is that?'

'I haven't a fucking clue.'

He sighed then shook himself out of it.

'Anyway, mate. We're having a wee celebration tomorrow night. I'd have told you before but you were in another world. Literally. Are you okay for it? My place eight o'clock?'

It sounded good to me. 'Lesley's mum going to be there?' I asked mischievously.

'You leave Lesley's mum alone.' Barry took another sip, 'So, seeing Christine tonight?'

Actually I had all but forgotten about Christine.

'Yeah, I'll call her after I leave here.'

138

'You told her about the wedding, right? I mean the Caribbean thing?'

'Yeah.'

'I thought so. The jungle drums are sounding the alert already. I saw Brian Kelso...'

He saw my look. 'It's okay, okay, you're still the best man. Anyway I think Christine may have told him about it. Brian'll be there anyway, in Barbados, that is. They'll both be there tomorrow as well. He knows he's first reserve.'

'That's okay. When I'm sitting in my luxury recliner on Virgin's Upper Class he can come up front and beg.'

'He's pretty sure you won't make it. He knows you too well.'

'Fuck him.' My glass was almost empty. 'So, Barbados, eh?'

'Yeah, Almond Beach. Lesley's over the moon.'

I caught that, just Lesley, no 'we'.

We finished our drinks and left with the agreement that I'd see him at his soiree with Lesley and her colour charts. It was gone seven and I hadn't phoned Christine so I thought I'd just go up and surprise her. She had one of those fancy doorbells that plays the 'Hallelujah Chorus' when you ring it.

'Gordon.' She had a towel covering her body. 'You should have called.'

'That's okay, I see you're ready for action.'

'Just having a shower.' She just stood there.

I made to enter the house but she didn't move.

'Christine?'

'I really wish you'd called.'

I thought I saw some movement behind her so I pushed the door wider.

139

'Oh Jesus Christ, Christine. Not Brian Kelso.'

'Gordon, you should have called. It's not as if we've pledged to love honour and obey, is it?'

I walked past her into the hall. Brian Kelso was standing there also draped in a towel; they'd obviously been in the shower together.

'Hi Gordon,' he said nervously.

I ignored him and turned to Christine. 'Seriously? Brian Kelso?'

'Now look here, Gordon,' said Brian.

'Look where, Brian?'

'It's not what you think.'

'You're both standing there all but bollock naked, it's exactly what I think.'

'I love Christine, Gordon.'

Even Christine rolled her eyes at this. She took control of Kelso.

'Brian, love, why don't you go and put some clothes on while I talk to Gordon?'

'If you think you'll be safe.'

I put my hand in my jacket pocket. 'I've got a gun, Brian.'

'Oh my God.'

Christine rolled her eyes. 'Brian, he hasn't got a gun and I'm perfectly safe so please let us talk.'

He scampered into the bedroom. Christine looked defiantly at me.

'It's all your own fault.'

'*My* fault?'

We went into her sitting room where she sat down, lit a cigarette and crossed her legs. I could feel my anger dissipating already.

140

'Listen Gordon,' then she noticed my wounds, 'What happened to you?'

'Just an accident, you were saying?'

'The last time I saw you, you made some big promises then just pissed off. I've tried calling you but don't even get an answer. What am I supposed to think?'

She took a draw on her cigarette. 'We both agreed that we like each other and the sex is great, most of the time anyway, when you're reasonably sober, but that's it. We're both free agents and let's not kid ourselves, we're both fairly promiscuous, so what's the big deal?'

'But Brian Kelso, Chris.'

'Don't keep saying that. What's wrong with Brian Kelso?'

'Oh, come on. He can read a book and watch TV at the same time.'

'So he's cross-eyed. He's dyslexic too so they cancel each other out.'

That was actually quite funny and I tried not to laugh. 'He doesn't know whether he's coming or going,' I said.

'Oh, he knows when he's coming. The whole of Shawlands knows when he's coming.'

This girl was a one woman comedy show. She should try stand-up; she'd make a fortune. I knew when I was beaten.

'But Brian Kelso.' It was more a plaintive lament than anything else.

'Will you stop saying that.'

'But why?'

'Because Brian's got the wherewithal.'

'The what?'

She sighed and started to explain as if talking to a ten year old.

141

'He's not stuck for money and he's offered to take me to Barry's wedding in the Caribbean, guaranteed. I know you said you would too, but let's face it, Gordon, it's not going to happen is it?'

So that was it. And she went on. 'A girl's gotta do what a girl's gotta do.'

'And you're doing Brian, Chris.'

'Come on Gordon, I'm not going to marry him and I'm still, what shall I say, I'm still a free spirit.'

She uncrossed her legs and the towel partly fell open. She'd obviously seen Sharon Stone in 'Basic Instinct'.

'No sense in spoiling a good thing, is there? What's wrong with friends with benefits?'

I suppose she had a point there. What's a benefit or two between friends?

There was a plaintive cry from the bedroom.

'Can I come out now?'

'Yes, Brian, you can come out now,' said Christine with a suggestive wink at me. 'Gordon was just going, weren't you Gordon?'

Brian nervously came into the room having changed back into his shirt and slacks.

'No hard feelings, Gordon?' He put out his hand.

I looked at him and looked at his hand for a long moment.

'Nah, Brian, no hard feelings.' I shook his sweating palm.

'That's the spirit.'

I made my way to the door and opened it then looked at Christine. Brian was standing protectively behind her.

'Oh, by the way, Christine, I've got the all clear now but the doctor says you should get yourself checked out.'

All was quiet as I made my way down the stairs.

142

Time dragged a bit as it often does when you're waiting for something. I was beginning to understand a few things about time. Einstein was right; everything is relative. Time seems to move at different speeds depending on the observer. Spend a half hour in a dentist's chair and it seems like every moment stretches out proportional to the degree of pain inflicted. You can almost hear people speaking as if it's like a recording played at a half speed. Watching a half hour episode of Coronation Street, something I am occasionally compelled to do when I'm with Christine, easily takes an hour despite what the clock says. Yet a few hours spent between the sheets with a new and willing woman seems to rattle by in minutes. Even now, in my thirties, I see the minutes turn into hours turn into weeks turn into years like a runaway train swiftly gathering speed.

That's not what Einstein meant at all, of course, but I think it's a much easier and more understandable explanation than using hieroglyphics to try to hoodwink us all into believing it's all to do with the speed of light.

I was anxious to get back to 1957. Katie was there and there was unfinished business between the two of us, we both knew that. Christine's dalliance with Brian Kelso didn't really bother me as much as I thought it would and that was probably because of Katie. It was more the fact that it was with Brian Kelso that got on my wick.

There was also the prospect of becoming very rich indeed. Things were going to be very interesting back then. But first there was Barry and Lesley's little party to attend.

Queen Margaret Drive sits in an elegant part of Glasgow just behind Great Western Road, far enough away from the centre to be desirable, near enough to get there in a few minutes on the subway. It's close to the Kelvingrove art galleries and a little more than a stone's throw from Glasgow University. There's a lot of student life around this part of the west-end and it's just about the best place in Glasgow to live. It's perfect for the restaurants and pub life on Byres Road and I could walk up there from my pad in the less salubrious quarter of Partick.

By the time that I arrived, more than fashionably late, the party, or 'wee celebration' as Barry called it, was in full swing. Not wanting to arrive empty-handed I had brought a bottle of Prosecco from Waitrose which I handed to Lesley at the door.

'Gordon, Prosecco, you shouldn't have.'

'Oh, it's nothing.'

'I know. You shouldn't have.'

'Oh come on, how about a big hug and a kiss for the best man.'

'I don't know if he's here yet.' This was said half jokingly and wholly in earnest. 'Come on in – my God – what happened to your face?' She had just noticed it.

'Fell out of bed.'

'Whose bed?'

What is it with women these days; are they all auditioning for the Michael McIntyre Comedy Roadshow?

'Barry says you're still planning on being best man.'

'Barry would be right.'

'If you aren't able to do it I'd understand.'

'Wild horses and all that.'

144

'Don't let us down, will you. And please, please, don't offend anyone in your speech. And keep away from mother.' Lesley's divorced mother was looking rather glamorous chatting to a personal fitness trainer called Forbes who Lesley occasionally used to keep herself in shape.

'Aw, Lesley, your mother has nothing to be afraid of, I'll be on my best behaviour.'

'It's not *your* behaviour I'm worried about.'

I followed her into the lounge which was filled to every corner with people who I had mostly never met before, business colleagues of Barry, friends and colleagues of Lesley and assorted hangers on. I'm sure there was a hint of an aroma of an illegal substance in the air. I waved an airy hand to all and sundry but they paid no notice. The drinks were laid out on a large trestle in the hall so I dodged back and got myself a Stella. Sensing someone behind I turned to see Brian Kelso who fixed me with a look from one eye while the other took in the decor.

'Hey, Gordon, look, are we okay?'

'Okay as we'll ever be, Brian,' which was no less than the truth.

He breathed out a sigh of relief. 'I didn't want us to fall out, us being mates and all.'

'Mates, yeah.'

There was an awkward silence which I eventually broke.

'How's the book coming along?'

'Book?'

'The Kennedy thing, you know.'

He thought for a moment. 'Oh, yeah. Fine, fine. Takes a lot of research you know so I'm still at that stage. A lot of interest out there though, lot of interest.'

'So, You've got a publisher?'

'Not exactly. Lot of interest though, lot of interest.'

There was another drawn out silence.

'So, you know I'm taking Christine to Barbados for the big do?' he said awkwardly.

'You're the man, Brian.' I chucked him on the shoulder.

He sort of shuffled nervously and looked at the floor. Or one eye did, I wasn't sure where the other one was headed.

'You planning on going?' he asked.

'Brian, I'm the best man.'

'Right, right. It's just that Barry wasn't sure.'

'I'll be there, Brian.'

'I won't be needing the speech then.'

I looked at him. 'Wait, wait. You wrote the speech already? It's three months away.'

'Not exactly wrote. It still needs tweaking.'

Jesus. I shook my head in despair. 'Excuse me, Brian. Gotta mingle.'

Barry caught sight of me and made his way through the throng.

'Glad you made it.'

'Seems to be quite a party. What, just fifty of your closest friends?'

'A lot of them are Lesley's. I don't know half of them.'

I did a quick survey. 'Is that Lesley's brother? That's Tom isn't it?'

Lesley's brother preened, patronising and smooth, dripping unction like a leaky tap yet positively reeking

146

superiority. If he fell into Rothesay Bay he'd create an oil slick a mile wide. They'd have to rescue seabirds. A Hugo Boss jacket that had that trendy, slightly baggy look, hung open to reveal a monogrammed designer black crew-neck shirt. Just the right amount of gel kept his streaked hair rakishly out of place. A brushed silver ingot of a Rolex Oyster weighed down his left wrist. He had clearly taken a lot of time trying to achieve a carelessly dressed at the last minute look. He reminded of Carol King's ode to Warren Beatty or whoever, 'You're So Vain'. He was, in short, what is known in discerning circles as a LOMBARD. Loads Of Money But A Right Dickhead.

'The very man. Lesley would really like him to be my best man but she knows it's my choice. I'm not that keen on him either. He's an investment banker in London now.'

'You almost said that right.'

At that Tom spied us and made his way over. 'Hi Baz.'

'Tom,' Barry acknowledged.

He turned to me. 'It's Gordon, ya?'

He held out his hand to shake and I took it for a second. I had to wipe it down my trouser leg afterwards. If anything sets my teeth on edge it's people who say "ya" for yes to end a sentence.

'Yes, Barry's best man.'

'Really? Heard you might not make it, ya.'

'What gave you that idea?'

'Lesley thought you were going through a bad patch. What happened to your face?'

'Tripped over my wallet.'

'Hah, good one. Oh well, catch up in the Windies, ya?' He turned away to find someone else to leak oil over.

'Windies?' I looked at Barry questioningly.

'West Indies.'

'I hate bastards that talk in code.'

Barry looked around the room and nodded towards Christine.

'Seems she's playing the field. Hedging her bets, as they say. Brian tells me he's the official escort to Barbados. He's like a dog with two tails.'

'That's okay. It was dying on its arse anyway.'

Barry looked around the room and I followed his gaze.

'Plenty of tottie here,' he observed.

Indeed there was and a lot of it unescorted as well so I thought I'd do the rounds. Lesley came over to take Barry away, I think she thought I was a bad influence and she's probably right. I took a good look at her wondering what it was that I saw in her that had made me lust after her. She was attractive, certainly, willowy tall and blonde, just turned thirty and she'd probably be a rabbit in bed but I saw now that she and I had nothing in common. She was clearly a social climber with crampons and I had about as much height as Holland and less depth than Tibet.

I looked to see where Christine was and saw her pinning a high flyer I had never seen before against a wall, but who was something big in the city according to Lesley, and was engaging him in earnest conversation. Very earnest by the look of things. Christine was very keen on sex toys and this guy apparently had two of the best; a Maserati Gran Turismo MC Stradale in signal red and a forty-eight foot Fairline Targa 48 GT moored at Inverkip. Christine was approaching the peak of orgasm on the spot. Brian was in a corner somewhere thumbing

148

through a copy of National Geographic. Brian had a lot to learn. I caught general snippets of conversation as I trawled the room.

'I wouldn't be seen dead in black...'

'I had tramlines all down my back, had to undress in the dark...'

'Who's the guy with the black eye...'

'Mary, I said, I said, Mary, I said to her, no really...'

Brian was trying to muscle into Christine's conversation with Maserati man. For some reason he was talking about wedding fireworks displays, maybe because he'd heard that Lesley had that on the agenda. Maserati man looked bored.

'I don't think they're worth it,' Brian was saying, 'The last one I saw barely lasted two minutes – it was such a disappointment.'

'I know just how that feels,' said Christine with heavy irony turning her full attention back to Maserati man who smirked.

Brian moved away, crushed. There were food smells from the kitchen so I eased my way past a heavily breathing Christine to grab some food. Lesley had certainly done Barry proud. There was anything and everything as long as it was from Marks and Spencer's so I busied myself with some bacon wrapped chestnuts and a handful of pigs in a blanket.

'Nice, aren't they?'

The voice belonged to an attractive woman with dark hair flowing to her shoulders which she swept back with a shake of her head just like they do in the L'Oreal adverts. What held my gaze was her hooded sloe eyes like someone who's just had sex although I was sure she just hadn't. Her voice was caramel smooth. If she was a singer she would be a contralto. There was something distantly familiar about her and I thought I may have seen someone like her in a film. She certainly had the looks.

'Delicious.' It might have been better if I'd swallowed what was in my mouth first.

'Sorry.' I brushed my shirt with my hand but she just laughed.

'I saw you come in. I always find men with a black eye and a limp fascinating. They usually have history and a story to tell.'

Baby, you wouldn't believe it.

'Had an argument over a ladies honour.'

She laughed again, 'Yeah, right.'

'There were three of them but I could handle myself.'

'Obviously,' she said, playing along.

'I had them really worried for a while.'

'Okay.'

'Yeah, they thought they had killed me.'

More laughs.

'But I adopted an old Navajo Indian trick that I learned.'

'What's that?' she asked.

'Oh, generally screaming and begging for mercy.'

She laughed and I said a silent thank you and apology to Woody Allen for using one of his lines. I had a whole stack of them ready for any occasion.

I put out my hand, 'Gordon.'

She shook it. 'Susan.'

'You here with anyone, Susan?'

'No, you?'

'No. I'm Barry's best man.'

'I'm a friend of Lesley's.'

150

'Right. Are you going to Barbados for the wedding?'

'Yes. I'll be one of the maids of honour. Frankly I can't stand all that crap, I think they should just slip off together and do it but that's not Lesley's style. She wants the whole Mardi Gras thing.'

'I don't think Barry knows what he's letting himself in for,' I said.

'I *know* Barry doesn't know what he's letting himself in for.' She popped another chestnut into her mouth. 'Mmm, these *are* good.'

'So what do you do, Susan? I'm thinking super model or film star.'

'Yeah, right.' She gave me a look that said don't be corny. 'I work for social services. Care homes.'

'Okay, interesting.'

'Not really. I just make sure all the records the homes keep are up to date and that the rules are followed, that sort of thing. It's all got to be coordinated so that we know who's where. You can't be too careful nowadays.'

'For all of Scotland?'

'God, no. Inverclyde.'

'So there's a central register?'

'Sort of. Mostly regional, but we can't have a bunch of unregistered care homes or unlisted, well, inmates, for want of a better word. We prefer "clients".'

'I suppose there's a lot of chancers out there.'

'Can't be too careful.' She took another chestnut. 'What about you?'

'Computer I.T. I work for myself. I do all right and I might have something big coming up.'

I do like to embellish and, besides, with all that was going on it wasn't too far from the truth.

'Something big, huh?'

151

There was a hint of a sly smile that made me think she thought my reply was some sort of double entendre.

'Modesty forbids.'

The party was in full swing in that the music was blaring out some heavy metal, drinks were being slopped and peanuts were being ground into the carpet. Lesley didn't seem to mind, secure in the knowledge that a team of decorators would be shortly undertaking a transformation under her specific instruction after which you'd only be able to get in wearing forensic coveralls.

Christine was halfway down the throat of Mister Maserati, any further and she'd need a Davy lamp. Lesley and Barry were doing the rounds and doing very well as the hosts, pressing the flesh and being the life and soul. In short, as a party, it was everything I hate.

Susan looked at me. 'Do you want to get out of here?'

'You've been reading my mail.'

'Your place? I'm out in the sticks.'

This was a woman who didn't believe in wasting time.

'Sounds good. I'll check it's clear to split. When you hear me say 'let's go, let's go, let's go', the last two are echoes.'

We were out of the door, laughing, while Lesley and Barry were trying to separate Brian from Mr Maserati.

Susan was well worth grabbing a taxi for and we were at the close of my building within minutes. When I switched the lights on in my place Susan gasped. 'My God, you've been burgled.'

'Sorry, haven't had much chance to clean up. Take your coat off – make yourself at home. Drink?' Please God, let me have some booze in the place.

'Whatever you've got. Are you sure you haven't been burgled?'

I found the remnants of a bottle of Bacardi and I knew that there was some of last week's coke in the fridge.

'Best I can do.'

'Looks good to me. Pour and bring it into the bedroom. Hurry.'

She was in bed by the time I came in with the glasses, I had to wash them first, but it only took me seconds borne of practice to get my clothes off and join her.

'You'll have to be careful,' I whispered and I explained the problem with my bruised testicles as a result of the contact with a steel toe capped boot.

'Poor baby, I'll be gentle.'

She tenderly squeezed the afflicted area. I wonder of the neighbours heard my screams.

Chapter Fifteen

I love the smell of bacon in the morning.

I didn't have any bacon. I padded through to the kitchen, actually it was more of a scullery, to see Susan turning bacon in the frying pan with a spatula. The frying pan that last night looked like a Petri dish in my sink, the sink which was now miraculously clear of any plate or utensil.

'Hi sleepy.'

'Hi yourself. What's going on? Why aren't you at work?'

'It's Sunday. It always follows Saturday.'

'Oh, right. What time is it?'

I looked around the place. It wasn't exactly pristine but it was a lot tidier than I could remember. Clothes had been folded and books put in a pile in the corner. Somebody had been busy.

'Half past nine. I thought you might like a bacon roll. I bought rolls as well. Morton's rolls. Don't say I don't spoil you. Tea? Coffee?'

'Tea. Milk, two sugar. Where did you get all that.'

'I just popped out a half hour ago. There's a wee shop on the corner.'

I could get to like this lady – a lot. She scooped the bacon onto the rolls and poured the tea. We both sat down on the sofa and ate. Oh, man. I must remember that. Morton's rolls.

'How are you feeling?'

'Good now.'

'No, I mean down there.' She nodded in the direction of my shorts.

'Recovering slowly.'

She smiled. 'Well you recovered three times during the night so you can't be too bad.'

Recollection dawned. 'Three times, eh? Care to go for the record after breakfast?'

This time she laughed. 'Well, it is Sunday after all. Mmm you're quite the lover, aren't you?'

'I practice alone a lot,' I said modestly.

She laughed outright. 'And a comedian as well. That's a potent combination.'

Back in the luxury of the double bed and after an hour or so had passed Susan propped herself up on the pillow, head in her hand, perfect right breast resting on top of the duvet, and looked at me.

'What?' I'm always on the defensive at times like this as I've usually fucked something up.

'Nothing. I just can't believe my luck, that's all.'

She couldn't believe her luck! A beautiful women invites herself back to my place, makes love to me three times, sorry four, tidies up my flat and clears my sink, makes me breakfast and *she* can't believe her luck. I knew it was time for her to leave. There were things to do back on planet Earth. She yawned as I got out of bed.

'There's no rush,' I said.

'I know. I have to go back and change. I usually visit my grandmother at the weekend.'

'My, you're a regular Florence Nightingale, aren't you?'

She gave a little smile. 'Not really. The poor dear is in a care home. I'm not sure if she really knows who I am any more but she loves it when I visit. She thinks I'm a

155

film star. Every time I see her she tells me she's seen me on TV the night before. She's in her nineties so I don't think it's Alzheimer's – just regular good old age dementia.'

I was sorry to hear that and I said so.

'Oh she's fine. Quite happy in her own wee world.'

Watching Susan dress was almost as much of a pleasure as watching her undress.

'Can I see you again?' I asked her.

'I certainly hope so.'

'I don't even know your surname.'

'Sharpe. Susan Sharpe with an "e".'

'I'm Gordon Lorne.'

'I know.'

'You know?'

'Yes, it's printed on the envelope of that final notice over there.' She pointed at the bin.

I looked at her.

'Oh, don't worry – I wasn't prying. I just saw the envelope. It's marked in red. Underlined.'

It could have been one of many. Give me couple of weeks and all will be well.

'Yet you want to see me again.'

'I told you. I like a man with a bit of mileage on his face. I've a feeling you could be very interesting in a flying by the seat of the pants sort of way.'

She had finished running a comb through her hair and adjusting herself. She found a pen and wrote on the back of an electricity demand.

'Here's my mobile number. I'll be mad if you don't call and you'd be embarrassed as hell when you had to dance with me in Barbados. Call me.'

'Of course. I want to anyway.'

'That's settled then. By the way, there's a pizza in the freezer – I thought you'd be hungry later.'

She came over to me, gave me a lingering kiss full of promise, waved and walked out the door.

Gordon to planet Earth 'How're you guys doing down there?'

Barry answered on the fourth ring. 'Gordon!'

'How goes it, man?'

'Where did you get to? I looked around and you were gone.'

'I took a lady home.'

'Ah, Susan.'

'Ah, Susan,' I confirmed. 'So how did it all go after I left?'

'You missed all the fun.'

'I promise you I didn't.'

He was almost right. Apparently Brian had challenged Mr Maserati to come outside but Mr Maserati hadn't waited and decked Brian there and then. Brian then called Christine a slut so Christine decked him as well. Lesley tried to intervene and a bit of a cat fight started between Christine and Lesley with Christine telling Lesley that she was a snooty, frigid bitch who wouldn't give Barry a second look if he didn't have a house, money and tickets for Wimbledon. Lesley screamed that she wasn't frigid and that Christine was a slag who'd shag anything with a pulse and stormed off into one of the bedrooms in a temper only to find Forbes in flagrante with Lesley's mother who shouted, 'Lesley, for God's sake have you no sense of decency?'

'That's quite a party, Barry.'

'Yes, went rather well, I thought.'

157

We arranged to meet in the Horseshoe the next day at lunchtime.

The Horseshoe was crowded when I got there at around half past twelve so I found a space towards the back of the bar and stood while I waited for Barry. He duly arrived dressed for a funeral. He informed me he was meeting a client and would stick to tomato juice and Worcester sauce.

'How's Lesley?' I asked a touch maliciously.

'She'll be all right.'

'I take it Christine and Brian are off the invite list.'

'Och no. It was just handbags at dawn. Christine phoned yesterday to clear the air and they had a long talk. You know what women are like.'

I have never had the slightest idea what women are like.

'And Brian?'

'Christine gave him the old soft soap and presumably a good seeing to later.'

'She's a regular peacemaker isn't she?'

'Actually, underneath it all, Christine's a trooper. You might not want to forget that and she's far too good for Brian. She just wants to get to the wedding.'

He was probably right but for now I had too much on my plate and Susan was another added complication.

'And Tom?'

'He fucked off when the big fight started. Said he had a reputation to protect.'

'The posh guy with the car and the boat? I can't remember his name.'

'Jonathan? He took off with some other guy. Rumour has it he's bi so Christine might not have been in with as much of a shout as she thought.'

'I should have known. A moustache and a tan is a dead giveaway.'

He looked at me. 'Your turn.'

'What? Susan?' I shrugged. 'Early doors but she's quite a lady.'

'Yeah. She was married before, a while back. Too good with his hands, according to Lesley. A wife beater.'

This was news; Susan hadn't said she was divorced.

'I take it you slept with her.'

'No, no. Well, I may have nodded off for a minute or two.'

He looked at his watch. 'I don't have much time, I'm afraid. This could be a big payday and I don't want to be late. Then I'm meeting up with Lesley. What's the update on the plans?'

I told him that I had given it some thought and that I needed to be sure that all the "t"'s were crossed. There was no point in sending off a pools coupon if Littlewoods came calling with a cheque and wanted to see some identification.

'All I have is a bankbook and that may not be enough. What if they want to see a birth certificate or a National Insurance number?'

'Can you check that on the web?' Barry asked.

I shrugged. There was also the problem of getting the present day value of the cash back with me.

'Let's put some serious thought into that,' I said to Barry.

He stroked his chin thoughtfully then shook his head. 'Okay. I'll do that. I have to run. Lesley's coming in later.

She wants the ring. A solitaire, she says. Look on it as an investment, she says.'

We both looked at each other for a moment in simultaneous dawning realisation.

'Diamonds!'

Chapter Sixteen

At least we had a possible solution but it was all becoming quite complicated. Before I could send away my winning football coupon I would need to be able to prove to Littlewoods, the pools company, that I was who I said I was. That meant some sort of documentation which I did not have. It seemed highly unlikely to me that some wee man in a bowler hat would just turn up and hand me a cheque just because my name was on the door. Come to think of it, my name wasn't even on the door yet.

Then, assuming that I'd overcome that hurdle, I needed to buy diamonds to the value of a hundred grand or more, bring them back, or forward actually, to the present day, find a reputable buyer and sell them. I knew nothing about diamonds other than a hazy knowledge that Amsterdam was or had been the diamond trading capital of the world and that women liked them, particularly on the third finger of their left hand.

To get to Amsterdam I needed a passport; to get a passport I needed a valid birth certificate showing I was Gordon Lorne born in the mid nineteen-twenties or whenever it was. That brought me back full circle.

The strategy was clear. Win a fortune in 1957. Buy diamonds with it. Sell diamonds in 2017 for a million or more. But how? Then it hit me. There was a Gordon Lorne living in Glasgow in 1957 born in 1924 who was in possession of a British passport and a birth certificate. He had been in Canada so he had to have a passport and

I assumed it was still in date. That Gordon Lorne also looked very like me and I assumed his passport photograph did too. That Gordon Lorne was my dead grandfather.

There was one person alive who would remember where he lived in 1957 because he married her: my grandmother, very much alive and always looking for an update on my sex life. It was perhaps about time for a visit. She lived in Netherlee, just a stone's throw from where we lived in Clarkston. I used to love walking down to the house on a Sunday when granddad was still alive knowing that the first thing I'd smell would be warm scones cooling on a baking tray. Afterwards they'd take me down to Linn Park and we'd stroll down the pathway to the little wrought iron bridge that crossed the river Cart, more of a stream, actually. We'd even play Pooh sticks. It was always rounded off by a visit to the Derby Cafe for a single nougat ice-cream wafer that traced patterns down my jumper as it melted or ran up my sleeve as I lifted it to my mouth. There were times when memories like these were almost a physical pain.

This nostalgia wafted through my mind as six o'clock saw me standing outside her smart bungalow clutching a bunch of flowers and a box of Cadbury's Roses.

'Gordon dear, what a surprise. You should have called, I might have had a gentleman visitor.'

Grandma looked genuinely pleased to see me. She had never made any concessions to incipient old age and her hair was a mildly lurid red cut short and spiky. Her top and pants wouldn't have looked out of place on Chris.

'Have you?'

'Of course not – he comes on Wednesday. Come in.'

162

She always has a can of beer in the fridge on the off chance I'll drop by and the sell by date had passed six months ago making me feel a bit of a heel. I looked around the neat and tidy lounge that held so many childhood memories. It hadn't been redecorated in a while but was as clean and tidy as ever. She was no stranger to modernity though and embraced progress wholeheartedly. A forty-four inch ultra HD curved screen television sat in the corner with Fiona Bruce in razor sharp relief reading the news. Grandma switched her off dismissively. A laptop sat on a small table and there was a wireless mouse and keyboard attached. She saw me look at it and closed the top down so God knows what she had been surfing.

'Would you like some dinner, dear?'

'Sounds lovely.' She could rustle up a surprisingly palatable stir fry in no time.

'Good, you can take me to that new Italian restaurant at Clarkston Toll.'

I've got to hand it to grandma, she doesn't miss a chance and I said a thankful prayer that I had cashed my Giro. Once seated in the small restaurant she had me order a bottle of Bardolino.

'Keep another on standby,' she ordered the hovering waiter.

After we had ordered, me the lasagne and she the lobster ravioli, she wanted to talk. Grandma is usually the one person I am pretty honest with – she can spot a lie at a hundred yards – but clearly I couldn't tell her about my time travel events. She asked me how I had come by a black eye and I waffled a bit mumbling something about walking into a door which didn't fool her for a nanosecond.

'And Chris? Still seeing Chris?'

'Oh yes, still hanging in there.'

'I should meet her.'

No you shouldn't, really. 'It's not that serious.'

'Time you were settling down, Gordon. You're beginning to look a bit, well, dissolute.'

'Dissolute?'

'Shagged out. Literally.' She doesn't mince words.

It was time to get off that subject.

'Mum and Dad send their love,' I said as I cracked a bread roll open.

'No they don't.'

'I haven't talked to them in a while but I'm sure they do.'

'And Lara?'

'Still living the dream,' I said.

'I'm sure she is. Not so sure about Keith though.'

I laughed at that; she was spot on as usual. The food came and it was delicious. The wine slipped down a treat and the second bottle was summoned. She was a bright and enlightened talker with a mind sharp enough to cut glass. Eighty was just a number to her. I eased into the subject that brought me here.

'You couldn't do this in the fifties - eat out,' I said

'Oh, you could, but there weren't many places to go and anyway people just couldn't afford it. Don't forget, there was rationing up until about 1952 and money was tight. It took a while.'

'Was it tough for you?'

'No more than anybody else, your granddad earned a decent enough wage back then and we lived quite well. We even bought our own house.'

'Really, where?'

164

'A four in a block in Kings Park just round from the State cinema. Ground floor flat with a wee garden. We loved it there. Your granddad grew veggies and we had a greenhouse.'

'Granddad never had a hankering to go back to Canada then?' I asked.

'Oh, no. I didn't fancy it and anyway I was pregnant with your dad. Kings Park was lovely then. I had a lot of friends. We used to do coffee mornings at the church on Tuesdays and bridge on Wednesdays. There was something for everyday of the week.'

'So the passport just rotted away, eh?'

'He never needed it again. It was just shoved in the tin in the dresser drawer with the rest of the documents, birth certificates and so on.'

So that was that. I had an address near enough, and I knew where the passport and birth certificate were kept then. I just needed to find a way to use them for a while.

'It was strange.' Grandma looked far away.

'What was?'

'We needed to get his birth certificate for something one day and we never could find it. The passport had gone too. He swore blind he'd never touched them but they'd just disappeared. Strange.'

She was clearly in a talking mood and astonished me with her next topic of conversation.

'I had a lover, you know.'

'Grandma!'

'Oh don't be so coy, Gordon, you're the only person I ever confide in. We're so alike, you and I.'

I shrugged. 'Okay, tell me more.'

'He wasn't Scottish. I met him at the Highlander's Institute, I used to go there with a couple of pals once a week. Your grandfather didn't mind, he got his night out with the boys, or that's what he told me. I won't say we had an open marriage but we gave each other space.'

I was fascinated. I always knew my grandma was a wild child but I had no idea what granddad got up to.

She went on, 'Anyway there was this man, from Italy, he had been a prisoner of war up in Helmsdale or somewhere up that way, and he asked me up to dance. Well that was it.'

'What was what?'

'It was electric. I could have powered Busby.'

'Grandma! What about granddad?'

'He knew nothing. Anyway, Francesco - that was his name - danced with me all night. I met him again the next week and he asked me to go away with him.'

'I don't believe I'm hearing this.' I was astonished. I couldn't wait to hear more. 'And?'

'Yes, so I went away with him – to Dunbar. Oh my God, it was glorious.' She laughed at the memory.

'Did granddad not suspect anything?'

'Maybe, I don't know. Anyway he was fucking half the south side at the time. I told him I was off to the Chelsea Flower Show.'

'What happened?' I should have been writing this down.

'Gordon, what do you think happened? It was the swinging sixties –free love – flower power - I had a son but I sure as hell wasn't going to miss out. We both knew it was a wild fling but I've never felt so alive. What is the saying now? An Italian stallion. He was all that – hung like a horse.' She chuckled at that.

This was way too much information. She saw me looking at her, mouth agape.

166

'Close your mouth Gordon dear. Listen to me, these Latinos knew all about love. He *wooed* me, Gordon! It was incredible. Look, I don't mean to offend you but Scottish men know nothing about sex. They're not very good at foreplay, or afterplay, and they're not so hot at the bit in the middle either. Your grandfather was very much from the wham, bam, thank you ma'am school of bedroom etiquette.'

I didn't know whether to laugh or be offended but I took note to review my own technique in that department.

'So what happened to him, your- Francesco?'

'He went back to Italy of course, somewhere near Verona. I never saw him again.'

I shook my head in wonder. 'Wow, What do you know, grandma had an affair.'

'Well, there may have been others,' she said airily as the waiter approached. 'Ah, the dessert menu.'

She ordered a tiramisu and went on. 'My big regret is that I didn't leave your granddad and disappear off to San Francisco and fry my brain with all that pot and get into that Haight Ashbury free love scene. Gordon, your mouth is open again.'

There was nothing else to possibly talk about after that so I asked for the bill.

Grandma being grandma, wonderful lady that she is, wouldn't hear of me paying and sent me on my way with a loud admonishment not to leave it so long next time and if I wasn't getting married yet to be sure to wear a condom. Well, I'll just not go back to that restaurant again.

Tuesday was bright and clear if a little windy so I thought I'd see if my body was up to a three mile run and I took off towards Kelvingrove and did my usual up Kelvin Way to Gibson Street then cut across to Byres Road then over Dryburgh Road to Hyndland making my way to Crow Road and eventually back to Partick. I actually felt not too bad after it, the bruises on my ribs didn't look nearly so lurid and after a steaming hot shower I felt ready for anything.

I wondered if I should call Chris but decided to leave it for a day or two. She was probably working anyway. By rights I should have been at the college beavering away at computer programming but the usual ennui had set in. To be honest, computer programming is without doubt the most boring job on earth, ranked just below the person that counts out the orange Smarties for the tubes in the chocolate factory, and I signed up for it because it was the only course that would have me. Half of the time of programmers is spent making up jokes that nobody else will understand. Train spotters are the very soul of wit compared to your average programmer. Here is an example: Q: how many programmers does it take to change a light bulb? A: none, that's a hardware problem. No? Me either. They have them rolling in the aisles with that one.

They are all brains and acne. In 2004 Bill Gates predicted that in two years the problem of spam would be solved and John McAfee forecasted in 1988 that computer viruses would be extinct within two years. How is that working out for you, John? See what I mean? Computer programming glitches have variously nearly caused world war three, closed down Los Angeles Airport, delayed the launch of the A330 by several

168

months, released dozens of violent criminals from prison and, worst of all, delayed by ten days a Giro payment that I was desperately relying on to buy essentials like beer. And to cap it off they think that I am a promising student. I think I'm doing them a favour by staying off today.

That left me with Susan's telephone number. We had talked a lot without really finding out anything about each other. I had no idea where she lived although she said it was in the sticks wherever those might be. The number was an 041 code so she was in the Glasgow area somewhere. Barry's comment about her having been married before to someone who used his hands on her also intrigued me.

I was actually hankering to get on with the business of making money and by now the pools coupon should be lying behind the door in Nithsdale Road so I thought I'd give Susan a quick call then plan on making a trip back to the past.

The phone was answered on the fourth ring.

'Hello?' I said.

'Hello,' the voice at the other end said.

'Who are you?' I said.

'I'm Susie's husband,' the voice said. 'More to the point, who the hell are you?'

Susan's husband? The wife beater? The man of violence?

'Er, I'm Gordon. Gordon Lorne. Father Gordon Lorne.'

'I'll tell her you called, father.'

Chapter Seventeen

I was beginning to feel like Stan Laurel -another fine mess you've got me into, Ollie. I dropped the phone onto the table as if it was smouldering hot. The last thing I needed was a jealous stroke angry stroke violent husband on my tail and I felt fairly sure that my inspired induction into the priesthood wouldn't fool him for too long. When Barry had told me Susan had been married before I assumed the husband was long gone. So what was he doing at her house? Beating her up? Should I call the police? Why has he got her phone? Why did I give him my real name? Was he bigger than me?

Several scenarios played through my head from Susan lying in a pool of blood and him standing over her with a smoking .22 at one end of the spectrum, to her sitting with a cup of tea and two ginger snaps folding the alimony cheque at the other. She now had my number on her mobile so she could call me if she wanted. The problem was that he also had my number. Time to make a sharp exit.

Seven fifty seven, Central Station nineteen hundred and fifty seven, and sixty years of safety between me and Susan's husband whoever he might be sounded like a wise move. She had sent me a text not long before I walked through the clock's time portal; *Sorry about earlier. Can we meet up and I'll explain? Nothing to worry about. XX. Father ??*

I sent one back to her. *Sure. Won't be around for a few days but I'll call when I get back. RU OK? Just been promoted to bishop.X.*

As usual my imagination had been running riot and at least she seemed fine. My gut instincts told me to leave well alone but I had a few days to think it over and when did I ever listen to my gut instincts except when they told me I was hungry?

The stroll out to the south-side was cold but pleasant and it took me about half an hour to reach my house. On the mat behind the door was a square buff envelope with the name 'Littlewoods' printed across the top so that was one more step forward on the road from rags to riches. It was cold inside but there were a couple of electric heaters that I put on at full heat but as it was still chilly and an hour before pub closing I nipped out while the house warmed up to an igloo and found a likely looking bar on Pollokshaws Road at the corner of Allison Street called M.J. Heraghty. I liked that. No pretensions to anything grandiose, just the name of the proprietor. Fortunately I had left some spare change in the house, easily enough for the price of a drink or two.

It was as warm and pleasant inside as it looked from the outside with a large oak bar ringed at the bottom with a brass foot rail, behind which was an ornate wooden open cabinet well stocked with an assortment of whiskies. Various pictures of old Glasgow, antique maps and photographs of local worthies hung from the wall above a long leather banquette. Tables just wide enough to hold your drink and possibly have a game of dominoes were fixed to the floor. There were perhaps a dozen customers inside and the not unpleasant warmth of hazy cigarette smoke caught my throat. There was a

171

low hum of conversation. A rather jolly looking man in his forties and wearing an apron and a cloth slung over his shoulder welcomed me.

'Evenin'. What can I get you?'

'A pint, please. Is that light?' I pointed at a pump.

'Pint of light it is.'

He talked as he poured. 'Haven't seen you around before.'

'I've just moved into a house over in Nithsdale Road. Just temporary for the time being.'

'Oh well, might be seeing a bit more of you then?'

'You might at that. This looks like a pleasant enough place,' I said as I looked around.

He finished pouring, 'Hear that, Phil?' the barman called to a man at the end who was deep in conversation with another two. 'Gentleman here says this looks like a pleasant place. He hasn't met you yet obviously.'

Phil was quick on the response, 'Any more o' that and I'll take my slate elsewhere.'

They all laughed.

'Pay no attention to him. If it wasn't for us he wouldnae have a pub at all,' said the man called Phil.

Phil was a mountain of a man, tall, about six three, seriously large around the middle. His shoes must have been built in Clydebank by John Brown's. I felt drawn to him, not because I thought him physically attractive in any way, you understand, but because he generated his own gravitational field. It all sounded very good natured banter, mainly football or politics but interspersed with a great deal of humour. I gathered that Harold McMillan had just been made prime minister and taken over from someone called Anthony Eden. Two of the group were very disparaging but one was more in favour.

172

'You're not saying much, son.' Phil brought me into the conversation. 'We need a bit of fresh blood here.'

'I never talk about politics or religion. It only gets me in trouble. And as far as football's concerned I'm a Partick Thistle supporter so that doesn't count.'

'Your right there, it's no' a plan of attack they need, it's a map. I'm a Firhill man maself - it helps you to deal with life's disappointments all right,' said Phil ruefully as he shook his head.

'Come on, you look like a Tory to me,' said one of the others to me, a tall thin man in a shapeless raincoat.

I was actually Scottish National Party but I had no idea if they were around; I hadn't heard them mentioned. I hedged.

'I think it isn't going to make too much difference. Scotland will be at the back of the queue as usual.'

'You're right there, son,' said a man in what looked like his fifties, an open trench coat and a scarf draped around his neck. The others called him Benny. 'That's why you need Gaitskell in there. McMillan's just another toff who doesn't live in the real world. He'll look after his own.'

'Och, yer arse in parsley. You need somebody that knows how tae run a country.'

This was the sole dissenting voice, his name was Eric, the tall, thin man. 'We've never had it so good, he's right, things have never been better. I think you should give him time.'

'Aye, twenty years and no time off for good behaviour,' said Benny.

That raised a laugh.

I thought I'd try one. 'What do nappies and politicians have in common?'

'I don't know,' said Phil.'

'You've got to keep changing them because they're always full of shit.'

To their credit they laughed although they had probably heard it before. The clock in the middle of the drinks cabinet nudged towards quarter past nine and the barman, Jim was his name, shouted last orders. I couldn't get used to this closing early when things were just warming up. I had only just got here. Phil produced a packet of cigarettes and offered them around. Eric shook his head and reached for a pipe and proceeded to undertake a ritual known only to pipe smokers which requires the tobacco to be squeezed down, the bowl to be lit at least three times and the resulting sparks to burn holes in your jumper. I shook my head but thought I'd recognise their camaraderie by offering a drink.

'One for the road?'

They looked at me and Phil said, 'That's very protestant of you. I'll have a half pint.'

The others nodded likewise so I looked to the barman and told him to have one himself. There was still plenty of change from five shillings, just twenty five pence.

'We're in here most nights for a pint so you're welcome to join us,' he went on, 'What line are ye in anyway?'

I should have seen this coming but I remembered the spiel I had spun Katie so I thought I would stick to that. It was fairly vague anyway.

'I work for myself. Forecasting and statistical analysis. General consultancy work, you know.'

'I haven't a bloody clue what you're talking about,' said Phil.

I laughed, 'That's okay. Most of the time neither does the client. Bottom line is that I try to see what's in the future so they can plan accordingly. It's crystal ball stuff really.'

'Sounds a lot better than working. I'm in the newspaper business, a journalist.'

'Reporter,' interjected Eric.

'Journalist,' Phil went on as if he'd never been interrupted, 'and Eric here, he follows me about in his dirty mac with his box Brownie and takes snaps.'

'It's a Rollieflex and I'm a photographer. We both work for the Express.'

I assumed he meant the Daily Express and I nodded my interest.

'Benny's a policeman, plain clothes.'

Benny, a medium build, quite bland looking man with precisely combed and Brylcreemed dark hair, raised his half pint. 'Cheers.'

Phil looked at the remnants of damage to my face. 'What happened to you? Did you come home with a shilling short in your pay poke?'

'I had an argument with a couple of heavies. They won.'

Benny the policeman looked at me with professional interest. 'Anybody we know?'

'Wouldn't think so. It's no big deal.'

'It looks like a big deal by the look of you.'

'I just got too lucky with a bookie.'

'Oh aye, which one then, let me guess. Sandy Corcoran? Guy with a face like an Abernethy biscuit?'

I was amazed, 'How did you know that?'

'Sandy. Oh he's a very bad loser is Sandy. You're lucky you're still walking.'

'He's done this before?' I asked.

'Oh aye.'

I don't suppose it came as any great surprise to hear it but it still bothered me.

'Yet he's still out and about.'

'He's very well connected is Sandy,' said Benny and there was a touch of chagrin in his voice.

'You don't sound too happy about that.'

'I'd lock the bastard up and throw away the key if it was up to me. Got a finger in a lot of rancid pies, has our Sandy. He's got a wee man's Napoleon complex. He's so small that he's suing the council for building the pavements too close to his arse.'

We all laughed at that one.

'That's not going to happen, is it?' Eric asked, 'Locking him up.'

Phil said, 'Just get him where it hurts then.'

'I've got enough bruises thank you. My balls are the size of cricket balls and about the same colour.'

'So where are his weak spots then?' Eric asked Benny, obviously intrigued.

Benny took a sip from his glass then put it down. 'You'd best leave well alone. I've a job I like and it's time I was away.' He made to leave. 'None of my business, of course, but he's got a couple of greyhounds he races. That's his big passion. The word is he's training one up for a big race at White City next week. It's supposed to be a sure thing.' He drained his glass. 'It would be a shame if it lost.' He looked at me meaningfully.

We all drank up and said our goodnights at the door and I made way along towards the house with Benny's enigmatic comment in my head.

Just because I took a beating from Sandy's boys didn't mean I had to give up making good money altogether. I only had to make sure that I didn't go back to any of Sandy Corcoran's shops again so the next day I decided to get well out of Glasgow for my next foray. After a visit to the bank to withdraw twenty pounds in funds, much more than I would ever need, I took an express train from Glasgow through to Edinburgh. Even in the twenty-first century I had hardly visited the capital but whenever I did I wasn't sorry. It's a glorious city easily comparable with the world's best and a joy to walk around. It was almost a shame to take its money. I got off the train at Waverley Station and nipped around to where the two o'clock London express was ready to pull out on the east coast trip down to Kings Cross. A sleek blue Gresley A4 sat at its head, 60033 'Seagull' for you aficionados, and at the guard's whistle it eased out towards Calton Hill in a cloud of smoke and steam. Someone waved from a compartment as it passed. I had my camera with me and snapped off a few shots of her as she left.

Climbing out of Waverley steps on to Princes Street I had to stop and admire the view. Edinburgh wasn't as industrial as Glasgow in the fifties and so its Georgian buildings hadn't taken on the black hue of its sister city.

To my left Princes Street Gardens gave an airy open aspect to the town and of course, its crowning glory, the castle glowered magnificently on the hill. Maroon trams trundled up and down Princes Street off to Leith and leafy Corstorphine. Glasgow as a city had been virtually demolished by municipal vandalism but Edinburgh looked much the same then as it did sixty years later except that the trams were different. I preferred the old ones.

There is no doubt about it: Edinburgh is a wonderful city. Pity about the people who are generally a bunch of toffee nosed, superior, holier than thou, you'll have had your tea, arses. In Edinburgh they believe that breeding is good form; in Glasgow we believe breeding is good fun. There was an Edinburgh girl talking to a Glasgow girl and said that she was scandalised that she had got her knickers torn at a party. Astonished, the Glasgow girl says, 'Knickers?! At a party??'

Dismissing these blasphemous thoughts as a tad unkind I turned right at the top of the steps then right again at the North British Hotel and made my way up the South Bridge to the Royal Mile then walked down towards Holyrood Palace. Halfway down in a small offshoot, almost invisible as if it was trying to hide its shame from the surrounding grandeur, was a betting shop. It was nondescript place so I won't describe it, with a man marking the field and results on a blackboard with various coloured chalks and an elderly woman taking the bets. There was the grand total of three other punters in the place when I entered. I went through my usual routine, losing a pound for effect before betting on a triple that I knew should return me around sixty-five pounds. Sure enough, without as much as a second glance from the woman, I walked out an hour later counting my money.

I took great care to ensure that I wasn't being followed and within half an hour I was on a train back to Glasgow. There was nary a sign of Sandy's heavies or of the wee man himself. Clearly his reach didn't extend much beyond Glasgow. Having been successful in

Edinburgh I planned to leave it alone for a while and maybe head for Ayr or Motherwell for my next attempt. By the time I got to Glasgow, I figured Katie might be ready to hear from me. She was.

'The prodigal has returned.'

I thought I detected a slight tartness in her voice.

'Back to the fatted calf, and all that,' I replied, keeping it light.

'Been anywhere nice?'

I was ready for that and could reply with at least a half truth. 'Edinburgh. Just doing some financial projections. A profit and loss thing.'

'Welcome back.'

'Thank you. I was wondering of you'd like to meet up.'

'When?'

'Whenever suits. Tonight, tomorrow evening?'

'Tomorrow would work. I'm going out with my friends tonight.'

'Oh. The Plaza night.'

'No. We're just going to the pictures.'

I liked the way she called it "the pictures" instead of the cinema.

'Right. What's on?'

''Friendly Persuasion'. With Gary Cooper and Dorothy McGuire. It should be good.'

'Well, what about tomorrow. Maybe I can take you to the Plaza.'

There was a longish pause as if she wasn't sure but then she was quite positive. 'That would be lovely.'

'It's a date.'

'When will I pick you up? Do you want to grab a bite to eat first?'

179

'Where?'

'I don't know, I'll think of something. Say about seven?'

'Lovely.' She paused again, 'George?'

'Yes?'

'I'm glad you phoned.'

Yesss.

Chapter Eighteen

Being a modern day man, a man of the twenty-first century with all that we take for granted, it was difficult for me to get my head around some of the fundamental differences between the middle of the twentieth century and that of sixty years later.

For a start, there was hardly a restaurant to speak of. Not a Chinese, not an Indian, no Italian trattoria, and precious little pub grub. People just didn't eat out. I had no idea where to suggest to Katie so I thought I'd just wait until I saw her and take it from there. And another thing; apparently the Plaza started at eight o'clock and finished at half past eleven. I didn't normally plan on going out until well after ten. Try going out at eight in 2017 and you'd be on your own, mate.

My house had no central heating, a luxury apparently as yet unheard of, no fridge, not that it needed one, and worst of all, no shower. I am fully aware, since it has been pointed out to me by various acquaintances that I am a fully paid up member of the slob union. My Partick flat was such a mess that I had to wipe my feet before I went outside but I showered every day and sometimes twice depending on the quality of the date. Surely people here in the fifties didn't have a bath every morning? The way my boiler worked I'd have to start running it before I went to bed.

I found a hardware shop that sold those little rubber shower hoses with a nozzle for each tap so the best I could do in the morning was either kneel or stand in the bath and hold it with one hand while I lathered with the other. A wank was out of the question.

One thing was for sure, I smelt a lot better than anybody else. The only after shave I could find was a concoction called 'Old Spice' which was fifty percent right in its branding because any hint of the Orient was conspicuous by its absence but it certainly had an odour redolent of undertakers' embalming fluid. Having said that, it helped clear an annoying sinus blockage that had been pestering me for a few days.

I deposited most of the money into my account and then took a train to Motherwell where I found a backstreet bookie and went through the usual routine. Within a couple of hours I was back in dear old Glasgow over fifty pounds richer.

A couple of the most modern and efficient electric heaters I could find set me back a fiver and I treated myself to some more clothes which could only be described, in my eyes, as retro. But they were the standard mode now so later I made my way out to Govanhill looking quite trendy in my Daks sports jacket, cavalry twills and mustard Munrospun tie. As Streisand sings, '*If they could see me now...*'

Katie was almost ready when I arrived which as most men know means not ready at all. I developed a neat little grid matrix with Chris where I was able to cross reference her degree of readiness into a Microsoft Excel spreadsheet. 'Soon be ready' translated to 'You still have time to nip across to the pub and have a couple of pints then get back and change'. 'Almost ready' indicated 'I have my knickers on but I can't find my tights.' 'I'm ready' read as 'Just a bit of makeup and let me run a comb through my hair.'

I sat myself down in a tidy little living room which in my real time would be considered art deco but was simply furnished in the mode of these times. A small television stood in the corner, the screen couldn't have been more than sixteen inches, and there was a 'Dansette' record player on the floor beside it together with a handful of 45 rpm records and a couple of LP's one of which was Sinatra's 'Songs for Swinging Lovers,' and another of Ella Fitzgerald. The overall decor could be described as "spartan cosy".

'Be a dear and give my shoes a quick wipe, would you,' she called from the bathroom, 'I'm nearly ready.'

Clearly I was good for another twenty minutes. 'Sure. Where's the cloth? Should I give them a quick polish while I'm there?'

'If you think they need them. The stuff is under the sink,' she called from her bedroom.

I could hear wardrobe doors opening and shutting and the sound of coat hangers falling on the floor. I picked up her shoes from the hall.

'What colour?'

'Nigger brown.'

What!!

'What did you just say?'

'Nigger brown. You'll see it on the tin. The other one is a tan and it's too light.'

'Are you serious?' I asked incredulously.

She stepped out from the bedroom adjusting an earring. She looked stunning.

'Yes, why?'

'It's — well, it's just not a very nice word.'

183

'What –brown?' She looked puzzled.

'No, nnn, nnn,' I could hardly bring myself to say it. 'Nigger.'

'What are you talking about? – it's written on the tin.'

I went into her kitchen and looked in a box under the sink and sure enough, there written on a tin of Kiwi shoe polish were the words 'Nigger Brown'. Christ, what other colours did they make? 'Honky White'? 'Chink Yellow'? It dawned on me just how very different this point in time was and just how far we had come in terms of human understanding and lack of prejudice. I was fairly sure Katie wasn't a bigot or a racist, she just didn't know any better and neither did those nice people down at the Kiwi shoe polish company. Nigger Brown, dear sweet Jesus.

'What's the problem?' she said as she came into the kitchen.

'No problem, sweetie,' I ran a brush over her shoes, 'There, you can see your face in them.'

Katie was somewhat bewildered at the plans to eat out before going dancing. This, apparently, was unheard of in dancing circles unless it was a wedding, a birthday, or a funeral. The best that we could do was a fish tea in a fish and chippie on Allison Street that had a few tables available for sitting in.

A quick haddock supper, far and away better than anything I had tasted in my own world, and a taxi ride after saw us at the door of the Plaza Ballroom and very grand it was too. The hall was busy without being full and a ten piece band plus a male and female singer provided the music. They both sat quite primly on chairs in front of the band waiting for their cue to sing. In the middle of dance floor stood an elegant fountain and the

184

dancers seemed to go around it in an anti clockwise direction rather like fairground dodgems. Hanging from the ceiling was a ball inlaid with hundreds of mirrored squares that revolved usually during a slow number and reflected little sparkles all around the ballroom. Every male wore a suit or sports jacket and tie and every woman, without exception, wore a dress. There was an empty table at the side of the floor so I ushered Katie over to it.

'What would you like to drink?'

'An orange juice will be fine,' she smiled.

'Cheap date you,' I joked. 'Nothing stronger?'

'What do you mean?'

'A G&T or a glass of wine?'

'You can't get alcohol in here, surely you know that. Dance halls don't have licences except on special occasions. I'll have an orange juice, though.'

'Really?' I shook my head.

She looked at me oddly so I thought I'd better say no more.

The dancing itself was a revelation and I loved it, every minute. It was all so organised and civilised. Don't get me wrong, I love the ear –splitting, anarchy of the music of today. I like Aurora, The Cranberries, Radiohead, most phsycho punk stuff in the clubs and I like to throw myself about a bit. Mumford and Son works for me too. I'm thirty-five going on twenty sometimes and going on sixty others. For just listening, though, I'm a lot more retro. I like the folk scene and I'm not ashamed to admit to liking Neil Diamond and Orbison is a legend in my book. Just listen to his composition. He rarely goes for the two regular verses then a bridge. Listen to 'In Dreams' and 'Running

185

Scared' and you'll hear what I mean. He soars. Dylan sounds like a dog resisting a bath but, boy, does it ever work! And I can listen to James Taylor or Don McLean any day of the week. Simon and Garfunkel, well, I'd travel to see them as the Martini ad says, anytime, anywhere, and the Stones are eternal and are still here to prove it. One look at Keith Richards and I realise there's hope for me yet.

Anyway, there was nothing like that here. There was a lot of up-beat Sinatra stuff like 'Come Fly With Me.' And the lady vocalist obviously modelled herself on Ella except she was the wrong colour and shape, oh, and voice. The dancers held onto each other all the time even when the music got a bit hip like when they played some of Elvis's early stuff like 'Heartbreak Hotel' and 'Hound Dog' although the male singer definitely hadn't got the hang of what Elvis was all about. It was like Pavarotti singing 'Hey Jude' except Pavarotti could sing. Two or three couples started to jive at these numbers much to the admiration of those at the tables. One of the many things about then and now was that you could talk or sing along to the music, not always a good thing, but pleasant for the moment. I was used to a three day tinnitus attack after a night at The Sub Club or Viper where the only means of understandable communication was semaphore.

Best of all was the slow foxtrot. Up until now I thought a slow foxtrot was waddling to the toilet when you badly needed a piss. I mean, why call it a foxtrot? I've seen a few foxes and I've never seen one trot. I've seen them run like fuck with a pack of beagles behind but never trot. But I did like the concept. I got to snuggle up nice and close to Katie and after two or three

186

of these I eventually had both arms around her waist and she had hers around my neck and we were cheek to cheek. By the time the band played 'Love Me Tender' the fox had pretty much slowed from a trot to a shuffle.

During the interval the band disappeared presumably to the Star Bar across the road where they could get a decent drink leaving the paying customers to themselves, their orange juices, and a lone violinist who played Mantovani melodies until such times as the band had managed to shift a couple of pints and a chaser and returned feeling the better for it. The break gave us a chance to sit and talk over an orange juice given that not only was alcohol not available, the word 'cappuccino' had not yet arrived in Scotland. I was getting high on orange juice and I'm sure my teeth were getting stained. As I looked around the hall I did notice a few women, as opposed to ladies, take a flask out of their handbags and furtively pour some clear liquid into their glasses.

'Is that what I think it is?' I asked.

'Yep, probably gin or vodka. It doesn't smell. If they get caught they're out on their ear, though.'

Hmm, interesting. 'I don't suppose ...'

'Certainly not.'

Oh well. I looked at my watch; nine thirty.

'When does it close?'

'Usually at half past eleven. Why? Getting bored?'

'No, no, no, no, not at all. I'm really enjoying tonight,' I said, and I was.

She took my wrist and turned it to look at the watch.

'What on earth is that?'

Shit. It was a Seiko, not expensive, but although it was analogue it had a digital timer on the face for when I wanted to boil an egg or time myself having sex, usually about the same. Actually it was a Christmas present from my dad who had forgotten to take the card out from the wrapping showing that it had been a gift to him the previous year. From me.

'Oh, it's a stopwatch. Just a new fancy idea. It'll probably not catch on.'

'How does that work?'

Reluctantly I showed her how you set it at the side and then stop it.

'That's amazing. I've never seen anything like that before, not anywhere. Where did you get it?'

I could hardly say H. Samuel so I made up some cock and bull stuff about how it involved some market research for the company who were testing out a new product and this was just a prototype. I was babbling by the time I finished and Katie knew it.

'There's definitely something weird about you, George.' She sipped genteelly at her juice. 'And I'm going to find out what.'

I'm pretty sure Chris said the same thing to me sixty years down the line but that wasn't the point. I was going to have to be careful what I had on my person the next time I crossed the bridge of time.

The band started to filter back in and I was saved further difficulty by the pressing need to try my hand at a cha-cha, whatever that might be. It turned out to be something I wasn't very good at but I got a C+ for effort and she only got a few minor bones broken on her instep.

Later, as we strolled back to her place arm in arm along Victoria Road unmindful of the chill February air, Katie snuggled in.

'Thanks, George, it's been a lovely night.'

'Me too, I've had a ball – no pun intended.'

It was true, I'd really had a ball. I never realised before now that dancing could be a rather pleasurable form of communication on a number of levels rather than the frenzied, brain numbing, solo calisthenics that I had previously indulged in. We walked on in silence for a bit, content in each other's company and eventually arrived at the entrance to her house. She let go my arm and smiled at me.

'Don't be angry, but I won't ask you in and I'm a bit too old for a quick snog and a grope in the back close. But I would like to see you again.'

I really wasn't expecting anything else, truth be told and it was fine by me, which is probably the most amazing thing I've ever admitted. I was on a high and let my emotions get the better of me.

'I'm not angry and, anyway, I wouldn't want to spoil things. Plenty of time for that.' I realised what I said. 'Not that I'm going to spoil things – you know what I mean.'

She laughed and gave me a kiss on the lips that held future promise.

'So - phone me?'

The lines of communication between my brain and my mouth went down for a critical moment.

'Why don't we go to Paris for a few days?'

Chapter Nineteen

She laughed then looked at me again. 'Wait a minute – you're serious.'

The line was still down. 'I'm serious.'

'That's impossible.'

'Why? Nothing's impossible.'

'I've never been out of Scotland in my life. Okay Scarborough, but that doesn't count – it was during the Glasgow Fair and half of Scotland was there. Anyway I don't have a passport.'

'Look, you said you wanted to see the world – Paris is the perfect place to start.'

'I couldn't afford it – I don't have that sort of money.'

'It was my idea and it's on me.'

'Certainly not.'

That was my chance and I knew it. Communication had been re-established between brain and the rest of my anatomy and I now had a get out.

'Remember what you said the last time we met? About you needing a wee bit of excitement in your life right now? You won't get a better chance.'

Dammit, line fault again. This time she hesitated.

'How would we get there?'

That was a good question, I was fairly sure that there wouldn't be any flights, at least not from Glasgow.

'We make a trip out of it. Train to London then the "Golden Arrow" to Paris – doing it in style. Dinner at Maxim's, stroll around Montmartre, drinks at the top of

190

the Eiffel Tower, a sail down the Seine at sunset, shopping in the Champs- Elysées, a suite at the Georges Cinq.' This was laying it on with a cement mixer.

'You're really serious, aren't you?'

I nodded my head. 'Oh, I'm serious.'

She looked a bit nervous. 'That would mean – you know?'

Ah, sex, the elephant in the room. 'It's not a precondition but let's face it, we're both adults now, so very probably.'

She didn't say anything.

'Why? Does that bother you?'

She smiled shyly, 'No, of course not. But I wouldn't just want it to be a dirty weekend type of thing. I 'm not expecting a proposal, I hardly know you, but I would need to know that there's something between us.'

I put my arms around her. 'I think we both know that there is.'

'And there's something very mysterious about you.'

'Isn't that part of the attraction?'

She looked straight at me. 'Well, only up to a point. I've been hurt once already by someone who could have been your twin.'

She was right.

'Look, I won't knowingly or wilfully let you down, that's all I can promise, but I can guarantee that with me you'll have a bit of fun and adventure.'

'I must be crazy.'

'Is that a yes?'

'I don't know, but it's not a no. I need to think about it, okay?'

I nodded again. 'If you say so, but there's nothing really to think about.'

She gave me another kiss on the lips. 'Phone me, okay?'

I walked back to my flat literally in two minds. One mind was cursing me for my impulsive stupidity. What was I thinking? This was all getting me into a mess that would be impossible to wriggle out of. Sooner or later somebody was going to get hurt and that somebody was Katie, she was right on that score. I could always walk away through the time portal that was the clock in Central station and there could be no possible repercussions because my actions of today would immediately become sixty years old. My guilt would be assuaged by the fact that I could tell myself that it was all so long ago. Who was I kidding?

My other mind was telling me that I had a beautiful woman eating out of my hand. I could show her things that she would otherwise never have been able to see and places where she always wanted to go and even when it all went tits up, as it was bound to, then I had only added to her life's worth. Christ, even to me that sounded patronising crap, but really, where was the harm?

Regardless of my self-justifications, fate was sure to plant a hidden bunker on the fairway of life, it always did.

Back in the flat, every heater in the house switched to full and the disc in the electricity meter spinning faster than my head after a session in the Horseshoe, I opened the Littlewoods envelope and looked at the coupons for the next three weeks. Today was Thursday which meant that this weekend's matches were out of the question so I looked at the games for Saturday 26th January. There were eleven draws in the couponed games that week according to my research so I figured that would mean a lower payout if there were a number of winners. The following week looked not much better but the games on 9th February showed eight draws; that was more like it.

The pools company paid out on correctly selecting eight draws or on seven draws and an away win if there wasn't eight draws that week. The best way to do it was to select a permutation, or "perm" as they called it, of any eight draws out of a selection of ten or eleven. Apparently a perm of any eight draws from ten at a penny a line would cost forty-five pennies which in old money was three shillings and ninepence, or eighteen pence in 2017. All I needed to do was to make my selection, fill in the plan number, add my name and address and also, very important this, tick the 'no publicity' box. The last thing I wanted was a pack of press hounds at my door and a postie's bag full of begging letters. I should know, I was a dab hand at sending them.

There were names there of places I never knew existed. Hartlepool United, Rotherham, Tranmere Rovers. Did Aston live in a villa? And did Stanley own Accrington? Did Stockport have its very own county? Anyway I marked off the eight draws plus two other matches and filled in all my details. I would have to buy a postal order in the morning.

My rash offer to Katie meant that I would need to "win" a bit more ready cash. I figured that the first class Pullman return from Victoria to Paris would be around £30 return plus, say, a tenner for the return from here to London. Three nights at the Georg Cinq, who knows, maybe ten to fifteen pounds a night so I was looking at a couple of hundred to cover meals and incidentals. I felt I was erring on the side of caution here but I topped it up to two fifty to be doubly sure. I needed two or three lucrative visits to my friendly bookmaker or any friendly bookmaker.

So that's why the next day saw me standing outside Stirling station in good time to hit the nearest bookie. Other than a few admiring looks from those less fortunate than me and a sour look from the cashier the event was unremarkable save for the fresh sixty-seven pounds burning a hole in my pocket. I had a quick look around the town and a stroll up to the castle, a swift pint in the Station bar then caught the train back to Buchanan Street.

Not being one for my own company, after a fish supper I made my way back to Heraghty's. This was a bar that was easy to like. It wasn't too big and it was friendly. Some bars are just that – bars. You go in, have a pint and then leave. They are more like places to quench a thirst than any real focal point. Some, particularly those owned by the breweries, are ersatz clubs. Heraghty's, well that was a good honest to goodness pub where you could meet up with your mates and pass an hour or so in the most convivial of atmospheres and not a drunk to affront you. It was a man's pub.

The barman greeted me with a nod and I smile. 'It's yourself.'

I could hardly deny it since I was standing there; I recognised myself in the mirror.

'A pint of light if I'm not mistaken.'

He had the pump going and the beer flowing before I could confirm his assessment. This was my kind of place.

194

'Benny was in last night. Asked if you were around,' he said as he put a head on the pint.

'Oh aye?'

'He'll probably pop by tonight. Eric and Phil too as like as not.' He placed the glass in front of me and I paid him with a few coins.

'Thanks, Jim.' I remembered his name.

The beer slipped down a treat, cool and dark, leaving me with a white moustache that I licked off with my tongue. A couple of people wandered in and I nodded at them as Jim went over to serve them. I found a seat at a table in the corner and had only sat down a moment or two when Benny came in, saw me and sat down beside me.

'I was in yesterday, you're looking a lot better,' he said.

'Feeling good - pint?'

'Is it not my shout, what'll you have?'

I nodded at my three quarters empty glass. 'Thanks, light.'

Just at that the terrible duo of Phil and Eric walked in, Eric almost eclipsed by Phil's Jovian mass.

'Christ, you two smell it being poured?' laughed Benny, 'You'se have got a great sense of timing.'

'It's an art, Benny,' said Phil, 'You've either got it or you've no'.' He turned to look at me. 'Well. If it's no' Benny Lynch. How's the eye?'

I had no idea who Benny Lynch was but I figured him for some sort of fighter so I mugged a boxing pose.

'Oho, a southpaw, eh?'

'Nah, I'm ambidextrous, I can get knocked out with either hand.'

They laughed at that, they clearly liked my nonchalant, self-deprecating style. They didn't know it came naturally

195

after years of helpful training with my mother and various girlfriends. If I wasn't self-deprecating they did it for me so I just saved them the trouble. My mother didn't just put me down; she dropped me from a great height.

Cigarettes were passed around like some sort of camp fire, pipe-of-peace ritual although I declined. These guys were serious smokers, Phil passed around a brown packet of Capstan full strength which probably contained enough nicotine to kill an entire laboratory of research rats in one go. Phil's lungs must look like fruit cake filling, a fact which he confirmed by a rough throaty cough after taking a long, satisfied draw which reduced the length of the cigarette by half. I now realised the significance of the 'no spitting' notices on the top deck of the tram. Eric proceeded to the ceremonial lighting of the pipe. Another couple of miniature holes appeared in his maroon cardigan and a slightly acrid smell of burning wool permeated the air.

'Why were you looking for me, Benny?' I asked.

'Just a wee bit of information you might be interested in.'

'Oh, what's that?'

'Your pal, Sandy,' he said through a pall of blue smoke.

Sandy? The bookie? I had almost forgotten about him. Almost, but not quite.

'What about him?'

' Remember I mentioned he had a dog he was training up for a race at White City? Well it's running tomorrow night, I don't know what race. Word is he's purposely held it back before so that he'll get longer odds, but it's a sure thing I'm told.' He eyed me over the rim of his glass. 'He wouldn't be a happy man if it didn't perform.'

'Didn't perform? Like in not run you mean?'

'No, no. If it lost. Sandy will have a lot of money riding on it on bets placed all over the shop. I'm told he needs the cash.' He tapped the side of his nose as a sign of confidentiality.

I was puzzled. What did he think I could do, nobble the race?

'What can I do?' I shrugged my shoulders.

'Nobble the race,' said Eric.

'What?'

'Listen here,' said Benny, 'I'm a policeman so I can't be party to a crime so I'm just talking generally here, by way of conversation like. But just say somebody, hypothetically speaking, happens to find himself at White City, and just say that somebody has a white steward's coat and a badge, and that somebody just happened to find himself alone in the vicinity of a certain dog and he had two or three meat pies in his pocket and the dog somehow, well, managed to eat them just before the race. Might hold him back a bit, don't you think?'

'I'm bound, sorry, *somebody* is bound to be seen. The place would be jumping and Sandy would be there.'

'Actually no. What if there was a wee diversion for a minute or two? Sandy would be back up in the stand. You would just be another steward.'

'Diversion? What kind of diversion?'

'Oh I don't know, maybe a wee altercation. Just to divert attention for a couple of minutes. Nothing physical, just words.' He sipped at his drink and looked at me over his glass. 'There's always a couple of police there.'

197

I looked at him. 'You?'

'Oh no, it's nothing to do with me,' he said airily, 'but they're good lads. But just supposing that all happened, it would give you a moment to slip Lucky Lord – that's the name of his dug, by the way – slip it a couple of Bradford's pies.'

'Bradford's pies?'

'Or City Bakeries, it doesn't matter.'

The other two were listening in to this with obvious amusement.

Phil said, 'Peacock's would be better, they've a bit more filling in them. I don't think you would get anywhere near the finish line with a couple of them inside you.'

'Not at all. The best real quality pies are Ferguson's – have you seen the meat in them? And their sausage rolls.' Eric wasn't going to miss out on a discussion of the relative quality of pies.

'For God's sake, it isn't the Cookeen pastry cook of the month - it doesn't matter whose pies they are, as long as the dug eats them,' said Benny in exasperation.

This was getting surreal. 'I don't have a white coat – and I don't have a badge.'

With a nonchalant whistle Benny slipped his hand into his jacket pocket and produced a badge for White City Dog Track Racing with a name on it that identified the wearer as 'Donald Morton –Steward' and slid it across the table.

I looked at it dubiously, 'What about the police?'

'As I say, they're good lads.'

I sipped at my drink. 'I'll think about it.'

'Aye, you do that. Just a chance for you to get old Sandy where it hurts – in his pocket.'

198

'I already did that and look where it got me,' I said sourly.

But I liked the idea of getting my own back for the beating I took from Sandy's thugs and the way I read it he could stand to lose out on winning four figures if his dog lost.

We dropped the subject and went on to other things. One of the advantages of having lived in the future is that things which are old hat to you are brand new to everybody else. Like jokes for instance. Now I'm no Kevin Bridges or Billy Connolly but I can tell a joke and hold my own in company so I was able to throw in some good lines like Billy Connolly's famous Parkinson story where the guy murders and buries his wife with her backside sticking up through the ground so that he has somewhere to park his bike, and another about Jean Pierre, the famous French fighter pilot who pours brandy over his girlfriend's fanny and sets it alight so that he can go down in flames. I did that one with a fairly good French accent borne of practice. Even though I say it myself, I had them all in stitches. It turned nine-thirty before we knew it and it was time to take my leave.

'So, maybe no' see you tomorrow then,' said Benny meaningfully.

'Maybe not,' I replied. 'We'll see.'

Chapter Twenty

Glasgow's White City stadium has long since ceased to exist and its site is now ignominiously covered by the M8 motorway but back in 1957 it housed greyhound racing and motorway racing on its cinder tracks although not on the same night, not intentionally anyway. To call it a stadium was rather like calling Norman Wisdom funny; it was more like a running track and a shed. Ibrox stadium, home of the mighty Rangers was literally a stone's throw away assuming the biblical David was doing the throwing and you could see its red brick frontage from inside the White City. The entry fee was one shilling and sixpence, seven and a half pence in decimal coin, but judging by the Spartan crowd it was still too expensive. I've seen bigger crowds in Tesco.

It was a typical January night for any year, a biting, gusty westerly driving needle sharp squally showers into my face as I trudged along Paisley Road West. Under my raincoat I had on a white coat that made me look like a doctor except that doctors don't carry two Galloway's pies in their pockets. The final consensus was that Galloway's pies would appeal most to a hungry dog. I felt ridiculous.

The great red brick edifice of Ibrox Stadium loomed out of the grey mist to my right, still preserved in 2017 although with new steel braces holding up the modern day seating. Now, as I passed, it was still all standing terraces and open to the elements at both ends. My father had been at the stadium that bleak January day in 1971 when sixty-six fans had been killed in a crush at the Rangers end as the final whistle blew. He knew nothing about it until he got home to his frantic parents who had listened, with mounting horror, to the disaster unfold. I recalled the photographs of the twisted railings on the stairway exit now replaced by the modern east stand where everybody had a seat instead of standing tight together experiencing the warm glow of someone behind you pissing down your leg. It was at a Rangers Celtic game, or should I say battle, that I learned in the nick of time never to accept a can of lager from anyone, however friendly, particularly if it was unusually warm and frothy.

Sandy's dog was running in the third race, so to avoid any unnecessary communication with anyone I waited until just before the second race was due to start before making my way into the ground. I picked the darkest entrance and flashed my cardboard pass at an uninterested steward who nodded me in. Once inside I reversed my clothing so that the white coat covered my raincoat. The sound of the occasional dog bark and yelp of excitement led me to the kennel area where the dogs were kept in anticipation of the starting gate. There was a sound like the steady thump thump of a disco nearby and it took me a minute or two to identify it as the exaggerated beating of my heart.

A policeman strolled around in a desultory way. What he was doing there God alone knows but he looked hard at me which only added some cymbals to the sound of my heart's drum beat. What the fuck was I doing here? I started to walk around the paddock or whatever it was they called it for dogs as if I knew what I was doing.

'Hey you.'

I looked around.

'Aye, you, What's your name?'

'Gord.' Christ, what was it again? I trawled it up from the memory bank. 'Donald, Donald Morton.'

'You need to get over and get Waltzing Matilda out and ready for the next race.'

'Right.'

I had no idea where Waltzing Matilda was. A dog's a dog to me and they all look the same, a leg in each corner and a tail stuck between the back two. Okay, I know they come in different sizes. I looked around.

'Over there look. For fuck's sake do I have tae dae everything?' He pointed over to a row of traps. 'Number two. Just get it out and let it get some air.'

I nodded and made my way over to where there were some dog traps and stewards or handlers fussing about. A couple of the dogs looked at me with interest as I came over and sniffed and whined. Jesus, they must smell the pies. The traps had hand written cards on them each with the name of the dog inside and I saw the one with Waltzing Matilda written on it in a large spidery hand. Two traps down from it was Lucky Lord according to the name on the cage and inside was a greyhound that looked a bit more agitated than the others. It looked like it had just had a double shot of extra strong Colombian espresso laced with cortisone. This was one wired dog.

I remembered being a guest at an evening of amateur boxing bouts in the Kelvin Hall, presumably one of Barry's guests must have called off, I don't recall, but as the boxers were led out to be introduced there was one young lad who ducked and weaved and shadow boxed as he walked around the ring. I marked him down as a sure thing to hit the canvas in the first sixty seconds and sure enough the bell had barely stopped resonating when they had to carry him out as if he was a trencher of beef, his bewildered opponent looking at his right hand glove wondering if his second had slipped some lead into it. Lucky Lord reminded me of that guy. Clearly Sandy knew something I didn't because I wouldn't have bet on it to beat Casey's drum.

A muted roar, well more like a ragged half hearted cheer went up from above me and I assumed that the last race had just finished. Just how on earth I was supposed to get the two pies out of my pocket and slip them to Lucky Lord was a mystery but then two things happened almost simultaneously. First of them was the sound of an altercation breaking out no more than ten yards from me as two stewards started arguing with intent to inflict extremely minor damage on each other thus attracting the attention of most of the others in the area including the exaggerated interest of the solitary policeman who gave me a long look and a wink and then a glance at the abandoned Lucky Lord as he loudly intervened. The second event was the appearance of Sandy Corcoran who clearly wanted to take a personal interest in his meal ticket for the night. He paid no attention to the raised fists and voices nearby but came straight over to his dog who whined in recognition. It didn't sound happy.

'Hey, who's mindin' the dug?'

Fortunately the area was badly lit and I was positioned in whatever shadow was offered but nonetheless Sandy saw my white coat.

'You, over here – stupid lookin'. This dog needs careful handlin'.'

I looked around wildly but everyone else was engrossed in watching two fifty year old men arguing over nothing and doing it with as much enthusiasm as if they were washing the dishes.

'Aye you. Are you comin' over or what?' Sandy got a closer look at me. 'Do I no' know you from somewhere?'

I was good at accents so I put on my best Belfast twang. ' I don't think so now.'

He looked at me strangely. 'Aye ah do. I never forget a face. It'll come to me. Just gie a minute.'

Fuck, that's all I needed – Sandy getting his heavies to finish what they started a week ago. If they got to me again I wouldn't have much of a face left to remember.

A voice brought the tannoy to life. 'All dogs for the third race – five minutes.'

Fortunately this detracted Sandy. Lucky Lord by this time was whining and pawing and clearly anxious to be chasing a toy rabbit or getting the hell away from his master. There was no way I could slip a couple of pies to the dog with Sandy standing there. By this time the handbags at dawn had stopped and the policeman looked over at me. I shrugged and he turned away.

'Are you gonnae take the dog out or what?'

Sandy clearly thought that I was the designated handler and he expected me to take it around and parade it in front of what passed as a crowd. I have on occasion taken a dog out for a walk as a favour to a friend. I have even, on occasion, picked up its shit into a small plastic bag while it looked at me as if to say, 'remind me, who is the master here, again, and by the way my arse needs wiped.' However, I have never paraded one in front of a crowd, however spartan, as if it was a mannequin parade and I wasn't about to start now.

'Well!?'

 I had a flash of brilliance.

'It's not my turn.'

Genius or what?

'I'll take him Mr Corcoran.' A grizzled old guy intervened just in the nick of time but I still had the pies in my pocket.

'Thank Christ somebody knows what they're doin'.'

The old guy glared at me and took over the care of the dog precluding any further action on my part.

'It's a pleasure, Mr Corcoran.'

'This place is going to the fucking dogs,' muttered Sandy with no apparent sense of irony.

 He turned away from me and made to go up to the viewing area but then he stopped in mid pose, like a kid playing statues at a party.

'I know who you are,' he roared, making the dog jump. 'You're the bastard that tried to rip me off. I'll Bic fuckin' Biro ye. I'm gonnae sort you out good and proper.'

I'm pretty sure that's what he was saying but he was speaking to thin air, or more accurately, to a vacuum as the surrounding air hadn't had time to fill the space, which was the medium I had apparently just vanished from, such was the speed of my exit. I was out of the stadium and down Bellahouston Road so fast I would have been hot favourite to beat Lucky Lord by a couple of lengths myself. I was nearly at Paisley Road Toll before I stopped for breath. That's when the fear started to abate and the hunger pangs started to kick in. I had hardly eaten a thing all day but by a stroke of good fortune I just happened to have two Galloway's pies in my pocket and do you know what? They were too good for Sandy and his daft dog. I wolfed them down hungrily as I walked over towards Shields Road. It was too late to go back to Heraghty's and besides, I didn't feel like owning up to failure without a bit of alcoholic fortification. So I didn't nobble Sandy's dog, so what? There were more important things in life, -like having a life.

It was Saturday night, usually a time when I would be out having all sorts of fun involving music, drink and Christine's body coated with a perfumed Levantine oil but here I was on a cold, dark 1957 Saturday night in a city that had locked itself in and thrown away the key. This was a different Glasgow to the one I was used to. No wonder the average life expectancy of the male was sixty-seven; it just seemed like eighty. A red telephone box buttressed a gable end and I phoned Katie but it just rang out. I even pressed button 'A' by mistake and lost my four pennies. Probably at the cinema with her pals, I imagined.

Suddenly I longed for the bright lights of the next century all its freedoms. I started to feel sorry for myself, sorry and lonely, but then I realised that's the only time you do feel sorry for yourself – when you're on your own and nothing to do and nobody to do it with. Miserably I turned the corner into Nithsdale Road and decided I needed to go home for a few days, home to the future where I belonged. It was in a mood like this that I recognised the truism of the old cliché – nostalgia ain't what it used to be.

Chapter Twenty-one

What is it with mobile phones that it usually takes a minimum of two attempts to answer them? I got to it on the fourth ring but pressed the red button by mistake. Of course, when I checked the caller I.D. and tried to call back it was engaged because the caller was trying to redial me. The caller in this instance was Susan and clearly something was wrong. It was the tears that gave it away. It was so bad that my end of the phone was wet.

'Calm down, calm down – what's wrong?' I said, trying to pacify her.

'He's been here.'

'Who'se been here – there?'

'Fingal.'

'Who the hell's Fingal?'

'My ex – you talked to him, remember? You told him you were a priest. I think maybe he figured out that you weren't.'

There were so many alarm bells going off in my head that I could have been in the flight deck of the Hindenburg.

'So?' I said somewhat hesitantly.

There was another burst of sobs that took a few moments to subside. 'He hit me.'

What?!

'What?'

'Oh, Gordon, he hit me, it feels like my jaw is broken; and he punched me.'

Dear God, this was serious. This was assault and battery serious.

'Look, you have to call the police, do you understand? This guy is a criminal. Is he still there?'

Stupid question, Gordon, of course he isn't or she wouldn't be phoning.

'No.'

'Listen, Susan, phone the police, right away. I'll come over, okay.'

She quietened a little. 'Okay, hurry. But I can't call the police – he'd kill me.'

'He won't kill you, right. People like him are just cowards. Little men taking out their inadequacies on defenceless women. What does he do anyway?'

'He's in the Royal Marines. – Gordon – Gordon, Are you still there?'

I cleared my throat, 'Let's not be hasty, Susan.'

'What do you mean, "let's not be hasty"? I'm all alone here and I'm scared, Gordon, and I need some help. I need someone here in case he comes back. I need you here, Gordon.'

The tears flooded down the line again. I was in danger of electrocution.

'Okay, okay, I'll be right over.' I hung up.

The phone rang again almost immediately making me jump but it was Susan again, a little calmer. 'Haven't you forgotten something?'

I racked my brains. 'You want me to bring wine?'

'My address. You don't know where I live.'

'I don't?' I cleared my throat. 'I don't.'

'Near the Battlefield Rest. 29 Lochleven Road – red sandstone tenement top floor right.'

'You got it – twenty minutes, okay?'

I made it in eighteen. Susan had stopped crying and I gave her a hug as soon as she let me in, but the hug set her off again. It was clear that she had taken a beating, the side of her eye was red and swollen and she was going to have a real shiner in a few hours. Her lip was slightly cut and it was also swelling up.

'Jesus, Susan, what did he use? A sledgehammer? Did you call the police yet?'

She shook her head. 'I don't want to get him in trouble.'

'You don't want...' I looked heavenwards. 'Susan, he is already in trouble. If you don't report this he'll just keep on doing it.' Something occurred to me. 'How did he get in anyway? You are divorced, right?'

She shook her head and walked into her lounge. I followed her and looked around to see that it was unintentionally minimalist in style. There were a couple of pictures on the fireplace wall, both prints, one was Renoir's 'The Boating Party' and the other was an indeterminate landscape of what was probably somewhere in the Med or the Italian lakes. There were two or three ornaments on the furniture as well as some framed photographs although none of them featured what could be taken for a husband, not even a wedding photograph. The room was clean and fresh but clearly needed money spent on decor. There was nothing to suggest a man's presence, no computer or golf magazines or slippers lying around, and certainly none of the male detritus you would expect in my place such as empty beer cans, odd socks with holes in them, or Miss February 2015 from a 'Hustler' magazine I bought in New York and to whom I have sworn eternal and undying devotion.

209

'I thought you told me you were divorced.'

'Not divorced – separated,' she shrugged. 'What the hell does it matter?'

'So how did he get in?' I asked again.

'He had a key.'

'You gave him a key?' I said incredulously.

She nodded miserably, then shook her head.

'No, it was his key. This was our house until he left.'

'And you never changed the locks?'

Her voice was so quiet I could hardly hear her. 'No.'

'Why?'

She shrugged and twisted her hanky around her fingers. Then the penny dropped.

'You want him back, don't you?'

She started crying again then looked at me.

'You're in no position to judge. Nobody is, okay?'

I said nothing and we just looked at each other for a while.

'Not any more, not after this,' she said, almost to herself.

'He's hit you before, hasn't he?'

She didn't say anything.

'Come on, Susan, it's common knowledge from what I've heard.'

She looked at me again, frowning.

'Barry may have said something,' I said apologetically.

'Christ, he probably knows I slept with you. What did you tell him?'

I prevaricated, meaning I lied by omission.

'I didn't need to tell him anything, we left together in the middle of his party, remember? We might as well have taken out an ad in The Herald.'

'Fuck.'

210

'That's my girl.'

She stopped crying and this time there was a look of defiance in her right eye, the other was too swollen for me to determine anything. I thought of something.

'So why did he come round. Was he planning to hit you? Was he angry when you let him in?'

She looked away.

'Susan?'

'I think he realised after he put the phone down on you that you weren't a real priest.'

'Oh, what gave it away?'

'I'm a Wee Free.'

'What?'

She was referring to the Free Presbyterian Church of Scotland, a sect that was so bigoted and radical that John Knox was viewed as a left wing liberal and any contact with a Catholic occasioned a visit from their military wing from their base in Uig. Any form of enjoyment was frowned upon and they even made sure that the swings in the kids play park were chained up on a Sunday, for fuck's sake. Lochmaddy wasn't twinned with anywhere but it did have a suicide pact with Kabul.

'Actually, I'm not,' she went on, 'I can't be bothered with all that rubbish, but my father is so it's hardly likely that I'd know any priests.'

'Did you tell him who I was?' I tried to hide the rising panic in my voice; I was fed up being a human punchbag.

'No.'

Chivalry took over now that I was safe. 'Maybe you should have. It would have saved you a lot of pain.'

She shook her head, 'No - that's the last time. Now I'm going to kill him.'

211

'That's great. Let it all out. Get rid of your anger. You don't need a man like that and anyway anybody who stoops to hit a woman isn't a man, he's a bully and a coward and he's probably got penis envy.'

She got up and went into the kitchen and came back with a knife, not just any knife but a black handled, serrated edged, nine inch long, pointed monster that could be used for jungle clearance in Laos in an emergency.

'Susan, what are you going to do with that?'

'I'm going to kill the bastard, I told you. Come on.'

'Come *on*? Are you out of your mind?'

'Never saner.' She went to get a jacket.

'Whoa, whoa, Susan,' I ran into the hall after her. 'Let's think about this for a minute. You can't kill an officer of her Majesty's forces and hope to get away with it. They'll lock you up and throw away the key.'

'He's not an officer, he's a drill sergeant.'

'This is no time to be pedantic.'

'Are you going to help me or are you just another spineless wonder.'

'How many spineless wonders do you know?'

'Now who's being pedantic?'

This was getting ridiculous. How in God's name did I get myself into a position where I was facing down a potential crazed murderer wielding a machete and, more to the point, how was I going to get out of it. There was always the window but this was the top floor and I couldn't recall if there was any shrubbery outside to break my fall.

'Susan! Give me the damn knife!'

'Either help me or get out, but I'm going to end this once and for all.'

There was a demonic look in her eye and I figured that I would be able to convince a lawyer to cop an insanity plea.

'Susan! There are better ways to kill him!'

Excuse me, did I just say that?

'What are you talking about?'

I tried to placate her using the normal palms down hand motions while slowly moving towards her. I had seen it in an old rerun of Starsky and Hutch.

'Just give me the knife. I've got a better idea.'

She looked at the knife, at me, then at the knife again then leant backwards against the wall and all the fire seemed to go out of her. She dropped the knife which buried itself an inch into the wood flooring, then she started to cry again. I put my arms around her and led her back to the lounge leaving the knife oscillating gently in the floor.

'Why don't you tell it to me from the beginning?' I said in what I hoped was my most comforting voice. So she did.

It was the usual story of domestic abuse, of course. Whirlwind romance, all lovey dovey at the beginning and then the gradual controlling dominance started to manifest itself. Drink fuelled his rages. No she couldn't go out with her friends; no she couldn't have more money; no your parents can't come over; no, no, no. And then the abuse started, verbal at first; you're just a slut; you're a no hoper; you can never do anything right; if it wasn't for me nobody would want you, and so on. Then he started hitting her. First a bit of slapping then it got harder. He used his fists. She got pregnant. Then after one drunken bout with his army buddies one night

213

he came home and punched her in the face then the stomach. She lost the baby.

'For God's sake, Susan, the man's a sadist. He should be in jail.'

By this time the tears had stopped; she had cried herself out.

'It was after I lost the baby that I threw him out. Actually I'm not sure whether I threw him out or if he just never came back, it was about six months ago. He would be away for months with his unit. I should have changed the locks, I know.' She looked at the floor. 'I'm a fool. Maybe he's right.'

'Bollocks to that, Susan. Don't you dare make excuses for him.'

I let the pause lie there for a while until she broke the silence.

'So what's your plan then?' she asked dully.

I smiled at her then asked, 'Would you really have killed him?'

She smiled a little then. 'Maybe if he had been there at that point, but I doubt it. I'm not really the killing type. I'd maybe just have gone for his balls.'

'Well why don't we just do that, then?'

She looked at me in disbelief. 'You're going to cut off his balls?'

'Only metaphorically speaking.'

'What are you talking about?'

'What does a guy like that fear more than anything? Not bullets, for Christ's sake, he's in the army. He's big, he's macho and he probably thinks everybody admires him. He's got tattoos, I bet he's got tattoos.' Susan nodded. 'Probably the regimental emblem or some jingoistic shite. He kills Arabs for a living so what's the worst thing that could happen to him?'

Susan shrugged, 'I don't know.'

'For people to think he's just a coward, that's what I mean by cutting his balls off.'

She stared at me. 'How would I do that?'

I looked around her flat noticing again the spartan cleanliness of it, as if she was scared to show that it was her home instead of a house in which she lived. On a small table in the corner of the room was her computer, a PC which didn't look all that new.

'How long have you had that?'

'What?'

I nodded over to the table, 'Your computer.'

'Oh I don't know, maybe two, three years – longer, I can't remember. I just use it for emails, Facebook, that sort of thing.'

I saw a glimmer of light. 'Did he use it at all, for his emails?'

'Yes, I think so.'

'Do you know his email address?'

'I don't know, why would I? He never sent me any.'

'Do you mind if I look through your emails, you can sit with me and let me know if there's any you don't want me to see.'

She smiled another of those sad smiles. 'Chance would be a fine thing.'

So we trawled through her files and eventually came across one from him to his contact list in which she had been copied, avengerscot@gmail.com. How very fucking original.

'Any idea of his password?'

215

She shook her head. I asked her to think of anything, anything at all, a phrase or saying, that he might have used but she couldn't come up with any ideas.

'He was very secretive about things like his password. Every time I passed when he was on the computer he would switch screens or close it down. God knows what he was looking at.'

'You could have checked his history.'

'I did, but he cleared it after every session.'

'What about football?' I asked.

'He followed Celtic a lot but he wasn't a fanatic.'

How was that for an oxymoron?

'He used to say that people never looked in the obvious place for anything. He said that to hide anything, hide it in plain sight.'

This made me think and the thought I came up with was so obvious anybody would be a fool to use it, so I discarded it, but then I realised who I was dealing with. So I brought up Google and hit on the Gmail icon. It prompted me for my email address so I typed in 'avengerscot@gmail.com' and hit the enter button. It then prompted me for my password. I knew I would have only three attempts before it through me onto the security window so I hesitated then typed in the most obvious password, 'Password'. The screen flagged up a message telling me that it was an incorrect password. Shit. I tried '12345678' but with the same result.

I sat back and thought. 'What's his name, again?'

'Who?'

'Your ex husband, do keep up.'

'Oh, Fingal.'

'You're kidding me.'

'No, Fingal, like the cave.'

216

Hmmm.

'Does he have a lucky number?'

She thought for a moment. 'Actually he does. It's sixty-seven, it's the year that Celtic won the European Cup.'

I took a deep breath and typed in 'Staffa67' and the computer took a few seconds as if it was thinking about it then the words 'Welcome Fingal' appeared at the top right of the screen. I was in.

'Now what?' asked Susan.

'We send a few emails,' I replied.

'To who?'

'To his entire contact list.'

I explained to her what we were going to do. I would take photographs of her bruises. We would prepare an email purportedly from Fingal detailing his abusive behaviour to his wife including the beatings, the miscarriage, the bullying, but now that he had found God he wanted to confess his sins to all his friends and beg their forgiveness and understanding. He would go ballistic, of course, and protest to his friends and acquaintances, (and I was delighted to note that there were a number of women on his contact list so maybe one was a girlfriend and, better yet, his mother), but mud sticks, particularly when there is photographic evidence to back it up. His superiors in the army weren't going to take too kindly to it either. If the army want to beat up women and children they prefer to do it with tanks and long range rocket launchers and do the job properly.

She was aghast, 'He'll kill me.'

She had a point there.

'First of all, we change the locks so he can't get in. You need a spy hole in the door so you can see who's there. Also a good time to do it is when he is just about to go back to his unit for a few weeks. That way he's out of harm's way, or rather, you are. Any ideas when that might be?' I was beginning to enjoy the challenge.

'I've no idea, I don't want anything to do with him,' she said.

'Wait a minute, we can check his sent emails, simples.' I gave a click of my tongue just like Aleksandr Orlov, our cheerful cartoon meerkat who never ceases to get on my tits.

So I trawled through his mail and, my goodness, there were some interesting revelations.

'Susan, did you know that your ex needs Viagra?'

'No!'

'Yes.'

'It might be to help with this lady, for want of a better word, called Lynnette that he is apparently, and I quote, "going to screw you to the floor so hard you'll need a carpenter with a full set of tools to get you up again".' I looked at Susan, 'You do suppose he means sex, don't you?' I read on. 'Ah, no, definitely sex, see this bit here, the bit about "after that you can ride me like it's the last furlong of the Grand National and you're winning by a short head".'

'Jesus Christ,' said Susan, 'It was more like a pony ride on Saltcoats beach when he was with me. A quick trot and it was all over before you got your money's worth. I will say this, though. He was very competitive. He always liked to come first.'

I was glad to see that she was getting some of her composure back. I scrolled down his email list a bit more until I came to one that was headed 'Duty Roster' and to which he had replied. It seemed that he was due to leave

218

for Germany two days from now for a three month stint in Gütersloh.

'That's it,' I said triumphantly, 'We'll put together an email and attach a few pictures and send it to all his mates and to,' I looked at the list again, 'Ah, yes, Lynnette, I wonder if that's her real name.'

For the first time today, Susan smiled as I typed away.

'Do you want to stay over?'

I hesitated.

'Please.'

How could I refuse?

Chapter Twenty- two

I should have refused.

We had a pleasant evening and she made a spag bol that came straight from the plains of Tuscany and an excellent Chianti from which the only thing missing was a raffia covering. The rest of the night was taken up with numerous bouts of lovemaking that were the most satisfying that I can ever recall, even including the one night stand I had with a limbo dancer in Key West whose body described a set of oscillating curves that would have caused a riot in a monastery. We were in the middle of an early morning session of the four-legged foxtrot and I was just getting to the vinegar strokes when we were loudly and rudely interrupted by the sound of the front door crashing open and the noise of a silverback gorilla snorting its way towards the bedroom. The bedroom which enclosed the bed in which I was a millisecond earlier enthusiastically enjoying Susan's finer points.

The door flew open and bounced against the rubber stopper on the skirting board and rebounded temporarily slowing the figure in the frame which had now, in the greying light filtering in through the curtains, assumed the shape of a six foot six, two hundred and twenty pound male dressed in the khaki uniform of a trained killer of Her Majesty's government about to demonstrate the finer skills of his art.

I looked at Susan in horror. 'You didn't send the email yet, did you?'

One glance at her was enough to confirm my fears.

'Oh Jesus, Susan.'

Her ex let out a roar that may have twitched ears in Carlisle.

'You fucking bitch! You fucking bitch, I'm going to kill you this time!' He was beyond rage.

As he made his way around the bed I grabbed my mobile and pressed a few buttons. Beside me Susan whimpered. 'Fingal, please don't, please leave. Don't make matters worse,' she pleaded desperately.

'Worse? *Worse?* How could they be any fucking worse?' he roared at a decibel count approaching that of the front row of a Motorhead concert. Plaster dust trickled from the ceiling. 'You've trashed me to most everyone I know. *Worse! Fuck!* So now it's your turn, you bitch. If I don't kill you you'll wish I had – they'll be picking your tits off the pavement by the time I'm finished.'

He pulled the duvet away revealing our nakedness. He looked at me and sneered.

'Not such a big man now, eh, *father?*'

To be fair, any man in my position would have been the same. It's a scientific fact that when the male is threatened with violence his reproductive organs automatically retract into the body as far as possible. It's a self preservation thing. Consequently there wasn't much difference between me and Susan right now to look at in that department.

'You leave her alone or I'll...'

'You'll what?'

Actually that was a very good question but at least I had diverted his attention away from Susan who was frantically trying to find something to cover herself with - an invisibility cloak would have been perfect.

'Just leave her alone. Or maybe you prefer to hit women,' I shouted, with more conviction than I felt.

'You know what?' he hissed, 'First I'll kill you then I'll kill her.'

That wasn't quite the solution I had in mind. He made a swing at me but I blocked him with my eye. I could hear Susan screaming. He made another lunge and I kicked away the sheet that was hindering me and hit him with the nearest object I could find. A pillow. Oddly, it didn't seem to do much damage but he lost a second in swatting it away. There was a small table light at the side of the bed which had a heavy base so I yanked it but the cord came away at the on/off switch on the cable leaving the lead dangling. Susan, abandoning any attempt at modesty, jumped on him from behind and pulled a sheet over his head. Fingal easily threw her off but her interjection and his temporary disorientation gave me just enough time to grab the lead coming from the socket that sent the electric power to the on/off switch which now had only the bare wires showing. Fortunately they had not touched and short circuited so I grabbed the cable and jammed the wires into the area of his testicles. The convulsed scream told me that I had hit the bulls-eye as 240 volts earthed through his dick. I held it long enough to immobilise him but not long enough to do him serious damage; or so I hoped. Anyway the wires in the flex met and there was a simultaneous flash and bang as the plug fused. Fingal slumped to the floor with a strangled groan, clutching at his crotch.

222

As he lay there semi –conscious Susan asked me when the police would get here.

'Police?' I asked, somewhat bewildered.

'I thought that's who you were phoning when he came around my side of the bed.'

'No,' I said, 'I pushed the recording buttons. We've got the whole thing on tape, him threatening to kill you, kill us both. The sounds of the struggle, it's all here.' I tapped the phone. 'When he comes around we play it back to him and tell him it's on another email just ready to send unless he gets his arse out of here and leaves you alone.'

I looked at the groaning figure on the floor. He seemed to be trying to speak and I was amazed to realise that eunochs do indeed talk in a high tenor voice.

'Bastards,' he squeaked.

'Don't try and speak,' I said, 'I trust you heard all that? Just nod.'

He drew me a look that had murder written all over it but eventually he just moved his head. Susan had found a sweat suit and had put it on and she stood over Fingal with the knife that she had been wielding the night before appearing like magic in her hand. She stooped down and put her face next to his and spat out at him while jabbing the point of the knife at his crotch.

'Here's what you're going to do.' She turned to me. 'Gordon, after I tell you, put your phone on record again.'

I nodded.

She spoke to Fingal. 'Here's what you're going to say. You're going to say that you're a serial wife beater and you need help. You're a sexual pervert and a masochist. You have a sense of inadequacy which brings out the

223

worst in you. You'll state your name, rank and serial number. If you ever try to talk to me, see me, or in anyway disturb me, this recording will find its way to everyone you ever knew or anyone you are likely to know in the future. Do you understand?'

She jabbed him in the balls again with the knife just to make sure he got the point which he did, both literally and metaphorically. He duly spoke into the phone and in a voice several octaves higher than normal but still recognisably his, he dictated Susan's text almost verbatim. As he did this Susan went through his pockets and retrieved her house keys. By the time she finished Fingal was able to struggle to his feet.

'Now get out!' Susan hissed.

I was beginning to get a bit nervous that Susan would just lose it and rip him apart with the blade.

'Just go, Fingal,' I told him, 'She means it.'

He looked us both then limped towards the door and turned to us before leaving.

'I don't know how and I don't know when, but I'll get you for this, Susan, you see if I don't.'

With that the silverback, now more a yellowback, stumbled out the room and was gone. I had a feeling that they would be using his balls for Christmas tree lights for some years to come and his chances of fathering any little Sharpes for posterity had taken a serious dip. Susan and I looked at each other for the longest time. Then she came over and pinned me to the wall with what I can only describe as not so much a kiss, more a search for my Adam's apple with her tongue. This was enough to ensure that all my equipment had come out of hiding and was back to full working order and, what with all the excitement and all and some business yet unfinished, a

224

full mattress workout seemed in order just to confirm that diagnosis.

Later that day, in the early afternoon, Barry met up with me in the usual haunt. This was not the Barry of old, the high-flying, devil-may-care, free and easy, carpe diem, Barry of a few weeks ago. This was a Barry who appeared to have physically shrunk since I last saw him. This was a deer in the headlights, back against the wall, worse for wear Barry and I was amazed at the change.

He had a diet coke in front of him and he eyed my pint wistfully.

'I'm cutting back a bit, Lesley thinks I need to lose a pound or two before the wedding. She's right, of course, I was putting it on a bit.' He didn't sound convinced; he sounded beaten.

'So, still no regrets about taking the plunge?' I asked, a trifle provocatively.

'Oh God, no. Best thing I've ever done. Really mate. She's a terrific girl, yeah. Really terrific.' His voice trailed away and he gazed wistfully into the distance or it could have been at the gantry.

'That's great, Baz.'

'Better stop calling me that, she hates it. She wants people to call me Barry.'

'Jesus, Baz, Barry, sorry.'

We both looked into our drinks for a minute or two then Barry spoke.

'She *is* great, Lesley, you know. It's just that she doesn't seem to have a moderation control switch. Everything is full on with the wedding, you know? All she's interested in is having us look at catalogues, traipse around stores and shops, endless discussion about wedding invitations. And can she spend money! It's doing my head in, Gord.'

'You only get to call me Gord if I can call you Baz.'

He smiled at that. 'Yeah, fuck it, call me what you like.'

'Listen Baz. It's all up to you and I can't interfere. But if you want an opinion, well that's different.'

'Ok, I'm listening.'

'First of all, have a pint. You're your own man. Secondly, if you start out this way you're doomed. She'll walk all over you and when you're worn out like an old carpet she'll throw you out. You have to take a stand now,' I explained as if I was a personal advice columnist with an answer for everything.

'Yeah, you know, you're right. Fuck it, I'll have a pint.'

'You want me to get that?'

He looked at me with one of those looks.

Sure,' I said hurriedly, 'A pint.'

The barman took my order and moved away to the pump. It was interesting to see how the Horseshoe had changed over the years yet still retained its original style and atmosphere. My eyes roved over the walls at the photographs. There were a couple of the inevitable tramcars and another of the Jamaica Bridge with a Clyde steamer waiting opposite the Broomielaw to take the summer hordes "doon the watter". There were two or three of the pub inside and out and one took my eye so I went over and took a closer look. I couldn't believe it. There I was standing with my half pint while a barman looked ready to pour another. It was faded to the point of almost turning sepia and in the white border someone had scrawled, 'Horseshoe, 1957'.

226

I came back a few minutes later with a couple of foaming glasses and told Barry to come and see and to his credit he was impressed and went over to look at it.

'Look at that, Barry. If proof were needed you have it right there. To me that was taken just a few days ago.'

'Jesus, Gord, that's, that's – I'm lost for wards.'

A thought occurred to me. 'You know, I've never noticed that here before, have you?'

'Can't say I have, mate.'

We sat back down and Barry took a sizeable gulp and sat back contentedly.

'What if I do what you just said and it doesn't work?' he asked, returning to the topic at hand.

I thought about this for a moment, deliberating a number of possible different scenarios, trying to figure out what the Daily Mirror's agony aunt or whoever was the latest guru in print for the lovelorn would say, then took another sip.

'Well?'

I looked at him and squarely in the eye and gave it him straight.

'Basically, you're fucked.'

He thought about that for a long minute or so then looked steadily back at me.

'Hmm, that's what I thought.' He sighed then changed the subject. 'So, what have you been up to?' He peered a little closer. 'Is that another black eye or the same one?'

I touched my face tenderly. 'I'm thinking of signing up for the professional circuit. You should see the other guy.'

Barry looked at me questioningly.

'No, seriously, you should see the other guy.'

I told Baz all about Susan's wacko ex husband, his early morning courtesy call and his high voltage adventure.

'Jesus, Gordon, you want to watch yourself, that guy is bad news from what I've heard.'

'No shit, Sherlock.'

He sighed and put down his pint. 'Beau Geste may be the least of your worries.'

'What do you mean?' More trouble I needed like a full elevator needs a fart.

'Christine's on the warpath. She hasn't heard from you and she thinks you're avoiding her.'

'Does she, indeed?' Actually I had forgotten all about her. 'I thought she was shacked up with Brian with the roving eye.'

'I get the impression he doesn't quite measure up, no double entendre intended, and for all your imperfections, and she numbered them in some detail, she hasn't quite given up on you yet.'

'That could be a problem,' I said, frowning.

'Indeed.'

'But she still plans on going to the Caribbean for your nuptials with the boy wonder?' I said hopefully. With Susan now very much on my radar, not to mention Katie I was quite happy for Brian to take a load off.

'Let's just say that he's the back-up although he doesn't know it.'

'Okay, I'll call her.'

Barry nodded. 'So how goes the grand plan?'

I told him about recent events and my new found friends in Heraghty's and my burgeoning relationship with Katie. My adventures at the race track brought a welcome smile to his face.

'Jesus, Gordon, how are you going to keep all these women apart?'

'Well, right now one of them is in her nineties if she's still alive. She only features in my other life sixty years ago. But you're right, it can get complicated.'

He really brightened when I told him that we were set for a big win on Saturday 9th February and that all I needed to do was to go to Amsterdam, buy some diamonds, bring them back and sell them.

'You think you can do that?'

'Sure – money talks.'

'Yeah. Right now it's saying goodbye. Thank God for that, I could do with the money. Lesley seems to think I have an unlimited supply.'

'You do now,' I told him.

'So when do you go back?' he asked..

'I'll give it a few days. No rush.' I stretched out a yawn. 'Think I'll take it easy for a couple of days –it's nice not to have to worry about the little things – like money for a change. My Giro came in and that'll see me through comfortably until the serious cash arrives. Hey ho.'

Just at that my mobile rang. I checked the caller I.D. and saw that it was my mum, which was slightly odd as I rarely heard from her unless she wanted something.

'Hi mum,' I said cautiously, 'What's up?'

'Your father's had a heart attack – he's dead.'

Break it to me gently, why don't you.

Chapter Twenty-three

In the medical sense, it wasn't a heart attack at all. A heart attack is caused by arterial blockages restricting the blood flow through the heart and, if caught quickly enough or if the restriction isn't severe, is normally survivable and a full recovery is the usual prognosis. In my father's case the electrical impulses that control the heartbeat fluttered wildly out of control for a few seconds then stopped. He was dead before he hit the ground. It was as if a fuse had popped but there was no way of reversing the circuit breaker. It's really not a bad way to go if you are ninety-two and in bed with a twenty-something flat belly, but dad was still in his sixties and had a full cocktail cabinet in front of him. Apparently it happened just at the start of happy hour in the Lionheart Bar. Who says the gods don't have a sense of humour.

My mother was desperately cut up about it even although she had been sharing her life and her bed with another man for a number of years. I met her later over a tearful drink in the city when she rattled on about what a wonderful caring guy my father had been.

'He was a loving father to you and Lara, you know, and a wonderful husband,' she sniffed, dabbing her nose with a tissue. This was an observation at variance with my own recollections but I let her have her head. 'He was so proud of you.'

This was laying it on a bit thick. Lara definitely and I'll reluctantly admit, with some justification, that of the two of us she was the real go-getter and my dad adored her, but me? No, I don't think so.

She took another sip of Chardonnay. 'He used to make me laugh. Now look.'

'You're happy with Mark, aren't you?' Why is it the other man is always called Mark?

'Yes, of course. But still – I never stopped loving your Dad.'

I didn't know how much more of this self serving bullshit I could take so I tried to get on to firmer ground. 'What about the arrangements?'

'Arrangements?'

'The funeral, the death certificate, all of that stuff,' I explained.

'Oh. Right. Lara is taking care of all that.'

Well of course she was. What she meant was that Keith, would be taking care of it while Lara would be supervising operations from the lofty position of the settee with a coffee and a clipboard in her hand.

'It was the drink, Gordon, the demon drink.' She emptied the last of the Chardonnay into her glass. 'If it hadn't been for that we might still have been together. He practically drove me into the arms of another man.'

'Oh yes, Mark.'

'No - Kevin, Mark was after.'

I looked at her.

'What? Oh don't be such a prude, Gordon. You don't know the half of what I had to put up with. I'm just about to turn sixty this year and I can look back with a degree of wishing for what might have been. And by the way, your father was no angel either, look how he met

231

me. God knows what he got up to on those four day Sydney layovers. Sydney legovers we used to call them.'

So much for the loving husband, I thought.

'How's grandma?' I asked, changing the subject again.

'That old cow.'

Patience, Gordon. 'Have you talked to her?'

'Yes. She's very upset.'

'I'll go and see her. You'll let me know when the funeral is, won't you?'

'Yes, Lara will probably be in touch with you about that anyway.'

Later, after I had left her at the station it occurred to me that not once during the whole time I was with her did she ask me how I was doing. Plus ça change.

Deeply depressed, I walked back to Partick hoping the cold air would help but it only served to dampen my spirits further. Just to put the tin lid on it, Christine had let herself into the flat and was sitting there with a face like an Easter Island statue.

'Hello, I'm Christine. I don't believe we've met.'

Sarcasm wasn't her strong suit.

'Christine, before we start I...' But she ploughed on. Once Christine got started it was a bit like a 100,000 ton oil tanker, she wouldn't stop until the full forces of nature eventually prevailed.

'I call, I leave messages, I text, I send emails, nothing. Christ I know we're not love's young dream but I think I deserve better than that. I'm not just some cheap shag, you know, I have feelings. I've lent you money, quite a lot as it happens, and this is how you treat me. Look, I know you've been shagging someone else, Susan Sharpe if I'm not mistaken, and that's okay, I understand you weren't too happy the last time we met, but for God's

232

sake Gordon, I thought you were bigger than that. Where, the fuck have you been? I've tried everywhere and...'

'Christine...' It was hopeless.

'I haven't finished. And now Brian won't come near me because he thinks I've got the clap or something, what was all that about, eh? You promised you were going to take me to Barbados or the Bahamas or Bermuda or whatever bloody 'B' Barry's getting married in, first class if memory serves...'

'Christine, my father just died!' I hadn't meant to shout but it was the only way to stop the tanker.

She paused and looked at me. 'Jesus, Gordon, you'd better not be kidding.'

'Well, I wish I was kidding, what sort of dumb thing is that to say?'

She looked at me again then her shoulders sagged and she came over and put her arms around me and gave me a hug.

'I'm sorry, Gordon.'

'I know, I know. It's okay.'

'What happened?'

I gave her the whole story and the more I told it the more depressed I got. He wasn't a bad guy, my old man, he just couldn't control his desires any more than my mother could, His was the bottle, hers was the solace of other men. I wasn't any better; it was just different. By this time it was almost dark so I put the lights and the kettle on.

'I'm sorry I haven't been in touch and, yes, I have seen Susan Sharpe – I don't know what else to tell you. I don't even know whether it's serious or not. But there's also something else going on and I can't share it with you

233

– it's not anything you need to concern yourself about – it's not drugs or anything illegal – look at it as a business venture if you like, but for a few weeks I'm going to be gone quite a lot.'

The kettle started to whistle.

'Coffee?' I waggled a cup at her.

She nodded and sat on the couch so I made a couple of cups of cheap instant and flavoured them with a spoonful of sugar. Christine took the steaming cup from me, tucked her legs under her body and waited.

I continued, 'That's why I haven't been in touch. In effect I've been out of touch.'

'You could have texted, at least,' she pouted.

'I know this is hard to believe in this day and age, but actually, I couldn't.'

Her upset smouldering look said it all.

'Chris, just trust me on this, okay?'

She gave me a long hard look again and I shrugged. Wisely, perhaps, she sighed and dropped it but I could tell it was just for the moment. Women never forget things, they just file it away in the pending tray for future reference.

'I'm sorry about your dad.'

'Yeah, me too.'

'Do you want me to stay?'

'Okay, but I won't be up to much,' I said.

'That's okay, we can just cuddle.'

That would be a first.

Lara phoned me the early in the morning, and I mean early. My watch told me it was eight o'clock, my body told me it was six and Chris told me it was positively fucking primeval in as many words.

234

'Gordon?' Who else was she expecting, I wondered.

'Hi, Lara.'

'It's about Dad.'

I assumed he was still dead.

'Yeah, I'm sorry, Lara. I know you and he were close. I feel bad too.'

'I've been working on the arrangements.' By that she meant Keith had. 'The earliest we can fix the funeral is two weeks time. There have been a lot of deaths recently, apparently it's the cold and damp, they drop like flies this time of year.'

Quite.

'It's two weeks yesterday at the Linn Crematorium, Wednesday the 8th at 2pm. You'll be there.'

It was more of an order than a question.

'Of course I'll be there, he was my father.'

She steamrollered on, 'I've booked the Busby Hotel for a reception afterwards. I've briefed mum.'

Briefed? For fuck's sake! 'Okay Lara, I've got that.'

There was silence on the line and I thought that she had hung up but then I heard a sob.

'Lara, I'm desperately sorry and I feel shitty too. Thanks for doing everything, I appreciate it.' I couldn't think what else to say.

She seemed to pull herself together. 'Yes I know. See you later, Gordon.' Then she hung up.

Chris got up around ten. She was on shift at two and had some things to do so she left me with a peck on the cheek and the ominous admonishment, 'we need to talk', probably the worst four words in the English language a man can hear from a woman after 'go see your doctor'.

So I called Susan's mobile to see how she was doing. She was doing okay apparently, and sounded quite jaunty. She told me that she'd had the best sleep in weeks and that a weight had been lifted from her shoulders.

'You were right, Gordon, I did want him back, God knows why, but now I never want to see the bastard again.'

I told her about my father and she was genuinely upset for me but I told her I was fine and that I'd fill her in with the details another time. It was nearly lunchtime and I wondered what she had planned but she was out undertaking some assessment for a nursing home in the south side and then she was going to visit her grandmother who was in a care home in Twechar. We agreed that I'd call her tomorrow. Where, in God's name, is Twechar?

Today was Thursday the 24th and I thought it was time I was heading back to my little grey home in the past so I figured on passing under the station clock tomorrow at the allotted time. I still had Chris to face and somehow placate her and I needed a few days to get away. There was nearly two weeks before dad's funeral and Lara had everything under control. I imagine she had a spreadsheet going.

Chris was on a twelve hour shift so I wasn't going to have to deal with that today, thank God, so I put on my running gear and went for a long five mile run around the west end, through the Botanic Gardens and all the way to Anniesland making my way back through Broomhill and Hyndland. There is nothing like a good work out to get rid of the toxins in the brain and the body and with every step, every pound of the Nikes on the pavement, every intake of breath I could feel the oxygen purifying my red blood cells. It was like cleaning out the cupboard under the stairs and getting rid of all

236

the crap. Halfway around I got to thinking of my old man lying cold in a mortuary somewhere. I remembered the trips to Disney and the hours playing with the Hornby and the Saturday morning support at the school's football matches where I was always inevitably subbed at half time. I had forgotten all the good times and now they came rushing back. Like the long hours trying to get me to grasp the fundamentals of geometry and algebra; like the way he sat up with me all night holding my hand when I could hardly take a breath when asthma wracked my lungs. I realised that I had become bitter at him for no longer being that man without considering that I might no longer be that boy.

Thankfully a gentle rain started to fall, disguising the tears that rolled down my cheeks as I counted off the miles.

I phoned Susan the next morning and she was happy to hear from me. 'When do I get to see you, my knight in shining armour?'

'I've got to take off again but I'll be back in a few days.'

I could almost sense a pout but she said, 'Hurry back, I'll miss you.'

'Sure I will,' I said without conviction, 'How was grandma?'

'Gramma? Oh she's fine, just lives in the past but I think it was an interesting past so that's okay.'

'You be good, right, and don't answer the door to anyone in uniform, not even the postie.'

She laughed, 'Or the electricity meter reader.'

Tying up loose ends I called my mother but she was out so I got Mark.

'Hey Gordon, long time no speak. Sorry about Ronnie.' He seemed quite genuine and it was no use blaming him for the events of the past. He was just an innocent bystander caught up in the whole thing. Well, maybe not quite so innocent, but still.

We talked a little and he promised to let mum know I'd called and we parted on friendly terms.

And with that and a couple of pints in the 'shoe I headed over to Central Station and the previous century.

Chapter Twenty-four

The house was dark and cold but started to look and feel cheery after I switched all the lights on and blasted it with a few thousand watts of electricity. I had a good look round and then sat down. For some reason I felt better than I had a few hours before and it took me a moment or two to stumble upon a possible reason.

Right now my father was almost alive and somewhere out in Kings Park my grandma was pregnant with him. His life wasn't over; it was just about to start. He hadn't met my mother yet, not by a long way and I was merely a random atom floating somewhere in the universe, but here in 1957 he was all but alive. It was an odd, strangely comforting thought that warmed me after making my way out to the cold flat in Nithsdale Road and I slept all the better for that.

The following morning was dull, the slate grey clouds scudding across a low sky threatening more squally rain. I withdrew twenty pounds from the bank, still not quite used to the fact that this was a small fortune for most people just now whereas back in my real world it would hardly see me through the day. I was about to more than treble it as I took a train out to Greenock. It was a six carriage train, all with individual compartments hauled by a side tank engine running bunker first. The first stop was supposed to be at Paisley Gilmour Street but it pulled up at signals at Shields Road station and inevitably somebody tried to board which elicited just about the funniest comment of the week when the guard shouted. 'Ye canny get oan – this train doesnay stop here.'

I was amazed at the amount of shipbuilding cranes forming a guard of honour virtually all the way down the Clyde from Glasgow to Paisley. The shells of half completed ships sparked with the occasional electric blue of a welders' torch that lit up the sky even from this distance. The Clyde was a different place back then and all the better for it. The train rambled on until the river widened as we puffed through Langbank, stopped for a minute at Port Glasgow then reached Greenock.

A bookies shop in West Blackhall Street happily took my first bet of ten shillings which lost as planned but a treble on which I had put a pound yielded a return of sixty-two pounds much to the chagrin of the bookie himself and the admiration of the half dozen out of work punters hanging desultorily about, but there was no sign of Sandy and having learnt my lesson, this bookmaker wouldn't see my face again.

I took a stroll around the town. I had only been in Greenock two or three times and thought it was a sorry looking place with a main street half pedestrianised and the inevitable array of charity shops and everything under a pound stores. I thought of the old joke of the girl who asked her boyfriend to kiss her where it was wet and smelly so he took her to Greenock. That always cracked me up. The people looked tired as if beaten and hammered by life. I was there one day when a cruise liner had docked, filled with Americans and some from the south of England. It had come from Southampton, I seem to recall, and was the something-or-other Princess. Most of its passengers had wisely decided on a shore excursion to Loch Lomond or the Burns' Country or

240

even over to Bute to see Mount Stuart House but I saw a couple walking around in bewildered aimlessness wondering what had happened to 'Bonnie Scotland'. Brigadoon Greenock wasn't.

Now, back in 1957 it seemed altogether more prosperous and vibrant although by no means pretty. The people had purpose in their step and down at the quay there was an abundance of small craft loading and unloading their cargo. The old Clyde puffers lay along Customs House quay in proliferation while dray horses pulled carts loaded with coals and boxes of general wares. A little further to my left the warehouses that were derelict and weed strewn on my previous visits positively hummed with activity while the steel ropes from a huge crane rummaged about in the hold of a Blue Funnel Line steamer as if it was some kind of seaside lucky dip. I took a stroll along the esplanade and saw in the distance the paddle steamer 'Jeannie Deans' making its way from Craigendoran over to Dunoon. Not for the first time I wondered whether the old guys who nattered on about "the good old days" hadn't got a point.

The train took me back to Glasgow where by this time darkness had started to add its weight to the grey gloom. There were no supermarkets carrying an array of pre-cooked meals so I just grabbed a fish supper in a chippie on Bridge Street before heading back home. Looking at my watch I thought that Katie would be back from work so I found a phone box and gave her a call. By this time I had figured out the button 'A' and button 'B' thing and after a moment or two she answered with a breathless 'Govanhillfourtwoonethreewhosespeakingplease' on the fourth ring.

'Hi there.'

241

'George?'

'The very same, were you expecting somebody else?'

'It's so good to hear you. What great adventures have you been up to, I've missed you?'

For someone who just a couple of weeks ago couldn't catch the eye of Medusa I was suddenly Mister Irresistible.

'I've missed you too,' I said and I had. 'What's your plans for the next few days?'

'Oh, nothing special. I'm going out with the girls tonight, just to the pictures but other than that, nothing much.'

'Tomorrow?'

'Great, Sunday. I've got nothing on.'

'There's no answer to that.'

'George!' but there was a giggle in her voice.

'Do you fancy going away for the day?' I had come out with this on sheer impulse, I don't know where it came from.

She squealed with excitement. 'Oh my! But where would we go – it's January and it'll be dark by four.'

I hadn't thought about that, as usual my mouth was engaged before my brain was in gear.

'What about Edinburgh? A stroll through Princes Street Gardens, lunch at the North British. There's a train called the 'Queen of Scots', it goes to London and stops in Edinburgh. It's a fancy Pullman affair. We'll go in style.'

'Oh my God, George, I've never even been in Edinburgh.'

'First time for everything, sweetie.'

As we were talking I realised that I was just as excited as she was, well almost anyway. It's sometimes really

242

great to see something or somewhere through somebody else's eyes and, in any event, although I had been in Edinburgh many, many times and loved its style and elegance, apart from that brief trip to place a bet, I hadn't seen it as it was in 1957. This would be fun. Katie and I talked a few minutes more about how she was and what she had been up to, which wasn't much, and about the latest film she had seen. She asked me the same and I was pretty evasive.

'So, should I pick you up or meet you at the station?' I asked, getting off the subject of my recent past.

'I'll meet you there. What station?'

'Queen Street, say half past ten. I think the train is sometime before eleven. I'll have the tickets and everything.'

We said our goodbyes and hung up.

The 'Queen of Scots' was a train I'd known about from my musings through the various railwayana that I'd bought, sold and lost over the years. It was a relic of a bygone age, this age actually, a sedate train that meandered down to London in nine hours of Edwardian splendour where the elite were served three course lunches and dinners by liveried, white gloved attendants. Some of the gleaming umber and cream carriages were named; Arcadia, Ione, Marcelle were but three. The interior decor was plush and ornate to say the least, with curved iron light sconces, heavy brocade upholstery and lace curtains, shaded table lamps on the table between each seat, walnut, beech and elm wood inlay panelling, and a general air of a design style best described as 'early bordello'. I had seen one in all its glory at the National Railway Museum in York and I had also seen a full train of the coaches hauled by a couple of EWS diesels on an

243

excursion to Oban as it lumbered through Partick but needless to say, I couldn't have afforded the price of a glass of water, let alone a seat at the pinnacle. This was a treat to savour even if it was only for an hour to Edinburgh, and in the company of a beautiful woman too.

It was around seven o'clock before I made my way round to Heraghty's. I had been putting off showing my face and admitting my failure at putting the nobble on Sandy's dog but it was time to get it over with. Sure enough, they were all there, Phil, Eric and Benny, crowded round the bar, dissecting the results of that days' football. Both Rangers and Celtic had both won handsomely but Phil wasn't so happy as he was a Partick Thistle man and they had been Rangers' victims to the tune of three goals to one. Regardless, when they clocked me they appeared genuinely pleased to see me again. Before they could start ribbing me about my lack of success at the White City I thought I'd dampen the effect by getting a round in.

'Okay, okay, I know – drinks first though. Jim, set them up again and one for yourself,' I said and the barman set about this quite happily.

'So, young George. Congratulations.' Phil raised his glass and drank the last of his pint.

Benny patted me on the back. 'You're a brave man, I hear. I never thought that Sandy'd be down in the traps with you. Bit of a risk, eh?'

Benny didn't know the half of it. 'You'd better believe it. He recognised me, you know. I was out of there so fast you'd have thought my arse was on fire. He was not a happy camper when he saw me.'

244

'He was a lot less happy by the end of the night. I'm told he'd placed a grand all over town. Thought he was gonnae lift about ten grand at the end of the day,' Benny said.

Little bells started to go off in my brain. 'So...the dog,..?'

'Came in fourth,' Eric finished for me.

After all that, all the damn subterfuge and risk and not actually giving Lucky Lord the Galloway pies, the dog still lost. My initial doubts on its ability had been right.

'So, how did you manage to slip the dug the pies?' asked Phil.

'Oh, it was nothing,' I said modestly, 'I just had a second or two after the argument started and Sandy appeared. It was a close run thing though.'

Jim placed the pints in front of us and I counted out the coins.

'Aye,' said Benny, 'You must have been fast, Duncan said he never saw anything so quick. In fact he never saw anything at all. Fair play to you.'

'Duncan?'

'Aye, Duncan, he was the polisman on duty, remember?' He raised his glass in salute. 'I'd keep well away from Sandy's shops though, if I was you, just in case he puts two and two together – know what I mean?'

I knew what he meant.

'Actually, I've got a confession to make,' I said.

'Oh aye,' said Eric, 'What's that?'

I hesitated, 'It was just the one pie – I ate the other.'

They laughed and we started talking about anything and everything as men in pubs do whether it's in 1957 or 2017 or probably 2057 for that matter. Football, the weather, sex, football, women (as opposed to sex).

245

Benny got in another round although with the clock all too quickly making its way past the nine o'clock hour mark there was only another half an hour of drinking time left. No wonder there were a few drunks on the streets; they poured as much down their throats as they could to beat the clock. Mind you, things hadn't changed much by the twenty-first century. We shut the pubs at one in the morning and the human debris was everywhere, I should know, I was frequently a piece of it.

Benny turned to me. 'Just watch yourself, okay?'

'What do you mean?'

'I'm talking about Sandy, it'll no' take long before he puts two and two together and he's a sore loser - you already know that. He'll have put the word out in the betting fraternity – so just a word to the wise, okay?'

I nodded and took another couple of gulps of my pint just as Jim shouted out that it was closing time. Then Phil took me aside.

'Did you no' say that you were into forecasting and all that?' he asked.

I racked my brains for a minute trying to remember. I think I'd said something about forecasting or research and statistics, something vague so as not to appear interesting. Now my sensors were on amber alert.

'That's right, Phil. Crystal ball stuff.'

'See it's just that I do a wee bit of feature writing as well as reporting – I'm a journalist – and I wanted to do a piece on what's happening. There's been a lot of change since the end of the war, stuff you couldnae imagine and if you're into predicting trends, well, maybe you can give me some pointers, you know?'

I didn't see any harm. 'Eh, sure Phil. What sort of stuff?'

246

'How'll work change, leisure time, holidays, that sort of thing. Nothing science fiction, if you know what I mean. We're no' talkin' man in the moon stuff or robots, just the sort of things we can expect in the next ten or fifteen years. That's your line, isn't it?'

If only he knew.

'Let me work on it, Phil.'

'Thanks, George.' He patted me gently on the back, loosening some minor vertebrae.

Ten-fifteen Queen Street station and I had already bought two first class returns and the supplement for the Pullman seats as I meandered around the platforms. The supplement was a whopping two shillings and sixpence – half a crown – twelve and a half pence. A stopping train to Edinburgh had just pulled out and there was an ancient side tank loco at the head of a couple of vintage coaches ready for the short trip out to Kirkintilloch. Sitting at platform seven were the six gleaming Pullman coaches that made up the Glasgow portion of the 'Queen of Scots' and I watched as a Gresley A3 Pacific, *'Prince Palatine'* slowly backed up and kissed the leading coach ready to couple up. I had my camera with me and snapped off a few. A couple of spotters took notes in their books which made me feel superior with my single lens reflex dangling over my shoulder. I nodded at them as they looked over, brothers in arms recognising each other. I think they were at least seventeen.

The weather was grey but dry and the sounds of the trams moaning their way around the bend in George Square echoed around the concourse. Five minutes early, Katie came in from the Dundas Street entrance and saw me before I saw her so she was by my side

247

before I knew it and I got a peck on the cheek and a hug just for being there. She looked resplendent, I must say, dressed as she was in a fox fur coat which went very well with her nigger brown shoes - in 2017 there would be a tin of red paint over it to go with it. A liveried attendant met us at our carriage door and showed us to our seats. Once we were inside our carriage and seated in the single seats across from each other and she took in the unashamed opulence she turned to me in amazement.

'So this is how the other half live,' she said.

'The other five percent, more like.'

She sat back with a sigh, looked around her, shook her head and gave me an inscrutable look.

'I don't know what to make of you, George, I really don't.'

The whistles of the guard and porters followed by the loud 'chuff-chuff' of the heavy locomotive as it strove to get a grip on the damp steel silenced us and we watched as the station receded and we entered the long tunnel up to Cowlairs.

I imagined us as a mysterious couple on the Orient Express rushing over the Lombardy plains or eastern Austria hatching some John le Carré intrigue but the dull council houses of Croy soon dispelled that notion. The arrival of a waiter serving tea and scones revived the romance of it all however and Katie was enchanted, seemingly reading my thoughts.

'Imagine travelling to Vienna or Venice like this. Dinner, wine. Dreamy piano music, a sleeping car across Europe. I've dreamed of this sort of thing. It's so- so - *romantic*,' she said as we rattled over the points at Polmont.

'You don't need to imagine, you know.'

248

She lowered her eyes then sat back and looked at me. 'Paris?'

'It's a start.'

She took my hand as she gazed at me. 'Can we talk about this later?'

Magnanimous to a fault I shrugged. 'Sure.' Bogey couldn't have done it better.

We pulled into Waverley just before twelve and walked up the ramp into a watery bleak sun with ragged clouds scudding across the sky occasionally revealing patches of just enough blue to make a pair of sailor's trousers, as granny used to say. I had a sort of itinerary mapped out in my mind so we walked down Princes Street arm in arm while Katie ooohhd and aaahhd at the sight of the brooding castle and the houses on the Mound looking down on the gardens. We walked around the gothic, middle age rocket ship of the towering Scott monument then turned left past the National Gallery and strolled over the railway to the Mound.

By the time we got to Castlehill and walked up to the Esplanade it was almost one o'clock. A kilted soldier of the Royal Scots Dragoon Guards stood sentry at the gatehouse entrance to the castle underneath the shield bearing the Royal Banner of Scotland, the Lion Rampant and the engraved motto below, 'Nemo me Impune Lacessit', the translation of which is, 'No-one provokes me with impunity', or the more basic battle cry, 'Wha daur meddle wi' me!' A friend of mine, and this is true I swear, overheard an American tourist ask the sentry, for what must have been the hundredth time that day, what the motto meant. Standing rigidly to attention and his head held erect, bayonet at his right hand side, he said

249

without hesitation, 'No four tonners beyond this point, sir.'

We walked through the gate and round the cobbled lane to the ramparts just as the one o'clock gun was fired scaring Katie almost clean out of her fox fur coat and she clung on to my arm tightly.

'What was *that*?' she said when she recovered her poise.

I explained the tradition and she relaxed. We made our way down the Royal Mile and stopped at a tea room for a cuppa.

'I thought we'd have an early dinner and then get the train back. There are plenty of trains but the Pullman back is at eight. How about that?' I said as we walked.

'It's just perfect.' I got another squeeze and a peck on the cheek for my trouble.

So there we were, we two, ambling around old Edinburgh, talking, sightseeing, laughing and generally doing what two people tentatively finding their way towards a relationship generally do. Edinburgh behaved itself, the sun came out as we made our way down Victoria Street, through the Grassmarket and back to the gardens. Katie had read the story of Greyfriars Bobby at school, the tale of a Skye terrier who guarded his master's grave for fourteen years until he died. Katie was enchanted by the story and wanted to see the monument to it at the corner of Candlemaker's row so we made our way there where she gazed at it, all dewy eyed.

'It's such a sad story,' she sniffed.

I, of course, agreed, secretly keeping to myself the view that, like most Scottish myths, the whole thing was just a load of shite cooked up for the American market. Call me a cynic if you like but I don't believe in Robert

250

the Bruce's spider, The Loch Ness Monster or that carrots make you see in the dark either.

We got to the North British Hotel at around half past five where I tipped the maitre d' a couple of bob (don't you just love the way I slip into the 50's lingo?) for a decent table and sat down to dinner. The North British then was owned by the railway company and looked it. There was a sort of faded colonial glory about the place, a bit like a gentleman's club in Rangoon, but it impressed Katie which was the object of the exercise after all.

After a pleasant, if, to my mind, average meal and a bottle of Chablis Katie leant over and took my two hands in hers and said, 'So George, tell me about Paris.'

So I told her about Paris.

'Does this mean that you want to go?' I asked.

'Yes.'

'With me?'

She laughed, 'Of course with you. Who else?'

'Huh. Right. Well. Wow.' Say what you like but there are times when I can be erudite and eloquent and sculptured phrases trip off my tongue like honey. Clearly this wasn't one of those times. 'You're sure?'

'I've given it a lot of thought and I'm sure.' She paused. 'So what now?'

'When do you want to go?'

'Well, I have time due to me, so pretty much anytime. How about the week after next?'

I'll say this for the girl, once she decides on something she doesn't let the grass grow under her feet.

'Perfect. Works for me.' Then I remembered. 'Shit I can't that week. It's my father's funeral.'

'*What*?'

'I'm sorry – I clean forgot.'

251

'You forgot your father's funeral?'

'Yes – no – of course not. I just hadn't tied the dates together.'

'My God George, that's awful. I'm so sorry.'

'What about the week after?'

'George, your father has just died, you can't think of anything else right now. What about your mother?'

'No, she's still alive.'

'George, that's not what I meant.'

I explained about the divorce and how that although we all still kept in touch we weren't that close any more. Katie looked shocked; apparently divorce was a bit of a stigma in the fifties.

'How awful. What did he die of?'

'A heart attack I understand, but it was probably the drink at the end of the day.'

Katie was really upset for me, probably because she'd had such a close relationship with her own parents.

'Where's the funeral?'

'The Linn,' I said without thinking.

'The Linn?' she said, perplexed.

I realised I had made some sort of mistake by the puzzled look on her face.

'You know what, my sister is making the funeral arrangements, so maybe I've got it wrong. I'm still a bit shell shocked.'

She patted my hand, 'I'm sure you are.' But she still looked at me a bit oddly.

I realised now that the Linn crematorium looked fairly modern and probably hadn't been built yet. Hell, maybe they didn't cremate people in 1957, maybe it was all burials. I remembered that there was a cemetery between Cathcart and Muirend.

252

'I think it's probably the cemetery near Linn Park.'

'Oh, Cathcart cemetery.'

'Yes, that must be the one, that's what I meant to say.'

'Would you like me to come with you?' she offered.

'What? No – no. It'll just be a family affair.' It would have been a neat trick though, I thought.

'Well, if you sure,' she said doubtfully.

'I'm sure, now about Paris.'

She smiled that smile and said, '*Are* you sure, George?'

'Hey, that's supposed to be my line.'

So we agreed the week after dad's funeral would work for us both and she seemed delighted. I asked if she had a passport.

'Of course not, why would I need such a thing?'

'You will now so you'd better get cracking.'

'I don't know where to even start,' she said with a worried look.

'Not a problem. There must be a passport office in Glasgow. Get the forms, fill them out, get a couple of passport photos, take it in and you should get it in a week or so.'

'Have you got one? Of course, silly me, you must have.'

Actually, that was a very good point and it was time I did something about that.

We finished our meal and took our time walking round to the platform for the Pullman trip home where we rounded off a perfect day by enjoying a liqueur.

'I don't ever remembering having so much to drink before, well maybe that's not true, but it was a long time ago,' Katie said as she relaxed into a Drambuie. 'Anyone would think that you're trying to get me tipsy so that you can have your way with me,' she said, looking at me steadily.

'My intentions are honourable,' I said, crossing my heart.

'Let's not be too hasty,' she said with a glint in her eye.

The train rolled on through the evening, the darkness outside, only interrupted by the gas lamps of railway stations flashing past and the distant house and street lights somehow made the carriage seem more intimate, that there was only this small world in here and nothing else.

We pulled into Queen Street just after nine.

'I'll get us a taxi,' I said as we walked out towards North Hanover Street and she didn't demur. When we pulled up to her house I got out to make sure she was okay and I was about to tell the driver to wait when she said no, it was fine. I looked at her questioningly.

'I'm working in the morning but why don't you come up anyway.' She led the way.

Once in she switched on the electric fire and we sat down on the chairs opposite each other. She got up and put Ella on the record player.

'I can't offer you a drink, I don't have any in the house,' she said. 'I have tea, though.'

'Oh, I'm just fine. I think I've had plenty anyway, don't you?'

She looked me straight in the eye. 'Will you stay the night? I'd like that.'

'Yes.' Anything else would have been superfluous.

'I'd like us to be lovers before we go to Paris, do you know what I mean?'

'I know what you mean.'

254

'And it's been such a perfect day and this is just how I want it to end,' she said as she came over and kissed me properly and then led me into the bedroom.

We made love again before she got up to go to work (and that's about as much detail as you're going to get) and I rose also and made us both tea and a slice of toast.

'When will I see you again?' she asked.

'I'll telephone but in a couple of days, probably. Then I'll be gone a while, what with the funeral and there are a few other things that I've got to do. Work, you know?'

She looked over the rim of her cup. 'Yes, work,' she said meaningfully.

There was a long silence before she spoke again.

'George?'

'Yes?'

'You won't let me down, will you?'

'Of course not, we'll go to Paris just like we planned, I promise.'

'That's not what I meant.'

I got up and put my arms around her. 'No. I won't let you down.'

We kissed.

'Don't let old Mrs McConnachie see you leave, will you? Otherwise I'll be the talk of the steamie.' She pushed my nose with the tip of her finger then with a laugh, turned and left.

Twenty minutes later I left too and as I crossed the street and looked up to see old Mrs McConnachie peering out from behind her twitching curtains. I waived and she ducked back in. What the hell, they have to learn sometime.

I pondered Katie's words and my promise. Of course I would let her down, what else could I possibly do? And the sad part of it was, I think she knew it too.

Chapter Twenty-five

The Mitchell Library in North Street near Charing Cross backs on to the magnificent St Andrew's Halls, said to have the best acoustics in Europe. At least it did in 1957; a few years later the great halls burned down after a careless punter dropped a lit cigarette on to the floor during a boxing match and a few hours later the conflagration could be seen from miles around. Fortunately the Mitchell and its priceless collection of books were spared.

It was here, at a desk with a map of Glasgow and a Kelly's Directory before me, that I tried to pin down the exact address of my grandmother and grandfather somewhere in Kings Park. Kelly's printed this massive red bound tome which should have been delivered to my desk by block and tackle instead of by a double herniated old man with a club foot. It listed Glasgow's streets and showed not only the streets but the names of the inhabitants at each point on the street and grandma had said that they lived round the corner from the State cinema. The map showed me the location of the cinema and the array of roads and streets that led off Castlemilk Road on which the State stood. Browsing through the pages, Ashcroft Drive and Midcroft Avenue didn't show anyone by my surname but when I checked Castlemilk Crescent, there, listed at number twenty-seven, was the name Lorne. Surely that had to be it.

A recce was in order and as it was a cold, dry day, I decided to walk the three miles or so to Kings Park and walked through the Gorbals, past close to Katie's house then south until Hampden Park came into view. This wasn't the Hampden Park I knew, this was a vast stadium where up to one hundred and thirty four thousand screaming fans would gather every other spring to join in battle with the auld enemy – England. And every other year the chances were they'd come away with another glorious defeat, talked about for weeks as if it was a great victory. Some things never change.

Twenty minutes later and I was at the junction of Castlemilk Road and Castlemilk Crescent with my heart beating a good bit faster than normal. Not far along, there on the right hand side, was number twenty-seven, home of my grandparents and future father. It was a property that housed four homes, two up and two down. The upstairs properties were accessed by doors at either side while the two doors at the front were for the two ground floor houses. Number twenty-seven was the bottom right. I stood and looked at it for the longest time before I realised I would have to move or somebody would get suspicious and call the police so I walked around the crescent to the main road and walked slowly back again. I was going to have to figure out a way of making sure my grandma was out of the house at a certain time so that I could get inside. That was another thing, how was I going to get in? Grandpa wasn't a problem, he'd be out at work. I knew that when I used to go along to the house in Netherlee grandma would leave the key under a flowerpot for me, or for a tradesman or anyone else she was expecting. Dad used to give her into trouble for that telling her that she was certain to be robbed but she just fobbed him off saying that she's never had any trouble before. So the key was always there, under the non-stop begonias. She kept on leaving it there right up until someone let themselves in, took all her Hummel figures, her seventy-eight rpm single record of 'O Mein Papa', an L.P of the sound track to 'Oklahoma', and a pound of mince that was lying out for dinner that night. Police suspected an inside job. This was winter and there wasn't a begonia in sight but there were some pots to the side of the front door. Maybe, just maybe.

I left and walked back to Nithsdale Road trying to conceive of a plan to make sure that grandma would be out of the house and eventually I remembered what she had mentioned the last time I had seen her. She had a coffee morning every Tuesday. That was tomorrow. I could come back tomorrow morning and as long as the coffee morning wasn't at her house I could try and get in, find the passport and birth certificate, and get out.

I phoned Katie later. She rushed through her routine of announcing the number as if it was just one word.

'It's only me.'

'Hello, only you.'

'How are you today?'

'Tired,' she said shyly.

'I just wanted to hear your voice,' I said, and I think that was the first time I had ever said that to anyone. 'And also to let you know that yesterday – and last night – well, it was all amazing.'

'Yes, it was – for me too,' she said softly. 'Thank you.'

We shared a peaceful silence for a few moments, not awkward at all.

'By the way, Mrs McConnachie said hello.'

'Oh, George – you didn't,' she giggled.

Another pause. 'So,' I said, 'still on for Paris?'

'Oh yes. I spoke to my supervisor today, I can get a few days off from Monday the eleventh. Is that okay?'

I did some arithmetic. The funeral was on the eighth, 2017 time, and I should have confirmation of my massive win on Littlewoods before that so no reason why not.

'That's great, so if I make reservations for leaving, say Tuesday the twelfth, we'll have three nights, plus maybe a night in London on the way there. What do you think?'

'I think it sounds unbelievable, it's like dream,' she sighed. 'Oh, I went to the passport office, it's just off Buchanan Street, and I picked up the forms. I'll get it done and I should have it in a few days. Anything else I need to think about?'

'Only me.'

'I've been doing a lot of that lately,' she said quietly. 'Will I see you soon?'

'Oh, I could manage tomorrow. What would you like to do?'

'Why don't you just come on over?'

'Do you think Mrs McConnachie's heart could stand it?'

She laughed, 'I don't know if mine can.'

'Okay, see you then.'

'Bye.'

Things were moving along quite rapidly now and I knew I was being stupid in complicating matters by getting so heavily involved with Katie but I was having more fun than I had had in years. I was a big man in this world and I could handle it. Yeah, cats' tails go all bushy when I say that sort of thing.

260

I mentally ticked off the things I had to do. Tomorrow morning go and rob grandma. Then go to a travel agent and book the Paris trip. I also needed to up the visits to some friendly bookmakers somewhere out of town to top up the funds although I was doing okay with money. I had a couple of hundred now in the bank plus another sixty or seventy in the house. This could be easily topped up to five or six hundred before I went to Paris. My nocturnal session with Chris's computer had given me a month's worth of race winners so I had plenty of wiggle room. Then, of course, the really big money would come in when the wee man from Littlewoods came knocking at the door. In the meantime there was work to be done. Better to skip Heraghty's tonight, I thought, I needed an early night; there hadn't been much sleep last night with Katie.

I felt a lot fresher in the morning and even went for a three mile run around the streets of the south side much to the interest of the passing public. Obviously jogging hadn't been thought of as much of a leisure or keep fit pursuit back then. According to the advertisements, smoking was better for you.

After a difficult shower juggling the rubber hose, it was time to bite the bullet and head out to Kings Park and by the time I walked out there it was about half past ten. I did a circuit of Castlemilk Crescent and couldn't see any sign of life inside number twenty-seven and hoped to hell that my memory wasn't faulty and that grandma was out at her coffee morning gossiping about anyone unfortunate enough not to be there. It all looked too quiet for it to be her turn. Taking a deep breath I strode up to the front door. An engraved brass plate,

261

gleaming in the light (grandma was *very* house-proud when she was younger, and still is to this day, or should I say...well. you know what I mean) announced the name 'G Lorne'. At least it was definitely the right house so that was a good start. After another deep breath I pressed the doorbell and a shrill ring came from the other side shattering the silence and making me jump. I hadn't expected it be quite so loud. This was a difficult moment; if she answered the door now I don't know how I'd react. Jesus, I don't know how she'd react seeing what could be a twin of her husband standing at the door. She was pregnant, she'd probably break her waters there and then and I had my new shoes on too but fortunately there was no reply.

I looked around but the street was quiet. Nobody seemed to have a car and there wasn't one to be seen either in any of the driveways or parked in the street. The first terracotta pot I looked under had nothing lurking there except a few earwigs scurrying for cover. Neither had the next one, but under the third was a Yale key just as I had hoped and expected. I inserted it into the lock, turned it and the door swung open to a small vestibule off from which there was a door to the left that took me into a tidy sitting room. Suddenly I was overwhelmed with emotion. This was my grandparents' home, for God's sake. It was a part of my history albeit I was never aware of it. My genes lived here. Suddenly I could hardly breathe and I had to sit down on the small sofa. Jesus, I had seen that sofa before. She had it for a while in the house in Netherlee before they bought a new G plan number that she never took the cellophane off for a year in case grandpa soiled it with his very existence. It was all I could do to stop from sobbing. On the dresser there was a photograph of grandma and grandpa on their wedding day, he standing tall and proud, she demure and pretty. An art deco style mirror hung above the mantelpiece and a cheap framed print of two Spanish flamenco dancers on the wall opposite was reflected in it. With another pang of deep nostalgia I recalled that the same picture still hung on a wall in Netherlee sixty years later. I had seen it on my last visit.

I looked again at the photograph on the dresser. The dresser! That was where grandma said that the passports and documents were kept. I went over and opened a drawer but it was filled with cutlery so I opened the one to its left. Inside was a tin that had once held McVittie's biscuits. I felt guilty and cheap opening it which was a bit rich since I had just opened the door to her house. Inside the tin was a stack of papers, some old and dog-eared, others less so. At the bottom of the pile was a passport, one of the real British navy-blue hard-back jobs that proclaimed to any foreign Johnny, 'Look here, don't mess with me, I'm British and Her Brittanic Majesty Requests and Requires you to bend the knee and bring me a gin and tonic while you're at it and be quick about it!' Written in turquoise ink in the little window on the top above the gold lion and unicorn crest was the underlined name, Mr G. Lorne. I flipped it open to the photograph page. It was uncanny. I could have been looking at a photograph of myself.

Quickly looking through the rest of the documents, I found his birth certificate and I slipped it inside the passport, put it in my inside jacket pocket and decided it was time to leave so I quietly pulled the sitting room door shut, stepped out of the vestibule and gently pulled

263

the door closed behind me. That's when I saw her standing there.

We looked at each other in silence for a long moment, long enough for me to realise that it couldn't be grandma. This was a woman older than my grandma would be, and she was heavier and grandma would never be seen dead with nylons rolled to her ankles. She wore heavy lensed glasses and her hair was covered by a turban. Not an actual Indian turban but a scarf that had been tied around her hair and knotted at the front. She wore what my grandmother would have called a 'pinny' around her substantial bulk. She was not - and I don't want to sound uncharitable here - a pretty sight.

'Oh Mr Lorne, ah didnae expect to see you - I thought you'd be at your work but ah heard the door.'

Dear God, she thought I was my grandfather. The only course of action was to feign recognition. 'Oh hello, eh, Mrs...'

She carried on as if she hadn't heard me. 'Ahv'e got a wee problem.'

And I've got a big one, I thought.

'Ye see, ah think ahv'e got a wee fuse and a wonder if you could mebbes fix it for me.'

I looked at my watch, 'Well you see Mrs..er... I'm in a bit of a...'

'That's awfy good o' you. Come away in.'

Dear Lord. She led me around the side of the house to her door which I noted had a name on it, E. Kennedy, and led me straight upstairs to her flat.

'Ah just switched on the kitchen light and there was a bang. Ah think the bulb blew. Bang, just like that. Ahv'e only had it a couple o' years. Must be that cheap

264

Japanese rubbish.' She wiped her hands on her pinafore in anguish.

I had no idea how to fix a fuse. I'd never had a problem like that. When I applied the two hundred and forty volts to Fingal Sharpe's testicles the only things that blew were the small fuse in the plug and the synapses in his brain.

'Where are they, Mrs K?'

'Awfy formal the day Mr Lorne, whit's wrang wi' callin' me Ethel? Where's what?'

'Sorry Ethel, the fuse box.'

'Where it always is, sure - just above the kitchen door.'

Sure enough there was a box over the door near the ceiling. 'Do you have a chair or ladders I can stand on?'

'Haud oan.' She pulled a chair over. 'Ahv'e got some fuse wire somewhere, wait you till I get it for ye.'

Fuse wire?

The box was held closed by two wing screws at either end and they turned with a squeak. When the cover was off all I could see was an array of seven rectangular ceramic plates each about an inch by two and a half inches. I had no idea what they were for.

'Mind and turn it off at the main. Ah don't want ye goin' up in a puff of smoke. Ah'd never get mah dinner.'

This was something that had never occurred to me. What would happen if I electrocuted myself here in 1957? How could I die before I was born? Would all evidence of my existence in 2017 cease to be. What about photographs? Would someone exist in 2017 that was me but wasn't? These existential musings were interrupted by Ethel's insistent voice. It was reminiscent of sanding wood. She had the voice of someone who

265

smoked for a living and was a year away from a voice box.

'Gettin' on okay?'

The big switch at the end was clearly the main so I switched that off and assumed that I was safe. I guessed that the ceramic plates could be pulled out so I tried one that eventually came away revealing a small wire link between two terminals. I pulled another one out and it was the same. On the third one I could see some scorch marks and the wire was broken. Ethel came back with a bit of card with various thickness of wires wrapped around it and it seemed clear that a piece of this wire should be attached to the ceramic fuse switch by looping it around a small screw at either end so that the link was renewed between the two terminals. Ethel found a screwdriver for me and I put it all together using 13 amp wire, put the fuses back in and switched the main on again. She had a spare forty watt bulb and I replaced the dud with it. And God said let there be light and lo, there was light.

'That's great Mr Lorne, ah canny thank ye enough. It must be great tae have a man aboot the hoose.'

'Oh, your husband...' I fished for an answer.

'Aye, a tragedy. Him lost in the war.'

'Missing in action, eh?'

'Aye. Ran aff wi' a dairy maid frae Picardy. Never heard frae him again.'

There was no answer to that.

'A wee cup o' tea for your trouble. Mr Lorne? Ah'm sure ahv'e got a wee chocolate digestive somewhere.'

There was a noise of a door closing downstairs from where I was sitting and I knew I had to get away fast without being seen.

'Thanks, but no Ethel. I just came back for something I forgot. I'm due back and I'm late already.'

'Okay then, Mr Lorne, ah'll see ye later. Mind and tell Jenny ah was askin' for her. And thanks. She's a lucky wumman your Jenny, havin' a strappin' man like you around the hoose. If she ever throws ye oot ye ken where ah am.'

I blanched at the thought. 'Cheerio, Ethel.'

Praying to God that my grandma wasn't looking out of her window, I tiptoed quietly away and disappeared. Mission accomplished.

The next stop was to make the reservations for the trip to Paris. In 2017 there were probably more travel agencies than there were sex orgies in Ibiza but they were pretty thin on the ground in 1957. I remembered that there was a branch of Thomas Cook in Gordon Street and working on the assumption that since he was the guy who first started the whole package tour craze in the nineteenth century then there was probably a Thomas Cook agency around in 1957. Not only was there a branch of it, it was in the same location as it was sixty years later, only instead of the rather twee heart symbol and the in your face Arial style bold font, the frontage merely stated, in a modest and unaffected way, 'Thomas Cook and Son' as if to say 'if you don't know who we are or what we do that's your problem'. The left hand picture window carried a large model of a Boeing 707 in the light blue Pan American livery, surrounded by cardboard cut outs of a representation of the Manhattan skyline. I climbed up the step leading to the glass swing door and a liveried doorman wearing a skip hat with the agency name written around the band opened it for me.

To my left was a long wooden counter and a number of clerks standing or sitting on high stools behind. I went over to the first one I saw free and a black nameplate with gold lettering told me his name was Mr W.Sherrie.

'Can I help you?'

'Yes, you can.'

I told him I what I wanted, first class tickets for two on the Royal Scot to London, a night at a really good hotel, Claridge's perhaps, first class on the "Golden Arrow" the next day and three nights at the Georg Cinq. Then back again to London on the "Golden Arrow" and two first class berths on the overnight sleeper home again. I gave him the dates and he wrote it all down on a buff form. He asked for the names and I told him.

'Might be a little problem, Mr Lorne.'

I suddenly realised that there was, in fact, a hell of a big problem. Katie thought my name was George Clooney, how the hell was I going to keep the fact that she was travelling with Gordon Lorne, name of her ex boyfriend and whose passport was the one under which I planned to travel? Shit, I'd have to deal with that one later.

'Oh, what's that?' I asked.

'It's against the rules for us to make hotel reservations for unmarried couples. In a double room, that is.'

I looked at him blankly then almost laughed. 'You're kidding, right?'

'No, absolutely serious.' This was unbelievable. 'I'm sorry I don't make the rules,' he shrugged.

I grasped at a straw. 'She's my fiancée.'

He shrugged again – any more and he'd crease his jacket. 'I wish I could help, I'm on commission here and it's a slow month,' he said mournfully.

Aahh. 'Look, Mr – eh – Mr Sherrie, is there a quiet room where we can talk. I may be able to come to a solution which would be mutually beneficial.'

He looked at me and considered it. 'Follow me, Mr Lorne,' he said, almost reluctantly.

He led me to a small office at the rear of the building, with a desk and some chairs where he motioned me to take a seat and he sat behind the desk.

He folded his hands in front of him on the desk. 'What do you have in mind?'

'Here's what I suggest. You reserve the hotel in London as Mr and Mrs Lorne, they won't ask for identification there, so that's not an issue.'

'But I think it might be against the law.'

'Gravity is a law, Mr Sherrie, all the rest are just rules.' I continued, 'You book the Paris train in our real names, no rule about unmarried people travelling together, is there?'

He shook his head.

'You book the Ceorge Cinq in our real names – this is Paris we're talking about Mr Sherrie, they don't give a toss over there who you sleep with. In fact if I'm not much mistaken sleeping with your wife in a hotel in France is considered a bizarre aberration.'

He smiled at that. 'The problem is, Mr Lorne, I have to send the request to our hotels department in London. They won't process it.'

'Ah, well, no. You phone the hotel direct, don't worry,' I held my hand up, 'I'll pay all charges.'

'Phone? To Paris?'

I keep forgetting this is 1957. 'Yes, I'm sure it's possible. You can send a pigeon if you want.'

He made a sideways sort of nod with his head.

269

'You said something about it being mutually beneficial?'

And there it was, back scratching time.

'Are you a gambling man, Mr Sherrie?'

'What?'

'A gambling man, are you?'

'What are you talking about?' he asked, puzzled.

'Bear with me, are you?' I pressed.

'The odd flutter, nothing serious, why?'

'I am going to give you the names of four horses running this afternoon at two different racecourses. They are going to win, don't ask me how I know, they just are. If you put a one pound bet on a roll up this will yield you almost two hundred pounds. That's a lot of money, Mr Sherrie, maybe, what, two, three months' salary, I'm guessing.'

I usually only bet on three horses but I figured this would be a one off for him so why not let him make a killing.

He looked at me as if I was mad. 'Are you serious?'

'Never more so.'

'Mr Lorne, I can't afford to throw away a pound.'

I sat back. 'I'll tell you what, Mr Sherrie. If you put that pound on and by some chance the bet loses, then I will not only reimburse the pound, but I will pay out myself when I come back tomorrow, how's that?'

He demurred, 'I don't know.'

'What have you got to lose? Oh, and as a gesture of goodwill I'll leave you a fifty pounds deposit until I see you tomorrow.' I took a wad of notes from my pocket.

He nodded slowly, doubt slowly dispelling.

'How much is this going to cost me anyway,' I asked nodding at his paper work.

270

'I can't say exactly until I talk to the hotels but I would say in the region of two hundred to two hundred and thirty pounds,' he said writing some figures down.

'There you are. Do what I tell you and you could go to Paris yourself.'

I wrote out the names of the four horses and got up and made to go. 'Till tomorrow then. Oh, just one more thing. Make sure you place your bet in a bookie's in St Enoch Square. To the right and up one flight of stairs.'

Sandy would be pleased.

Two down. I took a train to Johnstone, found a bookie there just off the square and made my bet, going through the same ritual of losing a small bet first. Before the winning races started I took a train back to Paisley and did the same in a side street then went for a cup of tea in a cafe until the races were over before going back and collected sixty-two pounds seven and sixpence. Then I went back up to Johnstone and collected the same amount. It all went off without a hitch and I made my way back to Glasgow wondering just how long I could keep this up without word getting out. I was amassing money much faster than I could ever spend it even taking into account my jaunt to Paris. I'd take a trip to Dumbarton and Helensburgh tomorrow and do the same thing there. Two days and that was Paris paid for.

Looking back on the last two or three days amazed me. I realised that not only was I in a different era, I was a different person. I had money, I was confident, I mean, just look at the way I had sorted out that Sherrie fellow, he'd be offering me his daughter tomorrow. The problem was, there were times I didn't want to go back

271

(forward actually) to my old life or the old me. And then there was Katie.

Ah yes, and then there was Katie.

I walked over to her place around sevenish to find Frankie singing 'Come Fly With Me' on her Dansette and Katie singing an unintentional harmony in the kitchen, she called it a scullery, preparing some food.

'Lamb chops okay?' she asked after blowing me a kiss.

'Sounds good to me,' I replied and it did.

I wiggled the two bottles of Beaujolais that I'd managed to find in an off licence on the way over. There hadn't been much choice and the shopkeeper had to blow a bit of dust off of them and I think they were the last two – or the only two. Wine clearly wasn't the tipple of choice yet.

'Oh my, let me see if I've got a corkscrew.' She rummaged through the contents of a drawer for half a minute before emerging triumphantly with something passable and I popped the cork and poured.

'I took the form to the passport office today. I had to get the minister to sign that he knew me and that I was a person of good character. If he knew what I was up to last night I would be eternally damned. He had to sign the photos as well.'

Katie was clearly sparkling with excitement at the prospect of going abroad.

She continued, 'He asked me where I was going and I told him I was off to Paris with a friend. I got the impression that he knew it was with a man. He just said he hoped I knew what I was doing.'

Inwardly I thought that I hoped I knew what I was doing.

'Have you booked it yet?' she called from the scullery.

272

I told her about my trip to Cook's and that it was all in hand but she wanted to know details. The more I told her, the more excited she got.

'First class! On the train. What about lunch?'

Yes, I assured her, we would be served lunch in the dining car.

'London! I've heard so much about it. Oh, George!' She held out her glass for a refill.

We could take in a show, I told her, The Threepenny Opera was on and she'd heard of Kurt Weill but maybe that would be rushing things when we got there.

'The "Golden Arrow"! First Class! This is amazing. Who'd have thought it. Katie McWilliam from Calder Street off to Paris in style. Wait till I tell the girls!'

I told her about the Georg Cinq and how Eisenhower stayed there immediately after the liberation of Paris barely thirteen years before. I told her about Maxim's where the Duke of Windsor and Wallis Simpson sometimes dined as well as Onassis and Betty Hutton. I had no idea who Betty Hutton was, I just saw it on Wikipedia, but the mention of her name was enough to set Katie off again. If we were going to get a table there, and it was a big if, I was going to have to grease a palm or two.

We talked some more then she grilled the chops and we sat down in a cosy corner of the room at a small table. They were not so much cooked as cremated but I crunched my way through them happily. I had learned that medium or rare cooked meat was unheard of; if it wasn't cooked until it could be used for a major shoe repair then it was considered raw and inedible.

When went to bed Katie was hyper with excitement, probably more to do with the forthcoming trip than the prospect of a tumble with me but perhaps I put myself down. I snuck out in the early hours to give Katie a chance to get some sleep and I could swear that when I crossed the street Mrs McConnachie's curtains opened slightly but it could have been my imagination. The cold air was damp on me so I speed walked home to Nithsdale Road, a happy man for the moment.

Chapter Twenty-six

The River Clyde was grey and mottled as molten pewter as the train passed through the shipyard country of the north side, through Singer and its giant clock near where Sandy's heavies had given me such a thumping. The train rolled on until we reached Dumbarton where I got off and looked for the inevitable bookie. You could always find one, illegal or not and the poorer the town the more they had. There was one in a street that ran down towards the famous rock and although it was early and racing hadn't started there were still a few hopefuls with the housekeeping money hoping for a big payday.

I put on my line which, all being well, would yield me over sixty pounds, then left and took another train on to Helensburgh where I repeated the procedure. Then I took the train back to Glasgow to see how my reservations to Paris were progressing. It meant that I would have to come back out again this afternoon to collect my winnings but there were worse ways to earn big money and in 1957 a hundred and twenty quid was serious cash.

It was after lunch when I got to Cook's. The same doorman opened the door and doffed his cap and Mr Sherrie looked up when he saw me and motioned me to the private room we had been in the day before.

'Good morning Mr Sherrie.'

'Good morning Mr Lorne.'

'So did you have a profitable day?' I asked, interested to see if he had taken my advice.

'I didn't put on the pound that you recommended, Mr Lorne.'

'Oh, why was that?' I asked somewhat disappointed.

'Actually I put on two pounds.'

I smiled. Sandy would definitely not be a happy man. 'And?'

'Thanks to you, Mr Lorne, I'm nearly four hundred pounds the richer. The bookie had to go out to the bank to get more cash. That's a fortune. I'm not going to ask you how you knew.' He looked at me as if he was asking me exactly that.

'That's good, Mr Sherrie, because I couldn't tell you. Now, about my booking.'

He smiled good-naturedly as well he might. That was half a year's wages in his back pocket. Good man that he was, he had everything fixed up for me just as I had asked and all the vouchers and tickets were tucked away in a snazzy little wallet. The total bill was two hundred and forty pounds, a bit more than I thought but he explained that he had to book a mini suite at the Georg Cinq as that was the best available. That was all fine by me.

'What about currency, Mr Lorne?'

'Yes, can you fix that?'

'Sure, do you have your passport with you? I can only give you a maximum of sixty-five pounds each because of currency restrictions but that should be plenty. Strictly speaking I should have offset your Paris hotel against that but as you say, it's only a rule.' He smiled at that.

'Sounds good,' I smiled back

He picked up an intercom and spoke to someone and a few minutes later a grey suited man with a protruding lower jaw came in with a folder filled with a large array of brightly coloured notes.

'There's twelve hundred and seventy francs there, Mr Lorne. The exchange rate is nine point eight francs to the pound. Okay? Anything you don't spend bring it back and I'll change it back to sterling.'

Although I planned on spending every penny, or should I say, centime, I agreed and he counted it out, entered it into the rear of my passport and stamped it together with an insert for Katie's when it came.

Then I counted out three hundred and seventy pounds to Mr Sherrie, shook his hand and said. 'Pleasure doing business with you, Mr Sherrie.'

'Pleasure doing business with you too, Mr Lorne.'

I turned to go then looked back at him.

'A word to the wise, Mr Sherrie – whatever you do, don't go back to that bookie again.'

The trip back out to Helensburgh and Dumbarton was uneventful and I picked up my winnings and got the train back. I planned a similar excursion tomorrow to Falkirk and Grangemouth. They can't hit a moving target.

The problem with living in 1957 is that there are no supermarkets, no ready meals, no Indian or Chinese restaurants, precious little pub grub and I'm not much of the kind of person that likes to cook in for one. There were a few eateries but the choices were very spartan. However the Horseshoe, even back then, did a pretty good number in bar meals and I was able to get a decent plate of soup followed by an excellent mince and tatties washed down with a couple of pints. Feeling very content with a good days' work I briskly walked out to Shawlands and Heraghty's where, true to form, Phil, the human dirigible and Eric and Benny were holding forth at the bar.

'Ah, the very man,' said Phil, in a voice that woke two sleeping children in Giffnock. 'We were just talking about you. Jim, a pint for the man here.'

'Oh, what's that all about then?'

It was Benny that spoke, 'Seems you've brought Sandy Corcoran nothing but bad luck.'

My ears pricked up, 'Oh, how?'

'Oh, whisper is that some punter walked in, put down a four horse roll up and a couple of quid and walked out with four hundred near enough. Any more of that and Sandy'll be out of business.'

I picked up the pint and took a sip. 'Lucky man.'

'Aye, right enough. No' a regular - just walked in, came back took the money and disappeared.'

'Poor Sandy, eh?'

'Aye', said Benny, 'Anybody you know?'

'Me?' I said in feigned surprise, 'No, if I knew that I'd have had money on them myself.'

'Right enough,' said Benny with a sly smile on his face. 'Word on the street is that Sandy's in trouble. I'm told that a few of the heavy brigade had a few pounds on Sandy's dog. They think Sandy was up to something and they want to talk to him. He hasn't been seen for a few days. Lying low by the sounds of it.'

'Poor old Sandy,' I mused.

'Poor might just be the word. I've a feeling Sandy has overstretched. He's been taking a beating and he's got a

278

few markers out. Word is he's broke – maybe done a runner.'

'My heart bleeds.'

'Come on over here you lot and sit doon,' said Phil leading me and the others over to a table. 'You were going to give us the benefit of your entrepreneurial wisdom.'

We took our drinks over to a table.

'What do you think I can help you with, Phil?'

'Well, as I told you, I'm a journalist,' he started.

'Reporter,' interrupted Eric.

'Do you want tae drink that pint or wear it, Eric – your choice?'

'Sorry, journalist,' said Eric with a wink at Benny.

'Right, where was I?' he went on, 'Aye, you told us that you were into – what was it? – statistical analysis or something – predicting the future.'

'No – I just analyse trends and marry it to ongoing technology so that business can plan ahead,' I said, I didn't want him to think I was some sort of astrologer.

'Plan ahead? You can hardly plan behind,' said Eric and Phil drew him a warning look.

'I just want to write an article for the paper that people might read and say 'That's interesting, I wonder if that will really happen?' - you know what I mean?'

I knew what he meant but I could hardly tell him.

Phil went on, 'I mean, where do you see the biggest changes?'

I thought about it trying to put into words something that wouldn't sound like science fiction on the one hand and make me look like the alien I was on the other.

'I've been working on a few things, Phil, and that stretches my imagination. Have you thought about medicine?'

'How do you mean?'

'What do you know about transplants?'

'Transplants?' asked Benny.

'Organ transplants, liver, kidneys, heart – that sort of thing.'

'I don't know anything about that,' said Phil.

Thank fuck for that, I thought, I knew bugger all about them either but in the land of the blind the man with one eye is king.

'Well there's a start for you then.'

'How d'you mean? Where are they going to get the livers and things?'

'Dead people.'

'You're fucking joking. You mean they'll kill people for their organs? Burke and Hare? Is this the sort of thing you forecast?' Phil was horrified; so were the others.

'No, no, no. There are people who die, sadly, in car accidents, falling off roofs, it could be anything. Why not use their perfectly healthy organs to save other lives?'

'Are you serious?' asked Phil, still clearly appalled.

'Listen, if your son or daughter or someone close like your wife...'

Eric laughed, 'Maybe no' his wife.'

'Okay, whoever – if you could have their life saved by getting a transplant I bet you'd jump at it.'

They all looked at each other and shrugged.

'And you think that'll happen?' asked Benny.

'Yeah, I do. Sooner than you think.'

280

Phil had a pencil and notepad in his hand and took some notes.

I carried on in full flow. 'How many people do you know that have had heart attacks, plenty I'll bet.'

'Joe Hunter died month, just forty-five he was,' said Eric. 'Dropped like a stone in the street, died in hospital that night.'

'Maybe if it had happened ten years from now he might have survived.' At that I thought of my own father and how nothing would have saved him.

'How so?'

'You know most heart attacks are caused by blocked arteries in the heart so the blood doesn't go through. Well, just suppose they were able to put a wee balloon or something in there to make it wider. Or maybe bypass it altogether, just put a new artificial artery around the blocked one.'

Phil was scribbling furiously in a mixture of shorthand and longhand.

Benny asked, 'How do you know all this stuff?'

'Och, I don't – but things move forward. If you think a lot of this stuff is science fiction just think of what people would have said three or four hundred year ago if you told them what would happen in the middle of the twentieth century.'

Eric looked at me.

'They used to cure you with things like bleeding, purging, cold baths, you name it. Anything but the thing that would cure you.' I knew about these things. I had seen 'The Madness of King George'.

They were all listening now, even Jim.

281

'What would they have said about penicillin, disinfectant, aspirin, antibiotics, statins.' In was in full flow now. Actually I was in overflow.

'Statins?' asked Phil.

'Yes, for your cholesterol.'

They looked at me the same way your mother looks at you when she's not sure whether you're telling porkies or not. I realised that I might have gone too far.

'Sorry, shouldn't have said that, that's classified information – about statins and cholesterol I mean. But I'll tell you this and I'll say no more – the three of you smoke like a Red Indian communications centre, so here's some free advice. If you don't give it up, statistically one of you at least will die early of lung cancer. Trust me on that.'

I took a large gulp of my four point five per cent alcohol by volume pint that gave my liver something to think about while they digested this.

'They say there's no evidence that smoking does you any harm,' said Benny looking doubtfully at his smouldering Capstan Full Strength.

'Who says?' I asked.

'The tobacco companies.'

I looked at him with one of those looks. He frowned thoughtfully as he stubbed the cigarette out.

'So Phil, there's a wee starter for you. Why don't you do a five day series. 'What the Future Holds', by Phil – what's your second name?'

'Gillespie.'

'By Phillip Gillespie.' I described a banner headline with my hands. 'Today, medicine; tomorrow, transport – then communications, leisure and so on.'

He smiled as he put his notebook into his jacket pocket.

'You know, George – you talk a load of shite. But I'll say this – it's good shite.'

They all laughed as did I and we drank up and agreed to catch up in a day or so.

A period of high pressure had eased in and the brilliant blue sky belied the bitter cold that numbed the skin. Miniature icebergs floated down the Clyde and there was a skin of ice across the boating pond on Queens Park. It was Wednesday and nearly a week had gone by since I left the comforts or otherwise of the twenty-first century and people would be thinking of reporting me missing to the police, or at least divvying up my collection of Beatles albums so I thought I'd give it another day to bring in some more cash before making the transition back again.

If it hadn't been for the pleasure of relieving the bookies of some of their easy earned cash the visits further and further afield might have been boring but I travelled back from Falkirk and Grangemouth, no two towns less likely to feature in a two centre holiday brochure, with one hundred and thirty two pounds tucked inside my jacket pocket. It was like taking candy from a kid, but where that would have been mean, I felt that by taking the bookies money I was simply redistributing wealth. Okay, I was redistributing it in my direction but so what?

Katie was happy to hear from me but she couldn't see me later as she had planned to go to the Plaza with her pals and that was fine by me. She was worried that I might be unhappy about it.

'Are you sure, George? I mean I can cancel it.'

'No, don't. Keep your friends close, Katie. You never know when you're going to need them.'

'If you're sure.'

'I'm sure. Oh, listen. I picked up all the tickets today for the trip so we're all set, that's the good news.'

She squealed in delight. 'Ooh I can't wait. Oh, what's the bad news?'

'I won't see you for a few days. I have to do some stuff for the funeral, you know, and something has come up at work and I need to, well – the thing is I'll be out of touch.'

'Oh', she sounded disappointed. 'When will you be *in* touch?'

'After the funeral. Soon as.'

'Hurry back.'

'Sure. Missing you already.'

'George?'

'Yes?'

'Where do you learn to talk that sort of rubbish?'

Chapter Twenty-seven

It was three minutes to eight as I walked confidently under the Central station clock and three minutes to eight sixty years later when I emerged into a rather different and quieter concourse somewhat startling a hen party dressed in pink sashes and precious little else for their night out on the town.

I had purposely left all my old money back in Nithsdale Road and I had no modern money on me and my cash card was back in the flat so there was nothing for it but to make my way home in the rain and by the time I reached Partick I was soaked through and through. At least I could have a decent shower and I languished under the sheer pleasure of it for twenty minutes rather than kneeling down in a bath with a rubber hose trying to get wet. Anybody from the twenty-first century seeing that would have thought that I was into some form of autoeroticism – nothing could be further from the truth.

Everything in the fridge was green. The butter was green, the bread was green, the cheese was green; the only thing that wasn't green was the remains of some lettuce which was black. I couldn't even face looking at it so I just closed the door. I was too tired to be arsed about anything anyway so I just went to bed. When I looked at my mobile the next morning it was text city. Barry, Susan, Christine, my mum, Lara, even one from Lesley. Half a dozen from Barry saying he wanted to catch up and another one saying he *really* wanted to catch up plus a half a dozen from Susan that descended from cheery to annoyance then to worry about my lack of communication. There were also a few from Chris that started badly then fell away. Lesley just wanted me to call her – odd. Lara and my mum just wanted to go over funeral arrangements. I met up with Barry first.

'Everybody wants to know where you were,' he complained.

'I could hardly phone, could I?'

This was not the Barry I knew and loved, as a mate that is, I don't want you to get the wrong idea. He looked jaded and had lost the sparkle and joie de vivre that had the rest of us look up to him, particularly the girl that he was on top of at the time. He needed a shave and he clearly needed the pint and the double that were sitting in front of him as we sat in a corner of the Horseshoe.

'How are things in post war Glasgow then?'

He asked this in a rather desultory way as if it was of secondary importance instead of being the road to his permanent financial wellbeing.

'Everything just as planned, Baz old son, I can still call you that can I? By the way, I see you're not giving in to the teetotal regime.'

He glowered at me.

'Okay, okay, I'll talk to Chris.' I went on hurriedly, 'Is she still hooked up with Brian? Is he still her official escort to the Barbados bash?'

'No.'

Shit. I was hoping he was. I was going to have to come clean with her about Susan. There was no way I could take Chris to the wedding and expect Susan to wear that.

Baz continued, 'He's not taking her because the whole thing's off.'

'What? Did they not see eye to eye?'

He looked at me witheringly. 'I mean me and Lesley.'

'Jesus, Baz.'

'Yep, so there's no Caribbean wedding. It's all over.'

'What happened?'

He finished his Scotch and pushed the empty glass towards me. I got the message and bought him another. He told me the whole story. After dragging him through John Lewis for the fiftieth time looking for the right shade of Crueset to match the new kitchen tiles that had been ordered at twenty-one pounds per square metre she had dropped him with a bombshell.

'No sex till after the wedding.'

'*What?*'

'That's right. She wanted us to have a wedding that was filled with purity of body as well as soul so that we would both be cleansed to start our future life together.'

'She expected you to go three months without sex with her? Has she been reading something in 'Cosmopolitan' again?'

'So it was to be no more hanky panky for a while,' he said mournfully.

'Just hanky, then.'

He looked at me through narrowed eyes. It was a wake- up call. Apparently since the engagement sex had been pretty well hit and miss anyway and Barry figured if it was like that before the wedding what chance was there afterwards. Looking at the state of his finances and the rate that Lesley was spending his money Barry thought that paying for a live in hooker would be cheaper and without the need to minutely examine paint tester pots.

'So what did you tell her?'

'I just went over to her place and told her straight that it wasn't going to work and could she make sure to get a refund on the Russell Flint signed prints. I wanted to stop it going any further before we booked flights and everything.'

It seemed her mother was there and there was a bit of a scene involving threats to sue for sexual assault on the grounds that he used the promise of marriage to obtain Lesley's sexual favours and it all went downhill from there.

'Barry,' I said solicitously, 'You did the right thing. She was a frigid cow. I never even got a feel of a nipple.'

He shot me a warning look.

'Sorry. It was a long time ago.' I shuffled my feet.

'The thing is, Gord, I know it would be a disaster, but the problem is, I still love her.'

'You'll get over it, mate,' I said jauntily, 'Give Chris a call. She'll have you on your feet in no time – or your back.'

Next up was Susan.

'Where on earth have you been?'

'I lead an interesting life. How have you been? Any more trouble from action man?'

'Not a cheep. He'll be in Germany now. Do I get to see you?'

'Tonight?'

'Tonight. Shall I bring a Chinese and we'll eat in?' I asked hopefully.

288

'Make it Indian. I hear spice is an aphrodisiac.'

Chris was less receptive.

'Where the fuck have you been?'

'Nice to see you too.' I was standing in her hallway waiting to be invited in.

'Don't!'

'Look, you said it yourself, you're a free spirit – we're not joined at the hip, all that stuff, remember?'

'I didn't expect you to take it literally,' she yelled with all the irrationality of a woman who wants to have her cake and eat it too.

'How else do you want me to take it? If I recall correctly Brian Bifocal was in your bed at the time.'

'So?'

As an argument that was unanswerable.

'Can't we be adult about this, Chris?'

'So you're dumping me for that slapper Susan Sharpe. That's what men always say. "Let's be adult about this".'

'I'm sorry Chris,' and I was.

She walked into her lounge and I followed.

She spoke in a more resigned tone. 'I really didn't want to go to the wedding with Brian. He's nice enough but he could bore for Scotland.'

'You'll not be going to the wedding with anybody. There is no wedding. It's all off – cancelled – over – finito.'

She was stunned, 'What?'

'You hadn't heard?'

'No – when?'

'I just saw Barry today – a couple of days ago, I think.'

She took this in and sighed. 'Fuck. I always wanted to see the Caribbean.' She looked at me dejectedly, 'Tell me, how much on a scale of Sydney Devine to The Stones do you like Susan?'

'Enough at the moment.'

'Damn and double bugger. I suppose a quick shag is out of the question, I haven't had any in four days.'

Leaving Chris's apartment with my dignity and all else still intact I thought I'd better call Lara to see what was happening. Lesley I had no intention of getting back to. In the end it wasn't necessary; she called me. She was almost hysterical although there were times it was difficult to tell the difference.

'You've got to make him see sense, Gordon.' She wailed.

I was under the impression that had already happened but I didn't want to say.

'I'm not sure there's much I can do,' I said wearily.

'Talk to him, for God's sake – you're his friend.'

'Look Lesley, better you both find out now.'

'Find out what, Gordon?'

'That it's not going to work. You don't want to spend the rest of your life in misery. Marry in haste and all that.'

'I thought he loved me,' she said, her voice breaking.

'I think he loved the old you, Lesley, but you have gone a bit over the top recently.'

According to Barry she had gone so much over the top she could have overrun the German trenches.

'I mean, the 'no sex' thing? Come on,' I reasoned.

She sniffed. 'I just wanted things to be perfect. Do you think there's someone else?'

'Barry? No – definitely not.' I didn't tell her that she had probably put Barry off women for a very long time.

290

'Just tell him I need to talk to him, will you do that?' she pleaded.

'I'll try. No promises.' I hung up.

I talked to Lara but she had everything under control for dad's funeral, even the insignificant details, like me for instance. I said I'd meet her at mum's house so that we would all drive together. There was a memorial service at Greenbank church organised and she had booked a mini bus for some mourners to go from there to the crematorium. I was clearly redundant so I went for a long run then headed over to Susan's.

I spent the next few days hovering between Partick and Susan's place while meeting up with Barry to try and ease his pain. He was torn between the anguish of breaking off with Lesley and the joy of seeing some financial relief, his bank account had been haemorrhaging money faster than a Jimmy Durante nosebleed. The news that in only just over a week he would be very rich indeed cheered him up to the point that he deleted Lesley from his contacts list. Good on him - he had resolutely refused to take her calls even after I told him she had spoken to me.

'It's for the best, Gord,' he said to me over a pint. 'I was suffocating. I was starting to feel like someone had put a plastic bag over my head. In fact it had come to the point when I wished someone *would* put a plastic bag over my head.'

He asked me how I was managing in my alternative life but I didn't want to talk about Katie and my Paris plans. I had a feeling he wouldn't understand and anyway, I didn't want to rub salt in the wounds of his enforced celibacy while I was copulating like a demented rabbit in two different time zones.

'When are you going back through the clock?' he asked as if I was Alice Through the Looking-Glass.

'After the funeral, I guess. I'll be there by the way.'

'Cheers, mate. Yeah – probably Thursday – day after the funeral,' I replied.

'And then what?'

'I'll probably be there for around a week to ten days trying to get everything sorted, you know. I haven't figured out how to get the diamonds. There could be a complication.'

'Oh, what?'

'Currency exchange restrictions. Back then you couldn't just take money in and out so I need to work out a way to beat the system. I'll come up with something though. Maybe this will be the last trip – it can't go on forever.'

'Good luck, mate –can't wait.'

Looking back on it now I should have had somebody from the Monty Python team attend the funeral then turn it into an award winning script. I realised this would be an event somewhat out of the ordinary when mum, Lara and I met at Lara's where the main mourners' car was to leave from. The living room was decked out in party balloons. I looked at Lara in amazement.

'It's not a time for grief, Gordon, it's a celebration.'

'Celebration? Dad's dead.'

'A celebration of his life. We shouldn't be sad, look at all the things he's achieved. We wouldn't be here without him, would we mum?'

Mum just looked bewildered, Mark stoically stayed in the background drinking his coffee, wise man, and Lara had Keith awaiting instructions.

'Just wait till you see the coffin,' Keith said sotto voce to me darkly.

I caught grandma's eye and although she was a drawn and muted, she looked over at me and winked.

We drove to the church in a stately black limo and I was gratified to see such a good turnout of his former colleagues many of whom were wearing their company uniform. Dad would have been proud - what he would have made of the coffin I couldn't begin to guess. It was a stout cardboard affair made from recycled materials and was covered with a variety of different photographs of my father at various stages in his life, each one framed inside a coloured balloon. On the top of the coffin was written a stanza from his favourite song, John Denver's 'Leavin' on a Jet Plane', clearly as a reference to his aviation career but I don't think Lara had thought this one through. I suppose it could have been worse. Barry's uncle had shuffled off to Queen's 'And Another One Bites The Dust'.

The mourners had all been encouraged to wear something colourful by way of celebration, a token that I thought was entirely appropriate. However some of the congregation had taken it a little too literally and the event began to look more like a university rag day. The minister manfully tried to cope with this and the fact that he was there to pay homage to a man he had never met in his life and who had latterly been a lush of epic proportion. I gave him an A+ for effort and a C for content.

Once outside the church Lara had laid on a minibus to take people to the Linn Crematorium. She should have perhaps checked out the company fleet first.

Emblazoned along the side was a picture of a clown and the strapline, 'Your Cheery Wee Bus'.

The pièce de resistance was the presence of the Strathclyde Syncopated Dixieland Jazz Band slowly leading the cortege up the winding drive to the crematorium playing a version, unknown inside any church, of 'Just a Closer Walk With Thee.' At least, that was what the trumpeter was playing, I don't know about the others. The Linn had seats for about two thirds of the attendees and as a result we were all squeezed tightly together. Although damp, it was an unseasonably warm day outside and the heating in the building had been turned up to maximum on account of the fact that it was a Scottish February and the expectation was of chilly temperatures. As a result the temperature in the inside of the chapel swiftly climbed to around eighty degrees and higher and steam from damp clothes rose ceilingwards. There was danger of clouds forming at one end and had someone opened the door and let in some cool air the two fronts could have met and started a shower.

Just as the last strains of 'The Lord's my Shepherd' faded away and the coffin slowly disappeared to the furnaces, the temperature reached ninety and I clearly heard someone, it could have been Barry, say sotto voce, 'And we think it's hot.' Back outside the Strathclyde Syncopated Dixieland Jazz Band valiantly tackled a spirited version of 'When The Saints Go Marching In' with a renewed vigour that made up for its lack of expertise and several feet were tapping in time to the beat including, I noticed, grandma's. Meanwhile from the chimney of the crematorium billions of my father's atoms swirled away to become part of earth's continuing evolution.

Grandma and I sat next to each other at the reception in the Busby Hotel.

'I don't know what to think, Gordon dear,' she said. 'I've been to grimmer weddings, my own for a start.'

'It was nothing to do with me, grandma, it was all down to Lara.'

'Yes it was, and do you know, I can't thank her enough. It may have been a touch irreverent but nobody here will forget it. I think I'll get her to do mine.'

Chapter Twenty-eight

The nightmare of Wednesday had passed. Afterwards I went back to Susan's house, I just couldn't think of being on my own. It was my turn to talk and it all came tumbling out, my father's slow spiral into alcoholism, my mother finally giving up, and my own miserable failure at making a life. Susan baulked at this and made a brave attempt to lift my spirits. We went to bed.

'Okay Romeo, on top or underneath?'

'Oh, on top, there's too many shoes underneath.'

'Oh ha ha. Somebody's got his sense of humour back.'

'You know what they say, laughter's the best medicine.'

'Yep. Unless you've got diabetes. Then it's definitely insulin.'

Now that was funny.

Afterwards in the dark with Susan slumbering peacefully beside me I pondered on the morality of what I was doing. Was I cheating on Susan with Katie? Can you cheat on someone who technically you slept with sixty years ago? The same went for Katie. Right now Katie was probably no longer alive or if she was she'd be in her nineties. How could I possibly be cheating on her? But I was, and I knew it and that only made me more miserable. I turned over but sleep still wouldn't come and I lay awake until light started to drift in through the curtains.

I had told Susan I wasn't going to be around for a good few days, probably over a week and she didn't question it so Thursday night saw me back sixty years in Nithsdale Road trying to get the frost off the inside of the windows and chipping ice out of the toilet bowl.

I calculated how much I had in my account at the bank and it was over six hundred pounds – a small fortune and Paris was already paid for. I thought I'd give it one more run at creaming the bookies just to keep my hand in and I spent the next day in Airdrie and Coatbridge and came back just over a hundred pounds richer. So far the plan had paid off handsomely and tomorrow, Saturday, should be jackpot day. I knew that the teams I had chosen were all going to play their part but I wanted to listen to the results on the radio just for the thrill of it. Then, just as a celebration that only I would know about, I thought I would treat Katie to a dinner at The Malmaison in Hope Street, almost opposite the One-0-One where we had our first fabulous meal together so I gave her a call and she answered in the usual breathless rush.

'Hi sweetheart, happy to hear from me?'

'Oh yes, yes.'

'Dancing tonight? Girls night out?'

'Yes, Plaza. You don't mind, do you?' she asked. 'How was the funeral? I was thinking about you.'

'Sad, but it's over.' I didn't want to go into detail.

'And you're sure you're okay?'

'I'm sure.'

'As long as you are,' she said doubtfully. 'Is Paris still on? I've bought a new outfit.'

'You bet. In fact I'll buy you another one when we're there.'

She laughed. 'No need. I've missed you.'

'Me too. Oh, you know what I mean. Listen, would you like a dinner on the town tomorrow night. Maybe the Malmaison for a change.'

'Oh George, that would be lovely but you're spoiling me, really. I could just come over to yours for a fry up.'

I didn't think this was a good idea. I didn't know if there was anything incriminating lying around and besides the place never seemed to get warm.

'Tell you what – we'll eat out tomorrow and when we get back from Paris you can come over and give me some home improvement tips.' I felt a heel saying this because I knew things were nearing an end. 'I'll see you at seven if that suits.'

'Okay George, see you then.'

I met up with the team in Heraghty's which was just what I needed; some let your hair down, Friday night banter. Phil was at his most expansive in every sense of the word.

'George, come away in. It's Eric's round. Come on ya tight bastard, dig deep and never mind the moths.'

'Aye, aye, gie's a break, will ye,' said Eric, 'Usual?'

I nodded a yes.

'So,' said Phil, 'My editor liked the idea.'

'What idea?' I was puzzled.

'The series. We're going to call it 'Windows on Tomorrow's World'.'

I remembered the talk we had the last time.

'So tell me more. Get out your crystal ball.'

'I told you, it's just reasoned analysis.'

But he wasn't listening, he was reaching for his notebook. 'What about transport? Everybody loves the idea of travelling.'

I sighed, 'Okay Phil, what happened in 1903?'

'I don't know. What happened in 1903?'

'The Wright Brothers. The first recorded aeroplane flight. Only a few yards and a few seconds, but still.'

'And?' asked Benny.

'Then Bleriot crossed the Channel. Then aeroplanes were used to bomb the trenches, then airlines started flying with passengers after the first world war.' Thank God for Wikipedia, I thought. 'Then there were passenger flights to Australia and America in the thirties. You see what I'm getting at?'

'No' really George. That's all very interesting but it's history - I could check that myself.'

'It's incremental is what I'm saying.'

'I don't follow,' said Eric.

'Just a wee bit at a time. Today it's DC7's and Stratocruisers going to New York in fourteen hours. What If I told you that by the end of the decade, in a couple of years, you could fly in a jet in seven hours?'

'Seriously?'

'Seriously. Why not?' I went on. 'And probably in half that again in another ten or fifteen years.'

'Come on,' expostulated Benny.

'The thing is Benny, if it can be done, it will be done.'

We all took a gulp of our drinks. I noticed that Benny wasn't smoking but I didn't say anything.

'Your aeroplanes today now carry what, fifty people. Soon it will be eighty, then a hundred, then two hundred and then five hundred.'

'Five hundred! Are you off your head?'

'No Phil, that's what I mean by incremental. A bit at a time. Technology just gets better every year, all you need is imagination.'

Phil shook his head in wonder. 'Is that what you get paid for, making these predictions?'

'Yes and no. I analyse trends. You've got to anticipate what the public wants. No use having big aeroplanes if you can't fill them. But don't tell me you wouldn't want to see the Statue of Liberty, Sydney Harbour Bridge, the Colosseum, the Taj Mahal? Want me to go on? If there's a demand, sooner or later it will be met. I'm not talking supply and demand, I'm talking demand and supply.'

They all looked at each other and Phil scribbled like mad.

'What if I told you that tomorrow you could get on a train at Central and be in London in about four hours?'

'No. Fastest is about eight, maybe seven and a half,' said Eric.

'Okay, you're right. But what if I said next week it's going to come down to seven and a quarter. Maybe a better engine or better signals or something. Possible, eh?'

'Aye, that's possible,' agreed Phil.

'And next year, maybe another fifteen minutes quicker. And so on. Incremental.'

They looked at me and nodded so I went on.

'Then you get a channel tunnel and you can whizz from London to Paris is a couple of hours or so.'

They were about to object then they saw what I was getting at. What I was getting at was the benefit of hindsight and some web surfing, but they got the point. We carried on in this vein until closing time, and Phil had another feature for the paper. All he needed to do was to use a little more imagination. I left him with the mind boggling thought of hen and stag parties colliding in Poland and causing a lot more damage than the Luftwaffe ever achieved.

It was five o'clock and I was huddled around the radio waiting for confirmation of my status as a seriously rich man. It started well, Bolton Wanderers, nil, Aston Villa, nil, just as predicted and I switched off after I got confirmation of the last of the eight draws, Aberdeen, two, Ayr United, two. So that was it.

The instruction on the copy coupon informed me that I should immediately send a telegram with a claim. How I was supposed to do that I had no idea. It was well after five o'clock but I went down to the local post office in Pollokshaws Road on the off chance it would still be open and I was lucky, it didn't close until five thirty and I made it with a couple of minutes to spare much to the annoyance of the clerk. I dashed off a claim as per their instructions. All I had to do now was sit tight.

In this euphoric state I waited for Katie outside the Malmaison and right on time she showed up. When the maitre d' took her coat and revealed her wearing a black, body hugging dress emphasising a figure that would have made Gandhi turn to drink and loose women I was momentarily speechless. This woman had curves in places most woman didn't have places.

It was almost impossible to capture the excitement of that first night at the One-0-One but it came close, call it a score draw. Katie had me describe in detail the beauty of the Alexander III Bridge, the Place du Tertre, the stroll up the Champs- Elysées and I could see that she didn't quite believe that she was really going to see the

Paris of the movies. Her passport had arrived and she brought it with her to show me, the thrill of it all mirrored in the picture on her passport, banded around the third page with little more than some wide sellotape and embossed with the Foreign Office seal. Over a rack of minted lamb she told me that she would love to sail down the Seine after dark, and daintily spooning a Cranachan, she sighed with pleasure at the thought of walking along the left bank, the sound of French accordion music drifting across the river. I hoped to hell that the Paris I was taking her to lived up to her expectations. I hoped to hell it lived up to mine.

We made long, slow love and slept together at her house and I slipped away early under the watchful eye of Mrs McConnachie, promising to be back soon. I needed to be at home to wait for a response from Littlewoods.

That response came at two o'clock in the afternoon in the form of a telegram asking me to telephone the number given. I made my way to a phone box at the corner of Nithsdale Road and got through in a few seconds. It took more than a few seconds for it to sink in that I had won the exact sum of one hundred and forty seven thousand, three hundred and twelve pounds, thirteen and six pence. Even in 2017 terms this was a huge fortune. They wanted to send a couple of people up to talk to me on Tuesday. I told them that, jackpot or not, I was committed to being away from then until the following weekend and they agreed to see me the next day. They tried to talk me out of remaining anonymous but I was adamant. I suspected that they wouldn't give up on that and would try again tomorrow

I was desperate to talk to Barry but short of slipping back and forward between the years that wasn't possible and I didn't want to chance anything until I had the money nestling nice and cosily in the bank. The fact was that I was fabulously wealthy with not a soul to tell. Sitting in my cold flat I felt that this wasn't how very rich people lived. That was about to change: big time.

It was two men and a photographer that arrived on my doorstep almost on the dot of two. They were both dressed in suits, ties and tan raincoats and even the photographer wore a sports jacket and tie.

'Mr Lorne?'

'That would be me.'

They introduced themselves as representatives from Littlewoods and had come up by train that morning from Liverpool. They had had an early rise. It was all very formal. One was Mr Collingdale and the other was Mr Lorraine and they looked a little like Lauren and Hardy but without the comedic touch. They didn't offer first names or introduce the photographer.

I looked at the photographer. 'You're welcome to stay but I don't think you 'll be needed.' He shrugged.

Once inside and after the ritual offer of tea and biscuits they tried again to change my mind.

'Word will get out anyway, Mr Lorne and sometimes it's better to get it over with. If you try and keep it quiet then friends and relatives think you're trying to hide something from them.'

'That's the whole point, Mr Lorraine,' I said, stating the obvious.

'Collingwood, I'm Collingwood he's Lorraine.'

'Sorry.'

'Quite alright, Mr Lorne,' he said magnanimously.

303

'In any event, the answer is still no.'

They were disappointed but stoic. They went on to request proof of identity and I showed them grandpa's passport, birth certificate and national insurance number. My heart was thumping noisily as they checked the passport and examined the photo against the real thing sitting opposite them. Without comment Collingwood nodded and took a note of the number and handed it back. There were a few forms which had already been partially completed in which they filled in some more details then asked for my signature. Then with as much ceremony as they could muster in a chilly flat on a dismal Monday afternoon in a Glasgow suburban tenement, they presented me with a cheque written in flowery copperplate hand in the amount of £147,312.17s.6d.

'Congratulations, Mr Lorne you're now a very rich man.'

There didn't seem to be much else to say and there was an embarrassed silence for a few moments before Mr Lorraine spoke to tell me that a vast array of Littlewoods' financial services and investment advisers were on immediate hand to offer the best advice on how best to cope with such an enormous windfall, 'for a small fee, of course,' he added.

'Of course.'

'You have a bank account, Mr Lorne?'

I told them I did and that the very moment that they were out of the house I would be knocking on the bank's door. By this time it was just after three and as the bank closed at three thirty they would understand if I didn't waste any more of their time. They gave me their business cards and left taking the redundant photographer with them. It was all as simple as that.

The taxi pulled up to the door of the bank with about ten minutes to spare and I stood in line with my pass book to make the deposit. The same Dickensian clerk with whom I had made a number of deposits recognised me and welcomed me despite the approaching closing time.

'Mr Lorne, always a pleasure.'

I handed over the cheque with as much savoir faire as I could muster and mumbled something about having had a "little good fortune". All credit to the man, he retained his grace and poise and was almost as imperturbable as Jeeves the butler.

'Indeed.' He looked at the cheque. 'It is rather a large amount to be depositing into a savings account. May ask if you have plans for it? I could arrange an appointment with our senior personnel to discuss it with you. Indeed it would be most advisable.'

'Thank you. Yes I will have plans. I have something to attend to for the next few days and I'd be grateful if you'd just deposit it for now. And Mr...?'

'Russell, Mr Russell.'

'Mr Russell, I know I can rely on your complete discretion.'

'Indeed you can, Mr Lorne, although a deposit of this size won't go unnoticed. But there's not much you can do with it anyway until it's cleared. Not that with Littlewoods that will be a problem.'

'No, I understand. Thank you and good day.' I nodded at him and left.

Good day! Jesus, Gordon, you're beginning to sound like one of them!

I called Katie later and got her down from high doh long enough to agree to meet at Central at around half past nine in the morning for the ten o'clock Royal Scot.

'Don't forget your passport!'

Too much had been happening over the weekend so it seemed a good idea to forego Heraghty's and be ready to leave with a clear head. Phil's column would have to wait.

Chapter Twenty-nine

Katie, fashionably late and dressed in a green coat and Astrakhan fur collar met me under the clock with twenty minutes to spare before the train was due to leave. She carried a mid size brown case for the trip. Thank God the fox fur was still in the wardrobe. I looked up at the clock as it ticked slowly onwards and hoped and prayed that the magic would work for just a little while longer.

We found our two first class seats in a comfortable compartment and I sought out the restaurant car manager and tipped him half-a-crown to make sure that he put aside a good table for two for lunch in the restaurant car, which he accepted with alacrity and a promise to personally take care of us. On the stroke of ten a cacophony of whistles blew and with the slightest of jolts, the huge 'Duchess' Pacific strained under the weight of the eleven coaches behind it and eased its way across the Clyde heading for Carlisle some two hours further down the line. I looked over at Katie, who had removed her coat to reveal a simple but classy finely knitted jumper and cardigan set off by a string of pearls, and a flared skirt, and smiled.

'Excited?'

'You have no idea. The girls want to know if you have any friends. They're positively drooling with envy.'

I was dressed in a sports jacket and trousers, a shirt and a tie all in keeping with the dress code of the nineteen fifties. The last time I travelled in 2017 it was on a stag flight to somewhere like Amsterdam or Berlin, it was so drink fuelled I can't really recall, although I remember one of the group stopping a number of locals and drunkenly saying to them, 'Y'ought tae see mah yacht. It's in the canal, ye c'nall see it', before staggering on to some other bewildered denizen so I assume it must have been Amsterdam. Anyway most of us wore tee shirts, jeans and trainers. There was a crowd of girls on the same flight, dressed more or less the same as each other except for pink sashes with messages printed on them. One of sashes proclaimed, 'I'm the Bride'. Another said, 'I'm the Bride's mother and I'm up for it'. Another, draped around an obviously pregnant woman had the message, 'I'm the Bride's sister and I was up for it.'

How we got from the attire of the nineteen fifties to the flamboyance, if that's the word, of modern day I don't know and I'm not sure which of the two I prefer.

The lush, green fields of rural Lanarkshire sped by the window, occasionally obscured by drifting smoke from the locomotive, and on the right, the looming mass of Tinto Hill dotted white with sheep slipped past the window. The Lake District and Lancaster eased by while we were enjoying the view from the comfort of the dining car – my tip had ensured an almost grovelling service – and it didn't seem long before the train flashed by the stations of the home counties and eventually coasted down the gradient into Euston. A taxi took us through the great Doric temple of the Euston Arch, since demolished in an act of civic vandalism in the name of progress, and fifteen minutes later deposited us in the heart of Mayfair at Claridge's Hotel.

I had decided against going to the theatre. It was six o'clock by the time we reached the hotel and Katie spent a good half hour looking into every corner of the room, inspecting the towels, turning on taps then generally doing what it is that women need to do before going anywhere. I contented myself just watching her getting attuned to this new, if transient, style of life. The fact was, I was just getting attuned to it myself.

We finally left the hotel and wandered through the streets of Mayfair until the cold drove us down into the underground where we took a tube to Piccadilly Circus. We could hear the bustle and see the brightness at the top of the escalator well before we exited into the kaleidoscope of light and cacophony of noise that was Piccadilly Circus. Katie gripped my hand tightly at the wonder of it.

'George, this is amazing. I've only ever seen it in black and white on a television.'

We walked slowly around then wandered down through Leicester Square to Trafalgar Square and to the top of the Mall where at the far end Buckingham Palace lay framed in the distance. By this time hunger had started to gnaw away at us and so we headed back towards Piccadilly to find a restaurant.

They say, whoever they are, that if you stand at the corner of Piccadilly Circus and Piccadilly long enough you will bump into everyone you know. How long is never specified but in the event it took me no more than three minutes. Considering that in 1957 I only knew or was acquainted with no more than half a dozen people, one of whom was standing at my side, it was more than amazing when I heard the dulcet tones of a voice I knew very well, too well in fact, filter through the noise and bustle.

'Well if it's no' Bic Biro, the man himself.'

I whirled around and there, standing about a foot shorter than me was the diminutive figure of Sandy Corcoran. I just looked at him then I checked around to see if he had his heavies with him but he was alone.

'You get about, don't ye?'

Katie looked at me then at him than back at me again. She had sensed the enmity in his tone. 'George?'

'It's all right, Katie.'

'Katie, is it?' He looked her up and down, leeringly appreciatively.

'Who is this man, George?' asked Katie, frowning.

'Oh, a name tae fit the face. Katie and George.'

'He's an animal lover, Katie. Horses, dogs, gorillas.'

'Oh, good one George. Quite a sense of humour.'

'What are you doing here, Sandy?' I asked.

He shrugged, then I got it. He was running away. Benny had said something about Sandy not being seen around and some Glasgow hard men were looking for him.

'This and that. Lucky meetin' you. See, the way ah see it is you have something belonging tae me.'

Katie was getting anxious. 'George, do you mind telling me what's going on?'

'Listen and learn, Katie darlin', listen and learn,' said Sandy. 'Ask him about a sick dog and a couple of lucky streaks on the horses.'

'I don't know what you're talking about, Sandy,' I said, taking Katie by the elbow, 'Let's go, Katie.'

'Ah can make it difficult for you, you know,' he said with contrived menace.

But I looked at him and what I saw was desperation. He exuded as much menace as a used teabag. He looked as if he hadn't shaved for days, his shirt was stale and sweaty and his suit was crumpled. Mind you he looked pretty much like that the first time I laid eyes on him but covering everything was a sheen of defeat. I almost felt sorry for him but the vestiges of the bruises on my body told me not to be so bloody silly. Still I had to get rid of him. I took him by the shoulder and walked a couple of paces away from Katie.

'Now you listen to me Sandy Corcoran,' I said with all the authority I could muster, which wasn't as much as I would have liked. 'I know all about you. I know you're broke, I know you're in trouble with some people back north who it's better not to be in trouble with, and I know you're here to get away.' I made an exaggerated show of looking up and down Piccadilly. 'No minders or hangers on now, Sandy, eh? Just a wee man in trouble and not a friend in sight.'

He looked at me with a mixture of contempt, fear and amazement.

I went on, 'I'm right on all counts, eh? So here's the scene, Sandy, you've got a choice. I give you twenty quid right now and you disappear - you get out of my face, okay.'

'Or?' he said this without much conviction.

'Or I make a call and let some friends of mine know that you're down here. It narrows the search a bit, doesn't it? And by the look of you you're pretty short of a bob or two, am I right?'

He looked at me, torn between his hatred of me and his need for some money. I took four five pound notes from my wallet and held them under his nose. The hesitation was fractional; he snatched the money, sneered at me and shuffled off towards Oxford Street. The look on Katie's face at that point was not one conducive to a romantic meal.

'Will you tell me this minute what's going on? Did you just give him some money?' She looked as angry as I've seen her. 'Are you a betting man, George?'

'Yes, and not really.'

'What?'

'Yes I gave him some money and no, I'm not really a betting man.' This last statement was true in the strictest sense of the word. There was no betting on my part; I already knew the outcome.

'So what was all that about dogs and horses?'

'Can we discuss this over dinner?'

'If we don't discuss it now we'll be discussing it on the night train back to Glasgow.'

Boy, was she upset. 'Katie, it's the middle of Piccadilly, let's eat and I'll tell you all about it.' I took her arm and she reluctantly came along. I needed a few minutes to think of something.

We walked in silence until I found a nice little Italian restaurant in Swallow Street. Some semblance of international cuisine had reached Britain it seemed, it just hadn't found its way north of Watford.

Katie didn't waste any time. 'Well?'

I took a deep breath, 'Sandy Corcoran is a bookie, a bookmaker, they take bets on horses.'

'I know what a bookie is, George,' she said impatiently.

'Yes, so you do. Anyway, I have contacts in the racing fraternity – they gave me some inside information on a couple of races so I put money on them.'

'You told me you didn't bet,' she said accusingly.

'That's right, I don't. But these were straight from the horse's mouth.' I laughed at the unintended pun but quickly stopped when I saw Katie's face.

'Anyway, as predicted, they won. I won quite a lot of money.'

'How much money?'

'A couple of hundred.' This wasn't strictly true but it wasn't a lie either.

'What? Seriously?'

The waiter came over with menus but Katie waved him away. 'In a minute.'

'He's a bookie, Katie, that's his business.'

'What about the dogs?'

'Dog singular. He had a dog that he had a lot of money riding on, a greyhound. He thought he had rigged the race but his dog lost. He's out a lot of money and he owes all over Glasgow.'

'What has that got to do with you?'

'Nothing,' I protested, and again this was not a lie except by a little bit of omission. 'He knows I took a lot from him on a couple of races and for some reason, I don't know why, he blames me for a lot of his problems.'

'How do you know all this?'

Christ, it was like the Spanish Inquisition. 'I have a friend in the police. I meet him and a couple of pals at Heraghty's for a pint from time to time. He told me the story – filled in the blanks.'

'Why did you give him money?'

'Bottom line? To make him go away. He's down on his luck and maybe I took a bit of advantage of him. I took him for quite a lot. Legitimately.' I added seeing her face.

'Not legitimately. Betting is illegal.'

'No it's not. If I'd actually gone to the racetrack it would have all been above board. The whole thing is an anachronism.'

She brooded on this then asked, 'What's your friend's name? The one in the police.'

'Jesus, Katie! What's that to do with the price of milk?'

She just looked at me.

I sighed, 'Benny, I don't know his second name- begins with an 'F' I think – he's not a bosom buddy.'

'Benny Frew?'

'That could be it.' How did she know that? 'Do you know him?'

'If it's who I think it is my father did. Dad was a policeman at Craigie Street, a sergeant. He'd be a lot older than Benny but he mentioned him a few times. Seemed to think a lot of him. A policeman's policeman he called him.'

The fact that I knew Benny seemed to mollify her somewhat and she sat back and opened the menu.

'Right, George, please – no more surprises,' she sighed. 'And what in God's name is tagliatelli?'

After what turned out to be a pleasant, if somewhat strained meal, we walked back to the hotel. Halfway there Katie took my hand and sighed, 'George, whatever are we to make of you?'

I assumed it was a rhetorical question and just squeezed her hand. We made love in the large feather bed in the hotel and it appeared that all was forgiven after the unfortunate encounter with Sandy Corcoran. Forgiven but, I suspected, not forgotten.

Wednesday dawned bright and cool, the four hundred miles separating London from Glasgow adding a touch of spring to the day. After a superb breakfast we took a cab to Victoria in plenty of time for the ten thirty 'Golden Arrow', a train I had often read about, renowned for its unashamed display of ostentatious luxury and romance. We were escorted to our two seats separated by a table similar to that of our recent journey on the 'Queen of Scots' although, if it were possible, this was even more luxurious. Our carriage, number 64, I noted, was named 'Christine'. She would have been pleased.

The Lord Nelson class locomotive, 'Howard of Effingham' (it worries me sometimes how I know these things) steamed us down to Dover in an hour and forty minutes and we decanted on to the first class section of the 'Canterbury' for the short trip across the channel.

Chapter Thirty

Paris.

The Pullman coaches of the 'Fleche D'Or', the French equivalent of the 'Golden Arrow' awaited the arrival of the 'Canterbury' at Calais, deep smoky blue and cream and written along the top of the carriage in gilt lettering were the words, 'Compagnie International des Wagon-Lits et Des Grande Express Europeans'. Inside the coach the opulence was even greater than that of its British counterpart. This was more than just a train, it was Versailles on wheels. Other less noble trains and carriages that were for the hoi polloi stood in sidings and were shunted into loops to let the 'Fleche D'Or' run regally past, whistling in derision. I don't know who was more excited, Katie or me but let's call it a draw.

Last night's bit of unpleasantness featuring the odious Sandy was parked in a distant bay for inevitable future retrieval but for now Katie was radiant with the joy of finding herself in a foreign land, not just any foreign land but one that had been the subject of such a rich tapestry through the ages. She flushed with pleasure as the smiling French attendant met us at the entrance to our car.

'Madame, monsieur, suivez-moi, s'il vous plaît.'

Katie looked at me. 'George ?'

But the attendant was already leading the way to our seats and invited Katie to sit, with the exaggerated Gallic flourishes that only the French can do in such style and panache. He wasn't quite so attentive to me but then again, I wasn't nearly attractive as Katie and we both knew it so that was okay, but a surreptitious ten francs squeezed into his palm restored the equilibrium for the moment.

Over afternoon tea I pointed out the Somme when we crossed it at Amiens and I just caught the name Chantilly as we roared through the station until presently we slowed as the outskirts of Paris approached and a few minutes later the train glided slowly into the wide expanse of the Gare du Nord. Chastened by last night's experience I looked around as we detrained but of course, there were no ghosts from the past, or the future, come to that, lurking in the folds of steam hissing from the Nord Pacific at the head of the train, an engine, I was happy to note, that had none of the style and class of the British Staniers or Gresleys. As we exited the station it was on the cusp of darkness but, true to stereotype, a number of people were sitting outside the cafés surrounding the Gare du Nord, wrapped up against the cool night air, sipping a coffee and pulling on a Caporal or a Gitanes.

A taxi took us at some speed through the back streets to deposit us outside the elegant portals of the Georg just off the Champs - Elysées where a doorman, uniformed to perfection in maroon, summoned a boy to take our luggage, little enough though it was.

'Katie, you sit there while I do the honours,' I pointed to a chair far enough away from the reception desk so that she wouldn't hear the clerk or me. She smiled and nodded.

Pulling the voucher from my pocket I handed it over together with our passports.

'Ah, monsieur. Bienvenu a Paris. Mademoiselle McWilliam et Monsieur Lorne,' he read from the voucher and passports. I looked over at Katie but she gave no sign of hearing.

'I wonder if you could do me a favour,' I checked his name badge, 'Phillipe?' I said quietly.

'Oui monsieur?' Only the French can ask a question with their eyebrows.

'The lady, my...er...partner, knows me by my nom de plume, I am a writer you see, Mr Clooney, George Clooney. Could you address me by that name when you see me, particularly in her company,' I said in a confidential man to man tone while slipping twenty francs into his fingers which disappeared faster than any Penn and Teller sleight of hand.

'Mais bien sûr – but of course, Mr Clooney,' said Phillipe smoothly, a bed in heaven to the man.

'I, er...I need something else.'

'Oui monsieur?'

'I need a reservation at Maxim's for tomorrow night, what can you do?'

The sharp intake of breath and the pursed lips were common to any language.

'That would be almost impossible, I think.'

I noted the word "almost" and the fact that the conversation was clearly not over.

'But not completely impossible,' I said dispensing another twenty francs.

'Very unlikely.'

'How unlikely?' Another twenty disappeared.

'Possibly only early, maybe around five o'clock.'

'How about seven o'clock?' Yet another twenty vaporised. At this rate his kids would be going through the Sorbonne without need of a grant.

'Leave it with me, Mr Clooney, and I will see what I can do.'

'Good man yourself, Phillipe, vive La Vieille Alliance.' Now I was just showing off, never a good idea with the French, but Phillipe was up to it.

'We have a special place in our hearts for Scottish people and lovers, Mr Clooney, and you would appear to be both. Bon soir.' He smiled and that was me dismissed for the nonce.

'You two seemed very chatty,' said Katie as we crossed to the elevator.

'Just my old friend Phillipe,' I said airily, 'He's taking care of Maxim's for me. It's usually booked out from now till doomsday but he owes me from the war.'

'My God, what happened?'

'Sorry, can't talk about it. Official Secrets Act and all that.'

She looked at me askance but said nothing.

The mini suite was actually a very large bedroom with a small sitting area in an alcove. The decor could have been lifted from the richness of the train except for the colour, all red velvet opulence and brocaded drapes folded back onto ornate curtain tie backs. The furniture was Louis XV although not original of course, though you never know. There was a writing table with an olive green leather inlay and all the usual accoutrements you would expect from a quality hotel. In short it had 'stuff'.

When I was in the travel trade I just called it 'stuff'. A decent hotel had to have 'stuff' in the room. Sachets of scented soap, shoe polishers, chocolates, iced water, a bowl of fruit, free movies (porn available for a supplement), writing paper and postcards, none of which was ever used except the chocolate and the supplemental porn, but the principle of the thing was you had to have 'stuff'.

I was once in a hotel in New York called the Royal Manhattan on Eighth Avenue which at that time boasted the novelty of a safe lurking at the rear of the wardrobe. Not one of the modern day affairs that you programme with a four digit code and looks like a microwave oven, but a tin box mounted on a pedestal and operated by means of a simple key. I was escorting a group of American football fans from Glasgow on behalf of the agency to watch the New York Giants in a pre season game against some obscurely named team from a place that even if it had an international airport would still be the middle of nowhere, something like the Fargo Follies or the Des Moines Dipsticks, I forget. Anyway, we had a night on the town which involved giving detailed opinions of the weak alcoholic mediocrity of American beer until we were quickly and predictably legless, followed by a trawl up Third Avenue to sample the singles bars and the renowned desperation of unattached New York women anxious to be seduced by the charms of a handful of guttered inebriates from the west of Scotland. Predictably no-one in the group, to their astonishment, got lucky; except one – me.

I snagged an enthusiastic amateur whose state of inebriation was one degree greater than my own and took her back to my room. I remember nothing of the subsequent events but it is unlikely in the extreme that I would have been able to raise an eyebrow let alone an erection and I came to the following morning with my

320

tongue velcrod to the roof of my mouth and my ear glued to the pillow with what at, first glance, appeared to be excrement, but on closer examination proved to be the melted remnants of the chocolate left on my pillow.

Of the object of my desire there was no sign. Neither was there any sign of the thousand dollars in cash, five thousand dollars in traveller's cheques and the two American Express cards with which I had been delegated to pay all costs associated with the trip. A frantic search of my jacket and trouser pockets and the drawers in the room revealed only scraps of paper, some assorted shrapnel and a polo mint. In despair I phoned back to my then current girlfriend to enquire as to whether I may have left six thousand dollars and a couple of credit cards lying on the dresser, much to her disbelief. There was nothing for it but to cancel the traveller's cheques and the credit cards then phone the office to confess my sins.

Some ten minutes later, just as I was about to call the police, in a state of hungover shock sitting on the edge of the bed with my head in my hands, I peered through trembling fingers and noticed, apparently for the first time, this odd box on a post at the rear of the closet and the first inklings of distant memory stirred. Searching through the bits and pieces of coinage from my pockets there was a small gilt key. This same key fitted the little box perfectly which swung open to reveal a cornucopia, a veritable Aladdin's cave of treasure, to wit, nearly one thousand dollars in cash, five thousand dollars worth of travellers cheques, (now cancelled), two Amex credit cards (also cancelled), one passport (I had forgotten about that), and return air tickets for a dozen people back to Glasgow. Come to think of it, it wasn't long after that that the agency folded. That little safe is what I mean by 'stuff'.

Here in the 1957 version of the Georg there was no little safe, you left it in a secure box at the front desk, but there was 'stuff' enough to induce Katie to think that the only thing missing was a Christmas tree under which to put it all. And it was good 'stuff' too, or so I was told. Powders and unguents from the top parfumiers, chocolates from the top chocolatiers, scented notepaper, and, of course, bathrobes and towels as soft as angel clouds. I could see her eyeing her suitcase to see if there was enough room to transport half of it home.

We left the room an hour or so later and headed for the Champs-Elysées where we turned left and meandered up the gentle slope towards Place Charles de Gaulle and the Arc De Triomphe. According to the little map I got from the concierge it wasn't called Place Charles de Gaulle in 1957 in honour of the imperious Anglophobe, that came much later, but was called Place d'Etoile in recognition of its star like shape with its twelve straight avenues leading away from the hub.

By this time it was well dark but pleasant enough for a stroll and we walked hand in hand just basking in the Parisian sights. This was a new Paris for me almost as much as it was for Katie. Dark green buses trundled up the avenue, with open platforms at the rear on which stood nonchalant men reading 'Le Monde' just like I had seen in old photographs and I ached to ride one.

We were beginning to feel a little hungry so we stopped at the top of the avenue and found a brasserie overlooking the floodlit monument and sat inside the canopy looking out. I couldn't help but sigh with the

322

sheer pleasure of it all and looking at Katie I could see a moistness in her eyes. She took my hand and squeezed it.

'Thank you for this,' she said simply. I smiled and squeezed back.

We both had steak frites and a carafe of vin du table then walked under the passageway to the Arc and looked at the eternal flame of the unknown soldier.

'His mother must be so proud of him,' said Katie, leaving me to ponder the intricacies of the logic of the female mind.

We ambled arm in arm down Avenue Kleber to the Trocadéro where we stood for a while and looked across the Seine to the Eiffel tower, the great symbol of Paris, as yet unlit but gleaming in the moonlight. Katie couldn't take her eyes off it and kept murmuring, 'So beautiful, so beautiful.'

We walked along the banks of the river to the Pont D'Alma then made our way back up to the hotel where we lost ourselves in the folds of the huge double bed and slept.

Paris on a cool clear morning is nothing short of perfection, especially when you have a beautiful woman hanging on to your arm who has never sampled the city's delights. I planned for us to walk across the Seine via the eternally and heartbreakingly lovely Alexander III bridge so we meandered down the Champs-Elysées to the Jardin de la Nouvelle France turning towards the bridge at the Grand Palace, that magnificent stone and glass structure built for the Universal Exposition of 1900 in the style of Beaux-Arts architecture, details of which I had gleaned from Wikipedia before we left. As we turned right to the river I looked across the road to the Avenue

323

de Marigny and saw rows of tented stalls and people milling around and browsing which set me to thinking and I stored the thought away for future reference.

After admiring the bridge, by common consent the most beautiful in Paris and by definition therefore, the world, and its four 'Fames' each on massive stone pillars which provide the counterweight to the arch, Science, Arts, Commerce and Industry, we looked over to Les Invalides, tomb of Napoleon, and the lovely gardens fronting the ornate buildings. A stroll down the left bank then took us to the emblem of all Parisiennes, the Eiffel Tower.

Still continuing my recently learned commentary and wisdom gleaned from a device not yet invented, I impressed Katie with my knowledge telling her that it was built for the 1897 World's Fair by Gustave Eiffel and was at first loathed by the cognoscenti of the day. It was supposed to stand for twenty years and then be dismantled but by that time it had become too valuable as a communications tower and opinions had mellowed somewhat. In fact the nearest it came to being torn down was in 1944 when Hitler ordered it destroyed along with the rest of the city but General Dietrich von Choltitz, the military governor of Paris, disobeyed the order, brave and wonderful man that he was for that act alone. We took the elevators to the very top, of course, and surveyed the city over a glass of champagne. Katie asked me to identify various landmarks.

'That's Sacre Coeur, on Montmartre – we'll go there later, maybe tomorrow,' I said as I pointed to a domed building to the north. 'Behind it is that little square I told you about. That's Notre Dame,' I said, gesturing with my arm, 'that's for later too. And see, up there, that's the Pantheon.'

She drank it all in, like an alcoholic desperate for more and, like an alcoholic, I could see that she was hooked for life. I knew the symptoms only too well. There is no known cure for that most insidious of all infections, travel lust. It is an itch that can never be cured, only slaked and quieted by the rattle of a wheel on a steel rail, or the whiff of kerosene at an airport or the deep blast of a ship's horn as the mooring ropes slip the quay.

After a lunch back at the Trocadéro from where we could gaze upon the tower I suggested that we take the metro to the Louvre if only to view its two most famous inhabitants, Venus de Milo and the Mona Lisa better known here as La Giaconda.

To my mind the best museum in Paris was as yet not a museum but a railway station, Gare d'Orleans, and ran as a suburban station into the 1960's which meant that while we were there steam trains still rumbled in and out. But I had visited it well into the twenty-first century by which time it had been converted into quite simply the most stunning art museum in the world, the Musée d'Orsay. Even my untutored and uncultivated eye couldn't fail to be impressed. Take that, Guggenheim!

The original building still stands, also in the Beaux-arts style, and houses a staggering amount of works by Van Gogh, including 'Starry Night over the Rhone' and 'Self Portrait', Renoir, including 'Bal du Moulin de la Galette', Manet and 'The Luncheon on the Grass', Cezanne's 'Card Players', 'Whistler's Mother', and a host of others by such names as Gauguin, Monet, Degas, Millais, and of course, Toulouse Lautrec. Call me a philistine if you like but I'd have one of Lautrec's works above the mantelpiece rather than ten of van Gogh any day. His pastels bring netherworld Paris to life more than anything Van Gogh ever did for France.

It also houses 'L'Origine du monde' by Gustave Courbet, a close up of a woman's widespread legs and, there's no delicate way of describing this, her dark and hairy, very hairy, vagina. The model, Joanna Hiffernan, was James Whistler's lover at the time which just goes to show how friendly the two artists were and a little too friendly if you ask me. God knows what Whistler's mother thought of it although by the vinegar look on her face in her own picture I think she may have seen rather more of her son's girlfriend than she would have liked. I don't think I've ever seen so much hair on that part of a woman before, not that I'm a connoisseur you understand; she had more hair there than Bob Marley had on his head. When she took a bath it must have been like fronds of seaweed swaying in the Sargasso Sea. It's said that John Ruskin never went near his wife, Effie Gray, after being shocked on their honeymoon night by the profundity of her pubic hair. God knows what he expected – pigtails? One look at this and he'd have had cardiac arrest. It was certainly enough to put me off the naked female form for at least, well, at least until tonight.

The English translation is 'The Origin of the World' but I think this was Courbet's pretentious way of justifying the fact that the kinky old goat was just a lecher. It was about as hot, steamy and erotic as a barber shop floor and I'm not sure how Katie would have reacted to it either but that point was moot given that the only hot and steamy thing coming out of the Quai d'Orsay today was 12.30 to Chartres.

Just for the record, lest you think that me being the dissolute, workshy, conniving scrounger that I describe earlier in this narrative by definition also means that I am therefore an uneducated, unappreciative philistine then nothing could be further from the truth. I know what I like and I'll spend as much of other peoples' money as I can to enjoy it.

Of that now there was no need, my pockets stuffed as they were with the satisfyingly large, in denomination as well as size, notes of the République. So we finished our lunch of paté and fromage and crispy French bread at the little Trocadéro bistro and took the metro through the tunnels with their 'Dubo Dubon Dubonnet' adverts on the walls and got off at the Louvre. Today the much derided, and not without reason, glass pyramid covers the entrance to the Louvre but here in 1957 the way in was by a door set in the main building. There was no line of any note and the huge museum was quiet. It took a little orienteering to find our way but we eventually found ourselves standing in front of the world's most famous and valuable work of art, the Mona Lisa. It never fails to disappoint. Just thirty inches by twenty one inches, for a start you can never get near it, or at least you couldn't when I last visited it. Now there was no protective glass and very few viewers so it was much more visible. Nah – still disappointed. I don't think Katie was overly impressed either.

Venus de Milo was interesting but to be honest, there were a number of just as desirable sculptures on view. However she is famous for her lack of arms and the fact that she is 2000 years old so we both paid homage to her then decided it was time go.

327

It didn't take us long to stroll east to the Pont Neuf and the Île de la Cité where we stood and looked up at the magnificent facade of the Notre Dame, and inside Katie lit a candle despite her Presbyterian upbringing, and good for her. I didn't ask her who it was for but she looked at me as she lit it. I refrained from telling the hoary old Quasimodo jokes about his face ringing a bell and dead ringers and so on. I had a hunch she wouldn't appreciate them.

There was time for an hour's cruise on a little boat on the Seine, under the proverbial bridges, and despite the cool air we stood up on deck and watched the enchanting city slip by. One of Katie's dreams had been ticked off on the chart.

The sun started to set and the winter chill settled on the Seine as afterwards we walked through the deserted narrow street that bisected Île Saint Louis so we took a bus back to the hotel, both of us standing on the open platform at the rear holding onto the rail for dear life as the bus swung round the Place de la Concorde fetching passing pedestrians little more than glancing blows.

On the whole it had been a day wrapped in perfection and tied with a polka dot bow.

God alone knows how Katie managed to pack what she did into her suitcase but in preparation for the night at Maxim's she was wearing a shin length gown that shaded from dark red at the top through maroon, purple through deep blue and she looked Parisian to the very core.

She gave me a twirl, 'You like?'

'Oh, mama!' I said in a fit of remarkable fluency.

'I'll take that as a yes then, shall I?' she said, flushed with pleasure.

Her light brown hair flowed well combed and wavy down to the back of her neck a la Lauren Bacall and a slender gold necklace sporting a Celtic cross hung around her neck. She liked to cock a snook at the Wee Frees did Katie.

'Well I don't think we're dining at McDonald's tonight,' I said without thinking.

'Where?'

'Never mind.'

Maxim's was simply splendid. The Art Nouveau decor, its magnificently ornate stained glass ceiling softly lit, red velvet chairs and banquettes, sinuously sculpted chandeliers and mirrored walls reflecting everything in quadruplicate was an assault on the senses. Phillipe had briefed me before we left the hotel and so when I was greeted by a maitre d' I knew to take care of him. Even he, well accustomed to the beauties that he welcomed nightly, bowed in appreciation at the sight of Katie as her coat was taken and her style and perfection revealed. We were escorted to a table set for two just far enough away from the small stage at which a dinner jacketed pianist was playing some Strauss melodies, but not so far that we couldn't see or enjoy the music. I couldn't help thinking that when I got back to 2017 with my million pounds this was the way I was going to live.

'George, this is sensational – how can I ever go back to being Katie McWilliam from Glasgow after this?' Katie gasped as she looked around her. 'I thought the One-0-One was grand, but this...'

I almost laughed at her pleasure for it was my pleasure too, doubled by her reaction to it all.

'I wonder how the poor live,' I said airily.

'Oh, don't. I almost feel guilty.'

'But not quite.'

'No, to hell with that. Tonight I'm going to wallow in the sheer hedonistic pleasure of it all and the devil be damned,' she said defiantly.

'You can't be at Maxim's and not drink champagne, this is where they invented the damn stuff.' I started singing 'The Night They Invented Champagne' in a very poor imitation of Maurice Chevalier.

Katie laughed at me. 'That sounds great, you should write it down.'

The waiter was solicitous without being patronising and I had enough of a smattering of French to get through the menu without resorting to asking for translation which would have seen my street cred plummeting like a ruined soufflé, not so much with Katie but probably with the waiter. We ordered the foie gras to start then I had the lobster and Katie had the sole with langoustine, and the waiter, blessings of angels upon him, never once corrected my accent. A bottle of Pouilly Fume complemented both to perfection. We both chose the warm chocolate Grand Marnier soufflé for dessert, a concoction so orgasmically sensate that sex later might seem superfluous – I stress "might".

It is impossible for two people to dine in Maxim's without being intimate, not necessarily in the sexual sense, but just in sharing confidences. Maxim's draws you close and casts its mysterious magical spell on you. The food is more than food, the music more than music and you, more than you.

330

I let Katie do most of the talking, mainly because I found talking about events of the past could only be an invention and talk of the future would be treading dangerous ground. But Katie wanted to talk about the future – our future.

'Where do you see us going, George?' she asked over coffee.

This was no time to be flippant no matter what the temptation but knowing the impossibility of the situation I fumbled for words.

'It's okay, really, George,' she said reaching for my hand. 'This whole adventure has been perfection – a dream – and if I wake up tomorrow and find that's what it was, well, I would be just as happy. But it's not, is it?'

'No Katie, it's not, and when you wake up tomorrow you'll still be with me in Paris and we'll still have another day,' I said.

She smiled and sighed, 'It's just that...it's just...well, you must know that I've very strong feelings for you. I've never met anyone like you and this...' she waved an arm at the surroundings, '...can turn a girl's head, any girl.'

I held her hand. 'I have to tell you, Katie, that I've, well, sort of fallen for you too.'

And I had. Wispy thoughts and ideas wafted through my mind, thoughts too outlandish to grasp and analyse and I let them drift away.

'This isn't real life, Katie, but it's what makes real life worthwhile, these dreams and fancies, and I can show you more of them. New York, Venice, Rome, you name it.'

'It's funny, how a person can have all this and still want more. But I'm not greedy, I just don't want to lose you.'

'I won't let that happen.' I squeezed her hand again.

'I'll just have to trust you on that then.'

Just then a small group of people made its way towards us heading for the exit. Katie grabbed my arm.

'My God, George, do you know who that is?' she hissed.

I tried not to look obvious but all I could see were two women and two men walking behind them. They were clearly well known by the way the waiters and the maitre d' fussed over them but I didn't recognise any of them, perhaps not surprisingly.

'It's Greta Garbo.'

'What?'

'Greta Garbo.'

'No. Really? I thought she was dead.' Had I been back in 2017 I would have been right.

'Of course she isn't. She's only about fifty and *look* at her, she looks younger than me.'

She may have been famous for wanting to be alone but she certainly wasn't alone now. Garbo swept imperiously past us but just as she did so the sleeve of her coat caught Katie's wine glass and knocked it over. It could only have been about half full and it was white wine and most of it went over the table cloth but the merest splash touched the side of Katie's gown. The waiters froze and Garbo looked around.
She spoke in that deep voice so often parodied.

'Oh my dear, I am so sorry, so clumsy of me.'

Waiters dashed over armed with napkins and started dabbing at the tablecloth.

'Pardon, madame, pardon, pardon,' said the maitre d' almost weeping, although his entreaties were directed more at Garbo than at Katie or me. Garbo took a dainty, embroidered hanky from her clasp bag and dabbed it against the spot that had landed on Katie.

'Such a beautiful dress, I am so sorry.'

'Och, that's all right,' said Katie magnanimously, 'A blind man running for a bus wouldn't see it.'

'You are not English?' asked Garbo, noticing the accent.

'No, Scottish.'

'Ah Scotland. So beautiful, I must go there.' She finished dabbing. 'There. I think now your blind man would not at all see it, as you say. Please, take this.' She offered her handkerchief to Katie.

'Oh, I'm fine.'

'Please take it, in case.'

'Thank you Miss Garbo,' and she took the hanky.

'Greta. Please.'

The other three in her party looked on and the maitre d' recovered some of his composure realising that disaster had been averted and there wasn't going to be a scene and the Foreign Legion could be stood down.

'And now I must go, I apologise again Miss...'

'Katie.'

'Katie, goodnight.' She turned to me. 'And to you also, goodnight.'

With that Garbo whispered something to the maitre d' and they swept out of the restaurant.

'Oh my God, George, this is *Greta Garbo's* hanky!'

'You could always wash it and send it back.'

'George!'

'Only joking.'

'What a night. What a night,' she said but I don't think she was talking to me.

Once the excitement had died down I called for the bill which was presented with discretion and a complementary brandy as a gesture of goodwill, the maitre d' waiting until Katie had gone to the ladies before slipping it gently beside my elbow.

'Apologies for the wine, monsieur, Madame Garbo has insisted that she pay for it. I have taken it from your account,' he said, almost bowing.

'Oh that wasn't necessary.'

'It is done, monsieur.'

I thanked him.

There was no doubt about it, it was serious money for 1957 even without the wine, it wasn't that cheap for 2017 come to that, about three hundred and fifty francs, thirty five pounds in sterling but I paid it with elan, counting off a wad of tissue paper notes and rounding it up to four hundred which had the man insisting upon my swift return 'with no reservation problem, monsieur'. I still had plenty of cash left and anyway I had taken the precaution of stuffing fifty quid into the heel of my shoe before leaving Dover to get around the currency regulations but the customs officer had paid me scant attention. There was plenty more where that came from.

We had another coffee at the foot of the Champs-Élysées watching Paris by night pass by before going back to the hotel and finishing the day with the sexual version of the Grand Marnier chocolate soufflé.

Katie loved the alfresco style of Parisian life so we had a kerbside breakfast of coffee, baguette and croissants opposite the Arc de Triomphe before taking the metro to Abbesses from where we walked along to the steps at the foot of the climb up to Sacre Coeur. The view from the top was glorious and we spent half an hour trying to identify the landmarks before wandering around to the Place du Tertre. This little square, above all others, captures the bohemian heart of Montmartre. On my previous visit the cafes and restaurants had taken over the square itself edging out the artists who made their living there painting at their easels while the visitors and locals looked on, occasionally buying. Now, with Katie, it was as it had been, the artists dotted all over the square dabbing away seemingly oblivious of the handful of us admiring their work.

'Picasso painted here,' I told her. 'He lived in one of these houses.'

She didn't say anything, just shook her head in wonder.

'He could double coat a room and kitchen in a day,' I continued and she just snorted and dug me in the ribs.

One painting took her fancy. It was a cut above the usual street scenes and old shop facades that get churned out ten a penny, a view of the square itself from slightly above with the basilica of the Sacre Coeur draped in mist in the background, like looking at it through a muslin veil. I haggled with the artist half-heartedly and got him down from sixty francs to fifty-five and he carefully rolled the canvas and put it inside a cardboard tube.

'This will have pride of place above the mantelpiece,' she said giving me a peck on the cheek. 'Every time I look at it, it'll bring it all back.'

There was a little cafe overlooking the square where we bought coffees and crepes while watching the artists work and a street musician, straight out of the cast of

'Gigi', dressed in a striped shirt and beret, played the theme from 'Moulin Rouge' on the accordion. I couldn't have staged it better myself.

We took the metro to the Père Lachaise cemetery and I showed her the tombs of Rossini and Chopin which somehow brought it home to us that they were real people and not simply names on sleeve notes. Katie knew nothing of Jim Morrison who years later would eclipse the two classical composers as the most famous inhabitant of the cemetery. I felt sure it was a distinction that he would have preferred to have avoided but that's what a needle full of heroin can do. I love the quote where he said, "*I think of myself as an intelligent, sensitive human being with the soul of a clown which always forces me to blow it at the most important moments*". You and me both, Jimbo, you and me both.

There's always too much of Paris for the time available but we finished off the dwindling daylight by walking along Rue Rivoli, through the Tuileries, and on to the Champs- Élysées to the hotel. No visit to Paris for the ingénue is complete without a visit to the Moulin Rouge in the Pigalle and my by now good friend Phillipe contrived, for a small fee, to get a pair of reservations. I had trawled the Pigalle with a couple of renegade friends in 2008 and the whole area was seedy and dissolute, perfect for guys like me. We had walked past the Moulin Rouge with its iconic windmill but didn't go in mainly because it was too tame for our tastes. Women covering their tits with fans were lame fare indeed, we wanted the full monty and there was plenty of that around.

It was a lot more classy in the fifties and I had no compunction about taking Katie there for dinner and the cabaret. The theatre had a great feel of the Belle Epoque about it or even a touch of Isherwood's thirties Berlin. The food was excellent without being up to Maxim's standard but who can take that every night. Charles Trénet sang 'La Mer' and it sounded infinitely better than the Bobby Darin version, 'Beyond the Sea', good though that is, and the evening was rounded off by, what else, Offenbach's terrific music played for the Can-Can. I was nearly on the table kicking it up myself, I can tell you.

As usual the waiters fussed over Katie and poured her more than enough wine so that she was perfectly in that zone where you are pissed enough not to care but not so pissed that you make an arse of yourself. It's a knack I've never been able to manage but at least tonight I was the perfect gentleman

As we walked back from Place d'Etoile a touch of bittersweet melancholy set in. We talked and held hands and I think we both knew that decisions had to be made. What those decisions would be and how I could make them happen was an entirely different matter. Once again I had thoughts that I didn't want to think and so I pushed them to the back of my mind. Impossible thoughts, crazy ideas yet the more I tried to banish them the more they crowded out my consciousness.

That night Katie made love to me with a hungry urgency and intensity that she had never displayed before and I knew then that she never wanted me to leave. I felt the same. However, I had to, but maybe for just one last time. Maybe my time was now here in my past and maybe, just maybe, that's where I should plan to be. These were the inchoate thoughts that kept rushing across my mind and the more I thought on them the more I thought, why not. Here in 1957, with Katie, this is where I want to be. Just one trip back to settle up with

337

Barry, to clean the slate and to make my peace with the
twenty-first century, the come back and be with Katie.

Why not?

Chapter Thirty-one

The Gare du Nord was bustling and busy at noon the next day as we were ushered to our seats by the conductor on the northbound 'Fleche d'Or'. It was a grey, sombre day with a touch of rain in the air, perhaps to match my mood because it had been a four day holiday of perfection, a break from reality, and like all such breaks, they come to an end sooner or later. We sat opposite each other as the train pulled out of the station in a cloud of smoke and steam and picked up some speed through the city's northern suburbs. I sat with my back to the engine and I could see the dome of Sacre Coeur on top of Montmartre receding into the distance as a light rain beaded the window.

Katie spoke. 'I want you to know that whatever else I do in my life, these last four days will never be anything less than perfection. I can never thank you enough.'

I leant over and took both her hands. 'This doesn't need to be the last time. There is so much more we can do,'

'Maybe, maybe so. But you're such a man of mystery and for all the glory of these days, I still really don't know anything about you, maybe even less than before, do I Gordon?'

'I know, but I can...' Wait a minute, she just called me Gordon.

'You called me Gordon.' I looked puzzled.

'That's right. You're not George Clooney are you? You're Gordon Lorne – not my Gordon Lorne but that's who you are.'

I started to speak but just stammered. She put her finger to my lips.

'Shh, it's okay, really it is,' she said gently.

'How did you know?'

'Oh, I saw your passport. I wasn't snooping – well maybe I was – I saw it sticking out of your jacket pocket in the hotel room when you were in the bathroom. The odd thing was that the photo in that looked exactly like the Gordon I knew but that's maybe just a coincidence. I don't think it is though.'

'Look Katie...'

'No Gordon, before you say anything let me speak, okay?' She didn't seem angry or upset or even disappointed and I let her have her say.

'I think I told you that first night I met you that there was something about you that wasn't quite right, but I trusted you, well, trusted you enough, to know that you wouldn't intentionally hurt me and you haven't. I said then that I knew you weren't on the level but I was happy to string along and enjoy the ride. And, boy, it's been some ride. I told you about my dull, uninteresting existence and now look. The trouble is that I doubt if anyone would believe me. You've blown half a years' wages and more in just four days and I've loved every minute.' She looked out at the rain. 'And now it's time to come back down to earth.'

'I'm sorry.' I couldn't think of anything else to say.

'No, don't be. But if we are to go any further I need you to tell me the truth. I need to know who the real you is, do you understand, Gordon?'

340

I sighed and shook my head. 'Katie, the lies I've told you, they weren't to impress you or to intentionally mislead you and certainly not to hurt you. But the thing is, if I were to tell you the truth, you would absolutely, guaranteed, think I was so obviously lying you'd get so mad and probably have me thrown off the train.'

'I don't think so, you've got the tickets.'

I smiled. She was still cracking jokes so all was not lost.

'I'm serious,' I said.

'Try me.'

'Right, but before I do there is something I can say. All the things I am about to tell you I can back up with evidence. Maybe not right away but I can tell you things and show you things that you will think are just magic, I mean real magic. But it's not, it's just the way things will be.'

'Okay,' she said with one of those hesitant, doubtful looks.

I took a deep breath. 'I'm from the future.'

'Jesus, Gordon!'

'Let me finish.'

'Christ! Really – is that the best you can come up with?' She was mad now. 'I deserve better than that, Gordon. If you can't be honest with me at this stage – then –then – just say nothing at all.' She was in tears now and I felt like shit.

'Katie, just listen to me.'

'Piss off, Gordon, you got what you wanted.'

'What do you mean?'

'Was all this just so you could sleep with me?' She gave me a look of pure contempt which I probably deserved but not for that reason.

341

I was indignant. 'Certainly not. If I want to sleep with someone I don't take them to Paris I take them to...'

I realised that I usually took them to the Sub Club or Bamboo but that would be difficult to explain.

'Where do you take them, Gordon? I note it's not singular.'

'I don't go around sleeping with women, Katie, you're the first this year.' This was technically true as it was 1957 but if you counted 2017 then I could be in trouble.

'It's only February, give it time.'

I laughed, she could still be funny.

'The fact is Katie, I took you to Paris because I knew you would love it and I knew I would love being with you seeing it together. I love being with you, hell, I just love you.'

If you ever want to stop a woman who's crying or start a woman that's not tell her that you love her.

'That's just the problem, Gordon, I love you too.' She dabbed at her eyes with a hanky.

'I hope that's not Garbo's hanky.'

She looked at it and shook her head.

'So what are we fighting for?' I went on.

'Because you're trying to spin some cock and bull story about you coming from the future as if that explains everything. You're just making a fool of me. If you're going to lie at least do me the courtesy of making it a believable lie.'

I looked at my watch. 'Katie, there's about an hour and a half before we get to Calais. Why don't I get us some coffee and I'll tell you all – and I promise I'm not lying. If you still don't believe me, or at least not prepared to give me the benefit of the doubt, then just walk away when we get to Glasgow.'

I called and the attendant duly brought us coffee.

'I *am* from the future. No, listen,' I held up my hand. 'I'm not from another planet or another galaxy or any of your Dan Dare nonsense but I am from the future, February 2017 to be exact.'

She gave me another "don't come it" looks but at least she was listening. I told her about the events of that January day and how I had travelled back and forth a few times and about what I was trying to do.

'Seriously? This is about making money?'

I nodded. 'That's how it started out. And it worked. But then you came along. I couldn't believe it when you called my name that day. It threw me for six.'

'But I don't understand. Who's my Gordon Lorne, you know what I mean, the one I went out...,' her voice trailed off. 'Oh my God, don't tell me he's your father.'

'No, that wouldn't be possible, but he is, was, is, my grandfather. I was named after him.'

'Is he still alive?'

'He's married and living in Kings Park, my grandma is pregnant for my father. Granddad dies in 2010 I think, but grandma is still alive, in 2017 I mean. This gets confusing, you know.'

'So he never stayed in Canada?'

'No, sorry.'

She thought about this for a minute. It didn't seem to upset her as much as I thought it would.

'How do you know all this?'

'I visited my grandma before we left, in 2017 obviously. I had to find out where granddad's passport was otherwise I couldn't have gone to Paris. I needed his passport because I knew I could pass it off as mine.'

'I don't understand.'

'I had to get it from their house in King's Park.'

'*You broke into your grandparents' house?*' She was aghast.

'No, there was a key under a flowerpot, she always did that.'

I told her about my adventures with Mrs Kennedy and at least she laughed at that.

The next question was inevitable.

'And was, is there a girlfriend, wife, fiancée, in this future world of yours. Gordon?'

I looked at her levelly, 'Yes, that is, there was.'

'Oh,' she said dully. 'What do you mean, '"was"?'

I told her about Susan. 'A girlfriend, sort of. Looks a lot like you actually, same eyes, same build. But I've been doing a lot of thinking and I have to break off with her.'

'Why?'

'You.'

'I see.' But I'm not sure she did.

'So that business with the guy in London, was that just some sort of coincidence?'

I told her about my forays into the betting market using advance knowledge and how it led to Sandy's fall from grace. I told her about the beating I got and the business at the dog track. She just shook her head.

'I did nothing illegal, you know,' I said defensively.

'Maybe. Tell me about "the future" as you call it.'

'Well "in the future", when we say it like that we use our fingers to make wee inverted comma signs above our heads.'

'What a good idea!'

'Trust me, it isn't.'

'And?'

344

'They don't use the word "nigger",' I made the inverted comas sign, 'And they don't wear fur and they use the word "fuck" a lot, even the women.'

Katie looked shocked. 'Gordon!'

'Yeah, well – you asked.'

A thought struck her. 'How were you able to find out the race winners? Oh, wait, the library I suppose.'

'The internet.'

'Now I'm lost.'

'There will be an invention called a computer, a bit slow and erratic at first, that you can use for just about anything. You can use it as a typewriter, to store photographs, to make spreadsheets, to play music, you name it. They will be portable and no bigger than your handbag,' I pointed to the bag at her side. 'It will be linked to the internet which is a massive web of any information you want. Instead of going to a library you jut Google it.'

'Google it?'

'Yes, I'll go into detail later. Anyway it took me about twenty minutes to find out every horse race winner for January, February and March. And football result too.'

It took a moment to dawn on her. 'You mean...?'

'You got it. And these computers I'm talking about – they're so small you can wear them like a watch. Oh, and wait till you see the phones. Want to know the name of a song, tomorrow's weather, time of the London train, just ask the phone and an automated female voice will tell you in a second. You can even programme the voice you want; mine's Marilyn Monroe.' I saw her face, 'Yep, some things were still better in the fifties.'

'This is pure science fiction.'

'So was the iron horse to the Indian.'

345

I told her a lot more, about a female prime minister, the twin towers, the Berlin wall, Jimmy Johnstone, Princess Di, (she gasped at that one), credit cards, debit cards, Billy Connolly, and much else but that was only scratching the surface and I still wasn't sure if she believed me but there was genuine doubt now.

The train slowed as it approached Calais docks and I could see the 'Canterbury' waiting at the quay.

'You said something about proof earlier,' she said as we munched delicate sandwiches and cake in the ship's first class lounge. 'What did you mean?'

It was a good question, all of what I had told her was compelling enough but it wasn't proof.

'Yes, I know, so I did,' I said, prevaricating.

'I mean, you could have just made all this up – all it takes is a good imagination.'

'You're right, but maybe there are a couple of things.'

I had a couple of coins in the house in Nithsdale Road dated two thousand and something. That would help. I took out my wallet and foraged about the corners where I found a small dog eared receipt from P.C World for a wireless mouse for twelve pounds fifty including VAT. I hadn't noticed it before and I should have left it behind but there it was.

'Have a look at this. See the date 07-01-2017, seventh of January two thousand and seventeen. And here, that's my credit card number, at least the last four numbers, they don't print them all for security.'

'You bought a mouse?' She looked puzzled.

'It's just a device for working your way around the computer. Much simpler than using the keyboard all the time.'

'What's P.C. World?' she asked.

'It sells computers and electrical stuff. It's a sort of Santa's Grotto for men.'

'Is this the price? My God.'

'That's not bad. The average salary is about twenty k a year.'

'"K"?'

'Thousand.'

'Good lord.'

She scrutinised it further. 'And VAT?'

'Value added tax. Legalised government theft.'

'Well, it's refreshing to see that some things never change.'

'Hmm, quite the little cynic, aren't we?'

She sighed, 'I don't know. George, I mean Gordon, I just don't know what to think.'

'Come with me to Central Station tomorrow and I'll show you,' I said. I thought I'd do the Barry trick in reverse.

'Supposing all this is true – where does that leave me? You're still going back to where you came from and that'll be it for us. I don't think I could stand being dumped by two Gordon Lornes. I'm just getting over the first one,' she said dispiritedly.

'I was thinking about that, Katie. Maybe I can figure something out. I want to be here with you. I told you that I loved you and I meant it. I will have to go back, just once and sort it all out, but then I'll come back for good. We can have it all –Paris, Rome, New York, Dunoon.'

She laughed at that. 'I'll tell you what – do your little time traveller thing and bring me back a newspaper. Then we'll see.'

I smiled and nodded.

'By the way,' she continued, 'Why George Clooney?'

'He's a twenty-first century film star that woman find instantly orgasmic.'

'Hmm,' she sniffed, 'I might have known.'

'There are certain similarities,' I said, hurt.

She gave a deep sigh, 'I don't know why I'm even thinking this might be possible.'

'I know.'

'I preferred George,' she said.

'What?'

'I preferred you as George.'

'I prefer me as George too. I think that's what you should call me then.'

'Okay – George - now tell me more about Camilla and Charles.'

We both slept fitfully in our sleeping car berths on the journey up from London, the rattle of the wheels on the rail joints, far from being a soporific, kept me awake. Katie too, apparently.

'George?'

'Yeah?'

'Would you come down here and just hold me?'

Chapter Thirty-two

The train pulled into Central just before eight and we made our way to the taxi rank. Katie turned and looked at me.

'So what now?'

'I take you home.'

'No. I need time to think – why don't you go on home and just give me a call tomorrow. I'll meet you here and you can show me this disappearing act of yours, okay?'

'If you're sure.'

'I'm sure. And, Gordon – George - thank you – seriously. It's been a wonderful four days, unbelievable in every way really, but wonderful and I'll never forget it. So thank you.'

'No need. If it was good for you then you can double that for me.'

She put her hand on my chest, then kissed me lightly on the lips. 'We'll always have Paris.'

'Here's lookin' at you, kid,' I responded, Bogeyesque.

'Of all the gin joints in all the towns in all the world, she walks into mine.'

'Hey, that's my line.'

'It's about the only film you seem to have heard of.'

The word 'dreich' was coined for Glasgow early on a drizzly February Sunday morning. No-one was around, the streets were deserted, not as much as a tramcar in sight so I decided to walk rather than take a taxi. It matched my mood. It didn't improve much when I realised that being a Sunday the pubs were shut and I couldn't even seek solace in a the warm embrace of Heraghty's and a pint or four so I spent a desultory few hours moping around the house then went for a four mile run and had an early night.

Monday was a bit better and I phoned Katie at work before sitting down and trying to figure out how I was going to get my hands on nearly a hundred and fifty grand's worth of diamonds. It was clear to me now that I couldn't just walk out of the country and head for Amsterdam with that amount stashed away. Nor could I transfer cash directly from my account to anywhere outside of the country without special permits and rigorous scrutiny due to the currency exchange regulations. So I decided to pay a visit to a jeweller in Glasgow and ask for advice. I didn't think one of the well known companies like Laing's and certainly not H.Samuel would be appropriate so I wandered along the Trongate and found a small jewellers in Candleriggs with a sign in the window stating that they bought and sold all kinds of jewellery. The name above the door simply said 'Martin Feldman – Quality Jewellery' and a little bell tinkled above the door as I entered. A sixtyish white haired man looked up, Mr Feldman himself I assumed.

'Yes, what can I do for you?'

There was no point in beating about the bush. 'Mr Feldman?'

He nodded.

'How easy is it to buy diamonds in quantity here, in this country I mean?'

He looked at me warily, 'How much diamonds are we talking about, if I may ask?'

I coughed, 'Er, rather a lot, actually – say just to take a figure - around a hundred thousand pounds give or take.'

He looked at me for the longest time before speaking. 'That's rather a lot of diamonds, Mr...'

'It's just an enquiry at the moment.'

'And the purpose of such a purchase?'

'Investment – purely investment.'

'I see.' He took off his wire framed spectacles and polished them with the end of his tie. 'I'm afraid that sort of purchase would be beyond my capabilities. For that amount of diamonds they would have to be imported from Amsterdam and there are currency exchange laws and so on. Besides, I'm really a small time merchant as you can see.' He waved his hand around the small shop.

'I understand. It's just that I don't know how I would go about it. I know about the currency issues.' I explained.

He finished polishing then put his glasses back on and looked at me over the rims.

'You will pardon the question, but I assume the wherewithal to make such a purchase is - how shall I put it – legal?'

'Perfectly – it came about as a result of a large windfall.'

He was silent again before speaking. 'Well, Mr ...,' he looked at me questioningly but I said nothing. 'I'm afraid I cannot help you for the reasons I have given.' He paused and took a card from his pocket. 'However, if you contact this gentleman, he is a chartered accountant and his partner is a lawyer. They – how shall I say? - specialise in the transfer of capital. They can arrange the purchase of goods from abroad and have many contacts.'

I looked at him. 'All legal and above board?'

'Let us say that they have ways and means, but yes.'

I looked at the card and saw an Edinburgh address.

'Tell them I recommended them to you,' he continued.

'I will. Thank you for your time Mr Feldman.'

'Good-day to you.'

It seemed logical not to waste any time so I called the number on the card and it was answered almost right away by a man. He confirmed that it was his name, Cameron Baxter Esq., on the card and said that he would be happy to meet with me that afternoon. I had the impression that dear old Mr Feldman had already briefed him probably as soon as the door had clipped my arse behind me.

Sitting in his office a couple of hours later he confirmed that he and his partner specialised in financial and commercial business transactions and through a myriad of contacts they could arrange the purchase of diamonds on my behalf, for a small fee of course. The fee was one and a half percent.

Cameron Baxter was a large, tweedy, expansive man with a cultured Edinburgh accent and his legal sidekick was small and mousy but his eyes glittered with a sharpness that showed he was the brains of the outfit. He didn't say much, in fact I don't recall him saying anything at all; he just took notes. I explained what I wanted to do. Baxter looked at his colleague whom he had introduced as Jack Smaill. There was a slight nod.

'I'm sure, we can help you Mr Lorne.'

He explained how it would work. I would bring him a guaranteed bankers draft for the agreed sum. He didn't even raise an eyebrow at the amount. The bankers draft would be dated for the date of me taking possession of the diamonds. That transfer would actually take place in London on Thursday at Berners Hotel where I would meet with an emissary from a diamond dealer who would travel over from Holland to meet me. Once I had viewed the diamonds and accepted them I would telephone Baxter and he would then bank the draft and I would walk away with the diamonds. I couldn't help but feel that this was a helluva risk with such a vast amount of cash but I couldn't think of an alternative.

'Nothing to worry about Mr Lorne. We do this kind of work every day, don't we Jack?' Jack nodded. 'I'll call you Wednesday just to confirm and you can take the early Thursday morning flight down, how's that? Just pop through with the draft beforehand, say Wednesday afternoon?'

He shook my hand vigorously before seeing me to the door.

The trip to London did allow me to undertake another enterprise that had occurred to me as Katie and I had strolled through Paris that first morning so it would be a busy day all in all.

I met Katie with a hug and a kiss as arranged at Central station just after seven thirty.

'Okay, Houdini, so this is where the magic starts?'

'You'll be laughing on the other side of you face when I show up with all tomorrow's news. I don't think you're convinced – well the proof is in the pudding.'

We walked around in a state of agitation for the next minutes and time dragged but eventually the big overhead clock clicked on to seven fifty-six and I gave her a quick kiss.

'Wish me luck.' And at that the hand tripped over once more and with one bound, as they say, I was back in familiar territory.

Of course I should have had it all planned out before I took the leap. Turning around I saw that the stationers and newspaper shop was W.H Smith down towards the Gordon Street entrance and I sprinted into it. Needless to say it was mobbed. Then I had to find the papers which ate up another valuable fifteen seconds before I grabbed that morning's Herald. There was only one person at the till and three waiting and I tried to plead that my train was just about to leave but got short shrift from an overweight woman in line holding a basket with enough chocolate in it to put a pound onto Cadbury's share price and another pound on to her waistline.

'Dae ye think ah'm just staunin' here fur the good o' mah health?' she said rudely, not requiring an answer.

The contents of her basket gave the lie to that but I didn't have time to argue, I was fast running out of time. There were three self service tills and mercifully one was free so I scanned the paper but of course the fucking machine rejected the first coin I put in and by the time that I eventually managed to complete the transaction, all for a fucking paper for fuck's sake (you could tell I was feeling pressured) I had five seconds to spare. It took me six to get to the clock. Just as I was a yard from being directly under it the minute hand clicked over to seven fifty-eight and that was it. Shit, shit, shit, shit!

Katie would be standing there wondering what had happened to me. Actually she wouldn't because although it was just a minute to me, it was sixty years to her.

Cursing fluently to the obvious discomfort of a passing nun I sat down on the little metal chairs that

354

were designed to provide five minutes relief and two days of back pain and pondered on what to do now. It wasn't a total disaster. I could go back to 1957 tomorrow and call Katie and explain what had happened. I still had the evidence and I could even bring her more proof, like my mobile phone which, though it wouldn't connect to anything, had a store of music and photos on its memory card.

However there was another problem. Save for the coppers in change I got from buying the paper I had no money, well I had but it was eight pound notes from the fifties and a ten bob note. Worse, my key for the Partick flat was back in time in Nithsdale Road in a glass jar on the sideboard – a dawning realisation that was about as welcome as Sammy Davis Junior at a Ku Klux Klan rally.

I reviewed my options. I could go to Susan's but I didn't feel right about that given my feelings for Katie and no amount of trying to rationalise it by telling myself that Katie was sixty years in the past made it any better. I could try and get hold of Barry. And of course there was always Christine. Christine won the toss.

'And you are?' she said with heavy sarcasm as I stood at her door.

'Come on Chris, I'm sorry I haven't called. It's a long story.'

'You remind me of someone.'

'Cut the sarcasm, Chris.'

'So what brings you to my door at ten o'clock at night without so much a by your leave?' Boy was she angry.

'I need a bed for the night.'

'Well you can fuck off for a start. Does it not occur to you that I might have a life? Has that snotty bitch kicked you out? Well good for her if she has.'

'No she hasn't. I mean I was never in, not as a live in anyway.'

I made a move to enter her flat.

'Ah!' she put her hand out to stop me. 'I might have company.'

She was dressed in a creased set of old grey pyjamas that had been a business class give away on a Qantas flight and two odd socks. I didn't think so.

'Do you have company?'

'No,' she said sulkily.

We looked at each other. 'You can sleep on the settee.'

'Thanks, Chris – really.'

'And don't even think about sex. It's a bad time anyway.' She turned and flounced away.

'Last thing on my mind.'

'Gee thanks.'

She disappeared into the kitchen and came back with a bottle of plonk and an opener and handed me both.

'Sorry about your dad,' she said.

'Yeah.'

'The funeral was a blast.'

I smiled, 'Yes it was, wasn't it?'

This was one of the things I loved about Chris, she was a giver. I had pissed on her from a great height and she had a right to be angry and she was but it quickly passed and she never held a grudge. Then again, she expected the same from everyone else and everyone else wasn't so forgiving. As a result she was always at the wrong end of the toilet flush, but I have to say this, she always came up smelling of roses. She really, really deserved a good guy. Unfortunately I wasn't him.

'I'm sorry about the Caribbean trip,' I said.

'Yeah, well. To be honest I wasn't too crazy about a week in the sun with Brian. He's got a premature ejaculation problem. I told him he should see a doctor about it.'

'Oh?' I raised a questioning eyebrow.

'Yeah. They say it's touch and go.'

We both fell about laughing. Poor Brian.

'That's unkind really,' she said once she had calmed down, 'He's a nice guy but I want more –someone halfway between you and him would be perfect.'

We were silent for a while, each in our own reveries.

'So what's really between you and Susan – is it the real deal?'

'I wish I could tell you but things are really weird right now – I wish I knew where I was.'

She stroked my hair. 'Poor baby.'

'Yeah? Why don't you finish it?'

'Okay. Poor baby my arse.'

She gave me a kiss, filled my glass then took herself and the rest of the bottle to her room.

'Sleep tight,' I said.

'That's the plan.'

Fortunately Chris had a key to my flat so I was able to go back in the morning and check on a few things like more final demands and the cast of Jurassic Park multiplying in my fridge, as well as picking up my mobile phone. It also gave me a chance to have another browse at horses and football in 1957 although I wasn't going to need any more of that. Old habits die hard. I gave the place a quick once over with an entire can of Glade that only made matters worse and made a call to Susan.

'I just wanted to say high. I miss you.' And I did.

357

'You don't need to, I'm right here.'

'I know. Any more news from action man?'

'Not a sausage. He's out of the country anyway. I haven't even thought about him.'

'That's good, that's good,' I said.

She didn't say anything, waiting for me to speak again.

'Look I'm sorry, but I'm out of action for a few days, till the weekend at least, but I'll call, okay?'

'Okay.'

Damn, I hate understanding women.

It was quarter to eight at the station and I was pacing about like a jaguar on speed. The minute the clock switched to three minutes to eight I was through again so I immediately found a bank of phones and called Katie.

'Katie, sorry about last night. It took me more than a minute...'

She interrupted. 'Gordon I hung around for an hour – I didn't know what to think. I still don't.'

'Can I come over? I have all the proof you need.'

'This isn't working for me, Gordon.'

'Don't say that, Katie. Give me a break.'

She was obviously torn and dispirited and there was a long silence before she sighed.

'Right, come over, but don't plan on staying.'

Fifteen minutes later I was at the house and she let me in.

'What time is it?' I asked her.

She looked at me questioningly then looked at her wall clock. 'Twenty past eight.'

'There you are, I came back through the portal or whatever it is you want to call it at exactly three minutes

358

to eight, called you right away, and, e voila, as they say in Paris.' I probably shouldn't have mentioned Paris.

'Yes, here you are,' she said drily.

'Now look at this.'

I produced yesterday's Herald, Saturday 18th February 2017, not normally my choice but it was all they had.

'See, look at the date,' I pointed excitedly.

She looked at it and I could see doubt cloud her face. 'But yesterday was Monday.'

'Not in 2017 it's not. The date is the same but not the day. And look at the headlines.'

Emblazoned across the top of the paper was 'INDEPENDENT SCOTLAND COULD JOIN E.U.'.

Katie frowned. 'What's all this about?'

'These are the things that are happening in my time. Scotland is devolved now and has its own prime minister, or first minister. Britain voted to come out of the European Union and Scotland isn't happy. You don't know anything about any of that, though - I'll explain later. Just look, though.'

I opened the paper. There was an article about Piers Morgan and J.K Rowling having a twitter spat, an article about the Panama Papers scandal that I couldn't give a shit about, a Naval ship rescuing a yacht in the Atlantic, the usual murders, Trump being made fun of, and a host of other things like global warming. Just another day in paradise.

'The first minister is a woman?' Katie was incredulous.

'The *Prime* minister is a woman Katie. She's the second we've had and don't ask about the first one.'

'My goodness! Who's J.K Rowling?'

'Oh my God, do I have lot to tell you.'

I dug the few coins I had from my pocket, a one pound coin, a twenty pence and two pennies.

'This is 2017 money, Katie. This is a pound.' She took the coin and examined it then she looked at the others.

'This is a pound? No notes?'

'Fivers and up only. There's a two pound coin too.'

'My goodness, it doesn't look much.'

'For what you buy for ninepence now you'll need this in 2017.'

She shook her head, amazed. We sat down and she made me some tea and toast while I told her about all the political shenanigans and Harry Potter and I explained some other items.

'Global warming?' she asked with a frown.

'Yes.'

'What's that?'

'Oh we're all going to fry,' I said nonchalantly.

'*What*? When?'

I looked at my watch. 'Twenty five to four on the thirteenth of July, nineteen twenty-six.' I was at my best when I was being flippant.

'Be serious.'

'I am being serious. Okay, not the date, but it's true.'

'Why?'

I told her all about carbon dioxide and cows farting and Hummers and the melting ice caps and George Bush and everything else I could think of.

'Oh my God.' She was shocked, as well she should be. 'So we're all doomed,' she exclaimed, appalled.

'Except Scotland.'

'How come?'

'It's going to be wetter and windier, wouldn't you just believe it. Everywhere else gets to bask in the sun,

360

slapping on fifty factor cream and we're going to spend the Glasgow Fair sitting in Nardini's in Largs watching a hurricane flattening Millport.'

'Why?'

'God knows. Personally I blame John Knox.'

She looked at the paper again and the weekend supplement, shaking her head in wonder all the while.

'The women wear trousers all the time.'

'Pants they're called. Not all the time but most of.'

She flipped the pages. 'Look at all these holidays! A thousand pounds for a Caribbean cruise. Who could afford that?'

'Just about everyone, kiddo – if you like cruising. It's a bit like a care home with lifeboats. I also brought this.' I took my smart phone from my pocket. It was an old IPhone but it still had all the whistles and bells. Katie sat beside me and looked at the blank screen on it curiously.

'What is it?'

'My phone.' I switched it on and the screen came to life with all its apps.

'I can't phone anyone because there's nothing in this period to recognise it but I can show you things.'

I flipped through some photographs being careful to avoid any with either Susan or Chris. There were a few of Barry's party and two or three of a day out at a 'T' in the Park concert and a few I took at a Mumford and Sons gig at the new Hydro including a couple of the outside of the Hydro itself all lit up in its rainbow colours. Katie was literally open mouthed.

'How did all those photos get in there?'

'It's complicated.' Then I had an idea. 'I'm going to take a selfie of us, okay?'

361

She looked nonplussed. I stretched out my hand with the phone in it. 'Say cheese.'

'A what?'

Click. I showed her the photograph, a good one as it happened – me smiling and her looking startled. Her hand flew to her mouth.

'That's impossible.' She examined the photograph. 'I don't believe it. Where's the film?'

'No film and not impossible where I come from.'

I explained that I could do a number of things with it such as download it (a word she had never heard) into my computer then print it out. I could do all sorts of tricks with it like turn it into black and white or colour just a part of it. The phone had an app that could put horns on her head or make her look like a cat. She was, and there is no other word, flabbergasted.

Then I took a pair of earbud speakers from my pocket and plugged them in and showed her how to put them in her ear. I searched for a couple of songs that wouldn't be too way out for her 1957 sensibilities. I found Neil Diamond's 'Sweet Caroline' and also Rod Stewart's 'Mandolin Wind'. She listened to them both all the way through.

'That's fantastic,' she gasped.

'Now do you believe me?'

'My God, it's really true.'

'Now say something.' I switched it on to video mode.

'What?'

'Smile – you're on Candid Camera. Say I love you, George.'

She shook her head in puzzlement. 'I love you, George.'

362

I hit the playback button and watched her face as she saw herself.

'I can't believe what I'm seeing here.'

'Welcome to 2017.'

Now that she believed me we talked a lot more about what life was like in my world.

'There's a line from a book about the past being a foreign country and it being different there, well, that works both ways, so is the future.'

We talked some more then I told her I had to leave because I had so much to do although I didn't tell her what that was. I couldn't tell her that I was going to the bank to lift out nearly a hundred and fifty grand, money beyond her imagination, then book a flight to London for Thursday, buy some diamonds, take them to 2017, and sell them for a almost couple of million. Some things are best left unsaid.

It took a couple of visits to the bank to get what I wanted but between times I paid a visit to my old friend Mr Sherrie who booked me on a BEA Viscount down to London Heathrow at eight o'clock the next morning and back again in the evening. Once I got the draft I needed from the bank I took the train through to Edinburgh and met up with Cameron Baxter and his partner again. They were delighted to see me.

'All set, Mr Lorne, are we?' he boomed as he took the envelope and examined the draft. 'Dated Friday, I see.'

'Just security Mr Baxter. I can't get back from London until late tomorrow so I can't cancel the draft after I pick up the diamonds and you can cash it first thing Friday.'

He looked over at Smaill who shrugged and nodded.

'Okay. Here's what will happen. You will meet a Mr Oosterhuizen at twelve o'clock at Berners Hotel. He's a representative of Prinzenschraacht Diamond Dealers and he will be in possession of diamonds to the value of the amount on the draft.'

'How do I know that they will be real?'

Baxter pulled himself up to his full height. 'Mr Lorne, we are a reputable firm with many testimonials and references. I can assure you Mr Oosterhuizen represents a long established business. Besides you will be supplied with full certification, receipts and documents certifying that you are the legal owner.'

'Okay I'm sure you're right.' I said with all the confidence I could muster.

'Besides, Mr Lorne. How else can you arrange the financial side of things?'

He had me there. I was just going to have to trust him.

I spent the night at Nithsdale Road in a fever of nervous energy feeling like some sort of secret agent on a covert mission and I hardly slept.

Renfrew Airport looked nothing like modern day Glasgow Airport except for some sort of futuristic arch bridging the terminal entrance. A couple of old prop jobs sat on the tarmac and I assumed one of them was for the London flight since it had 'British European Airways' painted on the fuselage. They didn't go in for fancy logos in this period. Check in was a simple affair and I realised just how much more pleasurable travel was in this day and age without long lines at security and scanning machines and spotted youths feeling me up and down.

The airplane was a Vickers Viscount and the flight was proudly billed as 'The Clansman' service to London Heathrow. The flight was about half full and I noted with some amusement that the overhead rack was a simple net affair for throwing your coat onto. Even more amusing was as the propellers pulled the aircraft away from the terminal a uniformed senior officer of the company, the station manager no less, saluted the departing aircraft smartly. I felt like Guy Gibson heading off to the Möhne Dam. Halfway through the flight, during which an excellent breakfast was distributed, a map of our route was circulated from the flight deck, duly signed by the captain and first officer. It was pretty much a straight line drawn from Glasgow to London just in case anybody on board might be under the impression that we might be taking a circuitous route via Keflavik and Dublin.

Two hours later we landed at a strangely provincial looking Heathrow and within the hour I was in the centre of London, a little early, at Berners Hotel.

Mr Oosterhuizen sought me out at a coffee table in a quiet corner of the hotel lounge having been previously briefed on my description. He was a small, balding, bespectacled man of around fifty and looked like a banker.

'Mr Lorne?'

'Mr Oosterhuizen.' I rose and shook his hand.

After a moment or two's pleasantries we got down to business. From a briefcase at his side he produced a velvet pouch and a chamois square. He opened the pouch and decanted about seventy or eighty, maybe more, glittering beads of what looked like crystal. They caught the light and sparkled it around the table like the revolving glass orb at the Plaza. I was mesmerised.

'These, Mr Lorne, are diamonds. Mr Baxter has specified the value and these you see before you, they are what my firm offers you.'

I looked at them not quite knowing what to say or do.

Oosterhuizen proffered me an eye glass. 'Look, look you can see. They are cut by experts to be sure, that is the art.'

He spoke in a cultured voice with a hint of accent that was enough to identify him as of low country origin but not German. I took the glass and looked at a couple of the stones without knowing what I was looking at.

'See the cut, see the purity, Mr Lorne?'

I nodded in assent. They looked brilliant. Oosterhuizen covered them with a cloth then caught the attention of a waiter. 'Coffee for two, please.' The waiter retreated.

'Yes we have time. Please take the time you need.' He reached into his briefcase. 'I have here the certificates of authenticity and of, course, documents recording the sale and transfer in your name as proof of purchase. I understand that this is an investment.'

I nodded yes.

'Very wise. Gems like these never grow old, never fade. They will never betray you like a woman will, Mr Lorne. They reveal their beauty to you at your bidding. They grow more beautiful with time. Keep them safe, one day they will repay you.' He rolled them lovingly across the chamois with his fingers, almost dreamily.

He covered the diamonds again to hide them from the waiter as he poured the coffee and we drank it while I looked at what I had come here to achieve. Here it was and here they were. In a few short days I would be back in twenty-first century Glasgow selling them for more money than I could ever have imagined. First Class to Barbados? Fuck that, I could charter a plane.

'Thank you Mr Oosterhuizen, it has a been a pleasure doing business with you. I'll call Mr Baxter and tell him he can cash the draft first thing.'

He held out his arm and we shook hands, then with a small stiff bow he left me with a small black velvet pouch and a bag of stones. Precious stones.

I still had one more errand that I wanted to make which took a couple of hours but I was still at Heathrow in plenty of time for the evening 'Clansman' back to Glasgow.

Back in the flat I took out the diamonds and emptied them onto the table just to watch them glitter and imagined the riches and fortune that lay ahead for me, little old Gordon Lorne from the south side of Glasgow, who would have thought it?

The following morning I phoned Katie who answered on the third ring just as she was about to leave for work.

'He's ba-ack,' I mimicked in my best Freddy Kruger voice but of course she had no idea what I was talking about. 'Any chance of dinner on the town tonight?'

'You certainly know how to keep a girl waiting, don't you?'

'I really want to see you Katie, I've been doing a lot of thinking.'

'Girls night out, remember?'

Damn. 'Okay, tomorrow? I'll take you to the Rogano. Best seafood in town if not the entire world. How about it?'

'Okay, Gordon, but we really need to talk,' she said, stating the words that strike the fear of death into the

367

hearts of most men from Scrabster to Sicily. The "we need to talk" mantra never, but never, heralds good news. My mother used it on me from an early age about the state of my underpants telling me she'd be shocked to admit I was hers if I was ever taken to hospital if I had been in an accident. It always seemed a touch callous that in the event of my being rushed to hospital having been mown down by a number 56 Shotts bus her most pressing concern was the state of my underpants. I imagined the doctor talking to her in the hospital waiting room. 'Bad news, I'm afraid, Mrs Lorne. You son is on the operating table as we speak and I have to tell you that the *state of his underpants is an absolute disgrace!*' My father used those words when he wanted to discuss the contents of my school reports cards, which, although being a step up from the contents of my underpants, were nonetheless chastening. At least three girlfriends used the phrase preparatory to dumping me along with the words, 'It's not you, it's me' although one was more blunt. Then, of course, there was the owner of the travel agency but we won't go into that again.

So it was with some trepidation that I agreed a suggested time of seven o'clock the next day outside the Rogano. Anyway it gave me a free evening to have a few pints in Heraghty's and that's where the three musketeers found me just after seven o'clock.

I set up the drinks and we generally basked in the glow of the knowledge that it was Friday night and the joys of the weekend lay ahead. Benny had some news.

'Did you hear about your friend, Sandy?'
I had no idea where this was going and I didn't want to mention my chance meeting with him in London.

'No,' I said.

368

'He'd been off the radar for a few days but he turned up in London.'

'Oh?'

'Dead.'

I nearly choked on my pint. 'No!'

'Aye.'

'What happened?' asked Eric.

'I don't know too much, the Met are handling it, but he was found with his head caved in at a lane off Covent Garden.'

'When?' I asked.

'A few nights ago. The grapevine is saying that he owed some guys out in Blackhill some big time cash and couldn't pay. You don't want to mess with these guys I can tell you. Anyway they caught up with him. Probably didn't mean to kill him but it just got out of hand.'

I shook my head. I didn't know what to say. 'I don't know what to say.'

'Nothing to say, is there? He was a bad lot so no big loss,' said Benny uncaringly.

'What'll happen to his shops?' Phil asked.

'The Blackhill mob will take them over, no doubt. I think that was their play all along.'

I made a mental note not to place another bet in Scotland again; I didn't like the sound of the Blackhill mob.

Phil changed the subject. 'My editor likes the stuff I've come up with for that wee series on the future. What about all the other points, communications and the like?'

We spent another hour talking about where I saw things going with my twenty- twenty foresight and he jotted away happily with the stub of a pencil. Pints were ordered and drunk but I couldn't get my mind away from Sandy's fate. He must have been killed within a day or so of me bumping into him, maybe even that very day. I hated to think that in some small way I had played a part in his demise but I shrugged it off. It was his choice to be a bookie after all, and he'd been responsible for a few broken spirits and probably a few broken heads over the years. Poor unlucky bastard.

We closed the pub as usual and staggered off to our various homes although not before a final word of caution from Benny.

'If you fancy a flutter, George, just mind where you get lucky. Glasgow might be the second city of the empire and all that, but it's still just a wee village.'

There was clearly a veiled warning in there and I had a feeling that Benny knew more than he was letting on.

'I'll bear that in mind, Benny – thanks for the tip.'

He nodded and we went our several ways.

Chapter Thirty-three

You could always count on Katie being on time and today was no exception to the rule. The minute hand of the Tron Church clock had just hit the hour when Katie appeared through the archway at Royal Exchange Square, the smile on her face dispelling any of my concerns of her "we need to talk" admonishment. She gave me a quick kiss on the lips before she even said hello.

The Rogano is, and always has been, one of Glasgow foremost restaurants especially in the field of seafood. I had passed its doors often before I was whisked off to 1957 and although I had never eaten in it I had on a few occasions had a drink there and had once attended a small wedding in its downstairs lounge, an interesting affair where the best man was whisked off to pokey and got six months for lifting most of the cutlery. It was, and still is, very much Art Deco in its style and has long been one of the places in which the cognoscenti can be regularly seen wining and dining. The then owner, Donald Grant, wanted the restaurant designed and styled like the Queen Mary which was still the only way to cross the Atlantic in the fifties. Apparently Rod Stewart when in Glasgow dines there and insists on table sixteen but that is some way in the future. Besides I have never seen him there but that is hardly surprising given my rather impecunious state at that time.

It was a first for Katie too although, what with all the fine dining in other establishments plus consorting with Garbo in Maxim's, she was beginning to feel not quite so out of place. I thought that she could never be out of place.

The menu was unashamedly maritime. There were Portpatrick oysters and Brora lobster; Whitstable crab and wild Tay salmon. For the carnivore there was Angus beef and Braemar venison. When you ate in Rogano you didn't need a menu; it was an atlas you wanted.

I had a scallop starter and ventured to share with the waiter the notion that it might go well with black pudding but that concept hadn't been imagined then and he just smiled indulgently. Katie had smoked salmon and a crab au gratin dish, and I had a shrimp and salmon main course. We polished off a bottle of Pouligny Montrachet just because we could. I silently toasted the late Sandy for his unwitting benevolence.

'I've been thinking about us,' said Katie over coffee. Was this the "we need to talk" time, I wondered.

'Me too.'

'I don't like being without you, in fact I hate it. You've brought so much into my life. I want us to be together.' She shrugged at the remains of the wine and waived her hand around the room. 'Oh it's not for all this, although, don't get me wrong, I love it – I do. It's because of who you are and what you know and what you want. It's what I want too. I want you to take me to the places you talk about and more. I want to be part of your life – 1957 doesn't come close but without you this is what I'm stuck with. You know I love you – there I've said it.'

That was the best "we have to talk" speech I'd ever heard. She should give lessons.

'I feel the same way too, Katie,' and I did. The thoughts, ideas and feelings I had been having started to coalesce into a firm resolve.

Katie started to speak again. 'So what I've been thinking is this – I want to come back with you.'

It took me a second to realise what she meant.

'You want to come forward with me you mean? To 2017.'

'Yes.'

I sat back and gave a silent whistle. I hadn't seen that one coming.

'Listen, Katie – there's a million reasons why that won't work.' She looked downcast but I carried on. 'Firstly, I don't think it would be physically possible. I was the one hit by lightning – it's my body that's programmed to go through this, this – this tunnel through time. It might even be dangerous for you to try, I don't know. Also – think of this – supposing you did make it through – who would you be? You have no identity, I mean you have no identity as a person. You wouldn't be able to get credit or earn money, open a bank account – you couldn't get a passport. You couldn't exist.'

I hadn't realised myself up until that moment all the things you needed to survive in a digital environment. You could pretty well adopt any identity in 1957 with a bit of ingenuity. It might be illegal but you could do it and it would be victimless. It was a different a story in 2017 unless you were a computer criminal specialising in identity theft and I couldn't get into that. In 1957 it was fairly easy to adopt the identity of a dead person and get a national insurance number which was pretty much all you needed. Not in 2017.

'Katie, there's another thing. I've been telling you all about life in the twenty first century. It's a life that you slowly evolve to – adapt to. But for you to jump into life as I know it would be such a culture shock for you I really don't know how you would cope.'

'I'm sure I'd manage,' she said dully.

'No I don't think you would,' I said. 'God knows I've enough trouble myself.'

'You manage alright in my culture.'

'That's because I know what to expect. I've seen pictures, I've read a bit about the history, listened to my parents and grandparents. It's easier to go back than go forward.'

I could see tears starting to glisten in her eyes.

'So what, then?' she asked.

I took a deep breath. 'I've been thinking too. If you can't come with me, then I can stay with you.'

It took her a moment. 'You mean you would live here in 1957?'

I nodded.

'With me?'

'With you.'

She looked at me. 'Would you do that? Do you really want that?'

'It's been on my mind for some time. Just think of what we can do together – what a life we can have. Because of the circumstances of what happened to me I am richer than you can imagine.'

'But what about your life there – your friends? There will come a point when you can never go back and anyway, I don't think I'd like the idea of you jumping back and forward.'

374

'No. That would be it. It would be a clean break. I'd never go back again. I just need to go back one more time to settle some affairs and make sure I have enough information that will keep us in some style for the rest of our lives.'

She digested this. 'I don't know. Do you think it would work?'

'Let me tell you this, Katie. I've had more fun being here with you than I ever had in my other life. I've felt more for you than anyone I've ever known and I never want to leave you. So, yes – it will work.' My mind was made up.

Her eyes started to tear up again and she held my hands in hers. 'I think that would be wonderful.'

'Agreed - it's deal. Let's seal it with a bottle of champagne.'

A waiter happily took our order.

'I just wish we could be together in the future, in 2017, I'd love to share some of your life with you.'

'That's just it. You will. We'll both be in our nineties but you will see all of the things I've told you about. The Beatles, jet planes, DisneyWorld, Celebrity Big Brother, texting, tweeting. You'll see it all. I promise.'

'So we will be together in 2017? I never thought of it like that.'

'Yes we will, I promise. You just get to live the bits in between.'

'And we'll always have Paris.'

'Here's looking at you, kid.'

I slept over at her place although neither of us got much sleep for a variety of reasons some of which are best left to the imagination but as I left her on that

Sunday morning both of us were bright with hope and excitement for the great future ahead of us. I just needed two or three days to wrap things up. I needed to split the diamonds and take Barry's share back with me. My own share I would just leave here and sell them off as I needed them. I regretted buying such an amount now but I didn't know that I would be making such a momentous decision. By now it was just before six and I had a couple of hours to tidy up so I made sure that I had everything I needed. I took my wallet and my mobile, I would probably be making a few calls then I thought of something on a whim, I don't know why but I did.

I left my share of the diamonds and my bank book which still had a few hundred in it, locked the door then left Nithsdale Road. They would be there when I came back. The weather had softened and the house wasn't so cold so it wouldn't be too bad when I returned.

Half past seven at Central station and the 'City of Glasgow' pulled the late running Royal Scot in to platform one and a Cathcart Circle chuffed out of an adjoining platform. I popped a stamped envelope into a pillar box, walked towards the clock and just as it reached the appointed time I walked through into 2017.

Barry met me in the Horseshoe the next day hardly able to contain his excitement.

'How did it all go?'

'Like a dream, old son, like a dream.'

'You've got the diamonds?'

'In my pocket.' I tapped the side of my jacket.

'Christ, let's see.'

376

'Not here, Baz. It's a bit public. Drink up and we'll go back to my place.'

'Okay, okay.' He gulped at his pint.

'So,' I said, 'what's the latest with you?'

'Oh, I should tell you. The wedding's back on.'

'*What?*'

He shrugged. 'We had a long talk about it.'

'Baz, are you thinking with your dick again?'

'Yeah, I had to have a visit to the clinic – oh wait, I forgot –that's you,' he said with his usual sarcastic venom. Nice to have the old Barry back.

'Right, point taken, but what happened? Last time I heard Lesley had cut off sexual relations and had boosted the John Lewis share price by ten points.'

'I think she came to her senses after I'd broken off the engagement. Plus Chris had a long talk with her. Basically told her she was being a drama queen and if she didn't come back to planet Earth nobody would want to know her and to fuck off and come back when she's seen some sense.'

'Sounds like Chris.'

'Yep, good advice too.' He took another swig of his pint.

I nodded at his glass. 'Another?'

'Make it a half.'

'So it's back to Barbados on Coconut Airways?'

'Actually no. We're getting married at Broomhill Church on Crow Road and the reception at Cameron House. We might do the honeymoon in the Caribbean - in fact that suits me fine – some sand, sea, sun, and sex, just the two of us.'

'And, not to be prurient, but what about...?'

'Oh, we're at it like rabbits.'

377

I wondered why he looked so smug. Go Barry.

We downed the drinks and took a taxi back to my place. For once Barry didn't make any comment about the spartan and run down look of the place. I think he was too eager to see the diamonds to take any notice of his surroundings. I took the velvet pouch from my pocket and then took the certificate of authenticity and the receipts from the envelope I'd brought with me. I laid the certificate onto my table so that Barry could examine it. Then I opencd the pouch and poured the diamonds out on the table top where they shone like, well, diamonds.

Barry breathed excitement. 'Wow!'

'Wow right enough.'

'And this is them all?'

'No, this is your share,' I said.

'What about yours?' he asked, a puzzled look on his face.

'Look, Baz, there's something I've got to tell you.'

'Go on.'

So I told him about Katie and my decision to go back to 1957 this time for good and how I left my share of the diamonds there and that's where I saw myself for the rest of my life.

'Gordon, mate – you're joking, right?'

'I've never been more serious. You're starting out on a new life, it's about time I did too.'

'But you're my mate.'

'Baz, let me tell you how it's going to be. If I stay here you'll get married, you'll have kids, we'll still be mates but your life will be with your family. Sure, we'll have a pint or two every week or so then it'll get less and less...' Barry started to protest but I held my hand up. 'No,

378

that's just life – it happens to everybody and I'm fine with that. But this is my life too and this is what I want.'

'Oh man, I don't believe this. What's Chris gonna say, and I thought Susan was the pin-up of the month.'

'I'll have to deal with that over the next day or so. By the way, how is the lovely Christine? Have you seen her?'

'Oh, yeah. I should have said. She's going out with Maserati man. Turns out he's not bi at all. Straight as an arrow and twice as sharp.'

'The chap from the party?'

'Yeah. Brian got the old heave-ho.'

I was strangely pleased. Chris deserved somebody who could give her a fun time and the wherewithal to provide it. I could see her swanning about the Clyde or Loch Lomond in a power boat with wind in her hair and enjoying the moment. She'd had plenty of losers in her life of which I was one of the latest. She deserved a winner.

'Anyway, Baz old son,' I said, nodding at the diamonds, 'You're a rich man now. Honeymoon at the Sandy Lane methinks.'

'It won't be the same without you around, Gord.'

I patted him on the shoulder, 'Yes it will, Baz. Yes it will.'

He sighed then looked at the diamonds. 'So what now?'

'We'll probably have to go down to London to sell them but maybe we should go into town to Laing's or someone and ask for a rough valuation.'

'Monday?'

'Make it the day after. I've got couple of urgent things I need to attend to.'

Barry looked at me questioningly.

'Stuff to do with my father, you know how it is.' I continued.

'Oh, sure, sure. Tuesday then?'

'Great. I need to get back to the old days. I've got hot date there.'

After Barry left I got around to thinking about what I should do about Susan. The problem was that here in 2017 I had strong feelings for her and I didn't want to hurt her but I had made my bed and my bed was in another time. I'm not the most moral man in the world, actually I'm probably near the bottom of the list somewhere, and I promised myself that I would be a different person in my new life. With that thought in mind I decided that one last act of cowardice wouldn't significantly add to the debit column so I decided to write a long letter and ask Barry to hand it to Susan after I had left. I could explain things so much easier on paper. It wasn't nice, it wasn't pretty but it was the best I could come up with.

I did the things I had to on the Monday then Barry and I met at ten o'clock on Tuesday morning. I had the pouch and certificates in my pocket. We nodded at each other in a "let's do this" fashion and went into Laing's jewellers in the Argyle Arcade. Feldman's in the Candleriggs was, of course, long gone. Laing's was renowned in the west of Scotland for probity and trust.

We entered into what at first glance looked like an executive lounge in an airport for a major long haul airline. There were a number of gold coloured chairs covered in velvet and some banquettes set into the wall. Small redwood tables lay between them and there was a reception desk. Discreet lighting from recessed lamps bathed the room in a discreet glow. A pleasant woman, early thirties perhaps, welcomed us.

'Good morning gentleman, can I be of assistance,' she flashed a flight attendant smile.

Barry nodded at me.

'Yes,' I said, 'I'd like a rough evaluation of some items with a view to selling.'

'And what would these items be?'

'Diamonds,' I said without preamble.

'And you have them with you.'

I brought the pouch out of my pocket but didn't open it.

'We normally ask clients who request valuations to leave them with us for a couple of days. There is a fee of course.'

I looked at Barry then spoke to the woman. 'Yes I understand. This may be a little different than what you're used to.'

'Really, you may be surprised,' she smiled condescendingly.

I opened the pouch and poured the contents on to a black cloth on the counter top. I could see she was impressed.

'Could I ask you to wait for a moment or two while I get Mr Ingram for you? This is more in his line. May I take one of the stones into him?'

I looked at Barry and we both nodded yes. We put the others back in the pouch. After about five minutes she reappeared and ushered us into a small tasteful room where there was a table and a couple of chairs in front and another chair behind. In this chair sat a man of around sixty, thinning grey hair swept back across his head. He wore a grey suit and a maroon tie and an expression of utmost gravity. On the table in front of him, on a small black cloth, looking splendid in all its solitude, sat our diamond. He stood and welcomed us and gestured to the seats. We sat down.

'I didn't get your names,' he said.

'I'm Gordon Lorne and this is Barry Marshall.'

He nodded. 'My assistant tells me you have a number of these.'

I took out the pouch and handed it to him and he emptied the contents on to the cloth and then examined a number at random with an eye glass. Gordon and I glanced at each other.

'Where, I might ask, did you get these?'

I brought out the certificate from the envelope I had with me.

'They belonged to my grandfather, his name was Gordon Lorne also. He got them from a dealer from Amsterdam I believe. I've got identification that confirms my identity if you need it. How or why they came into his possession I don't know.'

I handed him the certificate which he examined, and nodded

'I see.' He examined a couple more. 'I have to say that they are certainly the finest of their type I have come across.'

Barry and I exchanged smirks. He rubbed his hands between his closed thighs and I thought he might wet himself. I wasn't sure if I already had.

'Yes, quite the best of their type I have seen.'

He looked over at us. 'I can give you a rough estimate of their worth, certainly, but I am not in a position to purchase them.'

382

We nodded and he continued. 'Very fine stones indeed. However, Mr Lorne, you are labouring under the impression that these stones are diamonds. I regret to inform you that they are not.'

It took a second or two for this to sink in. 'Pardon?'

Barry spoke. 'But you said they were the finest of their type.'

'Indeed they are, Mr Marshall,' said Ingram, 'but their type is not diamond. These are zircons.'

'What?'

'What?'

'What the fu..., sorry, what are zircons.'

Ingram looked at us. 'Zircons are a semi-precious stone, the clear ones like these, are often confused with diamonds, although not by anyone who is trained to know the difference. Their properties are not unlike that of the diamond in many respects but a diamond is pure carbon. These are not.'

'But, but...does the certificate not state that these are diamonds?' I reached for it and read it again. The heading did state that the name of the company was Prinzenschraacht Diamond Dealers but when I looked at the invoice again it stated 'eighty four one and a half carat finest quality gemstones'.

'As you can see, the certificate, for what it's worth, is quite accurate.'

'Oh my God.' I could hardly breathe. If I had been wearing a tie I would have loosened it. By the look on his face if I had been wearing a tie Barry would have tightened it.

'So, what are they worth?' I asked in a strangled voice.

'As I say, they are the finest of their type, quality stones indeed.' He counted them out. I knew there was forty-two there; I had the rest back in Nithsdale Road half a century ago.

'I would say that each of these is worth around a hundred, maybe a hundred and twenty pounds. At a conservative estimate, say around four thousand, five thousand at a push for the lot.'

'Should we get a second opinion?' Barry asked hopefully.

'Absolutely. And a third and fourth. But I'm afraid that they're all going to tell you the same thing.'

I thanked him for his time and courtesy and we both staggered into the arcade in a daze and out into Buchanan Street as if in a trance.

Barry looked at me murderously. 'If you weren't going back to 1957 I'd fucking kick you there myself.'

I tried to pull myself together. 'Look, I'm sorry. I'm gonna go back there and kick the shit out of the guy who set me up.'

'Right. Your lawyer pal is going to claim he only did as instructed and you're Dutch pal has given you a certificate that's technically accurate. What exactly are you going to do?'

He was right. Jesus, I was angry, so was he.

'Okay, okay.' I took a few breaths to clear my head. 'Let's go somewhere quiet. We need to talk.'

'Shit. Not the "we need to talk" speech.'

I marched round to the Grand Central hotel next to the station and found a couple of seats in the deserted bar upstairs.

'Listen, Barry. It's not as bad as you think.'

'It's exactly as bad as I think.'

384

'No it's not. First off, you have four or five thousand in the space of a few weeks for a stake of a few hundred. That's a pretty good return,' I said.

He still looked mad but he nodded albeit reluctantly. 'Is there a second "off"?'

'Yes there is.' I pulled out another envelope from my pocket, opened it and spread the contents on the table in front of us.

'What's this?' asked Barry querulously.

'What does it look like?'

'Stamps.'

'That's right, Barry. Stamps.'

'I see that. You think I want to take up stamp collecting?'

'Not just any stamps, Baz. These babies are worth eight hundred thousand pounds.'

'What the fuck are you talking about?'

'I remembered some advice my father used to give me years ago about not putting all my eggs into one basket, so I, well I – diversified,' I said.

'I'm not with you.'

'I took a trip to Paris with Katie. We walked past the Avenue de Marigny and it gave me an idea.'

'What's the Avenue de Marigny when it's at home?'

I told him about an old film I'd seen - as it turned out he had seen it too - that was called 'Charade' and starred Cary Grant and Audrey Hepburn. The whole concept was that Audrey Hepburn's dead husband had left her his ill gotten gains in rare stamps. She only realised this when she was walking with her young nephew down the Avenue de Marigny where they have a major stamp fair in dozens of stalls three or four days a week. This gave me the idea of buying some rare stamps as well as

385

diamonds so that I would at least have some protection if things went badly wrong. Which, of course, they did. Spectacularly wrong.

'So I didn't put all my eggs into one basket. I diversified.'

Barry looked long and hard at the stamps. 'And these are?'

'These, Barry, are very rare stamps. Very rare indeed, and worth a lot of money.'

Barry peered at them. I took a pair of eyebrow tweezers from my pocket. 'Here, use these. Don't handle them.'

'What are they?'

I pointed at a few of them with my little finger. 'This one,' I said, pointing to a red stamp with an image of the god Mercury on it, 'is the Red Mercury stamp. It's Austrian, worth around forty thou. This one,' I pointed to a blue stamp with an almost indistinguishable background somewhat obscured by a cancellation franking mark, 'this is the Australian Inverted Swan stamp - fifty thousand.'

'You're shitting me.'

'No, Baz, but your eloquence does you proud.'

He looked the stamps, literally open mouthed.

I pointed to a few others. 'The U.S. Inverted Airmail – look – see how the biplane is printed upside down by mistake? Forty grand. And this, the 12 pence Canadian Blue of 1851, and look, the French one franc orange red of 1849, both around thirty thousand each.'

I sat back and watched his face as he examined them, turning each one over carefully with the tweezers one by one.

'There are twenty stamps there, Baz, total value around three quarters of a million to eight hundred thousand give or take. That's maybe four hundred k each.'

Barry then asked the inevitable question as I knew he would. 'Okay wise guy. You told me you had a fortune in diamonds that turned out to be not much better than cut glass. You've probably been conned with these as well. Who's to say?'

'No. When I went to London to meet with the diamond dealer...'

'Zircon dealer.'

I gave him a "give it a rest" look and continued. 'As I was saying, when I was in London I took another draft with me, made out to a reputable stamp investment dealer in London. I had the draft made out for seventy five thousand pounds and told the dealer I wanted stamps to that value. These are them.'

Barry shook his head. 'But that doesn't mean that they are worth a fortune today.'

'Yes it does.' I explained to Barry that the reason I hadn't met with him yesterday was nothing to do with my father's affairs. I had taken the early morning London flight and gone straight to Sotheby's rare Stamps and Coins evaluation department. I also took all the authentication documents from where I had purchased them in 1957, a firm well known to Sotheby's. It was them that confirmed their value as three quarters of a million at least and were prepared to put them up at auction with that amount as a reserve. I told them that the seller would be Barry Marshall and he would have a photocopy of the authentication certificate with him and

387

asked them to sign and agree that they had viewed and accepted the validity of the original.

'So, Baz, all you need to do is just pick any ten, I don't care which ones, and take them on down to Sotheby's and they'll auction them and you get four hundred thousand. Sotheby's will take their whack, of course, but, hey, you'll still be a rich man. I'll take my ten stamps back with me and resell them.'

'Fuck!' That's Barry, still eloquent as ever.

We ordered a drink from the barman.

'Geez, Gord, I don't know what to say.'

'No need to say anything. It's what we planned – almost anyway.'

He nodded. 'So you're really going through with this, setting up life sixty years in the past? I can't even ask you to write.'

I nodded.

'So when will you go?'

'Tomorrow. No sense in hanging around.'

'And you'll be okay - financially, I mean?'

'Oh yeah. These stamps are worth a fortune and I'm also going to visit every racecourse and bookie in England and, well, I'll be fine.'

He sighed.

'Oh,' I said, 'And I'm going to be famous.'

'How come?'

I smiled wickedly, 'Who do you think's gonna write some of these great songs? 'Hey Jude', 'Yesterday', 'Maggie May', 'Wonderwall', 'End of the Road', 'Bohemian Rhapsody', need I go on? Hey, I could write Phantom or Les Mis. Oh, and I almost know Harry Potter off by heart so you can forget J.K Rowling.'

'But – don't be daft -you can't,' he expostulated.

'Just you wait and see. Come on, time to hit the road.'

We wandered out of the hotel via the station entrance on to the station concourse and at that moment my whole world collapsed. Underneath the clock there was a tower of scaffolding, a cherry picker, and half a dozen workmen in high viz jackets and hardhats in the act of removing the clock from its ceiling support.

Chapter Thirty-four

Barry had to hold on to me to stop me sinking to my knees. Once the blood had returned to my head and the spots stopped dancing in front of my eyes I shook off Barry and ran, roaring, to the guys working on the clock.

'Stop that, stop that, *stop that at once*!'

People hurrying for the 13.40 to London stopped at my shouts. Christ, people *in* London stopped at my shouts. A dozen starlings that had been trapped under the huge glass roof for weeks rose as one and swiftly discovered the road to freedom. A small chihuahua, held close to its owner's bosom, sank its teeth into her in fright. Barry chased after me but it was all too late.

'What the fuck are you doing?' I screamed.

They looked at me in bewilderment.

'Is that a trick question,' one of them asked.

'I need that clock!' I shouted at them.

'How, have ye no' got a watch?' another asked.

One of the team, clearly the foreman as he was the one standing about not doing very much, strode over to me.

'What's your game, then?'

'You can't take that clock down,' I pleaded.

'Says who?'

'Look, you just can't okay. Can you not just leave it until after eight tonight - please?'

'Are you aff your rocker? This clock's going in for a refit. Whit's it to you anyway? Now piss off before I get the polis.'

It was all too late no matter what. By this time the gang had lowered the clock with a block and tackle onto the cradle of the cherry picker. The hands were stationary and obviously wouldn't be moving anywhere near three minutes to eight for some time.

It transpired that the clock was going in to be completely refurbished and brought back to former glories as part of some Network Rail customer awareness programme. Quite how it was going to ensure the punctuality of the five-thirty to East Kilbride or wherever wasn't explained.

'How long will it be down for?' I asked weakly.

'Nae idea, six weeks? Coupla months? Onybody's guess.'

I groaned. The foreman turned to Barry. 'Whit is it with yer pal? Ye need to get him away frae here. Like now.'

Barry put his arm around my shoulders and dragged me away.

'It's no use, mate. Too late.'

I was nearly in tears. No, I *was* in tears. He took me away from the public gaze and back in to the hotel where he sat me down, found a waitress and ordered coffee.

'Christ, Baz, she'll be there waiting for me wondering what's happened.'

He tried to comfort me. 'Listen Gordon, no she won't. It's sixty years later remember. Right now what's just happened to you happened to her sixty years ago. Right now, she's just an old woman or...,' he hesitated. 'Or...worse. It's all in the past.'

391

This was a nightmare and Barry was right, there was nothing, nothing at all I could do. The utter despair and helplessness that washed over me like a suffocating blanket was worse than anything I had ever endured before. My father's death a couple of weeks ago couldn't even come close. It wasn't just the feeling of loss – it was the knowledge that Katie would think I had failed her, that I had let her down just as I think she always knew I would. I wanted to scream out into the void so that somehow she would hear me, but of course, she couldn't.

Days passed, days when I would walk through the station hoping against hope for some miracle but where the clock had been there was only an empty space. I avoided Barry, I avoided everybody. Susan called, left messages until eventually those began to tail off. Chris tried once or twice but that was it from her and I don't blame her. If she had a thing going with Maserati man then good for her; she deserved it.

There is a line in that great iconic film, 'Breakfast at Tiffany's' when Audrey Hepburn in her role as Holly Golightly says she has the "mean reds". The mean reds are so much worse than the blues; the blues just get you down for couple of days, but the mean reds are when you're down and scared and don't even know what you're scared of. I had the mean reds in black spades.

Suddenly I wanted to watch the film again. (Just as a by the way aside – in my travel agent days I found myself in Savannah, Georgia. I saw the real Moon River which is the title of the song that Audrey Hepburn sings in the film. Henry Mancini didn't write it – I know – I know – just listen. Henry Mancini wrote dum dee dee, dum dee

392

dum dee dum; it was Johnny Mercer who wrote '*Moon River, Wider Than a Mile*' and it became so famous that the good folks of Savannah renamed that little creek I saw Moon River).

Anyway, enough of that, this story is about me and my angst and misery and failure - who cares about Johnny Mercer. I left the blinds closed day and night and I'm sure the neighbours must have been wondering about the possibility of a maggot eaten corpse lying festering behind the front door although not enough to do anything about it. I must confess I did let myself go a bit for a while, well certainly for almost a month, not eating, just feeling sorry for myself, feeling guilty, feeling suicidal, then feeling hungry again which I took to be a good sign.

I went through it all again in my mind over a Marks and Spencer individual cheese and spinach ravioli and a bottle of plonk but it wasn't going to change anything. I had let Katie down. It may not have been intentional but that is a fine point when it comes to the person affected. I browsed over my net contribution to the order of life, the universe and everything and came to the fairly obvious conclusion that in the ledger of life looking at the debit and credit columns, all my entries were almost all in the red. It was time to balance the books. I called Barry and he answered right away.

'Saw you on caller I.D., man, how are you doing?'
'Shitty.'
'You got it bad, didn't you?'
'Yeah. Wanna meet up? We probably need to talk.'
'Sure.'

I met him next day at The Horseshoe and he seemed very relieved to see me.

'Susan has been worried about you, you know? I told her just to let it be for a while and you'd come round. I told her you were just in a fit of depression about your old man. Hope that's okay.'

I nodded, 'Yeah, whatever. Thanks Baz.'

'You need to get your shit together now, though. Time's moving on.'

'What, you in a hurry?'

'As a matter of fact, yeah. Lesley and I have set the date and booked everything and you're the best man, remember?'

I had forgotten all about that when I was wallowing in my sea of self pity.

'Not Brian then?'

'Shit, no.'

I took this in and decided he was right. I needed to get on with things.

'So when are we talking about?'

'In case you hadn't noticed this is now the ides of March, so maybe that's a sign. The wedding is the 22nd of April so we don't have much time.'

'Still doing Cameron House?'

'Yeah – look – about that. We're not talking Barbados money here but it's still going to run at a cost. We're looking at a couple of hundred guests plus a honeymoon, yada, yada, yada, so I was wondering...'

'Shit – the stamps!'

'Good man – can I leave that with you? I know I can trust you,' said Barry, much relieved.

'Yeah, sorry Baz. I should have thought.'

He looked happy, and content as he set the next round up, the exact opposite of what my own feelings

394

were but recovery had to start somewhere and where else but the Horseshoe?

That recovery was slow I have to admit, but it happened nonetheless. I went back to Sotheby's with the stamps and they took them in for the next auction as agreed. Barry came over to my flat, a flat, incidentally, that had seen a remarkable conversion in terms of habitability. There wasn't a dirty dish in the sink, not so much as a water ring mark on any of the wooden furniture and the fridge had been emptied of an assortment of cultures that would have been more at home in Alexander Fleming's laboratory. It now housed a healthy, and I mean healthy, assortment of vegetables, meats and dairy products right out of the Jamie Oliver book of wholesome living. My clothes were either clean and ironed and hanging in the wardrobe or tucked away in a hidden wicker basket ready for the wash. A psychiatrist would have had a field day but it didn't take a genius to figure out that I had reassessed my life style and come to the conclusion that things had to change.

Anyway Barry came over and did all the usual double take stuff and comments about him must be being in the wrong house and could I tell him where Gordon Lorne lived.

'Yeah, yeah, yeah, get all the jokes out of the way now,' and I hauled him inside.

'So the auction was yesterday afternoon. Any word?'

'No – I thought I'd wait till you got here and then call them.'

He looked at me then said, 'Let's do it.'

I dialled and was put on hold for a minute or two and then put through. Barry, of course, could only hear my side of the conversation which consisted mainly of phrases like, 'I see', 'Is that so?' 'I understand', and so on. By the time I got off he looked as if he was in need of smelling salts.

'Well?' he croaked.

I looked at him for a long minute.

'For Christ's sake, Gord.'

'He was saying that they had to subtract their commission which is fifteen percent and then there was a lot of gobbledegook about minor tax adjustments for works of art blah, blah, but anyway...'

'Gordon, I swear...'

'Okay, okay. The bottom line is, after all that, net to us is,' I paused for dramatic effect, 'seven hundred and eighteen thousand four hundred and twenty two pounds.'

It took a while to sink in then Barry let out a whoop that lifted an eyebrow or two in Wick. He even frightened himself.

'That's — that's, Christ I'm so excited I can't count. That's three hundred and fifty nine grand each.'

'And two hundred and eleven pounds to be precise. Oh plus the five or six hundred that I owe you.'

He whistled. 'I was never stuck for a pound or two but this is serious money, Gordon.' He paused to think about it. 'So what happens now?'

'They're gonna send an email confirmation and we'll have a cheque within a week. But it's the real deal, Baz.' I thought of something, 'Listen, Barry, we should keep this quiet, know what I mean? Play it cool. Sure, we can splash the cash, you've a wedding coming and all, but let's not say anything. If we seem a bit flush, well that's our business.'

396

'Way ahead of you, my boy. Way ahead. But right now I think a wee celebration entre nous is called for – what do you say?'

'You're the man,' and I patted him on the back.

'No – you're the man.'

That was the turning point.

Every so often I would find myself in town, the first few times I couldn't even go into the station; I knew it would bring it all back. Then one day I walked through it going from Hope Street to Union Street but when I looked, there was still an empty space where the clock had been. I examined the ground underneath where it had hung but of the slight scorch marks of my brush with Thor there was no sign. Weeks of the shuffling feet of thousands of passengers and the evening machine clean had obliterated all the evidence.

Then one day as I was walking through the station not really paying attention, through force of habit I looked up and there, where the old clock had once hung, was a new clock or the old clock beautifully refurbished for it looked the same. I felt that familiar constriction in my chest as I gazed up at it. People scurried past as for me time stood still. Eventually I summoned up the courage to step forward and walk directly underneath. It was stupid, it wasn't even three minutes to eight so nothing at all could possibly happen and I wasn't disappointed; nothing did. But I did come back later that evening with Barry just for moral support.

Barry couldn't do enough for me. He was always a good friend, a great friend actually, and he never saw me stuck, but he now had new respect for me, not that I felt

397

that I deserved it or anything, but he knew I had lost more than I had gained.

We had a couple of the usual in the 'shoe and then wandered over to the station. I had taken the precaution of bringing the Nithsdale Road flat keys with me just in case and at five to the hour of eight I stood with Baz almost under the clock.

'The thing is, Baz, if by some miracle I walk under this thing and disappear then that's it – you won't see me again.'

'I know mate.'

We looked at each other and then gave each other a long man hug. Not too, long, you understand. I think the absolute maximum is six seconds otherwise you have to start chucking each other on the shoulder, talking an octave lower and discussing last night's heavyweight bout between 'Slugger' Steel and 'Sizzlin' Sam Bronowski or something. Heterosexual guys have rules about these things. Women don't understand.

The clock hand touched the fifty-seven mark and I walked under. Needless to say all anybody watching could see were two guys standing looking rather foolish as one of them walked back and forward under a clock a few times, looking up then shaking his head. I wasn't really depressed or disappointed. It was never likely to work. Whatever strange scientific chemistry, or kink in the fabric of the universe had occurred back in January had been ironed out, nature had not been thwarted. God was in his heaven and all was well with the world. Was it fuck.

There was nothing else for it but to meander back to the Horseshoe and drown my sorrows. I imagined my little flat in Nithsdale Road with its electric fires and little cache of semi-precious stones and a bankbook with a few hundred pounds and wondered when it would be opened. It was an exercise in futility since that was sixty years ago and it would all have been long since discovered. I thought of Phil, Eric and Benny, probably dead by now, or if not they damn well should be given the amount of tar clogging their lungs.

Oh well, I thought, as I downed my pint, at least the pubs now stay open till late. I said I would give Barry a call in a day or so and went back home.

The next day I started wondering about my old chums in Heraghty's. The south side was an area I hadn't given much thought to in the present era having left Clarkston, if not under a cloud, certainly under an unfavourable weather report. It was a pleasant enough day for March, a hint of the promise of double figures in the air, so I walked out past the boating lake at Queens Park to Shawlands where, mercy upon mercies, Heraghty's was still there, and not only still there, the sign over the door was just the same except it may have had an extra coat of varnish or two.

Inside hadn't changed much either, if at all. The seats and tables were in the same place if somewhat newer, the bar was exactly as it was with the gleaming, polished wood open drinks cabinet and mirror with the clock above. I remembered Jim looking at that many a night before he called 'time, gentlemen'. The clientele was of the same cut of cloth as those that I had left behind so long ago, honest, worthy men. The only thing missing was the coil of drifting smoke.

I bellied up to the bar to coin an American phrase. 'A pint of heavy, please.'

The pint was duly poured. The barman did what barmen do - cleaned glasses checked the till and served another customer and passed the time of day with us.

'Been here long?' I ventured.

'Oh, a good twenty years or so. Part of the family. It's a family pub.'

I nodded and supped at my pint.

'You new here? Haven't seen you before,' he asked conversationally.

'Aye, yes. My grandfather used to be a local though. Talked fondly of the place and the people. He liked the atmosphere in here.'

'Is that right?'

I wasn't sure if he was really interested but I pressed on. 'His name was Lorne – Gordon Lorne. He was pally with three regulars, Phil, Eric and – er- Benny I think was his name, Benny Frew - a policeman.'

The barman shook his head. 'Probably before my time.'

'Aye, right enough. It wasn't yesterday.'

'There was one old guy came in regular like – not long after I started,' the barman said, 'twenty year ago like, as I said. His name was Phil, I think – big fella. Used to bum his chat about how he was an award winning journalist – how he wrote some articles on, och I don't know – wait, I remember – My Vision For The Future – that was it. Fair old character but he'll be well dead now.'

He went off to serve another customer.

Well, well, well. Here's to Phil. I ordered a large Glenmorangie and toasted his health, then I realised and toasted his memory.

It may not have been Barbados, but Loch Lomond certainly gave the Caribbean a run for its money on the day of Lesley and Barry's wedding. An unseasonably warm April sun bathed the Cameron House gardens on the bonnie banks and some of the rhododendrons had started to bud early lending a touch of colour to the proceedings. Ben Lomond stood sentinel over the calm blue waters where two or three jet skis buzzed around like angry bees. Inchmurrin island lay lazily a mile or two offshore and the crimson funnel of the defunct paddle steamer Maid of the Loch splashed colour against the dark green foliage of Balloch Park a little further away.

Guests, some with a glass of champagne in hand, milled about the manicured grounds, the men mostly dressed in kilts and the ladies in all sorts of finery. It was the type of occasion to strike terror into the heart of a confirmed bachelor, some of whom could be seen nervously and anxiously avoiding the steady hard gazes of their girlfriends.

In the church Lesley was demurely radiant in off white while Barry, kitted out in a tartan that appeared to have been created for the occasion by Dulux paints, stood proud and happy as Lesley's dad escorted her down the aisle, milking the occasion for all it was worth. I'm not sure I would have chosen Leonard Cohen's 'Hallelujah' as the processional song but I liked Queen's 'Don't Stop me Now' for the recessional and I suspect that was Barry's choice.

Lesley's mother was on her best behaviour, well at least until the service was over, and she only hit on me once before turning her attentions to more likely prey, like the youthful looking minister. He seemed to be struggling with the concept of the validity of the seventh commandment and judging by the absence of the two of them for a short while during the cocktail break I think he might have overcome his doubts about his calling.

'Giving you ideas?'

I turned round to see Chris standing behind me hand in hand with Maserati man. She nodded towards the bride and groom so that I would know what she meant. I smiled at her.

'No, not really, but I'm glad for Barry. I think they were always going to end up together. A few bumps along the way, mind.'

'How are you doing, Gordon? We were all worried about you for a while, what happened there?' she asked gently.

'I just went through a bad spell, I guess,' I said. Only Barry and I knew about the weird time travel episodes of January and February. If we had told anyone else I would have been in the Carstairs institution for the criminally insane by now. 'So you didn't get to go to Barbados after all, eh? Barry fooled us all.'

Chris laughed. 'Actually he didn't. We're off to the Caribbean for a couple of weeks once this is all over. Turks and Caicos then Jonathan has chartered a yacht for a few days, haven't you darling?' She looked dotingly at her escort. 'By the way, this is Jonathan,' she said rather redundantly.

'Hi,' I said, 'we sort of met at Barry's party.'

He laughed, 'Oh yes, Barry's party. I won't forget that in a hurry. If I'd known I'd have brought my trainer.'

Chris looked at me seriously. 'Susan's here, you know. She's a lovely looking maid of honour. You should go over and talk to her.'

I nodded. 'I will.'

402

'I mean it Gordon – she's a keeper. Go – before it's too late.'

'I will – promise. Have fun in Barbados you two – I'd better go and rehearse my speech, I've just thought of another insult.'

Lesley, who had been doing the bridal rounds, came over.

'Hi, Gordon.'

'Hi, Mrs Marshall.'

'I know, sounds good, doesn't it?'

'It certainly suits you,' I said and meant it.

'Gordon, I just wanted to say thanks.'

'For what?' I asked.

'For being Barry's friend, for being his best man.' She glanced at her feet nervously. 'I'm sorry.' She looked me in the eye. 'I'm sorry I was such a – a – well, you know how I was. I was a bit mean to you for a while and I'm really sorry.' She then gave me a big hug and a peck on the cheek. 'I want us to be friends, good friends, okay?'

I nodded and she smiled. 'Good to see you looking so well. We were all worried about you, you know.'

Well what do you know, even Lesley was concerned. Hmm, how times change.

'Thanks, Lesley, I'm just fine.'

'Good, that's settled. Now I'll see you later, I have to mingle – but thanks.'

I looked around and saw Susan talking to a couple I hadn't seen before, probably relatives on Lesley's side, so I took a deep breath and sidled over. The couple moved away just as I approached her from behind.

'Love means never having to say you're sorry.'

'That's the biggest load of bullshit ever written,' she said without looking round.

403

'You're right – I'm sorry.'

She turned to face me and I saw in her face what had attracted me when I first met her, a hint of something I couldn't quite put my finger on but which drew me to her.

'I'm not going to make any excuses except to say I've been going through a bad patch.'

She softened a little at that, only a little but it was a start. 'I'm sorry about your father. I know he was still relatively young.'

'Yeah, well, what ya gonna do,' I said, sounding like Tony Soprano.

There was a long, slightly embarrassing silence which she broke.

'So you're a V.I.P.'

'Sorry?'

'You're the best man, a V.I.P.'

I laughed. 'Yeah, right. I'm not even an I.P.' then I said, a little more wistfully, 'In your book I don't think I'm even a P. I might be a non P.' I paused and looked at her, 'You looked beautiful in your role. In fact you look beautiful, period.'

She was silent again for a minute. 'You didn't return my calls.'

'I didn't return anyone's calls.'

'I didn't think I was "anyone".'

'No, you're not just anyone and again, I'm sorry.'

She looked around at the loch and at the leaves stirring slightly in the zephyr.

'It's lovely here. I love the hills and the water.'

'Susan?'

'Yes?'

'Is there any chance you could put this behind us?'

'I already have.' She took a sip of champagne. 'I've moved house, you know. No of course you didn't. I just wanted to get away from any trace of Fingal. He's in Afghanistan now so there's always the chance that he'll get a bullet up his arse. One can but hope.'

'I meant putting my wobbly behind us,' I said.

'Is that what it was? A "wobbly"?'

'Whatever you want to call it. I know I'm my own worst enemy.'

'I wouldn't say that, there's plenty of competition.'

'You've a right to be upset, I know,' I said. 'I want to see you again.'

'Take a good look, you're seeing me now.'

This was like swimming in treacle but she was entitled to make it hard for me. I got the feeling, however, that she was just testing my resolve so I kept at it. 'You know what I mean.'

'Give me one good reason.'

'I love you.'

There was a long pause.

'That's a good reason,' she said and looked away again then turned and looked me straight in the eye. 'Listen to me, Gordon Lorne. I don't know why I'm doing this but you get one more bite at the cherry. If you screw it up then I'll do to you what you did to Fingal - I've taken a course in household electrics. I'll wait until you're asleep of course then -bzzzt. You won't know what hit you.'

'Sounds fair,' I said unconsciously crossing my hands in front of me.

'Right. Now take me inside and get me a refill. Afterwards you can take me home.' With that she took my arm and we walked inside.

The rest of the afternoon and evening passed in a whirl of traditional wedding gaiety enhanced by the fact that Barry had splashed out on a terrifically good combo who did great justice to some Stones and Queen numbers while still getting the golden oldies up for Strip the Willow and the Dashing White Sergeant. My speech pressed all the right buttons with just the right amount of humour seasoned with a sprinkling of schmaltz to keep everyone, with the possible exception of Lesley's mother, happy.

I caught Susan's eye two or three times from my exalted position at the top table and I knew that the time was now, not tomorrow, not yesterday, but now. Tomorrow is an illusion and yesterday is a sheet of paper with the ink on the page already dry. It can't be changed or rewritten which is why I could never have claimed authorship of the songs and stories written by others as I had foolishly imagined. Nature always finds a way of finding its own level, like water, of creating equilibrium and balance. It is what it is.

Chapter Thirty-five

So Susan and I started living apart together in an oxymoronic way. I still had my flat in Partick and she had her new place out near Eastwood Toll. I gather that Fingal had been forced to cough up some cash and that, what with the profit on her Battlefield place and a small nest egg, she was able to afford a pad side by side with the landed gentry in the south side. It wasn't a bad place to live and I found myself spending more and more time there with her. The lease on my own place was about to expire anyway and I had a choice of dipping into my substantial gains from the sale of my share of the stamps and buying something of my own or simply moving in full time with Susan, paying my way of course; I'm no longer a leech.

We rubbed along, just fine the two of us, in a harmonic symbiosis, a bit like Mama Cass in the Mammas and the Pappas, getting better and stronger every day. I often caught Susan humming it to herself. And I had "got my shit together" as they say. Certainly, the security of a few hundred thousand in the bank has a way of doing that although there are plenty of people who, when hit with that kind of windfall, drown themselves in an orgiastic pool of hedonism. It doesn't make them bad people; it could have been a close run thing in my case to be honest. I started an I.T. company of my own, with a broad sphere of interest. I put together web sites and found that here was something in which I excelled. I knew what the public wanted from a web site, not what the clients thought they wanted. As a result I had developed algorithms that anticipated what the public needed making browsing a much more pleasurable experience. At least that's what the blurb on my web site said, I didn't understand a word of it. The company did other things as well - designing simple programmes, identifying glitches quickly, solving all the little annoying things that combine to create impulses that induce you to hit your laptop further with a three wood than John Daly can hit a golf ball. It washes its face which is to say that I cover my costs and pay myself a pittance without having to delve into my funds too much.

I was also in the throes of putting together a book for which I had found a publisher. My black and white photographs of the various steam engines and trains I had taken had caught the attention of a specialist book company and there was still a large interest in new material of old steam in the railway enthusiast fraternity. All of my prints were dated and carried a full description of all the arcane technical points that anoraks like I love.

Barry and Lesley are happy as sandboys (and girls) living the life of domesticated bliss in the west end and can be seen most weekends strolling around the Botanic Gardens or entertaining royally and Lesley not giving a damn about the mess. A weekly visit from Molly Maid certainly helps in that respect. Lesley is heavily pregnant much to her mother's outright disgust as her chances of wild sex with tennis pros in broom cupboards will diminish as soon as the appellation "grannie" is heard around the corridors of the local club. I see Barry regularly, I'm glad to say. Lesley, to her enormous credit, insists that the two of us have a pint or two together and I am always welcome over for a pasta.

Chris and Jonathan the Maserati man seem to be keeping the national debt of several small Caribbean islands to a manageable level but they still have time to come back to Glasgow to recharge the batteries. The six of us often get together for drinks and dinner but it's usually a fairly easygoing pleasant, affair. Barry has been true to his word and kept quiet about his windfall, even from Lesley who is under the impression that it's all part of Barry's super ability to create wealth. To a degree she's right; if it hadn't been for Barry and his financial support I would never have been able to follow through with the scheme. So he hasn't talked about it, not even with me. I have said nothing to Susan either and sooner rather than later I am going to have to explain to her that I am somewhat more financially secure than she ever imagined. I won't tell her about how I came by it, though. Some things can never be explained rationally, and not even to myself if truth be told. The past is past.

One Saturday morning lying in bed I asked Susan what her days' plans were.

'I'm going to visit gramma in Twechar.'

'I don't have a visa or I'd join you.'

She laughed. 'You'll not need a visa but you're welcome to come anyway.'

'Maybe I will, at that.'

'You should, before it's too late. She's a lovely old lady but I think I told you, she's got dementia.'

'Oh, that's too bad.' I said, playing footsie with her under the sheets.

'Oh, she's one of the happy ones. Some of them get very aggressive but gramma, she just lives in her own wee world.'

'How old is she?'

'Ninety-one I think, maybe ninety-two. She's up there anyway.'

'Okay, I'll come. I've nothing better to do anyway.' I got out of bed and started laying out some cereal and making coffee. Susan disappeared into the shower. I was tempted to follow but it would keep until tonight.

Later as we got into her car I asked her, 'Where actually is Twechar, anyway?'

'Out east, past Lenzie somewhere.'

'You learn something new every day. I thought it was a contagious disease. Did you hear about Bertie Sloan? – twechar of the kidneys –nothing they can do for him,' I mimicked.

She laughed as she steered the car on to the M80.

'Comfortable?'

'As well as anybody can be in a beetle. The last time my knees were this close to my chin it was on a Ryanair flight,' I said.

'Don't knock it – this is an investment. A friend of mine bought it in Mexico for five thousand pounds, drove it all the way to New York, shipped it home and sold it to me for seven and a half. It's worth ten thousand right now.'

'I'm impressed. Pity he didn't throw in seat cushions.'

I watched the road trundle by underneath us, Trabants overtaking us in third gear on the inside lane.

'So, tell me about gramma.'

Susan shifted into fourth. 'She's a grand old lady – last of her type – but the mind has gone. She's Cathy

Galloway. My mum was a Galloway until she married my dad.'

'Oh yeah?' Women like to give you the fine print. Men tend to give you the big picture.

'Yeah, she married my granddad round about the end of the fifties, nineteen fifty-nine or sixty, but it didn't last.'

'Why? A bit of a lad?' I thought about the ways of my own grandfather.

'Oh no, not at all. Apparently he was the homemaker. He was content to have a normal home life, according to my mother, but gramma was an adventurer – loved to travel.'

Good for gramma.

'Yes, she had my mother not long after she got married – I think it might have been a bit of a shotgun wedding to be honest – I don't know.'

'Right.' I stifled a yawn.

'It didn't last – the marriage, I mean. She dumped him not long after. My granddad brought up my mum mainly on his own but gramma always provided and took her on holidays and the like.'

'Quite a lady then.'

'She sailed to New York on the Queen Mary, you know – the original. Took my mum with her, spent a few days and flew back, first class on BOAC no less.'

We were near Mollinsburn and Susan slowed down for the turn.

'My mum says that gramma came into a lot of money when she was younger, before mum was born. I think it was serious money but that's as much as anybody knows. We don't know how – there was never any indication in the family history, but gramma always had money.'

411

'Go gramma,' I said to show I was listening.

'Yep. I think I was always the favourite grandchild. She'd tell me about the Taj Mahal, the Pyramids, Petra – she'd seen them all. I think it's these memories that keep her going.'

We neared the village and I saw the signs for the Campsie View Care Home, 'Elegant, Luxury, Exclusive Residential Care for the Golden Aged', coming up to my left.

'But she gets confused now and just lives in a world of her own and can't tell fact from fiction. I mean, I know she's been to all those places – she's got souvenirs enough to fill a museum. But other times, well it's just fantasy.'

'Oh, such as.'

'Every time I visit now she talks to me about Paris.'

'Paris?'

'Yeah, and about the first time she went there.'

'Tell me more.' I was really intrigued – this was a good story.

'According to her fantasy she went there like a film star – round about 1957 I think. She went to London on a fancy train, dining car service and all that – they stayed at a posh hotel – dined in style. Then they took another special train to Paris – stayed in a five star hotel near the Champs-Elysées. She talks about the Eiffel Tower and Montmartre and all the places she saw.'

My senses were on full alert now. Parts of my anatomy were sending up flares to other parts of my anatomy. Susan went on talking as he approached the turn to the drive up to the care home.

'And, get this, who do you think took her there?'

I couldn't answer.

'George Clooney! Is that not just the most hilarious thing?'

Terrific – I'm dying of laughter. No, just dying.

'I mean, as if George Clooney was even alive then,' she continued, 'and then, and then – she goes to Maxim's, drinks a gallon of champagne and bumps into Greta Garbo and Garbo spills some of gramma's wine and Garbo dabs it with her hanky and gives her hanky to gramma! She still has the hanky, heaven knows where she really got it. Marks and Spencer probably.'

She slowed at the main entrance to the ivy covered mansion and parked the car then looked at me.

'Gordon, Gordon – are you all right?'

No I'm not all right – I'm far from all right – I'm all wrong and I need some air and I think I'm going to pass out. I did some quick mental arithmetic. When did Susan say her mother was born? She said something about getting married at the end of the fifties, maybe nineteen sixty, and she was pregnant at the time. A shotgun wedding, or something. So it couldn't be possible, Susan couldn't be my granddaughter, thank God. The thumping in my heart eased enough to let me breathe.

I knew the answer to gramma's windfall in 1957. The last thing I did as I left Central Station that evening was to post an envelope to Littlewoods Pools – with Katie McWilliam's name as the sender. It was my last act as someone with the foresight to know the results. There may have been some unacknowledged doubt, perhaps an unconscious uncertainty on my part, that my best laid plans would fail and that I wouldn't see Katie again. Or maybe I just got greedy and thought that the two of us could be filthy rich. Whatever my motive was, I had completed a pools coupon in Katie's name and sent it

413

off. If Katie couldn't be rich with me she could at least be rich without me. I often wondered how she reacted when the Littlewoods men came calling at the door. She'd protest at first then realise what I'd done and she wasn't so stupid as to look a gift horse like that in the mouth. I wondered if it was Collingwood and Lorraine that visited her with the photographer in tow. It wouldn't matter, I had ticked the 'no publicity' box and Katie wasn't the type who'd want her name splashed over the papers.

'Gordon!'

'Yeah, fine. Just the sun on the windscreen and I got a bit queezy for a minute.'

'Oh no. Are you all right now?'

'Fine, I wonder if you shouldn't go in yourself.'

'No – gramma would love to meet you, I've told her all about you. Don't let her down.'

That was it, of course, I couldn't let her down.

I recognised her right away - that Rachel Stirling similarity with a hint of Juliette Binoche just enough to turn a beautiful face into a phenomenon. Although she was still lovely the looks were cloaked in the cloth of the passing years yet time had been kind to her. Her smile still radiated joy and warmth, her eyes still sparkled like the reflections of the mirrored ball in the Plaza and her hair, obviously lovingly dyed by Susan, still glowed with the same lustre of sunshine. Her eyes lit up when she saw me. I sat beside her and took both of her hands in mine.

'Hello, Katie.' I said.

'George, my George, I knew you wouldn't let me down.' She smiled at me radiantly.

I smiled at her. 'No, of course not.'

She turned to Susan, 'I told you he'd come back.'
Then she looked to me. 'I knew you'd keep your
promise, George.'

'Better late than never, Katie.'

She run her hand down my cheek and touched my lips
with her fingers and I had to turn away from Susan or
she would have seen the wetness in my eyes.

'Do you remember, George? Wasn't it wonderful?'

'It was wonderful Katie.'

She smiled, 'I still have the hanky, Garbo's hanky – do
you remember?' She reached into a drawer and pulled it
out. It was as fresh and clean as it was when I saw it in
Garbo's hand.

'You said we'd be together in 2017 and here you are.
It is 2017, George, isn't it?'

'It is Katie, and here I am.'

She sighed with pleasure. 'And here you are. I kept the
picture, George. Remember the little square where we
had crepes and coffee – up by the Sacre Coeur, and that
funny little man played the accordion – do you
remember?'

'I remember, Katie.'

I looked around her room and sure enough, there on
the wall, beautifully framed, was the scene of
Montmartre from slightly above the Place du Tertre with
the Sacre Coeur mistily shimmering in the background.
The glass frame sparkled with neither a spot or a blemish
to be seen.

I looked at Susan and smiled. She looked at me,
astounded. It was just then that I realised what the slight
familiarity was that I had seen in Susan and couldn't
place it. She had her grandmother's smile that crinkled

415

her eyes and her gentleness when she talked. I looked back at Katie.

'George?' she said.

'Yes?

'We'll always have Paris.'

'Here's looking at you, kid.'

Driving back Susan was quiet for a while before she spoke.

'Gordon?'

'Yes, sweetheart?'

'What just happened in there?'

'I don't know. Maybe I rekindled old memories for her.'

'It seemed as if she knew you. I know that's not possible but...' she tailed off. 'Thank you. I don't know how you did that, but thank you.'

'She's a wonderful lady, your gramma.'

'Yes she is,' she said. 'It's funny, but it's like you've known each other all your life. It was like she was expecting you.'

'I know,' I said.

We drove on towards her house.

'George?'

'Yes?'

'How did you know to call her Katie?'

'Didn't you tell me that was her name?'

'No, I said it was Cathy.'

'Oh, I don't know – it just seemed right.'

'Yeah? My mother said she used to be called before she married granddad but then changed it to Cathy.'

'Really?'

'Yes. How odd,' she mused.

'Isn't it, though,' I said, wanting to drop the subject.
She drove a mile or so before saying anything.

'Funny how the past comes back to haunt us.'

25050093R00246

Printed in Great Britain
by Amazon